Little
Jenny Parminter
is missing

Dennis Talbot

A
Whitecross Yard
Murder

Introducing the main character Will Dexter

Born in 1908, William "Will" Dexter is the son of railway-man, George Dexter. He was born and brought up in a two-up two-down terraced railway house in Derby, with his parents and two older sisters, Edith and Florence "Flossie".

Six years of age at the outbreak of the Great War, as the First World War was then known, he and his family, and their neighbours suffered the hardships and heartbreak of four years of conflict. George, too old for war service, educated his son about the benefits of being able to grow a few fresh vegetables for the family and cultivating the small area "The Plot" at the rear of the house. Throughout the tale, Will finds himself reminiscing on his lowly but happy childhood.

Will gained an electrical apprenticeship with a small but highly respected contracting firm and although he loved the work, his ideal job was to be a police officer, and he entered the Crammingdon Force in 1929 as a junior officer…

What readers have said:

An outstanding and gripping novel that is a MUST READ!
J McBride

This is a historical detective novel with a cracking story, couldn't put it down!
R Nauen

A brilliant story that captures the era so well, more please!
Dr Peter Meakin (Creative Director)

This novel expertly mixes Dexter's home life, [his] past, and the thrilling police work necessary to find the killer.

Britt13   On Line Book Club

About the author

Dennis Talbot was born and bred in Derby and loves to walk with his wife Pauline in the beautiful English county of Derbyshire.

Dennis wrote his first novel **'A Small Price to Pay, Sir'** at the age of 70. With his lifelong love of the novels of PG Wodehouse, this was bound to be a humorous offering. It reached the finals of 'The People's Book Prize 2016. Two further novels using the same characters, Josh and Ellingham followed.

During a spellbinding holiday in America and Canada, the seeds of a detective story set in the 1930's began to take shape. **'The Killing of Cristobel Tranter'**, the first in the Whitecross Yard Murders series was the result.

Also by Dennis Talbot

The Whitecross Yard Murders

The Killing of Cristobel Tranter

Death in the Back Row

Too many Wrong Notes

The Josh & Ellingham Novels

A Small Price to Pay, Sir

Best foot Forward, Ellingham

Look Lively, Ellingham

Dedication

To my wife Pauline

Acknowledgements

Once again to my late Grandfather "Heffield" who told of his experiences as a humble bobby in the 1930s.

1

Little Tommy Parminter was three years old. He was holding the hand of a next door neighbour, struggling to be allowed to walk with his dad. Ahead of him his mother and father walked arm in arm with heads downcast behind the coffin of Jenny, their eleven year old daughter. As if to rub salt into their wounds, the sun had come out after weeks of almost unbroken rain and the afternoon had become hot and sultry. I remember thinking, just for a moment of what my father had once said; *"If there is a god up there, he can be pretty bloody unfeeling at times"*. All of this I noticed as the funeral procession turned the corner in the cemetery path that led to the mound of earth beside the open grave. The neighbour Mrs Goodward picked the boy up and tried to console him as they reached the grave. Robert, the boy's uncle walked over with a half-smile of thanks and took him from her, and went to stand by the side of the boy's mother, but it was Dad that he wanted, and quickly Robert moved to Arthur's side.

There can't be many worse things for a police officer to have to perform than to have to inform the anxious parents of a missing child that a body, believed to be that of their child, has been found and to request one of them to make an identification. During my uniformed days it had occurred on several occasions. Being a member of the CID team, the investigation of such things was our responsibility and that made the sad event even more of a burden.

It had all started a month earlier, almost to the day. Monday the eighth of June 1936 had been one of the worst days I can remember. Crammingdon like many other places in the Midlands, had been subject to almost incessant thunder storms for the first few days of June, with sudden heavy squalls of rain and hail.

Normally missing persons are looked upon as very low priority. In most cases, where a husband or wife has walked out of the family home, they return within a couple of days and all is forgiven. Occasionally, as in the case of one poor chap I remember, an anonymous note suggested that he had killed his wife and buried her in his cellar, causing a major investigation which all came to nothing when a letter arrived explaining her reasons for leaving. But when the missing person is an eleven year old girl it is taken very seriously indeed. The investigating force and those surrounding it, pull out all the stops, and the police force nationally is alerted with the necessary information to be on the look-out for the child.

"Write a story about your favourite animal" had been the homework set for over the weekend, and Jenny had gone off to school on Monday with her story about "Smoky" the family cat, neatly folded in her school bag. Wearing a hand-me-down raincoat and shoes, she had arrived at school drenched, and been allowed to put her coat to dry in the school porch. Not surprisingly the rain had got into her school bag and the story had become wet at one edge. Jenny had been really upset, her teacher Mrs Leonard had stated, when questioned after it had become clear that something had happened to the little girl.

Mrs Parminter had not been overly worried when her daughter had not returned home at her normal time of around half past four. She had often sheltered at the house of one of her friends, Nelly Richmond, during the worst of the downpours and initially that was what Elizabeth Parminter had suspected was the reason she had not arrived at home. When eight o'clock passed, and the rain had stopped nearly an hour earlier, and there was no sign of Jenny she went to the Richmond's house to collect her. Nelly had told Mrs Parminter that Jenny hadn't wanted to shelter; she wanted to get home and show her dad the mark Mrs Leonard had given her.

PC George Douglas had been standing at his point on the corner of Long Yard and Duke Street in the south division area of the town, smoking a crafty pipe, when Mrs Parminter came running up and reported her daughter missing between gasps of breath. PC Douglas used the police box at the end of Duke Street to alert the south division station and the message was quickly passed on to CID at Whitecross Yard, Crammingdon's Police Head Quarters, and motor patrols were duly alerted.

According to Mrs Leonard's statement the next day, Jenny had left for home with the rest of the children at four o'clock. Her coat was almost dry and she had set off with her story with Mrs Leonard's remark "Well done Jennifer 9/10" now dry, though a little wrinkled, in her school bag. The teacher had found a stout envelope and put the story in it to protect it from the rain. Mrs Leonard had last seen the girl running out of the school gates with her friends, laughing and joking as they normally did.

On hearing the news that Jenny was missing, Mr Jellicoe, one of the boys' teachers, admitted picking the girl up.

'I had had a free lesson and managed to clear up the day's marking and set things out for the first lesson next day. Unusually I left the school at the same time as the children. My car was parked outside the gates at the rear of the school.' He had volunteered this information when I questioned him immediately following my interview with Mrs Leonard.

'Do you normally pick children up in your car?' I asked.

'Heavens no! One has to be a little aloof as a

3

teacher. The reason I had offered Jenny a lift was that the rain was absolutely pouring down. I lived in the tropics for a short while and the rain that afternoon reminded me of a tropical storm. I knew she lived on my way home! Lorna Mrs Leonard – had shown me Jenny's little story, knowing I encourage my pupils to write about their everyday lives. It was such a well written piece, I was intrigued how much input her parents had made. When I saw her running for home in that torrential rain I decided on the spur of the moment to offer her a lift.'

'Jenny accepted without question?' I asked.

'She got in with a little smile of thanks. I remember she pulled the door with the release handle and it didn't shut properly; I had to lean over her to close it safely.'

'From picking her up to dropping her at home, how long was she in your car?'

'Two minutes, no longer, say a half mile or so. I couldn't drop her at her door as she lives in a row of houses, down an alleyway. I dropped her at the end of the alleyway, she said thank you and ran off towards home.'

'What did you talk about?'

'As I said, two minutes was all it took to reach the point I dropped her off. I asked her about her story and she told me that her mother had helped her with the spellings as I had suspected. Nothing wrong with that of course! I like to see parents involving themselves with their children's education.'

'How did she seem?'

'Excited. She told me that Mrs Leonard had given her nine out of ten for her story. I knew that in any case, we had discussed it in the staff room at lunch time.'

'You had discussed it with Mrs Leonard?'

'We often do. The headmaster, Mr Colchester, believes that we should mark with a degree of consistency. You can't always of course, some of the less bright children often need a bit of a spur to boost them along.

The occasional mark a little higher than reality can often be enough to gee-them-up a little!' he smiled.

'Did Jenny need geeing-up?'

'A little maybe, from time to time, according to Lorna – Mrs Leonard – but we both felt that the mark was earned quite genuinely.'

'Thank you Mr Jellicoe. I might need to talk to you again: if you think of anything else, give me a ring, please!' I said handing him a card with my name and the number of Whitecross Yard and CID's extension number on it.

'Of course, anything I can do to help, though I can't see how she failed to return home. She had only fifty or sixty yards to walk, and she set off at the run, though the rain had eased a little.'

Having passed on the details of the missing child to Whitecross Yard, PC Douglas went with Mrs Parminter to her house in Canal Row and began a localised search of sheds and outbuildings on the area. Although it was summer-time, the dismal day meant that by nine o'clock it was nearly pitch dark and Sergeant Cummings of the south division called off the search until first light next day.

2

Having worked the previous weekend, Monday had been my day off, and Tuesday morning was a very special morning for me and DI Brierly had sanctioned the morning off with strict instructions to be in by 1pm prompt.

'Very smart, little brother!' Flossie said as I stood at the bottom of the stairs.

'Thank you, big sister, I wanted to look my best, even though Marco will never see it!'

'His big day?' she smiled.

'Yes, thirty years later than planned!' I chuckled.

As a police officer, I am always very sceptical of coincidences, things don't often happen to click together by sheer chance. Yet, that was exactly how things had panned out for my dear old friend Marco Tizoni. His career as a brilliant violinist had been cut short by sudden blindness when still a young man. The girl he was due to marry had fled, unable to come to terms with the loss of his sight. Marco had moved around France for several years searching for her, finally ending up in England in the middle of 1912. He had eventually made his living by playing his violin, harmonica or concertina at Crammingdon Market. This remarkable old chap had a vast range of musical pieces stored in his head, playing everything from memory. Early in 1930, whilst I was still a young police constable, I had been forced to arrest him when an over-zealous new market manager had accused him of begging. Incensed by that, the market traders had pressured the manager into making Marco a permanent fixture on the market by allotting him an open fronted covered stall. He had taken a young boy under his wing and was teaching him the violin. The lad quickly picked up the intricacies of the fingering and was beginning to be bored by only playing the few simple exercises that Marco could explain. Unable to teach the reading of sheet music he had asked me to find him a music teacher. Coincidence, chance, fate; call it what you will the teacher I found him, Miss Penworthy (Diana) was his very own unknown daughter. Tatiana Peignoir, his lost love had changed her name to Penworthy when she had moved to England in 1913 in search of Marco, to introduce him to his daughter and to ask his forgiveness. The reason for my smartness, as commented on by Flossie, was that Marco had asked me to be the best man at his wedding to Tatiana.

'It's so romantic, don't you think,' said Flossie.

'Like a fairy-story come true,' I agreed with a chuckle of pleasure.

'So when are *you* going to ask her?'

'Er… ask her?'

'Oh, come off it Will, you know what I mean: Diana!'

Over the past few weeks, Diana and I had begun to enjoy each other's company and things had started to become more serious, on my part at least.

'I already have, I'm waiting for an answer.'

'Oh, I do hope she says yes, the boys need a mother.'

'They think of you as their mother!' I said.

'I know and I love it, but you need someone in your life. I know no-one will replace Alice but Diana gets on well with the boys and I can see that you are fond of her,' she said, squeezing my arm.

'My only worry is that I'm being swept along with the romance of Marco's reunion. That I should marry his daughter seems, I don't know, unreal somehow!'

'When did you ask her?'

'Last week. I pointed out that she would be marrying into the police force as well, I think that's why she asked to be allowed to think about it,' I smiled.

'If she says yes, where will you live?'

'I don't know; she said she wanted to continue teaching music. I'm not sure how my lords and masters would see that!'

'We're ready Daddy!' said George, as my two lads, George and William ran in from the hall.

'Are we going in the car Daddy?' Will asked, as they danced around excitedly.

I looked at my twin sons, now five and dressed in their very first long trousers, looking really smart and happy. *Oh, how Alice would have…*

'Yes come on, we'll be late!' I nodded.

The complicated little ceremony took place in the local Roman Catholic Church, both of them being of that faith. Carried out mostly in Latin it was a bit of a mystery, but the joy on the faces of the main players in the event was a real heart warmer. The landlord at the Market Inn had laid on a little spread for the happy couple and we three had a sandwich and a drink with the pair. It was all over by lunchtime and I had the boys back to Flossie's, got changed and was off to sign on at Whitecross Yard. That was the first time I learned about the missing little girl Jenny Parminter.

Although I had lived and worked in Crammingdon for over six years I had never had occasion to go down Canal Row. It was in the south division of the town and although not one of the worst areas by any means, was definitely lower-working-class. From Duke Street, where PC Douglas had been standing at his point on the previous evening, a narrow alleyway ran between one of the houses on the left and a large paper mill end on to the road. The alleyway opened out slightly beyond the house and a row of eight houses ran parallel with the side of the mill, divided in two by a canal branch, which ran under an archway in the side of the mill. A narrow bridge ran over the canal joining the two blocks of houses. Although they were well built they were showing their age and with a gap of only twenty feet or so between the front of the houses and the side of the mill, they must have been starved of light on anything but the brightest of summer days.

By the time I arrived, DI Brierly had authorised the dragging of the canal and two uniformed officers were pulling a hooked dragline across the bottom of the canal. I'm sure they were hoping as I was that, their effort would prove to be wasted. So far, the sum total of items recovered amounted to an old tin bath, a bicycle wheel and an old handbag. After half an hour, it became clear that although the canal held several other unexpected treasures there was no sign of an eleven year old girl, much to everyone's relief. The daytime search of outbuildings and the mill, only part of which was still in use, had begun at first light and although it had been completed by the time I arrived nothing even suggesting that a young girl had been hiding or hidden had emerged. Everyone was totally baffled. The DI sent me off to interview the girls teacher and the outcome of that I have already related.

That Jenny had seemingly disappeared off the face of the earth within fifty to sixty yards of her home without anyone seeing or hearing anything was hard to accept. Mrs Parminter was distraught as might be imagined, and one of our women police officers was detailed to give her support and comfort.

DI Brierly had decided to concentrate on the mill as being the key to Jenny's disappearance, arguing that it was the only building big enough for there to be unknown hiding places, though why Jenny would want to hide when she was excited about showing her story to her father, none of us could explain.

We met up that evening at about 6 o'clock in the CID office to compare notes.

'The mill owner wasn't very co-operative! Didn't see why he should unlock the parts of the mill that he never used. I pointed out that our search was for a missing eleven year old girl and he reluctantly agreed,' said the DI.

'What was his problem?' asked DS Whittington.

'I think he's just one of those people who don't like to put themselves out.'

'Plenty of them about,' said DC Harrington and we all agreed.

'What did you find out at the school, Dexter?' ask the DI.

'Jenny had left for home at the normal time in the pouring rain, carrying the story that she had written the night before. Her teacher, Mrs Leonard, had marked it nine out of ten, and she hurried home to show her dad,' I said.

'In the pouring rain?'

'Normally in the rain she stopped with her school friend, Nelly Richmond, until it eased enough to go home but last night she had set off at the run!'

'To show her mark to her dad?'

'Yes, sir.'

'But she never got there?'

'There's a twist to the situation, sir; one of the teachers, Ronald Jellicoe, gave her a lift in his car,' I said, referring to my notes.

'Did he now – for what reason?'

'She lives on his way home and the rain was particularly bad so he took pity on her.'

'Is that likely? I thought teacher were very careful not to show favouritism: quite apart from the possibility of a less savoury side to that sort of thing.'

'He said he wanted to ask her about her story, wondering how much input her parents had in it, sir.'

'Not totally unlikely, I suppose. How long was she in his car?' asked DS Whittington.

'According to him no more than a couple of

minutes, and he did come forward with the information. No-one else said they had seen him pick her up so he had no need to volunteer the information unless he was unsure whether he was seen!'

'Covering his back?' asked the DI.

'Possibly sir, but he did seem genuinely worried about the girl.'

'Mm, not getting very far are we? At least she's not in the canal!'

'Has anyone walked the tow-path, sir?' I asked.

'One of the uniformed lads walked as far as the London Road Bridge without success. The lads who had dragged the canal, also dragged the canal basin the other side of the mill, again everyone drew a blank. Like I said, at least she's not in the water.'

'Gives us a degree of hope,' said the DS, and we all agreed.

'I can't say I knew that this bit of canal existed,' I said. 'Where does it go to?'

'It seems it's a branch of the Erewash canal, connected to the Trent and Mersey at Trent Lock, Long Eaton. It passes the odd factory and mill on the way and terminates in the basin the other side of our mill which is known locally as Clock Mill since it used to have a clock on the wall above the canal arch!' said DC Harrington.

'Blimey! You've done your homework Harrington, well done lad.'

'Thank you, sir.'

'If the mill is only partially in use, do barges still use the canal, sir?' I asked.

'Are you thinking kidnap?'

'Just a thought, sir.'

'And one we need to follow up. The mill owner will know, give him a ring Harrington.'

'Right sir,' he said, picking up the phone.

'Kidnap's not such a bad idea, Dexter! These canal people use their children almost as slave labour, opening locks and helping to load and unload the boat.'

11

'But they have to send their kids to school, sir,' I pointed out.

'It's only a token gesture in most cases, often the kids get their books signed in the morning by the teacher in the school they happen to be passing, then skip off back to the boat as soon as they can and off they go on their travels again!' he smiled.

'So it might be worth finding out if a boat was passing at the time.'

'It wouldn't be passing, Will! The mill is a dead end. The basin is to allow the boats to turn around. It would have to be there for a goodly length of time,' said DC Harrington, looking up from the phone.

'The canal is a good bit lower than the houses; a boat could pass up it to the mill basin and turn without necessarily being seen. With the way the rain has been of late most people with any sense would be indoors,' the DI commented.

'Rain on the windows of the mill would probably reduce the view outside as well, sir,' I said.

'I can't help thinking that the dirt on the *inside* of the windows would do that anyway, Dexter,' he chuckled. 'The point remains we need to check it out.'

'No answer from the mill, sir.'

'Much as I hate to say it, it looks as though we're not going to learn anything else until morning; meantime the poor kid could be lying injured somewhere,' the DI said. 'We'll have to leave it to the uniformed mob to continue the search. Whittington, I want you to stay to be on call until midnight, Harrington on at midnight to take over from the DS. Anything of interest, ring me. Dexter get some shut-eye, I want you bright as the proverbial button first thing in the morning. Back here at six to begin again, any questions?'

'No sir.' We all agreed and a few moments later we trotted down the stairs, leaving DS Whittington going through the information on the case on his lone vigil until midnight.

12

As I pressed the self-starter of my little Hornet, I decided to call in on Canal Row on my way home to see if anyone knew if the canal was still used. I asked at the last house before the side of the canal, not wishing to alert the Parminters to my thoughts, and was told that although the occasional boat came up and under the mill their quest was merely to turn round; the goods from the now depleted mill going out by road. No one was aware if a boat had been in the basin or close by on the day Jenny went missing. So, it seemed as though the case had come to a dead-end for the time being. I remember hoping that the phrase *dead-end* was not going to prove a reality.

3

As so often happens with police work, recognising that our resources are stretched to near breaking point, the criminal fraternity take that as an opportunity to pull a big job. Thursday was payday in most factories in and around Crammingdon. Because that meant that large amounts of cash needed to be transferred from banks to the wage departments of the various businesses, certain companies, Thornton & Mayhew being one, elected to have their cash delivered on the Tuesday and store it in their own strong-room overnight to begin the task of wage packet filling first thing on Wednesday morning.

We had assembled as requested by the DI at six o'clock Wednesday morning and DC Harrington briefed us on the fact that our uniformed colleagues had abandoned the search when two of their officers had slipped on the muddy tow-path and ended up in the equally muddy canal water, shortly after one thirty in the morning.

'Clumsy sods. Still, rather them than me!' chuckled the DI.

'They are planning to start again about now, sir,' Harrington said.

'Good, right Harrington, off home and get some sleep.'

'I'd rather stick with it, sir! If that's okay… it's a kiddie after all, sir.'

'If you feel up to it, okay by me,' the DI agreed.

'Thank you, sir.'

'The plan for today; is the canal still in use?'

'I called in on Canal Row on my way home last night sir. It seems that the occasional boat uses it but it seems unlikely that there was one there the day Jenny disappeared,' I said.

'Good work, Dexter. Alas it seems that the kidnap theory is out of the window, for the moment at least.'

'Sorry, sir!' I said.

'Don't be, it's just as important so see what won't wash, as what will. So eliminating that, at least for the moment, is a useful bit of knowledge.'

'But where does it leave us, sir?' asked DS Whittington.

'Search me! We seem to be drawing a blank wherever we look... I know our brave lads in uniforms have trodden the canal banks, even to the extent of measuring the depth of the water, all be it in an impromptu manner, but I feel we need to do our own search.'

'They reckon they've searched as far as the London Road Bridge, should we start a search beyond it?' asked Harrington.

'No, I'll get uniform to carry on beyond. You and Dexter go over the bit they've already done to see if they've missed anything.'

'It's hardly a bit, sir. It's nearly two miles,' Harrington pointed out.

'Well you'd better get a bloody move on then, hadn't you?' he smiled.

'Yes, sir,' we said together.

'Meantime we'll have another look in the mill and take a wander around the canal basin,' he said to DS Whittington. 'Then we'll go back to the school and see if anyone's remembered anything.'

'Right, sir,' said Whittington.

The sergeant in charge had already received his orders or he had taken his own initiative, either way the boys in blue had all moved down stream and where beginning their search beyond London Road, at least according to the humble PC who had been left at the mill.

Turning away from the mill and down the steps at the side of the bridge brought us to the side of the canal and onto the towpath. The rain had become that fine mist; "the kind that wets you!" Mam had always said. The canal was on our right with a strip of weeds a foot or so wide between it and the path. Then the towpath a yard or so wide and to the left, of varying width a strip of vegetation ranging from tall weeds to thick bramble hedges. To the right beyond the canal was near open countryside.

We began the walk to the London Road Bridge, covering again the route already walked by our uniformed colleagues. The rain had left puddles here and there in the gravelled surface and getting across them without wet feet was tricky in places. Clearly, there were no hoof marks from a towing horse, so it looked as though if there had been a barge it was one of the steam powered variety. We had no real idea what we were looking for, and I suppose neither did the uniformed lads, just anything that suggested that little Jenny Parminter had been there.

From time to time odd things seemed worth a look but nothing seemed to be relevant and we quickly dismissed them. That this particular branch of the canal was slowly falling into disrepair was obvious. An old car tyre, probably once used as the fender on a barge, lay half submerged the other side of the canal. Weeds were gradually restricting the width of the water and trees overhung the water mainly on the far side. A pair of Mallard with three fluffy chicks protested loudly at our intrusion of their territory.

I became aware of a deep panting sound; someone was following us down the towpath and making heavy going of it. I turned to find it was in fact a huge mongrel with canine fangs an inch long and tongue hanging out of the side of its mouth, loping along at a fair pace, oblivious to the fact that on its present course it would force us into the water. I grabbed Harrington's sleeve and hustled him away from the edge. The dog sailed by, running as though it had a mission. Suddenly, about twenty yards ahead of us, it stopped turned and came back towards us. We readied ourselves for its return passage but it had gone only a few feet when it stopped and bounded into the undergrowth. We thought nothing of it until we were actually at the spot where it had disappeared. We could hear it snarling and scrambling obviously trying to pull something from a thicket of blackberry brambles. It was impossible to see what the dog had found and since it seemed to be gaining in its task, we waited until it finally reappeared. It played with its prize for a minute or so, as we stood in amazement at what it had found. The size and look of the animal made it unwise to attempt to relieve it of its trophy, which was an old and battered school satchel, much the worse for wear, but the leather was well polished and the rain seemed to have run off it for the most part. The dog had tried to get into it, probably smelling the fact that it had held someone's lunch each morning, but had finally given up leaving it in the middle of the towpath and continued on its original journey.

'I don't like the look of this!' said Harrington, as he picked the thing up by the strap.

'I reckon it must be Jenny's; doesn't look good, it could only have got there by being thrown, don't you think?'

'Can't see it being anyone else's. What if the poor kid is in there as well?'

'I was just thinking that!' I agreed. 'We need someone to cut these brambles back.'

'You stand guard here, I'll take this back to the mill and alert the DI, see if we can get these bloody things cut back,' Harrington said.

'Okay, I'll have a little scout around and see if there's anything else. Ah, hang on a mo'. I wonder if

Jenny's story is in the bag?' I asked.

'Might as well look. The rain and that damned animal must have destroyed any finger prints,' he said, unfastening the two little straps and buckles.

The bag contained a few bits of paper, a couple of pencils, a rubber and the thing that clinched everything beyond argument; a large manila envelope containing her little story. Harrington looked at me and said, 'Oh, bloody hell, I hope she's not in there!'

4

Three things happened as I scouted around the bit of towpath, awaiting the return of DC Harrington, all unknown to me until much later, although I had heard the clanging of a number of bells. DI Brierly whilst negotiating a fire escape on the side of the mill had slipped and fallen and been taken to hospital with a suspected broken ankle. At almost the same time a heavy steamroller resurfacing part of the road outside the town hall had caused the collapse of an old brick culvert carrying Littleton Brook under the centre of the town, injuring several workmen and disrupting traffic. With the consequence if this, not only were CID short of the head man, but a number of uniformed officers were taken from the search for our little girl to control traffic in the town. As always, the small force was being divided to meet the most urgent need, delaying the search for Jenny Parminter. Just as DS Whittington, now in charge, had rearranged our troops to the most efficient use, a third thing happened. There was a wages grab from Thornton & Meyhew, a large building firm just outside our force area, but County Police asked us for assistance and a further couple of our small force of uniformed officers, were drafted across to assist.

Eventually DC Harrington returned to me with a pair of heavyweight gardeners who set about the task of removing the brambles with a will. Thankfully, after twenty minutes work the area had been cleared without any sign of the little girl. We left the workmen to tidy up and as we continued our search towards the London Road Bridge they were piling the brambles up for a future bonfire. The remaining mile and a half to the bridge produced nothing new and we retraced out steps. On returning to the mill DS Whittington, now in control of operations in the DI's absence, told us to return with him to the station; nothing new having been found at the mill.

'I'm going to take a radical step!' said Assistant Chief Constable Milford. 'I intend to draft WPC Parsons to your team. She's very keen and will probably be more able to deal with the family issues regarding the missing child. Has anyone any objections?'

'Not really sir: will she be assisting with the investigations, sir?' asked DS Whittington.

'That's the idea, does that cause a problem?'

'In a way perhaps sir. As a WPC she will normally have accompanied a male colleague. *We* often have to work alone, how does that fit in with a female officer, sir?'

'In the absence of DI Brierly, you are in charge Detective Sergeant Whittington, I expect you to deploy your team as you see fit. WPC Parsons is fully aware that there could be occasions when she might need to work alone. She sees no problem; she's a *big girl* and understands the pressures she could be under. She will be on your strength as from zero-eight hundred hours tomorrow morning, until further notice. That is all gentlemen, good afternoon.'

'Good afternoon, sir,' we all said snapping a smart salute.

We all knew WPC Parsons, and when the ACC said she was a *big girl,* he wasn't necessarily referring to the fact that she was a grown-up. At five feet ten inches, fit and well-muscled without being over-weight, she could no doubt handle herself in a tight corner. I for one was more than willing to give her a chance. Perhaps the female outlook on life might point us in the right direction.

'I know one thing!' said DS Whittington.

'What's that Sarge?' asked DC Harrington.

'One or two of her male colleagues will feel that their nose is a bit out of joint!'

'You reckon she'll face hostility?' I asked.

'I think the poor girl is in for a rough ride. Not from my team I hope!'

'No, Sarge,' said Whittington

'Nor from me, Sarge,' I agreed.

'Glad to hear it, I expect each of us to be willing to hear what she thinks. She's bound to see things differently to what we do, let's make use of it,' he said picking up the satchel.

'Right, this school bag you found; it's pretty certain it belongs to Jenny, the buff envelope and the story it contains clinches that. I don't want her parents to know we've found it as yet; understood?'
We both nodded.

'It brings back the possibility of her being abducted in a canal boat, Sarge!' I pointed out.

'It does indeed. In which case we need to attempt to find out if a boat was on the canal the afternoon of Jenny's disappearance. Right Will, get on to that now and I suggest we put WPC Parsons on to it in the morning if you haven't got anywhere. She can ring around the canal boat companies and find out if a boat was on our stretch of canal.'

'Won't she actually be an acting DC, Sarge?' Harrington asked.

'Plain clothes, I hadn't thought of that! I'd better ask the ACC. I'll pop over to Heaven, before he goes home,' he said, whizzing out of the door.
Heaven was our nickname for the posh offices above the old stables, the other side of the central yard, occupied by the ACC and the Chief Constable himself.

'Does it matter if she wears plain clothes? I asked.

'I can't see that it does, but there is something else. We are going to have to be aware that our language needs to be more… er!'

'Suitable for mixed company?' I suggested.

'As a serving police officer, no doubt she has come across language that could make her hair curl. But, she won't hear it from us!'

'Fair enough, I think we are pretty restrained anyway but point taken,' I agreed.

'I intend nipping in at the hospital on my way home to see how the DI is; coming, Will?'

'Yes, I'll run you there and we can annoy him for a minute or two,' I laughed.

'Always assuming he'll agree to see us.'

'More likely if the matron will allow it! We can always flash our warrant cards!'

'No chance. In seven years in CID I've never known a warrant card sway a hospital matron a fraction of an inch. We need to tell her that liaising with our chief is paramount to the investigation of the missing girl.'

'That should do the trick,' I smiled. 'I'll get ringing those boat companies.'

DS Whittington arrived back in the office just as the first of the boat companies answered my call. When questioned they stated that none of their boats had used our stretch of canal in the last five years, since before the mill closed down. They suggested that we contact another company, Canal Boats (Midlands) Ltd, who they thought had used the section from time to time. I thanked them and put the phone down.

'Ellen Parsons will be joining our merry band at eight tomorrow morning as an acting DC and as Harrington suggested she'll be in plain clothes. That should be worth seeing; she's a very presentable young lady. By the way I'm sure I don't need to point out we need to watch our language!' the DS said.

'We've already discussed it, Sarge,' Harrington pointed out.

'We're going to visit the DI in hospital when we've finished this afternoon, Sarge; room in the car if you want to come,' I suggested.

'Not much point, according to the ACC, he's been sent home with his ankle in plaster, and wobbling around on crutches. The ACC also asked us to have a presence in the office until midnight in case anything new comes in. Harrington, you are already dog-tired so get off home, Dexter you've a young family and your little-'un's are expecting you home, so I've volunteered myself for the task.'

'I'll get my boys to bed and relieve you at about half nine, Sarge,' I said.

'If you're sure? I'll take up your offer, thanks Dexter!'

'Don't tie me down to an exact time, the lads will have been playing with their little mate down the road and sometimes they're worn out and asleep by seven. Other times they are so wide-awake they just can't settle. But as soon as I can get away I'll be here.'

'Good enough!'

'They start school after the summer holiday, don't they?' asked Harrington.

'Yes, they turned five at Easter time but there's no place for them until the new school year.'

'That'll tire 'em out!' Harrington smiled, wistfully.

His wife had left him at Christmas the previous year and taken his little girl Penelope with her. Not the first broken marriage in the police force, and no doubt not the last; and also, no doubt the very reason that Diana Penworthy was thinking long and hard about becoming Mrs Dexter.

'Right! Any news on the boats?' asked DS Whittington.

'E. B. Clark reckon their boats haven't used our bit of canal since before the mill closed, but they suggested I tried another company Canal Boats (Midlands) Ltd,' I said consulting my notes.

'Give 'em a try, Will.'

I nodded but before I could pick up the phone it rang with an incoming call.

'Crammingdon Constabulary, DC Dexter speaking.'

'I hear your illustrious figurehead has broken his leg!' said a chuckling voice at the other end.

'Who is this?' I asked.

'Pete Warrell, Crammingdon Argus. Well has he? Word is the silly sod fell off a fire escape!'

'DI Brierly has broken his ankle in a fall. I can't tell you anymore, I've only just found out myself,' I replied.

'Yer, right! Look, is there any news on this missing kid? Not looking good is it?'

'We are following a number of lines of enquiry, as yet I can't give you any more details, except that we have all available manpower involved in the search,' I said.

'All available manpower: except the five officers outside the Town 'all makin' a right cock-up of directing traffic around that bloody great hole, I assume? Not to mention the wages snatch!'

'A number of other incidents are hampering the search, not to mention the weather.'

'I understand you and the other DC were searching the canal bank between the old mill and London Road Bridge this morning, an area your flat-foot boys had already searched. Not only that, you had a patch of brambles cleared! Why was that? Had you found something?' he asked, fishing for information.

'I'm sorry I can't give you any more information except that we are taking the girl's disappearance very seriously.'

'My editor's gon'a love that. Give us at least a decent quote.'

'We are doing everything we can to find her,' I said. 'I'm sure the Assistant Chief Constable will be issuing a statement in due course.'

'I'll quote that then. What you really mean is you're bloody well stumped!' he said and rang off.
It was hard not to admit, he had the case in a nutshell.

Canal Boats (Midlands) Ltd weren't able to give a lot of help. Rather than owning and running barges themselves, they were more a sort of clearing agency for lots of owner-operated boats. Their task was to locate loads and find a suitable boat to carry them. They admitted that many of the smaller boat companies never used their services as they already had regular work. They could only suggest that I rang the very company that had suggested *them*. It seemed we were doomed on that part of the enquiry, except that an idea had popped into my head that I intended checking out once I'd sorted it out in my mind.

Mrs Brierly opened the door to us at about six o'clock that evening.

'Come in. He's been like a bear with a sore head since he got home,' she said.

'Is that my merry band?' the DI asked, shouting from what was clearly the parlour.

'It is! Can I offer you a cup of tea and a slice of cake?' she smiled.
We both accepted.

'Don't get 'em bloody settled, they'll be here all night. Well come in, sit down, tell me what's been happening.'

'We found Jenny's school bag thrown in a bank of brambles,' said Harrington.

'Sure it was hers?' ask the DI.

'Her little story was still in it,' I replied and Harrington nodded.

'She's not still in the brambles?'

'We had them cleared; just the bag!' said Harrington.

'Thank god for that. Whereabouts is this bank of

brambles?'

'About half a mile from the mill, heading towards the London Road Bridge.'

'Missed by our wonderful boys in blue!'

'To be fair sir, I doubt we would have found it. A bloody great mongrel dived in and pulled it out,' I said.

'It means that the likelihood of a canal boat being involved in all this is still on. We need to check out to see if any have been up our bit of canal.'

'Already done sir, with no result,' I replied.

'Come on and sit to the table and help yourselves, I hate to see cups of tea and plates balanced on knees,' said Mrs Brierly, bringing in a tray.

'Blimey Doris, we'll never get rid of 'em now!' We sat ourselves at the table as requested and thanked her. The DI struggled his way up and took a seat with us, his plastered ankle sticking out just waiting to trip someone up.

'How's the leg, sir?' asked Harrington.

'Not bad now; I've broken my ankle, hurt like hell when the doctor yanked it back into place I'll be back to work tomorrow, all being well!' he shrugged.

'Oh no you won't Tom Brierly! These lads can manage without you for a few days,' said his wife.

'Babes in arms without me, and a man short,' he replied.

'Er… we've been allocated a new member, temporarily sir,' Harrington ventured.

'News to me, who's that then?'

'WPC Parsons, sir!'

'Ellen Parsons! Nice bright girl – see that she fits in!' he demanded.

'Already sorted, sir; we agreed between us that we would give her all the help we can, since some of her male colleagues in uniform might not take it too happily,' Harrington said.

'Good! Harrington have you been on all day?'

'Yes sir, Will is running me home.'

'The ACC has asked us to man the office until midnight. The DS is there now and I'm relieving him about nine, when I've settled my lads, sir,' I said,

'Right, Dexter get him home before he falls asleep where he sits,' he said and nodded towards Harrington, 'and I'll see you both in the morning.'

'Oh no you won't, Tom Brierly!' his wife snapped, as we took our leave.

The boys were nodding off over their evening meal when I arrived back home.

'Did you enjoy playing with your friend?' I asked as I sat myself down at the table.

Too tired to speak they both nodded.

'Will you read us a story, Daddy?' George asked.

'Provided you are washed and ready for bed by quarter past seven,' I agreed.

'I can read some of the words,' said Will.

'That's good, has Auntie Flossie been teaching you?' I asked.

'Yes and I'm better than George!'

'No you're not!'

'Yes I am!'

'I'm sure you're both very good and you should help each other, we always get better with help in everything we do. Don't we Auntie Flossie?' I asked.

'Yes, and they are both very good anyway,' she smiled.

'Auntie Flossie taught me to read before *I* went to school!' I said.

'Coo!' they said together.

'I'd forgotten that! Yes we used to sit by the kitchen fire in Gamma's old house and I helped your daddy with the words,' she said and smiled at the happy memory.

'Was our daddy little like us?'

'Yes, of course. Now come on eat up and ready

for bed.'

'Now he is big and a tatective!' said Will.

'Detective!' said George, matter-of-fact as ever.

'I know, I just said it wrong!'

By eight o'clock they were fast asleep and I quietly slipped out of their room and down the stairs to the kitchen.

'I've made you a couple of sandwiches, seeing how you are going to be there until midnight.' Flossie said.

'Thanks, though I doubt I'll need them after that meal,' I smiled.

I'd parked the car down the drive by the gate, out of the way in case Henry had an emergency call, and far enough away so as not to wake the boys as I started the engine.

DS Whittington sat in the DI's chair with his feet on the desk, his head was lolling to one side and he was snoring gently as I entered. I quietly retraced my steps to half way down the stairs, sneezed loudly, made a far from quiet ascent of the stairs and entered this time wiping my nose.

'Evening Dexter, all quiet, nothing to report, I'll get off home and see if I can catch a night's sleep. How was the DI by the way?' asked the DS now bright eyed and alert.

'Seems okay, reckons to be back with us in the morning but his missus sees it somewhat differently,' I chuckled.

'He should take it easy, he took a hell of a tumble. Oh yes, Mr Parminter came in about an hour ago with a photo of Jenny. A pal of mine is a dab hand with the photography thing and he's agreed to get it copied; should have them here before midnight,' he yawned.

'Okay, how many is he doing?'

'I asked him for as many as he can manage; he

reckons about ten tonight, more if we need them tomorrow.'

'I'll get 'em distributed as soon as they arrive,' I suggested and the DS agreed.

'Okay, that's me, I'm off. Knock off at midnight, back here six in the morning sharp.'

'Righto, Sarge.'

The DS's mate, a thick-set chap with thick lensed glasses and a smile that spread from ear to ear, arrived with the photos a few minutes before midnight.

'Bloody rain! Summer ah? Not as yer'd bloody know it,' he said continuing to smile as he took off a sou'wester and shook it on the DI's square of carpet. He opened a leather pouch and took out six of the photos.

'Thanks, that's really helpful,' I said as he handed them to me.

'Not as clear as the original, mind you that's not all that good. You lose a bit of quality when to copy a photo, have to photograph it, develop the negative and work from that. Yer can still see who it is but it's not wonderful if you get me.'

'I'm sure they'll be a great help, do you need me to pay you?'

'Not bloody likely! If they help find this wee girl, they're on the house. I'll get some more done for the morning. Are them 'am sandwiches?' he asked pointing at my half-finished supper.

'They are! can I offer you one?' I asked though he was clearly fishing for the invite.

'Ta pal, a cuppa wouldn't go a miss, neither.'
The chap had put himself out for us, the least I could do was make him a cup of tea, and a ham sandwich. We sat and chatted for a while, as he made appreciative comments about my rapidly diminishing pack up. It's lucky I had had a good meal earlier I thought.

It was ten past twelve as I got into the Hornet, having left two copies of the photograph with the desk sergeant who agreed to make sure all of his chaps saw it as they returned to the station. By twenty-five past I was in bed, though I can't say that I slept. I just couldn't stop thinking about little Jenny Parminter, wondering where she was and what had happened to her.

5

We all assembled as directed at six the next morning. DS Whittington again sat in the DI's chair and looked at us both.

'Right Dexter, I know that my mate brought the photos in last night; anything else to report?'

'No Sarge. He's bringing in more copies some-time this morning. I've had an idea that I'd like to follow up, though.'

'What's your idea then Will?'

'I looked at the map last night after you'd gone. I got the sheets from the desk sergeant, the ones that cover the canal as far as its connection at Trent Lock. About half way there, there's a flight of three locks, any boat would have to pass through there if it was to end up at the mill!'

'Is there a lock keeper?'

'I'm not sure. There's a house marked but whether it's occupied – who knows?'

'It's out in hostile territory then?' he said refer-ring to the fact that it was out of our jurisdiction.

'I'll get on to county and get them to follow it up, Sarge.'

'No, we'll give 'em a ring and see if they mind us covering it. Since they've grabbed a couple of our chaps to help with the wages snatch I should think they'll play ball?'

'Do you want me to ring, Sarge?' I asked.

'No, I'll do it. You put the kettle on Will,' he grinned

It was the best part of an hour before the DS was

able to speak to the desk sergeant at County HQ. The phone was either engaged or just not being answered each time he tried to call. Even when it was answered, the chap on the other end wasn't able to give us the okay.

'He's promised to get back to us as soon as he can with an answer,' the DS said shaking his head in disgust.

'Assuming there was a boat, and that Jenny was abducted and taken away in it, how do we trace it? It could be anywhere by now,' I said.

'It seems like the only lead we've got, and if there wasn't a boat – God only knows what happened to the poor kid,' the DS shrugged. 'Even if she is in a boat she could be anywhere!'

'Not really Sarge, it's a canal boat and if she's on it, it must be on the system somewhere,' Harrington pointed out.

'That's true, where a car or a horse and cart can go anywhere, boats are stuck in the canal system,' the DS agreed.

'At Trent Lock the Erewash canal joins the navigable part of the Trent. Problem is at that point you can go any one of three ways, out to the Wash near Hull, out to the Mersey at Liverpool or down south towards Northampton and on towards London,' DC Harrington admitted.

'Well that narrows it down a bloody lot I must say,' the DS grunted, shaking his head.

The phone rang just before eight o'clock just as Acting DC Ellen Parsons entered the CID office wearing a smart, well-tailored blue skirt and jacket and an equally smart salute.

'Sit down Ellen, I'll be with you in a moment!' said DS Whittington, picking up the phone.

'Thanks,' she smiled.

'I'll make a fresh pot of tea!' I said, getting up to sort out the kettle.

'Could I have coffee? I don't drink tea!' she asked showing a little embarrassment.

'I don't suppose DI Brierly would mind me raiding his coffee,' I smiled.

'Oh, I'd better bring my own in the morning, I don't want to get into bad books before I even start!' she said with a grimace.

'I don't think the DI would mind on this occasion,' laughed Harrington.

Whittington replaced the phone, 'Good morning Ellen, welcome to the team.'

'Thank you, sir.'

'Right, we've got the go ahead to carry out the investigation wherever we need on county's patch. So we can go and see the lock keeper. Where is it by the way, Dexter?'

'According to the map the canal runs past Backridge, just this side of the village there's a flight of three locks. A lane runs down to the lock keeper's cottage.' I said.

'I know it! I used to play with some friends in the village as a kid!' Ellen said.

'Really?' asked the DS.

'Oh yes, we were always down at the canal watching the boats in and out of the lock!' Ellen smiled, clearly thinking of happy times.

'Well bugger me! That's a stroke of luck! Oops! Sorry!' said Harrington and we two fellows looked at him in censure.

'Oh, don't worry about me I've heard a lot worse than that in uniform. I want to fit in and that's not going to happen very easily if you are all looking at every word you say,' she chuckled. 'Relax, I want to be one of the team!'

'You already are, we've all agreed that you will be an asset and we'll give you all the help we can,' said the DS and looked around. We both nodded our agreement.

'Thank you, sir.'

'First rule of this department: we do not salute each other. The DI when he's here is "sir", I'm "Sarge" and you can address these two rogues how you see fit. Everything above the DI will be in uniform and you salute and "sir" as normal. Okay?'

'Understood! Thank you Sarge,' she nodded. 'But the lock, how does it fit in with the case?'

'We are working on the assumption that the child, Jenny, has been kidnapped on a canal boat. For what purpose we don't know. Dexter has suggested that the boat, if there indeed was one, would need to pass up and down through the lock at Backridge, since the canal ends more of less at Jenny's house.'

'That's right it does, but even when we were kids the boats going up and down were few and far between. You could count them on one hand; seven or eight a day.'

'Blimey, I bet you have a job buying gloves?' said Harrington.

Jenny looked puzzled for a moment then burst out laughing.

'Not since the operation!' she quipped. We all laughed.

'Settle down children, let's get back to business. Is there still a lock keeper, do you know?' the DS asked.

'There certainly used to be. We kids got quite friendly with him, he reckoned he was an old sea captain, told us the most amazin' stories. He used to let us operate one of the sluice-gates. Thinking about it, there will almost certainly still be a lock keeper, you need to know what you are doing. That sluice we operated added extra water to the lock.'

'For what purpose?' Harrington asked.

'The canal from the mill at the far end, to the lock is higher than the run to the Erewash. Each time the locks are used water is lost from the upper section, eventually it would run dry,' she said looking around us.

We all nodded.

'There's a couple of little streams run directly into the upper section but they are not usually enough to keep it topped up. A stream comes in at a lower level about five feet lower than the level of the upper lock. If a boat is going upstream it enters the lock through the lower gates, the gates are closed, water from the middle lock flows in and fills it. As the boat progresses upwards the sluice is opened as necessary. When the extra water has filled as much as it can, the sluice is closed and the paddles, little sluices on the upper gates, are opened to finish the fill!'

'So you only lose about half the water you would have done?' said the DS.

'Yes Sarge. I seem to remember the keeper telling us that there was a sort of holding pool close by, to make sure that there was always enough extra water available. I'm sure there will still be a lock keeper; it's a tricky job,' she nodded.

'Since you seem to know a good bit about it, go with Dexter and give him the lay of the land.'

'Right, sir... Sarge!'

It's a bit over four miles to the village of Backridge and the lock, and we set off at about a quarter past eight.

'Nice little car!' Ellen said.

'Thank you, I must admit I love it,' I nodded.

'It's yours isn't it?'

'It is; I've had it a couple of years. It has sentimental attachments so I intend to keep it as long as I can,' I smiled.

'You're sentimentally attached to a car?'

'It's a long story!'

'Sorry, I'm prying into your business; the copper in me I suppose!'

'Don't worry about it, I'll tell you the details sometime,' I smiled.

We drove down the lane from the road to the

lock; deep puddles filled the ruts and potholes. Proof if any was needed that the rain was still falling, adding a new dimension to the old saying "Flaming June".

'Oh, dear!' said Ellen. 'This place *has* gone downhill.'

'Not as you remember it?'

'No!'

'What's changed?' I asked.

'It must be fifteen years or more since I was last here, but I remember it as a well-kept place. The cottage brightly painted and the garden was a picture, not all weedy and overgrown like this. There used to be flower beds and a sign, "Backridge Lock" with gold lettering on a jet black background, it glinted in the sun!' she said almost tearfully.

'This must be the lock keeper!' I said, as we got out of the car and an elderly chap with a Charlie Chaplin moustache came walking towards us.

'Can I 'elp you?' he asked.

I could see that Ellen was itching to make the first move so I held off, nodding for her to take the lead.

'Mr Durose isn't it?' asked Ellen.

'Aye it is!' he said screwing his face up, clearly at a bit of a loss.

'Do you remember me? Ellen Parsons!' she said holding out her hand.

'Name seems to ring a bell but my memory's gettin' on a bit, like me!' he chuckled.

'I used to come here in the summer holidays, with the Davis twins and a boy call Willy Emmett.'

'Oh, aye; I remember you now. You four little buggers used to drink all of my missus's homemade lemonade. Never a drop did I get when you lot was around. You've made a handsome young lass, I'll say that for yer!'

'It must have been all that lemonade! How is Mrs Durose?' Ellen enquired.

'Middlin'; don't get around s' well as she used

to. She's in the house, pop in an' 'ave a word. I know she'd love to see yer,' he nodded towards the cottage door.

'I will before we go but I'm here officially. This is Detective Constable Dexter and I'm an Acting Detective Constable as well.'

'Actin', what, like on the stage?' he asked a bit puzzled.

'No I'm a WPC, but I've been placed in CID to help out!'

'So, he's your boss?' he asked nodding at me.

'Sort of,' I said, 'showing her the ropes.'

'So what brings you 'ere, 'ave I done summat wrong?'

'No!' I said taking up the threads. 'We are after a bit of information.'

'Summat as you think I'll know?'

'Only you can help us Mr Durose!'

'Oh, well in that case you'd better come inside,' he nodded and led the way to the door.

Three large sash windows, looking out onto the canal must have made the cottage surprisingly light and comfortable. He showed us into what was clearly the main room, lit by two of the windows. It wasn't a small room, yet a couple of hefty armchairs and sideboard full with well-polished brassware of all types, made the room look cluttered. A beam across the centre of what was clearly also the kitchen, held a copper post horn and horse brasses were everywhere. The massive kitchen table, surrounded by four dining chairs, held two freshly baked loaves of brown bread, and an apple pie. The smells reminded me of coming home to the fresh breads and pies that Alice used to bake.

'Ma; look who's come to see yer!' said Mr Durose.

'Well I never, is it our little Ellen; it is in't it?'

'Hello Mrs Durose, how are yer keeping?' asked Ellen.

'Not as sprightly as I was but I manage yer know. You look well. Is this your young man?' she asked eyeing me up and down.

'He's 'er boss; don't embarrass the gal, Ma,' said the lock keeper.

'Sorry, no offence: mind, you could do a lot worse from the look of 'im!' she chuckled, and Ellen coloured up.

'You were after some information.' Mr Durose butted in, to cover Ellen's embarrassment.

'Yes,' said Ellen, 'we want to know if a boat passed through the lock three days ago?'

'Ten or more boats a day when I started here in 1905, thirty odd years ago. Now if we get three a week it's a miracle. Three days yer say? Yes, up, turn round and back down again not a couple of hours later. 'Arry Sumpter picked up a load at Camfords; can't turn round there now, had to go on up to clock mill turn in their pool and back down again. Why do you ask?'

Ellen looked at me, clearly wondering how much we could tell the lock keeper. Clearly she wanted me to make the decision.

'It's an ongoing enquiry so I can't tell you too much. We think there could be some connection with the eleven year old girl who went missing three days ago,' I said.

'Oh, that poor wee lass. Have you not found her yet?'

'No Mrs Durose, I afraid we haven't,' I admitted.

'Her poor mother must be frantic,' she said, shaking her head.

'Accordin' to the paper, she lived by the canal up by Clock Mill. Are you thinking she's been kidnapped?' asked Mr Durose.

'It's one of our lines of enquiry. We need to speak to the boat owner, to be able to eliminate him,' I nodded.

'Can you tell us anything about him? Harry Sumpter wasn't it?' asked Ellen, taking out her notebook.

'I can!' said Mrs Durose. 'The poor chap lost his wife and daughter to the flu two – no three – years ago!'

'That's right he did, never been the same since! Never has no time to stop and chat these days. 'Sept, when he came through three days ago, he seemed more cheerful somehow, like he was comin' to terms with the situation; know what I mean?'

I knew exactly what he meant of course.

'Our problem is we've no idea where he'd go from here,' I said.

'That's easy; if he picked up at Camfords he's headed for Liverpool!' said the lock keeper with a knowing nod.

'You're sure?'

'That's the only place they ever send stuff to,' he nodded.

'That's really helpful, Mr Durose. But, how far will he have got by now, though?' asked Ellen.

'Three days, he'd probably be there by now, 'sept I 'appen to know he's probably still at Swarkstone!'

'How do you know that?' I asked.

''Cos some daft bugger has rammed the lock gates and brought everythin' to a halt,' he nodded.

'He's stuck there you reckon? Surely they'll be doing emergency repairs?'

'Aye, you'd think that wouldn't yer. This is the canal system though. We've not run at a profit since the railways came along, and now with road transport startin' to top even them; if it's repaired by Monday I for one will be most surprised. In fact, I've had a shillin' on it not bein' repaired before Monday night with the landlord at the "Lazy Shepherd" and I can't see me bein' out of pocket!' he grinned.

'Is it that bad Mr Durose?' asked Ellen.

'Yer used to be able t' get from one end o' the country to the other by canal at one time. Now there's great chunks of the system closed due to no traffic; so aye lass – it's that bad.'

'That's awful Mr Durose?' she said shaking her head.

'You've to move with the times, we're just too slow. Since the pressure that the Great War produced everythin's expected tomorrow, in some cases today.'

'You're sure he'll still be at Swarkstone?' I asked, bringing the conversation back to the subject in hand.

'Aye, he'll still be there, there's been no repairs, not as far as I'm aware.'

'What does Mr Sumpter's boat look like?' asked Ellen.

'Black hull, upper parts are a sort of deep red…'

'Maroon!' Mrs Durose corrected.

'Aye that's it Maroon, with yellow letterin', "Trent Wanderer – Sawley", on the cabin.'

'Are you on the phone Mr Durose?' I asked.

'Aye, you'll need tuppence, we 'ave to pay for our calls like a phone-box.'

'That's no problem Mr Durose,' I said fishing the small change out of my pocket.

It was two pence wasted as it turned out, since there was no answer from the CID office.

'I don't like going ahead without the DS's okay but I think we need to catch up with Mr Sumpter whilst we know where he is!' I said as I put the phone down.

'For what it's worth I agree with you,' Ellen nodded.

We said our goodbyes and Ellen promised to pop in and have a real chat with them both before too long. The Hornet started first try and we bounced our way back to the road.

'Swarkstone's south of Derby, on the Melbourne road isn't it?' I asked. It was an area that I knew only vaguely, even though I was born in Derby.

'Yes! I reckon we can save time by bypassing Derby. If we go through Borrowash and Elvaston we can be there in an hour or so!' she nodded.

After a couple of minutes silence, Ellen asked, 'Will… can I call you Will?'

'Of course, what's bothering you?' I asked.

'Nothing really… well what are the chances of me being kept on once the DI is back in harness?' she asked with a weak smile.

'If we can crack this case; pretty good I'd say!'

'It's only my first day, but the chance of seeing a case brought to a close is a real spur. It's what's missing from uniformed work; you see an arrest but you're not really connected to it, if you know what I mean?'

'I loved my time in uniform. I enjoyed talking to folk; my old sergeant, Sergeant Bell always said, "Never forget the value of a friendly chat with ordinary folk". He reckoned it was often the things they didn't say that was as much value as what they did,' I laughed. 'But I agree, following a case, being in on the twists and turns, that's what's important to me. That, and seeing wrong 'un's behind bars!'

'As a WPC I never got the chance of making an arrest, I always had to have a male copper as a partner, never really allowed to work on my own!'

'Never?'

'I was sometimes left behind to look after a be-reaved relative, make a pot of tea, add sympathy and support, but not out in the big world on my own,' she shrugged.

'We often have to work as pairs so there's no guarantee it's going to be any better here,' I said.

'But at least I'll see how things are progressing and have a chance to put my ideas forward without them being sneered at; then have them put forward a couple of days later as someone else's idea and cheered as a break-through!' she frowned.

41

'Was it really that bad? Did that really happen?' I asked. I hadn't had a lot to do with the three WPC's in my time in uniform, they had been used mostly in the south division of the town and I had worked the north.

'Yes several times, often by someone further up the chain. I suppose, so long as an idea gets used, or at least looked at, it doesn't matter but it would have been nice to get a bit of the credit for coming up with it,' she smiled.

'Now there I can put your mind at ease. Tom Brierly will always give credit where it's due. And back you up if he thinks the top brass might stamp on you.'

'Even for a female DC, acting DC at that?' she queried.

'I'd bet my life on it. DI Brierly will give you hell if you get it wrong, but defend you with everything he has if anyone else tries to tear a strip off!'

'I've only sort of seen him in passing, saluted him, said good morning, that sort of thing! What's he really like?'

'Unconventional, to say the least! I was in uniform and had been involved in a car crash that had put me in hospital. He managed to wangle me half pay even though it happened in my own time, but he suggested that if I came into his office to put his paperwork in order he'd have me seconded to CID, on full pay even though I'd be deskbound,' I smiled.

'That was good of him!'

'It was, you're right, but there was an ulterior motive; he'd been warned off following up a particular line of enquiry. He didn't want to let it drop, just because the person in question happened to be a big mate of the then Chief Constable, so my job was to follow up his leads without getting caught doing it. In at the deep end literally, I learned a massive amount in double quick time. Really good fun I can tell you,' I laughed.

'Sounds like it. I think I like him already!'

'He's great to work for and my guess is he'll be

in within the next couple of days!'

'With his ankle in plaster?' she asked.

'It'll take more than that to stop the DI taking control, at least from his desk, especially since we are looking for a missing girl!'

We turned off the Melbourne road up the lane to the small canal junction at Swarkstone, where it connected with a short branch to Derby. A bridge passes over the canal, almost over the lower set of gates. Five or six canal boats were moored in each direction held up by the damaged lock gates. A temporary wooden boom had been erected to hold the levels correct whilst the damaged gates were removed. A gang of canal workers were hoisting the old gate out as we arrived. The "Trent Wanderer" was first in line but pulled well back from the gate to allow the gang room to work. If the gates had been damaged, perhaps only ten minutes later, Harry Sumpter and his boat could well have been through the lock and miles away by now, maybe already in Liverpool as Mr Durose had suggested.

'We'd better find the lock keeper and explain why we are here,' I said.

'Do you want me to find him whilst you look for Mr Sumpter?' she asked.

'Yes, just tell him that we need to talk to Mr Sumpter.'

'Okay, I think that must be him, on the other side of the canal,' she said pointing to a chap in a dark blue uniform and peaked cap, as we made our way back over the bridge.

Although Harry's boat had a smoking chimney, of Harry there was no sign. Only one boat, the last but one, showed any signs of human life.

'Good morning, sir. I'm looking for Mr Harry Sumpter,' I said to a chap who had stepped off a boat onto the towpath.

'He'll be with the rest of 'em in The Crewe!' he nodded down the lane we had just come up.

'In the crew?' I asked.

'The Crewe & Harpur. The pub on the main road.'

'Oh, right. Funny name for a pub,' I commented.

'There's funnier I dare say,' he shrugged.

'You think he'll be there?'

'Don't know of another, and they all went off about an hour ago.'

'But not you?' I asked.

'I don't drink! Had to choose years ago; I like a pipe o' 'bacca, and if I drink and smoke at the same time I gets an 'ead like I don't know what. I couldn't do both so I chose the pipe. Haven't had a drop of beer for ten years or more,' he said.

'This pub, on the main road you say?'

'Down the lane turn t' yer right, follo' the road round to yer left and it's on yer right. Big place with stables; they reckon it was built expecting the road to become the Ashby turnpike but it never happened. Like I say big – yer can't miss it!'

'Thank you, sir.'

Ellen arrived back a few moments later.

'The lock keeper says he thinks the boatmen have all gone to the pub on the main road, Will,' she said.

'That's what this gentleman reckons,' I agreed.

As the boatman had suggested the Crewe & Harpur had been built on a grand scale, though like the canals it now served it had seen better days. A rowdy crowd stood at the bar, and another equally rowdy group sat around a roaring fire. Heads turned as we walked in and came to rest on Ellen.

'Can I help you sir, madam?' asked the barman.

'I'm DC Dexter and this is DC Parsons; we are looking for a Mr Harry Sumpter. We have reason to believe he's here,' I replied.

There was the sound of a chair scraping on the tiled floor and a man shot past us and out of the door. Ellen was after him like a shot.

'That's not 'Arry, that's Ned Farrier, he's just seen his bus to Melbourne turnin' the corner,' laughed a chap from fireside group.

Ellen had the poor chap by the collar as I shouted out through the door, 'That's not him! He's running for his bus!'

The bus had drawn almost level with the pub, and vaulting the low wall, I was able to stop it before it started to climb the bridge.

'Sorry sir, I thought you were the chap we need to talk to and you were trying to escape,' Ellen said.

'I wouldn't want to bloody try and outrun you lass!' the chap said, getting on the bus.

We looked at each other and began to laugh.

'Sorry Will. I thought he was our man,' she said.

'So did I, but you were quicker off the mark. No harm done, the chap made his bus and no doubt he'll tell the tale for many a long day,' I chuckled.

'Yes, and he'll think we were from the County force,' smiled Ellen.

'We'd better go and see the real chap if he hasn't made off in another direction,' I pointed out.

Back in the Crewe & Harpur we found Harry Sumpter standing just inside the door.

'You looking for me?' he asked.

'Mr Harry Sumpter?' I asked looking the chap up and down. He was, at a guess, a chap in his mid-fifties, wearing clothing that set him as a bargeman. His clean but well-worn dark grey, almost black, suit and waistcoat had a gold watch chain dangling across his brewer's paunch. A red and white spotted neckerchief knotted at the front was loosely tied around his neck and an equally well-worn bowler hat topped off what was most probably his Sunday best.

'Aye, that's me; who's askin'?'

'I'm Detective Constable Dexter and this is DC Parsons, I wonder if we might have a word, Mr Sumpter.'

'Talk's cheap enough and I'm goin' nowhere just at the moment,' he nodded. 'Though I can't see why the police would want a word with *me*!'

'Could we go back to your boat?' I asked.

'Warmer here, unless you think there's summat on my boat you need to see?' he said pointing to the table by the fire which had suddenly been vacated whilst we were outside.

'For the moment this will do just fine,' I said and we seated ourselves by the fire. I nodded to Ellen to make the first move, while I kept a close eye on Mr Sumpter's reactions.

'We have reason to believe that you were at Clock Mill on Monday the eighth of June. Is that correct?' she asked.

'Clock Mill in Crammingdon? Aye that's right. Not at the mill exactly, I used their pool to turn the boat. I know nothing about happenings at the mill!' he said looking from one to the other of us.

'Can you give me a rough idea what time that was?'

'I can do better than that. I can tell you exactly what time it was!'

'You can?' she asked.

'I looked at m` watch just as I went back under the mill arch. This old watch o' mine said seven minutes past four; it were my old dad's an' never misses a tick. I remember thinking I'll tie up for the night at Trent Lock, have a couple of pints in the tavern and meck an early start in t' mornin'.'

'We are investigating the disappearance of an eleven year old girl. She lives in the cottages by Clock Mill. She would have been returning home about that time. We were wondering if you saw anything of her,' I asked.

'Wondering if I took her; kidnapped her, yer mean,' he snapped.' I see why you wanted to look in my boat now!'

'We just want your help Mr Sumpter, the girl has just vanished,' Ellen said, with a friendly nod.

'I didn't see no girl, it's doubtful I'd 'ave seen 'er anyway. You're low down yer see, the 'ouses are way above the canal, and the bridge is higher still. I might 'ave seen 'er if she were lookin' over the bridge, but otherwise no chance,' he said shaking his head.

'We have reason to believe that she went along the canal, even if only on the towpath,' I said.

'So that's me still in the frame then?' he asked.

'You have to admit it seems suspicious,' Ellen pointed out.

'You'd better come and take a look in m' boat,' he snapped.

The tiny cabin of the narrowboat, roughly half the size of the boy's bedroom back at Flossie's house, had clearly once been a family home. Mrs Sumpter would have had a hard life cooking, washing and doing day-to-day chores in the confines of the tiny space. Mrs Durose, the lock keeper's wife had told us that Mrs Sumpter and their young daughter had both died of the flu and the missing womanly hand was obvious. What flat surfaces there were, were covered in an accumulation of dust, brass ornaments were tarnished and unkempt.

Nothing suggested that Jenny Parminter had spent any time in that tiny cabin. Ellen looked around for anything that might have given us a lead, without success.

'Satisfied – are yer?' asked Sumpter.

'You're sure you didn't see the girl on the towpath that afternoon?' I asked.

'In all that rain? The kid 'ud 'ave to be barmy to walk down by the canal, wi a warm 'ouse just over the bridge.'

'I didn't say she lived over the bridge Mr Sump-

47

ter!' I said.

'Are you tryin' t' catch me out?' he snarled. 'The kid must have lived at the far end of the lane, over the bridge or she'd have had to *pass* her house to get to the canal!'

'Why did you say, "Must *have* lived" rather than "Must live", Mr Sumpter?' Ellen asked.

'Bloody hell – yer've got t' watch what yer say wi' you lot, ant yer? I suppose I just thought, what must be in the back o' your minds, as she's already a goner!' he said shaking his head.

'We're trying not to think that way, but it seems odd that she failed to return home. We happen to know she had a lift to the top of the lane, and had less than a hundred yards to run to the safety of her home,' I pointed out.

'Look I'm very sorry for the kid's mam and dad and I hope she turns up safe and sound. But I didn't see her or kidnap her, alright?' Mr Sumpter said with an open-handed gesture.

'Thank you Mr Sumpter! You can't think of anything unusual from that afternoon, anything no matter how small or seemingly insignificant?' I asked.

'Aye, there was summat as made me think it were a bit queer. It's about a mile, no say a mile an' a half, from the mill t' the London Road Bridge,' he said scratching his chin.

'It is. I walked it yesterday,' I agreed.

'That stretch o' the cut is very weedy and silted up in places, so I was only trickling' along, barely walkin' pace, less in places. Didn't want to get m' propeller tangled up like, so it must have taken the best part of half an 'our to get there,' he nodded.

'Yes!' I agreed, 'it looks to be in need of a bit of attention.'

'Not a deal o' chance o' that 'appenin'!'

'Carry on Mr Sumpter.'

'Just as I was goin' under the bridge a chap was

48

walkin' down the steps from the bridge to the towpath. The rain 'ad eased a bit at that time. A posh lookin' chap wi a smart mac; well to do – not rich yer understand, just well to do,' he nodded again.

'What made you think it was unusual?' asked Ellen.

'He were carryin' a briefcase, like a lawyer or an accountant, but it was old and battered, wi' a strap that near dangled in the mud.'

'A leather briefcase with a long strap: what colour was it, can you remember?'

'I reckon it was tan, brown yer know, but it were the strap I remember like it should have been over his shoulder.'

'Can you describe this man Mr Sumpter?' I asked.

'I on'y saw 'im for a couple o' seconds!'

'Please try Mr Sumpter, I could be very important,' said Ellen.

'Right, let me think. He were about 'arf way down the steps when I first noticed 'm, so I remember his shoes, I got a fair look at 'em yer see. They were brown with them fancy patterns punched in the leather; there's a special name for 'em…'

'Brogues?' I suggested.

'Aye that's it, brogues. That's what I thought was queer! Would a chap with fancy, shiny brogue shoes be carryin' a tatty old briefcase like that? Then, when 'e saw me lookin' at 'im, 'e looked away; like he wanted to hide 'is face. "He's up t' no good" I thought, like yer do!'

'How was he dressed Mr Sumpter, can you remember?' Ellen asked, as she took out her notebook again and started to write down his description.

''E 'ad a fancy light grey raincoat like I said; good quality, not the best perhaps but good. My old dad used to call 'em Aberdeen but that's not it, a word like that but I can't remember!' he said shaking his head.

49

'Gabardine?' Ellen asked.

'Aye that's it. Nice it was, it'd be warm, keep the cold an' wet out. He 'ad a black trilby hat, I remember he had to grab at it t' 'old it on ag'in the wind,' he nodded.

'What sort of age would you say he was?' I asked.

'I'd guess he was forty, m'be a bit older. Been in the army I'd say, carried hisself well, been a Sergeant, Sergeant Major perhaps.'

'For a few seconds look you seem to remember quite a lot!' I chuckled.

'Funny that; I seem t' see it like one o' them fillums at the pictures!'

'Get to the pictures often, Mr Sumpter?' asked Ellen, trying to keep the friendly banter going, wondering, no doubt as I was, where it might lead.

'I took m' missus an' daughter a couple o' times. They both liked Charlie Chaplin. Couldn't stand the silly bugger meself but *they* loved him!'

'Thank you Mr Sumpter, that's been most helpful. One thing interests me. The briefcase this chap was carrying, what you thought was odd, out of place. Could you describe it a bit more?' I asked.

'Like I say, it were brown, old and battered w' a long strap. As 'e got to the bottom o' the steps it near dangled in the mud. Thinkin' about it, it sempt a bit small. In my experience, lawyers and the like generally have a big impressive one wi' gold coloured lock, this 'ad two little leather straps and buckles,' he nodded.

'Can you remember which hand he carried it in Mr Sumpter?' asked Ellen.

I remember thinking what a good question that was.

''E were comin' down the steps towards me and the case was nearest me, so 'e 'ad it in 'is left 'and. Aye that's right it were in 'is left 'and!'

'Thank you, that's very useful. If you remember anything else, could you give me a ring or drop me a line?' I asked giving him one of my cards.

'I will but I reckon I've told you all I'm likely to,' he replied putting it in the pocket of his waistcoat.

We got back in the car and moved off down the lane.

'I think we should take another look at the London Road Bridge on our way back to the station!' I said.

'Mm. I was going to suggest it. Could the briefcase this unknown chap was carrying have been Jenny's school satchel, do you think?' she asked.

'It seems there's a very good chance. I reckon Mr Sumpter happened to see this chap in the act of looking for somewhere to dispose if it!'

'That surely suggests a bad outcome to this case!' she said, flicking though her notebook.

'It doesn't look good, does it,' I agreed.

I was getting low on fuel, and called into a small wayside garage and had the chap put four gallons of petrol in the tank, I filed the slip of paper that he gave me in receipt in the glove box and we set off again to take a look at the bridge in question.

'What do you think has happened to her, Will?' Ellen asked, as we got rolling.

'I'll be honest. I fear she's already dead! I hope to god I'm wrong but I've a feeling in my stomach that's saying bad things,' I said.

'Could this chap with the briefcase or satchel be the chap who gave her a lift from school?'

'Roland Jellicoe? On the face of it he looks like a prime candidate,' I said.

'According to the Sarge this morning, didn't Mr Jellicoe come forward, offering the information on the first morning?'

'He did, it was me he spoke to; I was at the school asking about Jenny.'

'Looks like he's in the clear, then,' Ellen said.

'When we've looked at the bridge, we'll report back to the station and decide what the next move is.'

Where the canal passes under the London Road, it narrows to the width of a single boat. The bridge is made of brick with a shallow stone arch. The road rises slightly from each side to pass over the canal and a flight of steps connects the bridge to the towpath. I drove over it back towards the town centre and stopped in the little carpark of the "Bridge Inn". We walked back to the steps and down to the towpath.

'Mr Sumpter would certainly see the chap's shoes. There's a clear view from the canal,' Ellen remarked.

'I didn't see Mr Jellicoe's shoes, he was sent for and I sat behind the headmistress's desk, so that when he came in, his shoes were hidden to me,' I said.

'You were using the headmistress's room for the interview?'

'Yes, just for the few minutes I was talking to Mr Jellicoe.'

'Is he the sort of man who'd wear brogues and a gabardine rain coat?' Ellen asked.

'Probably,' I admitted.

'He's not bound to be left handed though is he?'

'Not bound to be but he was holding the case, whatever it was, in his left hand,' I pointed out.

'I guess we would in the same circumstances. We both held the rail as we came down the steps,' she said, nodding at it.

She was right, we had. The rail as you come down is on your right, making your left hand your free hand. The stone steps were worn and slippery; holding the rail was a must.

'We are assuming that this man is the person we need. He could be an innocent person who just happens to be walking along the towpath for some reason,' I suggested, though I wasn't really convinced myself.

'Going where?'

'Camfords, where Mr Sumpter took on his load, that's the place over there,' I said pointing to a small factory that looked nearly as derelict at the canal that served it. 'Clock Mill or any of the five or six properties that back onto the canal. But, to be honest I have to admit, the man on the steps seems to be our man and just at the moment Mr Jellicoe looks favourite.'

'How far is it to the place where you found Jenny's school bag?' she asked.

'About half way to Clock Mill, say three quarters of a mile.'

'Four miles an hour is a brisk walking pace, so say ten to twelve minutes each way, assuming that he turned back after throwing the bag away!'

'Longer dodging all of these puddles, and wearing a nice pair of brogues, I guess he'd be pretty careful,' I said.

'So, the best part of half an hour before he's back at his car?'

'I reckon that's about right!' I agreed.

'Meantime, Jenny is left locked in the car?'

'Unless he'd already deposited her somewhere: his house presumably. Nothing more we can do here, let's get back and report to the Sarge,' I suggested.

I parked the car in the rear yard at Whitecross Yard and we entered up the steps at the back of the building. At the foot of the stairs, we met Harrington coming down.

'Where have you two been?' he whispered.

'Interviewing our boatman,' I replied.

'Our acting inspector is on the warpath! You'd better have something pretty bloody good for him or he'll hang you out to dry, the pair of you,' he chuckled and continued on his way.

A look passed between us and we climbed the stairs.

What we told Sergeant Whittington closed his annoyance pretty quickly.

'So you reckon that Mr Jellicoe the girl's teacher has abducted her?' he asked.

'Mr Jellicoe actually teaches the boys. But yes, we think he's abducted Jenny.'

'Based on the evidence supplied by this Harry Sumpter?' the sergeant asked.

'It seems to add up. The time he was seen, seems about right; carrying what appeared to be a small briefcase, possibly a school bag. We both think we should have another word with our Mr Jellicoe!' I said and Ellen.

'Right, it's half past three, I'll ring the school and get him to wait. As soon as we know he's still there you two get off and have another word,' he said picking up the phone. 'Meantime, one of you put the kettle on.'

It turned out that Mr Ronald Jellicoe hadn't turned up at school that morning and his classes had had to be hurriedly rearranged. Neither Mrs Leonard, Jenny's teacher, nor Mr Colchester the headmaster had any idea where Jellicoe was.

'If Jellicoe hasn't abducted Jenny, have either of you got any other idea where she might be?'

'The only other place would be Harry Sumpter's barge but we're pretty sure that she's never been there!' I said and Ellen nodded her agreement.

'So the only logical step is to trace Jellicoe and see where that leads. You both realise that the longer it takes to find Jenny the worse the outcome is likely to be?'

'Yes Sarge!' we both said.

'We have some good news. DI Brierly is coming in in the morning to coordinate the operation. His wife doesn't like it but given the seriousness of the case she's agreed to allow him to show his face. I've arranged for one of the motor patrols to pick him up at eight o'clock in the morning. He's under strict orders to be back home no later than one o'clock!' he chuckled.

'Does that allow you to be out with us?' I asked.

'Once I've put him in the picture, yes. Till lunchtime at least!'

54

'How would it be if I popped in on him on my way home, gave him the state of play and then he'll be ready to start first thing?' I asked.

'Yes do that! So, Ellen, write all of this down and sort out the paperwork so that he's got all the details at his fingertips in the morning!'

'Right, Sarge!' she said.

'Will, get around to the school and see if there is any clue as to where our Mr Jellicoe has disappeared to. The headmaster and Mrs Leonard will stay on until you get there. Get an address for him.'

'Right, Sarge.'

'Off yer go then.'

I downed the rest of my tea and cantered down the stairs and out of the back door. As I reached the yard an old familiar voice shouted me.

'G'd afternoon Will, how yer keepin'?'

'Bong, good to see yer pal, I'm fine, and you?'

Bong had left Crammingdon a couple of years previously to take up the job of motor driver trainer at the Manchester force, including the promotion to sergeant. He's an ex-Australian policeman. I couldn't for the life of me remember what his real name was. He had always been known as Bong – short for billabong. Two years of teaching Mancunian bobbies to drive hadn't softened his Aussie accent.

'I'm great. I've put in for a week's leave, brought the g'd lady down to see her mother. We don't really see eye to eye my mum-in-law and me, so I've come to offer my services looking for your missing girl,' he said.

'I'm sure you'll be grabbed with open arms. Sergeant Whittington is in charge of the case in the absence of DI Brierly.'

'I was thinking about you on the drive down, about the day we first met on the way to the market-place, do you remember?'

'Never forget it pal, you had a badly bruised rib,

55

a back-elbow from your missus,' I grinned. 'I also remember why she did it!'

'Oh yes, I've never done that again!' he chuckled.

'Must dash, I've a call to make,' I said as we shook hands. It would be good to work with Bong again if only for a few days. As I drove to the school, I chuckled as I remembered the story of the bruised rib. Bong suffers, or at least suffered at the time from extreme flatulence. By his own admission, *"I could fart for Australia!"* he had said. I can't remember the exchange of conversation at the time, but it went something like this. Bong and his wife were in bed, she had got up for some reason, and when she returned Bong had put his arm around her and said something like *"I missed you sweetheart"*, fine so far. Then he broke wind, proving his World Class ability. Nothing new to his wife, I suppose, but unwisely he had commented, *"Got yer that time!"*, hence the back-elbow and the bruised rib.

The school was devoid of children when I got there a little after four o'clock. I was shown into the headmaster's office and Mrs Leonard was already there.

'We've tried to raise Mr Jellicoe,' said the headmaster, 'though we've had no success. He's not answering his telephone and I intend calling upon him as soon as I leave school!'

'He gave you no indication that he wouldn't be here today?' I asked.

'None whatsoever, in fact he was his usual polite self when we said good night as we left the school together last night!'

'I need another word with him, could you provide an address, please?'

'Mrs Leonard, would you be kind enough to write down Mr Jellicoe's address for Detective Constable Dexter?'

'Of course, Headmaster,' she answered, sliding

open the drawer of a small filing cabinet at the side of her. She took a slip of paper and made a careful note of the information in a beautiful copperplate hand, and passed it to me.

'Thank you, I won't keep you any longer. I'll go straight to his address and ask him to get touch with you, if you can give me a contact number, to explain why he didn't turn up today,' I said.

'Thank you that will save me a journey; he already has my home telephone number!' said Mr Colchester.

It was clear that Mr Jellicoe had not lied when he had said that Jenny lived on his way home. From the school to his house took me past Mill End. I stopped where I imagined that Jellicoe would have stopped and walked towards Jenny's house. It took less than a minute to her door, and a child running in the rain would have covered it in half the time. Jenny was an excited child, wanting to show her dad Mrs Leonards mark; she would not have hung about.

Mr Jellicoe's address was a modern semi-detached house on the Northdean estate, a new development of houses built by a wealthy German Jew who was rumoured to have left Germany on the rise of Mr Hitler.

The door was answered by an elderly lady who looked me up and down as I introduced myself and showed my warrant card.

'I'm looking for a Mr Roland Jellicoe, I believe he lives here?' I said.

'My son isn't in! He did not come home last night! I waited up for him until one-thirty this morning. It's not good enough, where is he?' she demanded.

'That's why I'm here! Mr Jellicoe didn't turn up at the school this morning. I need another word with him,' I replied.

'I suppose you'd better come in,' she said, moving aside and opening the door a little wider.

'Will this take long? I need to be going out at

any moment. I'm on the committee of a local charity.'

'You say you live with your son Mrs Jellicoe? But you've no idea where he is?'

'I do not live with my son! My son lives with me! This is my house!'

'Is your son not married then Mrs Jellicoe?'

'He is not! I have advised him that dealings with the opposite sex are the root of all that is wrong in this world!' she exclaimed.

'If your son isn't here and you've no idea where I can find him, then no I'll be on my way,' I said.

'Why do you need to talk to him, anyway?' she snapped.

'An eleven year old girl, Jenny Parminter, is missing from the school where your son teaches. You've perhaps seen it in the newspapers?'

'I do not buy newspapers. In any case my son teaches in the boy's section.'

'Your son admitted to giving this girl a lift from school to her home two days ago,' I pointed out. 'It seems that she went missing between him dropping her off and her house.'

'Missing you say? My son gave her a lift, why on earth would he do that?' she asked with a frown.

'It seems it was just a kindly gesture, prompted by the rain and the fact that he was going the same way,' I said, 'also he wanted to ask her about a story she had written.'

'This is just the very thing that I have warned him about. The instant the opposite sex become involved, not matter what age, trouble is never far behind! I fear he's getting himself involved with that woman teacher Mrs Leonard. He says that he isn't but I know the signs! She's always ringing, pestering him. She's a widow you know, and sees Roland as a future husband I shouldn't wonder. Over-my-dead-body!' she snapped.

'Thank you Mrs Jellicoe, if he does turn up would you ask him to contact me please?' I asked, handing her my card.

'If he's anywhere, he will be with that woman!'

'Mrs Leonard?'

'Unless there are others of whom I am unaware!'

Roland Jellicoe might well be our number one suspect in the disappearance of Jenny Parminter but I found myself feeling at least a little sorry for the poor chap, living in the clutches of a mother like that. As I drove to DI Brierly's house, I couldn't help thinking how lucky I had been; the unending love of my mother, and the few sweet years with Alice!

There was a minor mishap on the way to DI Brierly's house. I had been lucky with the little Hornet, only having had three punctures in the two years I had owned her. The fourth one happened about five hundred yards from his house. Strangely, on each occasion it had been the passenger side rear and that proved to be the case again. Thankfully, the rain had stopped and I took the opportunity to get it changed, rather than walk to the DI's house and repair it later. That set me thinking; the car had covered about fifteen thousand trouble-free miles since I had bought it with Alice's insurance money. Perhaps I ought to consider changing it, but the very fact that it had an emotional link with Alice made me loath to consider that, even though the thought had been in the back of my mind for a few weeks now.

As I lifted the jack out of its box I noticed that inside the lid there was a gold coloured transfer. "Supplied by Cox's Garage – New and quality second-hand cars – Guaranteed repairs, service and rebuilds. Crammingdon 777", I decided there and then to put the old girl back in his hands and have the engine overhauled and a new set of tyres plus anything else he recommended.

I arrived at the Brierly home at about six o'clock, to find the DI already well informed as to the state of the case. In fact, he was also well up to date with the wages snatch and the hole in the road outside the town hall, and able to put me in the picture with both. The County Force had tracked the gang over the border into South Yorkshire and was in the process of liaising with that force to gain information. The three bobbies loaned to County had also been returned then recalled late in the afternoon since it now seemed that the gang had doubled back into Derbyshire. Temporary diversion signs had been erected to take traffic away from the immediate area of the hole and our uniformed presence was no longer needed.

'I understand you will be back with us in the morning, sir?' I asked, at the end of his update.

'He will, with strict orders from me to be back here no later than half past one,' said Mrs Brierly, bringing in a pot of tea and three massive slices of her cherry cake.

'Doris, I've said I'll be back by one, trust me love. Those poor souls need my esteemed leadership to stop them floundering in the mire,' he chuckled.

'Mrs Brierly, I'm sure we will all make sure he's back on time,' I smiled.

'It's Doris, call me Doris. Come on, sit at the table both of you. That poor girl is still missing, then?' she asked, leaning the DI's crutches behind his chair.

'She is Mrs B... Doris, I'm afraid we seem no further forward,' I admitted, nodding my thanks for the cake.

'What's your gut feeling, Will?' asked the DI.

'I get a feeling that there's more to the fact that Mr Jellicoe gave the girl a lift. The bargeman, Mr Sumpter, reckons he saw a chap coming down the steps at the London Road Bridge carrying a small briefcase with a strap. Ellen and I both feel that it could in fact be Jenny's school satchel. Mr Sumpter's description was detailed enough to make Mr Jellicoe a favourite in the frame,' I said.

'He's not at home you say, no idea where he

60

might be?' asked the DI.

'None sir, he didn't turn up at school today and his mother has no idea where he is?'

'Does he live with his mother?' asked Doris.

'Yes, and she made it quite clear that the house is *hers* and that *he* lives with *her*! He's well under her thumb! She doesn't approve of him associating with the opposite sex,' I said.

'That's a recipe for disaster if ever I heard one!' Doris said, shaking her head and disappearing back into the kitchen.

'So that's how you'll find things in the morning, sir. I'll have to be getting home my two lads will be burning my sister's ears asking when I'll be home.'

'Aye, get yerself moving lad.'

'Goodnight, sir. Goodnight, Mrs Brierly,' I shouted.

'Doris! Goodnight Will,' she shouted back.

'Goodnight, *Doris*!'

'That's better,' she chuckled, poking her head through the kitchen door.

'Don't get the bloody idea you can start calling me *Tom*!' said the DI.

'No sir.'

Things had taken longer than I had expected, and with the added delay of the puncture, it was seven fifteen when I got home. The boys were already in bed but far from settled.

'They've had their dinner, and I've promised that you'll read them a story, if you're not too hungry,' Flossie said, as I hung my coat in the hall.

'I've been to DI Brierly's. Mrs Brierly gave be a huge doorstep of her cherry cake so I'm not exactly starving. I'll sort the boys out first,' I said.

They were talking quietly as I walked along the landing to their room. As I entered they both gave a big smile, so like the beaming smile Alice always gave when

I returned home each night. Then their faces clouded.

'Daddy, why is our Mammy have to be dead? We don't want her to be dead anymore!' asked George.

'I want my Mammy to kiss me night-night,' said Will, his bottom lip trembling.

Through tears, streaming down my face I explained as best I could just how much I wished the same but that the only place their Mammy and my sweet Alice could ever live was in our hearts. I was surprised how well they remembered her.

'Aunty Flossie says that the Angels have made a special place for Mammy,' Will sniffed.

'I'm sure they have,' I said, though I can't pretend to have Flossie's belief.

'Why?' asked George.

'Because your Mammy is very special I suppose. You remember my dear old friend Marco?'

'The wedding-ed man?' asked Will.

'That's right. He said that when we are sad about not having Mammy here with us, we should think about all the nice things we had done together,' I said. 'Try to think of the nicest thing that you used to do with Mammy.'

'Puddle jumping!' said George without a moment's hesitation and the smile was back again.

'Yes!' yelled Will.

'Jumping over puddles?' I asked. It was new to me.

'No!' laughed Will, 'splashing in the puddles – getting all wet!' They both laughed together.

'I bet that was fun,' I smiled.

'Mammy used to wash us in the tub by the fire in the kitchen. She dried us in your big white towel.'

'We don't do it now!' said George, suddenly sad again.

I looked out of the window. Although the rain had been stopped for an hour or so, there were puddles at the end of the drive where it met the road.

'Right!' I said. 'Find your welly-boots.' They looked at me with surprise, then beaming smiles.

I ran down the stairs with the boys close behind and darted to the kitchen and their boots.

'Flossie, I'll explain later but it's very important that I take the boys jumping in the puddle at the end of the drive. What clothes should I put them in?' I asked.

'Oh... er... leave them in their night-shirts. They are due for clean ones tomorrow,' she answered, with a puzzled look, 'But put their mackintoshes on.

A little over an hour later two happy little boys, clean and in fresh night- shirts snuggled down in bed and in less than two pages of their book, were fast asleep.

'They used to do that with Alice!' I said as I entered the dining room.

'They still miss her!' said Flossie.

'I miss her too!' I sighed.

'I know, but have you noticed their smiles? I think it's so much like Alice's!'

'Mm.'

6

There's a restroom at the back of the station used by the uniform boys as their mess-room. DS Whittington had commandeered it to save the DI having to climb the stairs and he had moved all of the files pertaining to the case downstairs ready for the morning. DI Brierly had settled himself rather clumsily at the makeshift desk, leaning his crutches within easy reach against the wall.

'Firstly I'd like to welcome Ellen to our happy little band and hope that she's being treated in a suitable way.'

'Yes thank you sir!' Ellen nodded and the DI smiled.

'Settling in okay?'

'Yes, enjoying it very much, thank you sir.'

'Good, glad to hear it,' he nodded then continued, 'I'd like to thank you all for keeping me updated with the state of play, and ask if there have been any overnight developments?'

'As you know sir, there's been a suggestion from Mr Jellicoe's mother that Mr Jellicoe is emotionally involved with Mrs Leonard, Jennifer's teacher at the school. I had intended asking Will and Ellen to check that out. I'm not sure if it's relevant but I think it needs to be brought into the open,' suggested DS Whittington.

'Agreed, talk to the other teachers and staff at the school, see if this Jellicoe chap makes a habit of giving the pupils, especially the girls, a lift home,' the DI said, nodding at Ellen and me.

'I'm going to ask DC Harrington to get a photo of Mr Jellicoe to go with the one of Jenny, and I intend to find out Mr Jellicoe's car registration number and get the lot circulated around the country,' the DS said.

'I'm happy with all that, but I've got an uneasy feeling about this case. I fear we might well already be too late. Can any of you think of anything we've missed?'

'I know it's a longshot and I don't really like even suggesting it,' Ellen said.

'Go on,' the DI nodded.

'I think we are *all* beginning to think the worst. The most obvious suggestion was that Jenny had somehow fallen in the canal and drowned!'

'Uniform dragged the canal as far as the London Road Bridge, thankfully without finding her,' the DI pointed out.

'I know, sir, but I read somewhere that the majority of murders are committed by the next of kin, or the very close family; often by accident, sir.'

'I think Ellen has just put into words what we are all fearing. What if Jenny actually arrived home and for some reason things went terribly wrong. It's something we need to keep in mind but I'm loathe to do a search of her house until things look more definitely in that direction. For the time being I still prefer to consider this as a disappearance or abduction,' the DI said. 'I know that you've all been giving this your best... continue pulling out all the stops, eh!'

'Yes sir,' we all agreed.

'Right, bugger off then and good hunting.'

We arrived at the school just as the first lessons of the day were already under way.

'To whom do you think we should talk first?' Ellen asked.

'If we can arrange it I think we should speak to Mrs Leonard. Find out if there *is* any sort of relationship with Mr Jellicoe,' I suggested.

'Do you think she would be more open talking

to me?'

'Possibly, do you want to try?'

'If that's okay with you, Will?' she said.

'We'll see what the headmaster can arrange.'

Mr Colchester was in his office and answered our knock with a curt "Come in."

'Good morning again Mr Colchester, perhaps we might have another chat with your staff? As I'm sure you remember, I'm DC Dexter, and this is my colleague DC Parsons.'

'Yes… yes, good morning. I can spare you a few moments, but my staff are extremely stretched at the moment, since Mr Jellicoe has once again failed to turn up. I was about to go and relieve his stand-in and take his English class.'

'We really want a word with Mrs Leonard first if that's at all possible?' I said.

'Please give me one moment, I will see what I can arrange. Oh dear, oh dear,' he said as he disappeared from the room.

The door opened a few seconds later and a lady in a kitchen smock entered the room.

'Mr Colchester has asked me to offer you a cup of tea. He said he's likely to be a couple of minutes.'

'Mm, yes please!' I said. 'My colleague doesn't drink tea, is coffee out of the question?'

'Mr Colchester always has coffee, so I should think he won't mind. Coffee for you as well, sir?'

'Coffee or tea, whichever is easiest for you, thank you.'

'Right ho, won't be a tick!' she said and left us alone.

'I wonder if I should have a little word with Mrs Tea-lady, she might be in the know about all sorts of things?' asked Ellen.

'Good idea, but not here. She'll talk more freely at home, pop and get her address, Ellen,' I agreed.

'Right; I'll go and help her in the kitchen,' she

grinned.

Left alone I began to look closely at the huge wall map behind Mr Colchester's desk. It was about four feet wide and two feet deep; it was the largest map of Canada I'd ever seen. I began to look at the familiar places marked, names that had become known to our family as the places where my sister Edith had emigrated, living there with her husband Joe and her two boys, like mine also named George and William. I traced with my finger the rail line from Montreal to Kamloops where they lived. There was a standing invitation to visit them, though on a DC's pay that seemed as likely as a landing on the moon.

The door opened and in walked Mr Colchester. He held it open for Ellen who was carrying two cups of coffee.

'Couldn't Mrs Eggleston have done that?' he asked.

'I offered to help her with it, we'd been cheeky and asked for coffee, and I thought it only fair to assist her,' Ellen smiled.

'I see...!' he said, clearly suspecting that there had been an ulterior motive.

'I was just admiring your map, Mr Colchester!' I said to help allay his suspicions.

'It is rather spectacular isn't it? My brother sent it to me when he emigrated out there at the end of the war. I was so impressed with it that I had Mr Babcock my woodwork master make a frame for it.'

'My sister emigrated out there and married a Canadian soldier. They live in Kamloops. I was just looking at it, a map this size makes it easier to understand the huge distances involved, doesn't it?' I said.

'Indeed so! The map is one issued by the Canadian Pacific Railroad; my brother works for them but is attached to their hotel division at a large hotel on the Bow River Falls!'

'My sister and her husband honeymooned there,'

I said shaking my head in disbelief.

'How extraordinary! They say it's a small world and there, my goodness me, is the proof,' he chuckled.

'I wonder if they ever met.'

'I don't suppose we'll ever know, but it certainly isn't impossible. Now, Mrs Leonard has a free period in about twenty minutes. Her class combines with another for physical exercise. You must excuse me I have that class to supervise. Please help yourself to the contents of my bookshelf, unless you have anything more pressing to attend to?' he said.

'Are we okay to use your office when Mrs Leonard is available?' I asked.

'Of course, please do,' he said and a moment later was gone.

I was again drawn to the map and followed the clearly marked line of the CPR as it made its torturous way towards Vancouver, crossing and re-crossing the Fraser River. Ellen came and stood beside me as I explained my interest and told her a little of the romantic story of my sister and her Canadian soldier.

'It's a lovely story!' she said, as I finished the tale by telling her of their two little boys. Not so little now I guess.

Mrs Leonard tapped on the headmaster's door and I invited her in.

'Mr Colchester said you wanted another word with me,' she said.

'Yes. Please sit down Mrs Leonard,' I said offering her a chair. 'Just a few points we need clearing up.'

'If it will help to find Jenny please ask away.'

'As you know Mr Jellicoe did not come to school today nor indeed yesterday, have you any idea where he might be?' I asked as Ellen took out her notebook.

'I'm sorry, I'm afraid I haven't.'

'Mrs Jellicoe, his mother seems to think that

there is some sort of romantic entanglement between you and her son. Is there any truth in that belief Mrs Leonard?'

'There is not!' she said quite indignantly. 'Ronald, Mr Jellicoe, is a respected work colleague that's all!' she snapped.

'Mrs Jellicoe stated that you regularly call him on the telephone.'

'I have telephoned him in the past, but I would hardly call it regularly!'

'Why would you need to call him Mrs Leonard?' I asked. 'Surely there are ample opportunities to talk here.'

'Indeed, and we often do discuss the progress of individual pupils. Occasionally we will miss each other and will call in the evening if a problem exists!'

'Mr Jellicoe rings you?'

'He has, but only a couple of times, maybe three, in the last two years.'

'How frequent are your calls to him? His mother gave the impression it was almost nightly,' I suggested.

'I rang him a few days ago, last Thursday I think it was. Prior to that, weeks even months ago.'

'You both teach English I believe?' Ellen asked, taking over the questioning at my nod.

'We do. It is one of the subjects we both teach; he teaches the boys, I teach the girls.'

'In normal circumstances you discuss any problems that arise in your classes here at school?'

'Correct, over a cup of tea or our packed lunches in the staffroom with the rest of the staff. Occasionally if one or other of us is on lunchtime duty and we fail to meet, then we will use the telephone in the evening but as I said, only if a specific query exists.'

'On the morning following Jenny's disappearance, I asked if you had any idea where she might be,' I said taking over again.

'You did, I remember feeling helpless. I had no

idea how I could help,' she agreed.

'After you had gone, I asked the other teachers to come and talk to me. Mr Jellicoe volunteered to be the first. He stated that the previous afternoon you had asked his opinion on a subject relating to the missing girl. Is that right Mrs Leonard?'

'I showed him a little story that Jenny had written, I wanted his opinion as to how I should mark it. The headmaster likes us to mark fairly and with consistency!'

'That certainly agrees with what Mr Jellicoe told us,' I agreed.

'Mr Jellicoe has a car I believe?' Ellen asked changing the subject.

'Yes. Though what has that got to do with anything?'

'Mr Jellicoe's car is also missing, Mrs Leonard.'

'I can't see that as being all that unusual. If a person has a car, they are seldom far away from it. If Ronald, Mr Jellicoe, has gone missing, I would imagine he has gone missing in his car. It's hardly a massive leap of imagination, surely?' she shrugged.

'Given that he is in his car, have you any idea where he could have gone?' I asked.

'I have not! I'm sorry I can't think of anything that I haven't already told you.'

'Is it normal for Mr Jellicoe to give pupils a lift home in his car?'

'Certainly not! Who has suggested that he has?'

'Can you think of any circumstances that might cause him to give a child a lift home?'

'I assume you are suggesting that he gave Jenny a lift on the evening she disappeared?' she scowled.

'I have it on good authority that he in fact did,' I pointed out.

'I find that hard to believe!' she said.

'I can assure you that is the case Mrs Leonard. However, changing the subject, was Mr Jellicoe in the army, do you know?' I asked.

'Yes, I believe he was a sergeant, though like many of the men who served in the Great War he is reluctant to talk of it. How will knowing that help to find Jenny?'

'What sort of shoes was Mr Jellicoe wearing on the afternoon you discussed Jenny's story?' I asked, ignoring her question.

'What sort of shoes?' she asked with a look of incredulity.

'Please bear with me Mrs Leonard, it could be quite important.'

'I think he was wearing the shoes he always wears,' she said, her brow creased with thought.

'Could you describe them please, Mrs Leonard?'

'Black, highly polished, with soft rubber soles, leather shoes make too much noise when moving around the school,' she said.

'Never brown... tan?' I asked, a little disappointedly.

'Only to go home in – never around the school.'

'He changes his shoes?'

'Night and morning, several of the male teachers do.'

'Could you describe his outdoor shoes, please Mrs Leonard?'

'Those are totally different, highly polished as you'd expect of an ex-soldier, but brown and fancy!'

'Fancy you say?'

'Punched leather, brogues, brown brogues,' she stated.

'Your homework for Jennifer and her class had been set for the weekend, is that correct, Mrs Leonard? I asked, changing the subject.

'Correct, all but one of the children handed it in on Monday morning.'

'That must have been a huge amount of reading and marking, yet you were ready to discuss Jenny's mark with Mr Jellicoe at lunchtime that day, how did

71

you manage that?'

'I think I told you when we spoke that day, Jennifer's story had become wet down one edge, she was very upset about that and I agreed to dry it for her while she got on with the set work for the morning. It was only one and a half pages, so I read it as it dried. The mark I arrived at seemed fair, but I checked it with Mr Jellicoe,' she explained.

'Thank you Mrs Leonard, you've been most helpful,' I said.

'I'm glad, but I can't think how. You're wrong about him giving Jenny a lift. Never in a million years,' she said as she got up to leave

'Would you be kind enough to ask another member of staff to pop in please Mrs Leonard?' I asked.

'I've agreed with the headmaster that I will relieve Mrs Balsam, I'll send her in.'

'Thank you Mrs Leonard.'

'Did you get an address for the tea lady, Ellen?' I asked, after the door had closed.

'Yes, Diamond Street next to the gasworks!' she smiled.

If ever a street was misnamed, it was that one. The houses are small and cramped like many others in the town and subject to the overpriced rent from uncaring landlords. Indeed if diamonds are involved in any way in Diamond Street, it is almost certainly from the profits of the rent.

'Have you arranged to see her?'

'Yes. She finishes here at three o'clock, I've arranged to meet her at her home about four o'clock; if that's okay, Will?' Ellen asked.

'Is she likely to be able to help?

'She seemed very guarded when I first walked into the kitchen, but when I suggested that we could talk at her home she lightened considerably. I get the impression that she will say at home what she would never say here!' she smiled.

'Good, we'll make sure one of us at least keeps that appointment,' I nodded.

'I wonder if Mr Jellicoe has a personal cupboard for his change of shoes and other things. If he has, perhaps a look in it could hold some clues,' Ellen suggested.

'Yes! We should do that,' I agreed.

Ellen's inquisitive nature was shaping up nicely. I could see her becoming a permanent fixture on the team.

'There's a school caretaker, he should have a spare key if there is a cupboard. I'll go and find him, shall I?' she asked.

'Yes, do that, please, Ellen.'

As she went out she met Mrs Balsam about to knock on the door and showed her in.

'Sit down please Mrs Balsam,' I said.

'Thank you,' she said and sat uneasily on the edge of the chair.

'As I'm sure you know we are here looking into the disappearance of Jennifer Parminter, and now it seems the whereabouts of Mr Jellicoe,' I said. 'You are not under suspicion Mrs Balsam, please relax,' I added, to help put her at her ease.

'Yes I know, though I don't see that I can help you. I know Jennifer of course, I teach her class in arithmetic and geography. She seems bright enough, though struggles a bit with the algebra from time to time,' she said.

'Did you teach her on the day she disappeared?' I asked.

'I anticipated that question. The last time I saw Jennifer's class was the Friday of last week. I could quite possibly have seen her in and around the school, at other times but not to speak to.'

'Have you any idea where she might be?'

'None whatsoever, I'm afraid. If I had I would have made it my business to inform you!'

'What about Mr Jellicoe?'

'I think Mrs Leonard is more likely to know that than I am. I do not seek Mr Jellicoe's company!'

'You don't get on with him?'

'I'm sure he's a very fine teacher, some of the work his boys produce is most commendable,' she said, looking down at her lap.

'That's not really what I asked, is it Mrs Balsam?'

'Although I use my married name, like so many others I am a widow! Mr Jellicoe was, I thought, a friend. Until Mrs Leonard appeared on the scene three years ago!' she sniffed.

'You were forming an alliance?'

'We were becoming close.'

'But Mr Jellicoe's attitude changed when Mrs Leonard joined the staff?'

'Completely, though to be fair I think Ronald's mother, he lives with her you know, turned him against me. And Ronald is strong in many things, but his mother rules him with a rod of iron!'

'His mother disapproved of you?' I asked.

'Ronald took me home to meet her one evening after school. Oh, she was pleasant enough, but you could see that I wasn't good enough for her precious son!' she snapped.

'So now you have become estranged?'

'An unusual use of the word, since nothing was ever formal, but I suppose it fits the situation.'

'Is Mrs Leonard a widow, Mrs Balsam?'

'No, she is not! She is divorced I believe, though perhaps you should ask her.'

'Mr Jellicoe's mother thinks they have some sort of arrangement.'

'I am sure I would not like to comment,' she said, and looked me straight in the eye.

'Thank you Mrs Balsam, that's all for the moment at least. If you think of anything that might be of use in finding either Jenny or Mr Jellicoe, please give me a ring,' I said handing her a card.

'I think Mrs Leonard is going to relieve Miss Bracknell so that she can come and see you!' she said slipping my card into her handbag.

The rest of the teachers came in one by one, none of them able to add anything to our knowledge. Ellen was gone for about twenty minutes then came back with a knock on the door just as I was thanking a mousey looking teacher, a Miss Upton for her help, though she too had been able to add nothing.

'The caretaker; he's a difficult chap to track down,' Ellen said, slumping in the chair beside me.

'You've found him though?'

'Yes, he's got a little lair down at the back of the boiler house. He's a Mr Dexter! Is he a relation, Will?'

'Not that I'm aware of! Did you ask him about cupboards and keys?'

'Yes! He's gone off to find the headmaster and get his approval to look in Jellicoe's locker. Apparently they've each got a metal locker in the staff room. I said we'd meet him there.'

'When we've done that we'd better get back and report to the DI before he goes home,' I pointed out.

'What about the teachers in the boy's part of the school?'

'We'll have a word with them this afternoon if the DI okays it.' I suggested.

Mr Colchester was standing with Mr Dexter the caretaker when we got to the staffroom.

'Go ahead Mr Dexter, open Mr Jellicoe's locker.'

'Very good, headmaster!' he said, producing a bunch of keys that must have contained one for every lock in the school and a few to spare. He inspected the tiny number stamped on the rim of the lock and shuffled through the keys until he found the one in question. He looked at Mr Colchester who nodded his approval, and with a little bow to the headmaster's authority, the key was inserted and the door creaked open.

'Thank you Mr Dexter, that will be all,' said the headmaster, much to the caretaker's annoyance, clearly he was as keen as we were to see into the little metal cabinet.

'Headmaster,' he said, with another little bow and shuffled off.

'Take a note of the contents please Ellen,' I said as I reached into the locker.

'Right.' she said taking out her notebook.

'One black Trilby hat, one raincoat dark grey, presumably a change of clothes he wears at school,' I said and Colchester nodded. One pair black shoes with rubber soles,'

'With the laces missing,' she pointed out.

'So they are!' I agreed. 'Make a note of that, it might be relevant.'

'Noted, carry on,' she nodded.

'Not much else, really; a couple of books on English grammar, a large dictionary and what looks like a handwritten manuscript of some sort. Ahh, and what I think is a diary!'

'Okay, I've got that.'

'Mr Colchester, might I have your permission to take this diary and manuscript? We will of course return it once Mr Jellicoe is found,' I asked.

'I suppose so if you think it will assist with finding Jennifer or Mr Jellicoe. I must ask you to give me a receipt for them.'

'Of course,' I agreed.

The DI was standing by the mess-room window, perched on his crutches, looking out onto the station yard as we drove back into Whitecross Yard.

'Any news?' he asked, struggling back to his makeshift desk.

'No-one seems to know where he can be. So far we've only had chance to talk to the female members of staff,' I said.

'The teachers for the girl's part?'

'That's right. There seems to be a bit of bad blood between two of the members of staff; we both interviewed Mrs Leonard, the girls form teacher, but Ellen went off to seek the caretaker whilst I interviewed a Mrs Balsam.'

'Why the interest in the caretaker?' asked the DI, nodding at Ellen.

'We wondered if Mr Jellicoe had a cupboard for his personal things; he had and the caretaker held the spare keys. There was a bit of a delay getting the headmaster's approval to open it up which meant I wasn't in on what Mrs Balsam said.'

'Okay, put us wise Dexter.'

'It seems Mrs Balsam, a widow lady, had what she at least thought was an understanding with Mr Jellicoe, but since Mrs Leonard became a staff member she has lost favour,' I shrugged.

'Nose out of joint, you reckon?'

'The way she tells it, Mr Jellicoe's mother put a stopper on the proceedings.'

'But she's no idea of the whereabouts of either of them?'

'No sir. And, I think she is telling the truth. Well, all of the staff are, as far as I can tell, everything rings true.'

'So we are no further forward?'

'There was a diary and a sort of manuscript in Jellicoe's locker. Though what that might tell us, I've no idea,' I said, handing them over to him.

'I'll look at these; it'll give me something to do,' the DI said. 'There was a message about an hour ago. They had to take it at the front desk; no use putting it through to the CID room when I'm down here. It makes no sense to me but if the silly buggers on the desk have got it right, it says – "Message for DC Dexter – The gates are open again and I'm on the move. I've just remembered; the bloke had black laces in his brown shoes!" Does that mean anything to either of you?'

'Yes!' we both agreed eagerly.

'In what way?'

'Harry Sumpter is telling us that the lock gates at Swarkstone are back in business and he's on the move again,' I said.

'Yes, and look at this, sir!' Ellen said, passing her notebook over to him.

'Apparently, Mr Jellicoe wears black shoes around the school,' I said as he checked Ellen's book.

'Right, so he had black shoes with missing laces. Brown brogues with black laces. He's snapped a brown lace, and replaced both of them with the ones from the school shoes until he can replace them. So the chap the barge man saw coming down the steps has got to be Jellicoe!' the DI said.

'Looks like it, sir,' I said and Ellen nodded.

'Now all we've got to do is find the bugger!'

'And hope that Jenny *is* with him and that she's okay,' Ellen said.

Ellen and I interviewed the four male teachers early in the afternoon, with little in the way of extra information. The only fact that we did gain was that Mr Jellicoe was a very fine amateur magician. It was stated by one of his colleagues that he often used his talents to fund-raise for various local charities. Quite how that fact tied into the disappearance of Jenny Parminter, if indeed it did, was hard to say, it was however one more piece of knowledge to add to our meagre store.

We kept our four o'clock appointment with Mrs Egglestone the tea lady in her neat little house next to the gasworks. After the introductions she invited us to sit down and offered us a drink, 'One tea and one coffee,' she beamed remembering it was coffee for Ellen. We both accepted with open arms, Ellen started the ball rolling.

'Mrs Egglestone, as you know we are investigating the disappearance of Jennifer Parminter, one of the pupils at your school.'

'It's not *my* school me-duck I'm only the tea lady and general dogs-body, but I know what yer mean. And I'm that worried for the poor child,' she said, putting three shining cups and saucers on the table and going back into the kitchen for the rest of tea and coffee paraphernalia.

'You've no idea where she might be?'

'That I haven't. An' now it seems Mr Jellicoe has gone missing too. Are they per'aps together do you think?' she asked, a worried frown creasing her forehead.

'How well did you know Jennifer, Mrs Egglestonne?' asked Ellen, ignoring the question.

'No more than any of the others, I don't really get to meet them other than out of class times, dinnertime and playtimes and such. I have had more to do with them of late, with all the rain. They've been allowed to stay in the school hall and a couple of the teachers take it in turn to supervise various games and activities for them.'

'I understand that Mr Jellicoe is an amateur magician; does he ever give magic shows to pass the times when the kids have to be indoors?' I asked.

'Oh no, I'm sure he wouldn't do that! I've seen him at the local orphanage, I help out there sometimes.'

'He gives shows to the children?' I asked, wondering if he was known to my pal Marco.

'Oh no; to adult audiences to help raise funds; makes a lot of money, he does!'

'If it's for adults he must be pretty good,' Ellen suggested.

'I've only seen him once; I was helping with the teas. That seems to be my level in life,' she shrugged, pouring out the drinks for the three of us.

'Nothing wrong with that Mrs Ecclestone. You

79

say you've seen him perform?' I asked.

'He's very good, very entertaining. He had one of the orphan girls help him on stage, just holding stuff, but he made it seem like the youngster had done the trick herself; she was so pleased!'

'Did he just pluck the girl from the audience?' I asked.

'It seemed like it, but now I come to think about it I think there was only this young girl sitting with the big-wigs on the front row; can't remember any other kiddies at all.'

Ellen caught my eye with a frown.

'What do you think of him as a person?' she asked.

'Well... he's a teacher, you see. They're all a bit hard to get to know. I think they must be trying to be... aloof... is that the right word? Not showing favouritism but approachable for the kids.'

'I think I know what you mean. You didn't have a lot to do with him, then?'

'I heard, not that I'm one for gossip you under-stand, that he had a thing going with Mrs Balsam, one of the other teachers. Thick as thieves they were, then sud-denly it's all over and done with and she's not speaking to Mr Jellicoe. Talk about givin' the cold shoulder! He seems to try to be friendly but she's havin' none of it. I don't know what he's done to her but she's mighty up-set!' she said taking a massive gulp of tea.

'Mr Jellicoe has a car; does he ever give the children a lift home, do you know?' I asked.

'I don't think he'd do that... favouritism, see,' she said.

'You wondered earlier if they happened to be together, Jenny and Mr Jellicoe, any reason?' Ellen asked.

'Only that it's strange both of them going miss-ing at more or less the same time. I don't believe in co-incidences, I reckon there's always a connection, just that you can't see it at the time!' she nodded.

'That's almost exactly what our inspector thinks!' I said. 'On the afternoon that Jenny disappeared, was there anything that struck you as strange, odd or unusual?' I asked.

'I have to tidy the classrooms before I go home. Monday afternoon Mr Jellicoe has a free session last thing and I often tap on his door to see if I can clear his room a bit earlier than normal. He was finishing some marking I think but he says I can make a start. I've got a big bin on wheels, that I dump all the rubbish and waste-paper into, with a brush and dustpan hangin' on the side. Halfway through sweepin' up, he picks up his briefcase and bids me goodnight, an off he goes. He was whistlin' under his breath; sort of between his teeth... know what I mean? Now that is odd; never heard him do that be-fore! I got the impression that a load had been taken off his mind, yes that's it, like he was suddenly free from something,' she nodded.

'Could you describe his briefcase, please Mrs Ecclestone?' Ellen asked.

'Oh, now; brown I think, but I can't be sure!' she said.

'Thank you Mrs Ecclestone, that's been very helpful and thank you for the drinks,' I said.

'I'm glad if I've 'elped but I can't see how.'

'We might need to speak to you again, would you prefer it to be here rather than the school?'

'Yes but better make it about five o'clock, I got off a bit earlier tonight. Mr Dexter the caretaker...' she looked at me.

'No relation as far as I'm aware!' I said with a grin.

'Oh, anyway he let me go a bit earlier tonight 'cos he wants to skip off early one day next week!' she smiled. 'Tit-f'-tat yer know.'

7

Diana gave me her answer the following day, Saturday. It finished off what had been a depressing day, with no advancement in the search for Jenny or Jellicoe, with yet more bad news. Although she enjoyed my company and loved the boys, she wasn't prepared to commit to marrying me, at least not as yet! I can't say that I was all that surprised. Police hours are hard on a marriage.

I had spent most of the day, it being a Sunday, with the boys and ended it with another session of puddle jumping. DS Whittington had been on duty and he promised he would call me in if there was anything he needed.

At the start of another week, things took on what on the face of it looked like an important step. Just after five in the morning, the body of a young girl, thought to be that of Jennifer Parminter had been washed up in the sleepy little fishing village of Stanger on the North Yorkshire coast. A young chap out walking his dog along the rocky shore had been alerted by his dog sniffing and yapping and nuzzling what he had initially thought was a bundle of old clothing. He had run to the local post office, hammered and banged on the door until he had been allowed entry. He had rung the local constabulary and they had alerted the local bobby who had in turn got the lifeboat men to recover the body, since the changing tide made it impossible to recover from the beach. The poor chap who had found it was in shock, according to the report received by the front-desk and DI Brierly had struggled to the phone to confirm the details.

'If this is Jenny's body it puts the whole thing on

a different footing. We now need to find Jellicoe from the standpoint of a possible murder enquiry,' said the DI, when he returned to his mess-room office.

'How long before we know if it is Jenny?' I asked.

'From the description we circulated, the North York's Police are ninety per cent certain that it is her. I've agreed to get one of her parents over to make a formal identification,' he sighed.

'Would you like me to break the bad news, sir?' Ellen asked.

'I wouldn't have asked you to do it, but I think you will handle it with the necessary tact, Ellen. Take DC Dexter with you,' he nodded.

'Could you give me the facts as you know them, sir?' she asked.

'Here, copy that in your note book and give it back please,' he said handing her a sheet of notepaper containing the details he'd written at the time of the phone call.

'Thank you, sir.'

'I believe Mr Parminter is currently unemployed?' said the DI.

'Yes sir; trying to get work but without much success. This situation is making it even more difficult for him as you can imagine,' Ellen agreed.

'I've arranged for one of our patrol cars to take you two and either Mr or Mrs Parminter over to York, the body is being moved there now for examination. Not a nice job for either of you, I'd go myself but with this bloody thing on my leg I lack the necessary decorum for the job,' he said.

'We'll treat it with appropriate respect, sir,' Ellen replied, and I nodded my agreement. 'Go and see them now Ellen, let them decide overnight which one is going to York!'

The police vehicle fleet; had recently been increased to include a large MG SA saloon as the head of the fleet. Driven by Police Sergeant Jim Byland, few vehicles could outpace it and this was to be our transport to York. The rear seat had a central armrest which could be raised into the seat back and make adequate room for three passengers. By seven thirty next morning it was waiting to take us to Mill End, to a meeting that neither of us was looking forward to!

We couldn't of course drive down Mill End so our driver waited for us on the road opposite and Ellen and I walked the fifty yards or so to the Parminter's house, just as Jenny should have done on the afternoon of her disappearance. The Parminter's were waiting for us.

'Mrs Goodward is looking after Tommy,' Mrs Parminter said. 'Will it be okay if we both come?'

'It might be a bit of a squeeze, but I'm sure we can manage it,' I agreed.

'I'll just put my hat on then I'm ready!' she said. The shakiness of her voice showed how much she was fighting to remain in control of her emotions.

There was the sound of a lavatory flushing and moments later Arthur appeared. 'A touch of nerves,' he said looking embarrassed.

At the car it was decided that Ellen would sit in the back with the Parminters and the choice was a good one. Quietly Ellen explained to them what they would be doing once we arrived in York.

That Sergeant Byland knew his stuff there was no doubt. He drove us smoothly and swiftly through the traffic in the towns on the way. Even so it was a good hour and a half before we pulled into the Central Hospital. The tension in the rear of the car could almost be touched. I turned to look back at them and Elizabeth was grasping her husband's hand so hard her knuckles were white with the strain. Our driver had obviously done his homework, parking us close to the pathology department door. He hopped out and opened the door for the Parminter's and I did the same for Ellen.

We were met just inside the door by a well-built chap of about five foot nine, with brown hair showing just enough grey to give him earned credibility. His face, which suggested that he had boxed or played Rugby at some point in his life and perhaps still did, showed a well-practiced degree of welcome without being offensive to those in grief and trauma.

'Good morning, I'm Dr Edwin Armitage, I'm the senior pathologist,' he said holding out his hand. The Parminters took it in turn and quietly returned his greeting.

'As I think you know the body of a young girl, believed to be about ten or eleven was recovered from the beach near Stanger, a little fishing village about twenty five miles north of here!'

'How did she come to be there?' asked Mrs Parminter.

'That I could not say, I'm afraid,' Armitage said.

'How long had she been in the water?' Arthur asked.

'My guess from the girl's condition would be a day or so, no more than two.'

Mrs Parminter sucked in a huge gulp of air and let it out with a deep, soul rending sigh.

'Would you like a cup of tea before you make the identification?' Armitage asked.

'Afterwards, perhaps; let's get it over with,' said Arthur looking at his wife.

'Very well. Firstly I must warn you that the nature of my work requires me to use strong chemicals, the odours of which can be somewhat overpowering when met for the first time,' he said.

Having attended autopsies and identifications on several occasions I knew he was actually softening the blow of the stench of rotting flesh that invades the room no matter how well scrubbed it might be. To be fair he had the body covered by a light green cloth, on a table in a small side room away from the autopsy theatre, meaning the smell was less invasive than it might have been.

'There is, I'm afraid, no easy way to soften what you are being asked to do. Identifying the body of a loved one is by definition bound to be traumatic. When that loved one is your own child, I can only begin to imagine what you must be going through and offer my heart-felt sympathy. If you are ready, do *you* wish to raise the cover?'

'Would you do it please doctor?' Mrs Parminter asked and her husband nodded.

'Certainly, I will start with the feet!' he said.
I guessed that the girl's body must have some easily identifiable abnormality to the legs. Armitage lifted the cover to just above the girl's knees and sure enough, there was an old scar just below the right knee making the corpse instantly recognisable.

'That's not her! Thank god, this girl is not our daughter!' Elizabeth Parminter said, burying her face in her husband's chest. Ellen rested her hand on Elizabeth's shoulder.

'You seem very sure, Mrs Parminter!' Armitage said, as Mrs Parminter turned to look at the body again.

'Jennifer's little toe and the next one to it on her right foot, are joined together, sort of webbed,' she said. Without thinking, she actually touched the girls flesh, and recoiled in horror.

'You are certain that this is not your daughter?' Armitage asked.

'That is not our daughter!' Arthur agreed.

'You didn't mention this in your description of your daughter,' I pointed out.

'She was always embarrassed about it, and I didn't think that the look of her feet counted!' Mrs Parminter snapped and her husband put his arm around her.

'I'm sorry you have been put through this ordeal, and hope that your own daughter is returned to you safe and sound,' Armitage said, holding out his hand.

'Thank you, and may God help you find this poor child's real parents,' Elizabeth said.

The return journey was only a little less traumatic. The Parminter's were quite obviously relieved that the dead girl wasn't Jenny, although that would at least have allowed them to grieve. As it was, they and we were no nearer a conclusion to the affair than we had been before.

We journeyed back at a more leisurely pace and dropped the Parminter's at Mill End, arriving at White-cross Yard about three in the afternoon. As we drove into the yard a little green GPO telephones van pulled in behind us. Thinking there must be some problem with the phones I passed it off and went through to the front desk to find a lady talking to the desk sergeant.

'Ah DC Dexter, I wonder if you'd have a word with Mrs Garret?' he asked.

'Certainly! Ellen would you pop upstairs and see if DS Whittington minds us using the CID office?' I asked. She nodded and hurried off. A few moments later she was back to say that it was okay to use the office.

'Would you mind coming up to our office and we'll see what we can do for you?'

'Thank you. I am a bit upset – well you don't expect it do you?' she said, picking up a sizable brown-paper parcel from the desk.

'Can I carry that for you Mrs Garret?' I asked.

'Thank you, but I can manage.'

In the office we invited the lady to sit down and offered her a cup of tea.

'Firstly can I ask your full name and address, please?' I asked as Ellen made the tea.

'Mrs Phyllis Garret, I'm a widow. My husband died three years ago.'

'I'm sorry to hear that Mrs Garret,' I said, beginning to commit the details to paper.

87

'I live at fifteen Belvoir Street opposite the laundry,' she began as she settled herself in the visitor's chair.

Very nice houses, I thought – well beyond a copper's pay.

'Oh yes, I know it. So what can we do for you?' I asked.

'We buried Arthur my husband three years ago, as I said. This is his suit!' she said unwrapping the parcel and laying it across the DI's desk.

'It's a very nice suit, Mrs Garret,' I said wondering quite where this was heading.

'It was his best. My brother-in-law found it in a second-hand shop in Derby!'

'Your brother-in-law found your deceased husband's best suit in a second-hand shop?' I asked to be sure I had got it right.

'It's not right; it isn't decent. It's dishonest, that's what it is!'

'Where *should* the suit be, Mrs Garret?' asked Ellen as she put the tea in front of the woman. 'Help yourself to milk and sugar.'

'Where should it be; where should it be? I'll tell you where it should be! On his body six feet underground, that's where it should be!' she said shovelling two heaped spoons of sugar into her cup.

'Are you saying your husband was buried in it?' I asked.

'That's right! So how can it be in a second-hand shop in Derby?'

'This is definitely his suit?'

'He had it made especially for our daughter's wedding.'

'How can you be sure that this is his suit?'

'My husband, my brother and my brother-in-law all had identical suits; made to measure,' she exclaimed.

'So that's why your brother-in-law noticed it in the shop?' suggested Ellen.

'Precisely, they looked very smart. Quite handsome the three of them looked.'

'You say they were made to measure; that must have been quite expensive Mrs Garret?'

'Thompson's on the Market Place did us a special price since he was making three suits, complete with waistcoats as you see,' she said opening the jacket.

'How long ago was this, Mrs Garret?'

'Five years, about two years before my husband passed away!'

'I wonder if they'd remember making them?' Ellen asked, reading my own thoughts.

'I should think so. The material had to be bought in especially; it was chosen from a sample book, not any old rubbish,' said Mrs Garret.

'So it's unlikely that they made another similar suit?' I suggested.

'I would think that was highly unlikely. I can see that you are still not convinced that this was, is, my husband's suit!' she snapped.

'What you are suggesting Mrs Garret, is a very serious matter. We need to be as sure as possible before making enquiries,' I pointed out.

'My brother-in-law said that you wouldn't believe me!'

'It's not a case of not believing you, what you are suggesting is that either your wishes were never carried out or someone removed the suit before your husband was buried,' I pointed out.

'He was in the suit the day before his funeral. I went to pay my last respects and saw the lid screwed onto the coffin. He was wearing the suit then,' she said, with a sniff.

'Where was the coffin overnight?' asked Ellen.

'At the undertakers, I wanted to have him at home overnight but they told me that they had no transport available.'

'It seems then that the suit was removed at

some point between your viewing and the interment,' I suggested.

'That is the only conclusion I can come to!' she said, dabbing a tear from her right eye.

'Which undertaker are we talking about, Mrs Garret?' Ellen asked.

'Watson and Marchbank, in Abingdon Street!'

'A very good company; it's hard to imagine them doing something like this,' I said.

'My husband had always been an extremely organised man. He made arrangements with them many years ago to carry out his funeral, when the time came, without further charge. He made an agreed yearly payment into an insurance scheme that they run to ensure that I had the worry of the cost taken away!' she smiled wistfully.

'That must have been a very comforting thought at a stressful time!' suggested Ellen.

'Indeed. But this is so distressing!'

'Could you leave the suit with me and I promise to find out what has happened Mrs Garret,' I said.

Then the worst possible thing happened, Nelly Richmond, Jenny's friend, went missing. Her mother came into the front desk at Whitecross Yard just as we were preparing to leave. Nelly had gone to school as normal, but had not returned home by her usual time, about ten past four. Amid tears, Mrs Richmond stated that when four-thirty came and went with still no sign of her daughter, she had been to the houses of all of her daughter's friends and had been told by them all that Nelly had not been to school.

It looked as though we were looking at best at a serial kidnapper, at worst a serial killer. I phoned Flossie to tell her that I had no idea when I'd be home, and told her of this new frightening turn of events. She said she would see to the boys, and hoped that the girl would soon appear unharmed.

Ellen took Mrs Richmond home and stayed with her overnight. The DI was informed, and came in around seven o'clock in the evening to organise the search.

'This is all we need, another missing child. Can you imagine what the press are going to make of this?' he said when he arrived in the restroom.

'Thank goodness I've got a phone now! They said they'd install one yesterday but I never expected to actually see one. This'll save a lot of running around.'

'I had to inform the Assistant Chief Constable, sir. He's at a dinner in aid of one of his pet charities. He's going to be speaking at about ten o'clock and has appointed you to take charge once I informed him that you were on your way in, sir,' said DS Whittington.

'I think we can let Jellicoe off the hook, unless he's come back for another victim. I assume we've not located him yet?' the DI said.

'Still looking, sir.' Whittington shrugged.

'Okay, you lot; any idea's where to start?'

'It makes it much worst that Nelly has really been missing since leaving home this morning,' Harrington stated what we were all thinking.

'Is it possible that this girl, Nelly, might actually know where Jenny is and has gone to join her?' the DI asked.

'Or thinks she knowns where she is and has gone looking for her friend,' I suggested.

'I assume you've already alerted our chaps in uniform,' the DI said.

'Mrs Richmond reported to the front desk and the duty sergeant put it out through all of the police boxes. All the lads should know by now, sir,' Whittington stated.

The new phone rang and the DI was over by the window, turning awkwardly towards it he said, 'You get it Dexter.'

'Right sir. I said picking it up and introducing myself.'

'Will, it's me, Ellen,' she said. 'Mrs Richmond has just told me that her daughter has been acting strange for a couple of days. She thinks Nelly has an idea where Jenny could be. It seems that in the summer the girls go off playing in the woods at the back of Longstaff Farm. She thinks that is where Nelly could be,' she said.

'But why would she not come back once she found that Jenny wasn't there?'

'Perhaps she is there and the pair of them are either playing or too scared to come home.'

'It would be nice to think so but I can't see it, can you?' I asked.

'Honestly – no, not really. I think we have to be prepared for the worst.'

Harrington and I went to the woods behind Longstaff farm, and together with a uniformed copper we met on the way, began a search as daylight began to fade. Searching a wood in the falling light by flashlight is a near impossible task. The woodland had seen little or no management and Harrington tripped and twisted his ankle on a protruding root, falling heavily among a thick bank of nettles and undergrowth. By the time we had helped him limp back to the car, it was already dark and our batteries were close to exhausted.

It was ten past nine and with Harrington's agreement, we called off the search. The uniformed officer, still on duty until six next morning continued his usual beat with the overriding task of looking for our missing girl.

'Thank goodness you're home,' Flossie said, 'the boys are still awake. They're in bed but can't sleep. George is worried that you're not coming back.'

Footsteps on the stairs announced the fact that they had heard me in the kitchen.

'Daddy, daddy!' they both shouted and threw their arms around my waist nearly knocking me over in the process.

'I'm home now, come on let me get you back to bed and read you a story.'

'Will was frightened that you had gone away and left us!' George said, though, according to Flossie it was him that raised that fear.

'How could I leave my lovely boys? Who would I go puddle jumping with?' I asked, giving them both a massive hug. 'Now, which story are we going to read?'

Within five minutes, two weary heads were fast asleep, gently breathing in rhythm, each with an arm around their well-worn teddy bears.

'Flossie tells me another girl has gone missing!' Henry exclaimed as I entered the kitchen. I told him the situation as far as I knew it, including the episode of Harrington's twisted ankle and fall in the nettles.

'Is he badly stung?'

'His hands and face were coming up in a speckle of rash by the time we arrived at the station. He was sore but he'll live!' I grinned.

'Is he likely to have anything to relieve the itching?'

'I wouldn't think so,' I grinned.

'I'll get him something to soothe the tingling,' he said and disappeared into his surgery, reappearing, a few moments later with a small bottle of calamine lotion and a small wad cotton wool. 'Tell him to dab it on, better still get Ellen to dab it on his face for him,' he grinned.

'Ellen – why?' I asked.

'You'll see.' He smiled.

'That's cruel!' Flossie chuckled.

'I'll suggest that he doesn't put it on his hands,' I laughed, suddenly understanding the joke. 'That way he won't notice!'

Harrington entered the DI's temporary lair about six next morning; his face aglow with a host of tiny pink, angry looking spots. I'd already given Ellen Henry's little bottle and put her wise to our little prank.

'Gosh that looks painful! I've some lotion for stings like that. Let me dab a bit on,' she said, feeling in her bag.

'Will it sting? This is bad enough already, I got no sleep at all with it last night.'

'Get the stuff on, I'm not having an officer of mine walking about looking like that!' the DI snapped.

'Right, close your eyes, I don't want to get this in them, you'll have to suffer the stings on your hands I don't think it's wise to put it on them,' she said.

'Oh, bloody hell, all right.' Harrington said, clamping his eyes tight.

'This will cool them and stop the stinging,' she said as the creamy-pink lotion left splodges all over his face. 'Keep your eyes shut.'

'That looks better already, less pink and fiery, don't yer reckon Dexter?' the DI asked.

'Much less red, sir.'

'It certainly feels a lot cooler,' Harrington admitted.

'All done, you can open your eyes now,' Ellen said, biting her bottom lip as she put the bottle and swab back in her bag.

'Can you put it on my hands, please Ellen?' he asked.

'I wouldn't like to take the responsibility for putting it on your hands. You might get it in your mouth, or rub your eyes. What do *you* think, sir?'

'Harrington's a big boy; he can make his own mind up. Let him put it on for himself then if there are any complications he takes the consequences,' the DI stated.

'Please Ellen, they're driving me mad.'

'On your own head be it!' she said, fishing out the bottle again, and the joke looked like being over before it started.

Strangely, although the lotion left the same pink blotches on his hands as he applied the calamine lotion, he didn't seem to realise the fact that it would be showing on his face.

'Right, come on you lot, uniform have been looking since first light, let's get out there and get this kiddie found,' the DI shouted.

'I think we've found her,' the desk sergeant said, replacing his phone as we entered the front office.

'Thank God for that. Is she okay?' we all asked together.

'The lads who found her have taken her back home, so I can't tell you much more than that at the moment.'

We reported the fact to the DI, who sent Ellen to have a word with Nelly at her home, and stood us down from our search.

Ellen returned about nine o'clock to tell us that Nelly had in fact gone to the wood behind Longstaff farm, believing Jenny would be in their summer hideout. Then had been frightened to return home when she'd have to admit what she had done. Finally, hunger and the noises in a night time wood had driven her home. Mrs Richmond had given her daughter a good talking to and put her to bed, with a full belly.

'So, case closed?' the DI asked.

'Yes, I think so sir!'

'Let's hope we find Jennifer Parminter equally safe and sound,' the DI said and we all agreed.

'Ho, bloody ho; very funny!' Harrington said, catching sight of himself in the restroom mirror.

For two days, there had been no further information about either Jellicoe or Jenny and the uniformed men were gradually moved to other duties, but to be on alert for the missing girl.

I got to thinking about my Australian mate.

'What's happened to Bong? He volunteered to

help with the search for Jenny,' I asked the DI one morning.

'I thought he went to Manchester, training drivers or something.'

'He's brought his wife here to see her mother and volunteered his services.'

'News to me, he's not on the team as far as I know!'

'Not like Bong to just disappear without saying good bye,' I said.

8

On Wednesday morning things suddenly changed, sending me off in a different direction, taking me away from the investigation of little Jenny Parminter. Overnight there was a huge art theft. The town Mayor, Alderman Tippett, had suffered a burglary, and Alderman Tippett is one of the Chief Constable's drinking and golfing pals. We first became aware when the Assistant Chief sent for DI Brierly and for some reason me, around nine o'clock that morning.

'I wonder what we have done now,' the DI said.

'Perhaps he's going to give you another talking to about the slow progress of the disappearance of the young girl, sir,' I suggested.

'Mm… probably. Oh, this is bloody hard work, struggling around on these things is killing me after a day and a half. When we get back, I'm not moving from that bloody restroom, no matter what!'

'Right, sir.' I nodded, helping him down the four stone steps at the back of the building to the yard.

When the rooms above the old stables were converted to offices, the old rough wooden stairs had been removed and a new and beautiful mahogany staircase had replaced them, as befits the high rank of Chief Constable and his assistant.

'I'll tell you one thing Dexter; once this bloody plaster is off I'm going to get a lot fitter than I am now! It's hard work up and down stairs on these bloody things!' he said shaking one of his crutches, in case I was unsure what he meant.

'I can see that, sir,' I nodded.

'I should have stayed at home like my missus demanded,'

'I don't thinks that's in your nature; like to be in the know, don't you sir!' I said as we made to climb the mahogany flight of stairs.

'Stay there,' the Assistant Chief called, appearing at the top of the stairs. 'I've arranged four chairs in the garage,' he added and nodded to the doorway on the left at the foot of the stairs leading through to what had been the stable, but now housed the Chief's shining car.

'Thank you sir,' the DI said as we both saluted.

'In you go then; the Chief will be with us in a moment,' the ACC said, starting a sprightly jog down the stairs to meet us.

I opened the door and was surprised how big the area of the garage was. Four chairs were arranged around a small table.

'Sit down gentlemen, I'll wait until the Chief gets here, I have to admit I've only half the picture myself!' he grinned.

'If this is about the slow progress on the Jenny Parminter case, I'd just like…'

'Nothing like that Detective Inspector,' the ACC cut in. 'Though I can understand why you are apprehensive about that matter. Is there anything new, any breakthrough in the case?' he asked, gesturing for us to take a seat.

'Slow progress, sir. It seems we take two steps forward and one step back all the time. Sometimes, even one step forward and *two* steps back. Each new piece of information seems to call into question what we thought we knew, sir,' the DI said and I nodded.

'That's police work, Detective Inspector, the nature of the beast!' he nodded.

We could hear the Chief, ambling down the stairs and we all stood up and saluted as the great man entered.

'Sit down please,' he said, returning our salute.

98

'This is a difficult matter to deal with, especially with the missing child so much to the fore. During last night, the home of Crammingdon's Mayor Alderman Tippett was burgled and three paintings taken. The total value, agreed by his insurance company three years ago is in excess of twenty-five thousand pounds. Alderman Tippett as Mayor is in a position to make things very awkward for us. He is close friends with the owners of the Argus our local rag, as I'm sure you know, and has no doubt already informed them. I want a high profile investigation on this!'

'I'm stretched to the limit as it is, sir. We are really struggling with finding the missing girl, Jenny Parminter, sir,' the DI replied.

'I am aware of that Detective Inspector, and I am mindful of your personal difficulties at the moment and thank you for coming in to run your department, when many people would have seen a similar injury as a means of divorcing themselves from responsibility. However, this matter is impacting on us as a department so needs clearing up as soon as possible. We don't look good over the Parminter case. We can't afford any more bad press!'

'What information can you give me at the moment, sir?' the DI asked.

'All I can tell you is; Alderman Tippett rang at eight-forty-five this morning and because of who he is, was put through directly to my office. I had just arrived and after a few seconds of disjointed, agitated conversation, I was able to determine that three paintings of extremely high value had been removed from his home overnight.'

'I see, sir. I assume he can give us an accurate description of the paintings in question.'

'He assures me that he has photographs of the paintings, taken for insurance purposes three or four years ago. They are of course at your disposal.'

'*I* would normally be leading the enquiry, but at

the moment I think, with your approval sir, I'll organise my troops like this; I will stay here at Whitecross Yard and co-ordinate both cases, with DS Whittington and DC Parsons looking into the missing girl. That allows DC Harrington and DC Dexter to look into Alderman Tippet's theft, sir,' the DI suggested.

'In the circumstances, I think I would prefer that DS Whittington runs the theft of the paintings; I think Alderman Tippett would be most unhappy to find himself relegated to a couple of DCs!' the Chief said.

'As you wish sir,' the DI nodded.

I don't like that anymore than you do. I'm wrong in the eyes of the press or public whichever way we play this! On the one hand I'm moving a DS from a missing child case, on the other I'm not giving the Mayor's theft enough priority if I send two DCs. We run with Whittington on the Mayor's theft. That is all, keep me informed of developments in both cases,' the Chief said, and raised to go, giving us a salute, by touching the peak of his cap with his stick.

'Certainly, sir,' the DI agreed as we both returned the salute.

We walked back across the yard and I helped the DI to climb the steps back into the main building.

'Right, I'm in here until further notice,' he said entering the mess-room. 'Get all the stuff transferred down, Dexter. I'll give our highly esteemed mayor a call and arrange for you and DS Whittington to take a look.'

'Right, sir,' I said and raced up the stairs to collect as much of the case paperwork and other stuff that I could carry.

'We're down in the restroom, until the DI is fit again.'

'Okay, come on let's get it over with, everything downstairs,' DS Whittington said, gathering up the paperwork and paraphernalia of the case.

With the makeshift office in full operation, DI Brierly allocated us to our tasks, as approved by the

Chief Constable. 'I'll ring county and get a fingerprint team to the alderman's house,' he said.

Alderman Tippett's house, stood behind a high, neatly clipped privet hedge, though certainly not a mansion, it was impressive to say the least.

'Behold the family pile!' Whittington said, with raised eyebrows.

'I wonder what the living conditions of his workers are like in comparison,' I nodded.

'You must remember how many people he keeps employed,' he grinned. 'Come on let's face the music.'

'I bet he's not a happy-chappy!' I chuckled.

The front door opened as we climbed the steps, and a bald-headed man of about sixty, clearly a manservant, asked if he could help us. DS Whittington introduced us, the man nodded and with an almost theatrical gesture waved for us to enter.

'This way, gentlemen,' he said and led us across an entrance hall as big as Henry's surgery waiting room, and tapping on the door of a room opposite a huge staircase, took us inside.

'The gentlemen from the Police, sir,' he said with an almost imperceptible bow.

'Good day, sir. I'm Detective Sergeant Whittington and this is Detective Constable Dexter.'

'A Detective Sergeant! Is that the best our illustrious police force can muster for an important crime like this?' the Mayor snapped. 'I thought we had a tame Detective Inspector, why isn't he here?'

'Detective Inspector Brierly, broke his ankle a couple of weeks back, and although he is at work, he's on crutches and very limited in getting about. I've discussed your burglary extensively with him and he is to oversee the case, most diligently sir,' Whittington said, though it was news to me.

'Aye – well, that'll have to do I suppose. You'd better come through to the music room,' he said and led the way across the hall to a large room containing a grand piano under a pale green dust cover. 'There see,' he continued pointing to three places on the wall where the paintwork was less faded that elsewhere.

'The missing paintings were hung there, were they, sir?' Whittington asked.

'And what else would be hanging on the wall!'

'Just confirming the facts of the case, sir.'

'Three Edmund Warrender landscapes, that's what they were!'

'I can't say I've heard of him, sir.' the DS said.

'Why doesn't that surprise me? For your information, Edmund Warrender, is one of Derbyshire's, probably England's finest artists; been rated an equal to Constable, Turner and Wright.'

'I see, sir. When did you first miss the paintings, sir?'

'About fifteen minutes before I rang your Chief Constable!'

'Are there any signs of breaking and entering?' DS Whittington asked looking around the room where we stood.

'There's a French window with one of the panes broken,' Alderman Tippett led us over to a curtained-off glass doorway. 'See, they broke the glass and opened the latch,' he pointed.

'From the size of the paintings, I guess they must be pretty heavy,' DS Whittingham said, looking at the patches on the wall.

'Not especially heavy but awkward, I'd say it would take more than one man to lift them off the wall and carry them away,' Tippett replied.

'Yet they failed to wake you!'

'It's a big house, we sleep at the front; this room looks over the rear garden of the house as you can see.'

'Could we look outside please, sir?' asked the DS as the front doorbell rang. A few moments later, the butler entered and informed Alderman Tippett that the fingerprint crew had arrived.

'Well show then in, you old fool,' Tippet snapped.

'Very good, sir.' the poor chap said and went out returning a few seconds later bringing in the two-man crew.

The Crammingdon force does not have its own fingerprint section, relying on the good will of the Derbyshire County Constabulary. This often means we have to wait a day or so before they can deal with our request. Amazingly, perhaps because of who the burglary victim was, they had responded quickly to what must have been the Chief Constable's request.

'Good morning, you'll need to start over by this window; it's where the beggars got in!' Tippett said.

'I'm sorry sir, would you mind leaving this room, so as not to contaminate the evidence. I will also need you to give me your fingerprints and those of your family and staff to eliminate you from anything we might find,' said the taller of two men.

'Turn me out of my own music room!'

'I apologise sir, but it really is necessary,' the tall chap said, and DS Whittington nodded.

'Oh bother! Come on you two you might as well take a look at the photographs of the stolen paintings, then at least you'll know what you are looking for,' Alderman Tippet said and led us through to his office.

'Are either of you familiar with the work of Edmund Warrender?'

'No, sir,' I said.

'I think I've seen a couple of his paintings, sir,' DS Whittington said, as Alderman Tippett sorted out the three photographs in question, from the ten or so in a manila envelope, and passed them over to Whittington.

'Warrender paints mostly landscapes in and around the peak district. That one is the village of Castleton viewed from Mam Tor,'

'Very dramatic, sir,' Whittington said and I had to admit he was right; the artist had captured a dark and threatening sky over the beautiful Derbyshire landscape.

'This one as you can see is Chatsworth House, viewed from the high point of the road through the park.'

'I know it well sir,' Whittington exclaimed. 'He's certainly done it credit, sir.'

'*I* think so. Now this one I can't place, several people have looked at it and offered different suggestions as to the subject. I personally think it is an interpretation of the peak district in general,'

'What sort of value would you put in them, sir?' I asked.

'It's not about the money, Detective Constable. It's about the loss of their artistic worth!' Alderman Tippett snapped.

'Of course, I understand, sir. I'm sure they must be insured, what figure did the insurance company put on them?' I said, repeating the question in a way that he had to respond.

'Twenty-five thousand pounds in all, though as I say, it's not about the money,' Alderman Tippett said, repeating the figure that the Chief had given us that morning.

'Have you notified your insurance company, sir?' Whittington asked.

'The instant I found they were missing!'

'Was that before you rang the Chief Constable, or after, sir?'

'Oh... er... er... I can't remember.'

'No matter, sir,' Whittington said, though we all knew that Alderman Tippett had fallen into the trap of almost admitting it really was about the money.

'I don't think we can do much more until we have the results of the fingerprints, sir. We'll get back and report in full to DI Brierly and get these pictures circulated.'

'I suppose you're right, ask DI Brierly to ring

me with any news. I want them back you know!'

'Of course, sir.' we said as he showed us out.

'Just one thing sir, where does your butler sleep?'

'Potter? Oh, he's not really a butler, manservant I suppose you'd say; sleeps up in the attic room.'

'He didn't hear anything I suppose?'

'You'd better ask him. Potter!' he yelled.

'Coming, sir.'

'These chaps want to know if you heard anything last night.'

'Heard the burglary? No sir!'

'That's all Potter.'

'Very good, sir.'

'Seems, *he* slept through it as well!' Alderman Tippett shrugged.

As we turned out into the road, DS Whittington asked, 'What do you make of that, Will?'

'I get the feeling, he knows where they are, and it *is* about the money,' I grinned. 'Admittedly the glass was broken from the outside but who knows.'

'He wouldn't be the first person to commit insurance fraud!'

'I find it difficult to believe that a burglar could break a window, then remove three hefty paintings, meaning three journeys to get them to a van, if there was only two villains involved. Then drive away without wakening the household,' I chuckled.

'Mm, I agree. What do we tell the DI?' he asked.

'Tell him what we think, we've no proof but we smell a rat!'

'Next thing we need to think about is where would he put them where they'd be safe and away from our search?'

'You seem to be suggesting that our illustrious

Mayor is trying to pull a fast one!' the DI said a few minutes later, when we had given him chapter and verse, on our talk with Alderman Tippett.

'Not really, not at the moment anyway, it's just that he rang his insurance company before he rang the Chief Constable,' Whittington said, 'but it's a thought.'

'Perhaps he considered, probably quite rightly, that the insurance office would be open before the Chief would be here,' the DI grinned.

'Yes, that's probably it!' Whittington admitted, and I have to admit that it seemed reasonable.

'There remains the question of how the thieves made off with the paintings without awakening the household. It could still be an inside job. This music room, describe it to me,' the DI asked, looking at me.

'Well, I'd say it's a room about twice the size of this mess room sir,' I said and looked at DS Whittington, who nodded his agreement. 'There's a sofa and a couple of armchairs and of course the grand piano.'

'A grand piano, eh. Very posh. Is it good one?'

'No idea, it's covered with a dust sheet, sir.'

'No matter; what else?'

'That's about it, sir. The floor covering goes from wall to wall in a plain light green carpet. The walls are a pale green distemper which has faded a little, you can tell that by the slightly darker shade where the paintings were hung. Anything to add, Sarge?' I asked the DS.

'Not really, so what's our next move, sir?'

'Firstly, how big are the paintings?'

'Including the frames, about two-feet-six high and three-feet-six wide,' Whittington said.

'Not exactly huge, would they be heavy enough to need two men to carry them?'

'These photos show the frames as well, they look pretty hefty, sir!'

'I wonder if the thieves already had a buyer,' Ellen suggested.

'Stolen to order, wouldn't be the first time. This artist, Edmund Warrender, is he any good?' the DI asked looking again at the three photographs.

'Neither of us has heard of him, sir,' DS Whittington said,

'Can't say I have,' Ellen said and Harrington agreed.

'So we don't know if he is recognised outside the UK?' the DI said, looking from one of us to another.

'No sir,' we all agreed.

'Okay, Dexter take these photos and get them copied, just a couple of sets initially and we'll take it from there, don't hang around waiting for them to be done, go and ask the local art dealers to be on the look-out for them,' the DI said.

'Right sir.' I said taking my jacket from the back of my chair and picking up the three photos.

'Make sure you ask how much they are worth to check against the insurance valuation.'

'Right sir.'

We don't have a regular photographer that we use for this sort of thing, just who happens to be most convenient at the time. I left them at the shop of Arthur Cornwell, who agreed to have three copies of each done for later that afternoon.

'Edmund Warrender... on the wane now of course. He's one of those artists who are all the rage for a couple of years then suddenly the public starts to look for something new,' said Andrew Davies an art dealer in Slade Street, off Commercial Row.

'Not as good as people expect, is that it, sir?' I asked.

'Not really, the paintings are well executed, he's a skilful artist, just lacks the certain something that changes a good painting into a work of art.'

'You wouldn't advise anyone to buy his work as

an investment, then sir?'

'It seemed a few years ago as though Edward Warrender was going to be that rare commodity, an artist who would be able to sell everything he produced. He could almost ask his price! Now if he'd died two or three years ago, no doubt they would have continued rising in price. But Warrender was prolific, chucking the damned things out like shelling peas. So tell me why the interest in them, Detective Constable?'

'No doubt it will be in this evening's Argus, so I see no reason why I shouldn't tell you. Alderman Tippett was burgled overnight and three paintings by Warrender were taken,' I said.

'No doubt Alderman Tippett had them well insured,' Mr Davies said, raising his eyebrows.

'I understand they were insured for a considerable sum, about five years ago, sir.'

'Can you describe them to me, Detective Constable?'

'I should be able to show you a photograph of them, later this afternoon.'

'You can't tell me the titles?'

'Er... one is simply called Castleton, another Chatsworth House, the third Alderman Tippett can't place, he thinks it just represents a romantic landscape typical of Derbyshire or the Peak District, sir,' I said looking at my notebook.

'That's very much Warrender's later work, almost as though leaving his studio had become too much trouble; possibly why he's fallen out of favour.'

'Can you give be a rough idea of the value of the paintings at the time Alderman Tippett insured them, sir?' I asked.

'Hard to say without actually having the actual painting to look at, a rough guess would be, and it is only rough, say eight to twelve thousand pounds.'

'Oh!'

'From the look on your face I'd guess that our

eminent Mayor has insured them for considerably more than I've suggested,' he grinned.

'I can't say how much but yes, considerably more. Out of curiosity, what would their current value be?'

'Six thousand, no more.'

'Each?'

'The lot… art goes up and down, Warrender is definitely going down. I'd say the Alderman's theft is rather fortuitous!' he said raising those eyebrows again. 'Don't take my word for it, ask around but I'll bet anyone in the know will agree with what I've said.'

I asked two other dealers in the town and heard much the same thing.

On the drive back to Whitecross Yard, I remembered my old pal Bong, and wondered again what had happened to him, finding it hard to believe that he would just drift off without a word.

Ellen was working with DS Whittington on various other matters. DC Harrington was detailed to fetch and carry for the DI, who was now managing to stay longer each day as he became a little more mobile. The search for Jenny was easing down, still active, but slowly taking a back seat. Continuing the search was down to me, likewise the less important case of the burial suit, with the Mayor's theft awaiting fingerprint results I decided to approach the tailor on the Market Place later today.

I arrived back at the makeshift CID office just as Ellen was telling the DI about the call she and DS Whittington had been on.

'…So then she said, "that old bat next door 'as been accusin' me of stealing her bloody carrots, I don't even like carrots an' I told 'er so, and she pushed me into the fence and broke it down, see. She called me a two faced little liar and that's when I 'it her. She fell an' 'it 'er 'ead on that brick." I asked her if she *had* taken any

109

of her neighbour's carrots and she said, "A few perhaps, now and then,' Ellen said, closing her notebook, with a shake of her head.

'The neighbour, Mrs Wallace, was it? She'd been taken to hospital you say! Do you know when she's likely to be home again?'

'DS Whittington has gone to the hospital now sir, to try to have a word.'

'Was she badly injured?'

'The ambulance man said he didn't think it was too bad, but head injuries always bleed a lot. Concussion was his real worry; he thinks they're likely to keep her in overnight, sir.'

'I see, we'll have to wait for Whittington to get back then. Dexter, what have you been up to?'

'I've asked several art dealers about the Alderman's painting and the general feeling is that they are worth about a quarter of what they are insured for sir,' I said.

'Now that *is* interesting, Dexter!'

'Yes, sir.'

'I can't see how we can progress the Alderman's theft any further until we have a report from the fingerprint boys. I'll let the Chief know where we are with it, in the meantime Dexter, look into the burial suit for Mrs Garret,' the DI said.

'On my way, sir!'

'All of our suits are made to measure, Detective Constable, only the very highest quality of material and workmanship. Our clients very rarely ask the price; they know we will give the best and are prepared to pay for that!' said Mr Melville Thompson, almost as though I was a potential customer, not quite up to his standard.

'I wonder if you could identify this suit as one that you have manufactured,' I asked, un-wrapping the parcel.

'We do not "manufacture" suits. We create suits

to correspond with individual requirements! Everyone has bodily irregularities no matter how slight, perhaps from poor posture or maybe an injury, skilfully reducing these to acceptable proportions is the work of a tailor. The reason why off the peg suits are never quite right, to the discerning eye,' he said somewhat pompously.

'Quite. No offence intended Mr Thompson. Would you be kind enough to look at these garments, please?'

'Of course, and indeed there is our label on the hem of the inside pocket. I cannot deny that this is one of our creations,' he said, carefully feeling the material. 'This is one of three suits I remember well. Unless I am very much mistaken they were made for a wedding four, no five years ago,' he smiled.

'How can you tell that?' I asked.

'The material was not one we stock, not quite up to our exacting standards. Nice enough; but not what we normally recommend. However since the order was for three suits I agreed to carry out the order. If you will give me a moment I should even be able to tell you the person for whom this suit was made!'

'That would be most helpful Mr Thompson,' I agreed.

He rang a brass bell on his desk and turned to a filing cabinet not unlike the one in Mr Colchester's the headmaster's office. A few seconds later a chap in a waistcoat and matching trousers, sporting a tape measure around his neck entered and nodded at me.

'Ah, Mr Duncan, would you be so kind as to measure this suit please?'

'Certainly, sir!' he said and with the speed of the skilled tailor he no doubt was, quickly called out several measurements, which Mr Thompson checked against a sheet of paper taken from a cardboard file.

'We made that suit for a Mr Arthur Garret, Detective Constable Dexter. The three gentlemen were similar in stature but the measurements Mr Duncan has given me could only be those of Mr Arthur Garret.'

'Thank you, that is most helpful.' I said.

I interviewed Mr Watson, of Watson & Marchbank, a short time later.

'What can I do for you Detective Constable?' he asked as he invited me to settle in his rather grand office.

'I am following up a complaint made by a Mrs Phyllis Garret of fifteen Belvoir Street,' I said.

'The woman complaining in last night's newspaper about our service?'

'Apparently you buried her husband about three years ago.'

'Give me a moment, I was about to look out the appropriate file,' he nodded, 'Three years ago you say?'

'That's right, almost to the day,' I said, consulting the notes Ellen had transcribed into my own notebook.

'Yes, here it is. Mr Arthur Garret. The deceased's interment to be carried out in an oak coffin complete with brass handles and red silk lining. Deceased to be dressed in a suit and waistcoat provided by Mr Garret's relict. Now what seems to be the trouble, Detective Constable?'

'Mrs Garret claims to have found the suit in question in a second hand shop in Derby!' I pointed out, watching the man closely and if I hadn't I think I would have missed his fleeting look of surprise and guilt. It was only for a moment and quickly replaced by a helpful smile.

'I fail to see how that can be. In any case according to my notes Mrs Garret viewed her husband's cadaver and approved the closing of the lid, which as usual was done in her presence!'

'She is adamant that the suit is in fact her husband's; it was one of three produced by a made to measure tailor.'

'Even so, there must be dozens of suits in second hand shops in the region. How, can she be so sure?' he flustered.

'The suit has been identified by the tailor who made it, even down to the person it was made for,' I pointed out.

'I don't see how that can be! There must be some mistake.'

Both Mrs Garret and the tailor are adamant that this is the suit in question. Which, if as you say, and Mrs Garret admits to, seeing the coffin closed, leaves only one conclusion; the lid must at some point have been removed and the suit taken from the deceased,' I pointed out.

'That is preposterous! Why on earth would anyone do such a thing?' he blustered.

'Can you think of another explanation, Mr Watson?'

'The only one that springs to mind is that perhaps the deceased was in fact buried in a different suit, and the client is now making some sort of allegation that cannot possibly be investigated!'

'For what purpose Mr Watson?' I asked.

'Why, to hold us to ransom, I should think. To threaten our good name unless we make some sort of settlement.'

'Mrs Garret doesn't strike me as that sort of person, sir,' I said.

'You asked me my opinion and I have given it. I fail to see how the matter can be resolved without an exhumation order.'

'I am convinced that the suit in question was the suit belonging to Mr Arthur Garret, the suit his wife swears he was to be buried in and the one she saw on his body as the coffin lid was closed.'

'What *if* the suit supplied for the burial *was* in fact a similar but cheaper one, supplied so as to be able to sell the correct one? What if this is an elaborate trick to extract money from us?'

'If that's the case why would she wait for three years before making this claim?'

'I regret I could not say!'

'According to Mrs Garret, she asked for the coffin to lie overnight at her home before the funeral the following day. She states that you were unable to carry out this wish due to a lack of transport. Therefore the coffin must have been in your premises overnight giving ample time for someone on your staff to remove the suit for the purpose of selling it!' I pointed out.

'That is a preposterous slur, Detective Constable! What you are suggesting is not only immoral but I believe is actually illegal. It amounts to the theft of goods; grave goods no less. We are a small, but well respected firm, Detective Constable. Often a newly deceased person has to be removed from their home or perhaps a hospital at short notice, that together with carrying out the necessary procedures can leave us short staffed or without sufficient vehicles in the short term. That and only that will have been the reason for us not ensuring that the wishes of the bereaved were carried out,' he remarked, slapping his hand on his desk.

'Mr Watson, would any of your employees have had access to the coffin in question after the lid was closed?'

'We operate on trust. All of our employees are free to and indeed expected to, carry out their normal duties unsupervised. If that trust is breached we look very seriously on the possibility of dismissal.'

'How often have you actually dismissed an employee?' I asked.

'One young man, Herbert Henchcliffe, was dismissed recently! He had been with us about five years. He was caught fiddling with clothes of the corpse of a young lady. Only the wish to control the likely damage to our reputation prevented me from reporting the matter to the police. The young man was dismissed on the spot!'

'So, you didn't report this to the police, sir?'

'I have to admit yes, that is the case, as I said I was mindful of our company reputation,' he said with a great deal of embarrassment.

'Would you happen to have an address for this chap?' I asked.

'He lived at the time in the small flat above our garage. I suspect he will have moved in with his widowed mother in Tyler Street.'

'If he lived on your premises, wouldn't he have had access to Mr Garret's coffin?'

'I suppose he would, yes. Thinking about it he certainly would!'

'Is it possible that he could, unbeknown to you have removed the suit in question?'

'Oh dear, I fear that looks increasingly like the case, Detective Constable Dexter,' he grimaced.

'Could you provide me with his full address in Tyler Street then please, sir?'

'I think the number is 36. It is a house in a terraced block, next to the shop of a baker!' he replied.

'Thank you, Mr Watson. I might need to speak to you again, I assume that will be acceptable?'

'Yes, of course!'

It was too late to interview Mr Henchcliffe, so I went on my way into work next morning.

9

Number 36 Tyler Street was indeed next to a bakery. Once again the smell of freshly baked bread lingering in the air brought thoughts of Alice's bread. I knocked on the door and a few seconds later it was opened by a young chap in his early thirties. He was tall and muscular with large hands, his face a little scary, unhandsome and pockmarked.

'Mr Herbert Henchcliffe?' I asked.

'Aye, who's askin'?'

'I'm Detective Constable Dexter,' I said showing my warrant card.

'What do you want?' he snapped.

'Can I come in please, sir?'

'Oh, aye, I suppose so,' he said, opening the door just wide enough for me to squeeze past him. 'I suppose you'd better sit down!' he said indicating a clean but well-worn sofa under the front window.

'I believe that until fairly recently you were employed as an assistant undertaker?'

'What has that old bugger Watson bin sayin'?' Henchcliffe snapped.

'He did suggest that he had been unhappy with your attitude, but I'm not here about the reason you were dismissed. What can you tell me about a suit of men's clothes that was supposedly buried with the deceased yet turned up, three years later, in a second hand shop in Derby?' I asked.

'I get it! He's been caught out at last an' I'm to be the scapegoat!'

'Are you saying that Mr Watson removed the

116

suit from the corpse of Arthur Garret?'

'Huh. Wouldn't be the first. The proud firm of Watson & Marchbank are not quite what they like people to think.'

In what way, Mr Henchcliffe?'

'We used to call old Mr Marchbank "The Kipper-box King". Oh, not to 'is face of course but among the staff,' he shrugged, a look of distaste on his face.

'Why was that?' I asked, a suspicion forming in my mind.

'Mr Watson was the undertaker, he dealt with the stiffs, Mr Marchbank was the joiner; cabinet-maker really I suppose. He could make the good stuff but he could also make cardboard-thin plywood look like finest teak or rosewood if he'd a mind.'

'So, they had different grades of coffin; presumably to suit different pockets,' I suggested.

'The clients were always shown a beautiful oak casket, finest seasoned English oak, with polished brass handles and fitments. Beautiful they were. The deceased was laid out in it and the relatives invited to view and observe the closing of the coffin. Then it was moved to the little chapel of rest. Like I said, they also made really nice lookin', but cheap plywood versions fitted with pretty looking brass plated handles, for folk who were a bit strapped for cash. Once in the chapel, they moved the corpse into the cheap one and screwed the lid on. They thought I couldn't tell the difference; didn't realise what they were doing in the dead of night!'

'Are you saying that they swapped the good coffin for a cheap alternative?'

'Now, not every time and I don't know for what reason; I'd say on average about one in three of the burials were fiddled with like that, the others were done right!'

'That's all very interesting but it doesn't explain how the suit ended up in the second hand shop,' I pointed out.

117

'Well, I don't know how that is, but let's just say that the coffin wasn't the only thing that they tinkered with!'

'Could you explain?'

'Well if a particular burial was one that I knew they had tinkered with, I'd nip down after they'd swapped the coffin and lift the lid again and take a dekko; often they'd taken the suit of clothes. I noticed that they only took men's suits, and then only the best, never the ladies dresses. I'm a big chap and liftin' 'em out is dead easy, unless they were really big. On m' day off I'd take them around the pawn brokers and second hand shops. I got a pound for a nice-lookin' suit and ten or twelve bob for a nice dress. They always want them buried in their best!' he grinned

'You took women's dresses as well?' I asked incredulously.

'Aye! That's what 'e caught me doin' the night he sacked me!'

'He suggested something, er…'

'I bet he did! He caught me removing the ladies dress and I suppose he put two and two together and made god-knows what number.'

'Are you admitting to removing the suit belonging to Mr Arthur Garret from his corpse after the closing of the coffin lid?'

'I can't remember that particular one! I had many a suit and dress like that, but only if they had already swapped the coffins. Chances are if it was a really good suit *they* would have already 'ad it!'

'As part of changing the coffin?'

'Mm, I've 'ad a lot o' time to think about it, add it all up, like. I reckon they save about fifteen quid with the cheap coffin, a cheap linin' and monkey metal handles. Plus, whatever they get for the suits. Nice little pick-up I'd say, wouldn't you?'

'You considered the corpse *fair game* in that case?'

'It was a way to get by on what the stingy beggars paid,' he snarled.

'Mr Watson has told me that you occupied a flat above the garage in their yard, is that correct?'

'Yes, they rented it to me as part of my pay. The flat an' fifteen shillings a week, not much chance of livin'-it-up on that would yer say?'

'It's hardly generous, I agree,' I nodded.

'So I borrow the clothes that the deceased is not really in a position to complain about and earn a few extra pounds like that. Only when they 'ad already swapped the coffin. If it was a genuine job I never tampered!'

'How many times have you done that?' I asked, incredulously.

'A couple of times a month, yer, about that I'd say.'

'A couple of times a month – for five years?'

'Blimey no! I didn't twig on to the coffin swap until I'd been with 'em about two years, just after I moved into the flat. I'm a very light sleeper, yer see; they're deadly quiet and the chapel o' rest is at the back of the main building so the chances of bein' 'eard by a normal sleeper is pretty slim. Anyway, like I said, I'd been in the flat about a month an' one night I 'ears a noise. Some bugger is breakin' in, I thinks. I slips me trousers on an goes to the window; it's *them,* the bosses, an I'm just in time to see a coffin with the lid propped inside bein' carried back to the showroom, and what looked like a suit of clothes over Mr Watson's arm.'

'So what did you do?'

'Not any o' my business, but I'm curious, see?' I nodded.

'So I goes down after they've gone to see what the heck is goin' on. Not that I 'aven't got a pretty good idea. Like I said, the joiner's shop makes all grades of boxes. The good ones are top notch, good as yer'll get anywhere, down to matchwood made to look good.

119

They'd swapped the top grade coffin for a nice-lookin' pile of firewood.

'What did you find?' I asked.

'I unscrewed the lid and 'ad a dekko. There's the poor bugger in shirt and underpants, not even the dignity of a shroud. I'd seen the corpse lyin' in the coffin when the relatives came to pay their respects. It was a top quality suit he was laid out in, now it was gone!'

'How often did this happen?'

'I never really took any notice, but I'd say probably once a week.'

'But they only took the top quality suits?'

'Aye, and left me the rest without knowing it… and the dresses. Only one lady went to her maker in her undies, didn't seem right somehow, so I bought some cheap single bed sheets and gave 'em the decency of a shroud.'

'Very good of you!' I said, perhaps a little sarcastically.

'Look, I've told yer what I know. Compared to them I've done nothing' and I'll deny sayin' any of this, except where it incriminates them!'

'I'll have to report this to my inspector. I will probably need to talk to you again,' I said.

'I'm likely to be 'ere, if I'm not job-'untin'.'

Back at Whitecross Yard the DI was again standing by the window looking at me as I drove into the yard. I nodded to him as I got out of the car and made my way in to the rear of the building. He was seated at his desk by the time I opened the door of his temporary office, with his bad leg up on another chair.

'You only just caught me Dexter, I'm expecting the car to take me home any second,' he said.

'I think you'll want to hear this, sir!'

'Go on then, I suppose a few minutes won't matter. Not that my good lady will see it that way,' he chuckled.

'I went to Watson and Marchbank, Mr Garret's undertaker.'

'Yes go on...'

'They weren't much help, but they did put me on to a young chap they'd dismissed...' I told him what was said.

'So let's get this right; this chap Henchcliffe is saying that his employers were swapping some of the coffins with a cheap version and nicking the suits?' the DI asked.

'But only the top quality suits, and never the ladies dresses.'

'Then he helps himself to what's not good enough for them?'

'So he said.'

'Well, bugger-me. Yer not even safe from crime when yer dead, Dexter,' he smiled.

'A bit hard to call them as a witness though, sir.'

'True. Look, you need to visit the undertakers again and question this Mr Watson about what we now know.'

'Always assuming that we can trust Henchcliffe's word, sir.'

'Did you think he was telling the truth?'

'He seemed genuine, unless he's a very good actor, sir.'

'I wish I could come with you, give our Mr Watson a bit of a roasting.'

'We could leave it until morning, sir. I could pop in and see the second hand shop in Derby this afternoon and see what they have to say.'

'Good thinking, Dexter. I'll give my opposite number in Derby a ring and get the okay for you to be on their patch. It shouldn't be a problem, we've helped them often enough. Meantime nip down to the yard and tell my driver I'll be a second or two,' he said, nodding through the window as the patrol car pulled up. 'I've got to go and show my face and express due concern at Alderman Tippett's house,' he shrugged.

'Right, sir.'

I parked the Hornet in a side road off Derby Market Place. Mrs Garret had explained where the shop was, locating it was easy enough. Although Saddler Gate had three such shops, only one could be considered to be at the Market Place end of the old timber-fronted street. The establishment of E M Chandler turned out to be part pawnbroker, part second-hand shop. The window displayed a wide range of goods but mostly shoes and clothing. A man's suit of a quality not unlike the one I had parcelled under my arm had centre stage in the display. A bell gave a little tinkle as I opened the door.

'Good morning, sir, can I help you?' asked a stout chap, probably approaching eighteen stone. Large round spectacles gave him the look of an overweight aging owl.

'I wonder what you could tell me about this suit,' I replied.

'Might I ask who's asking?'

'I'm DC William Dexter, Crammingdon CID. Although technically I'm out of my area, I have permission to carry out our investigation into the history behind this suit,' I said, laying it on the counter and unwrapping it.

'I'm sorry I don't quite understand your point!'

'Could you tell me if you recently sold this suit?'

'Possibly... This one – or one very similar. A woman came in with it a while back, she said it had been her husband's suit; *"too good to bury him in",* she said.

'I'm sorry, could you explain?' I asked a bit bewildered.

'Yes I reckon this is the suit,' he said opening the jacket and looking at the maker's label. 'This lady brought it in about six months ago; said it had been her husband's suit and was too good to bury him in, like I said.'

'Do you know the lady's name?'

'I'm sure I can find it. Being a pawnbroker it's force of habit to ask, for when they want to redeem, yer see.'

'It was brought in to raise money on a loan?'

'No! They wanted to sell it – short of a bob or two I'd say.'

'So you bought the suit?'

'Yes and no!'

'I'm not with you. Did you buy the suit or not?'

'I made an offer – what I thought it was worth. The lady looked down her nose a bit, like I'm trying to diddle her. Then she said, *"Will you sell it for me and take ten percent?"* I'm easy, no skin off my nose, so I agreed,' he smiled.

'That seems a strange arrangement.'

'Well, I can't lose can I? I sold it for two guineas. That's over four shillings clear profit for putting it on a hanger in the window. Mind you it was in the window over five months!'

'Can you tell me who bought it?'

'It's all in m' book, let's see; a Mr Garret – ah – of Crammingdon! He said he knew the suit. Tried to come the old con-trick, he reckoned it was his brother's! "Pull the other one" I said. Been in this game too long to fall for that one, I can tell you.'

'But in the end he bought it?' I asked.

'Yes, but he wasn't happy about it.'

'What date was that?' I asked and he looked at the book again.

'Monday the fifteenth. So what's the problem officer?'

'To be honest I'm not sure! The lady who brought the suit in, could you describe her?'

'I suppose ordinarily after six months, no. However, like I said, I'd sold the suit to this Mr Garratt on commission. I rang the seller a couple of days later to say I'd sold it and she could collect her cash, she came in that afternoon and I paid her. So, yes I can describe her pretty well; a bit of a looker as they say, black hair greying a bit here and there but only just. Cut short a bit like a boy's; like they did in the early twenties; a couple of inches shorter than you, and a bit of a flirt!'

The description he'd given could, with a little allowance for personal perception, quite easily have fitted Mrs Garret, though the name he'd written was Tremaine.

'You said you've an address for this lady.'

'I have, I'll jot it down for yer!' he said taking a slip of paper and pencil attached by a bit of string to the counter. 'Here, let me wrap that up again,' he added, seeing me struggling to retie the parcel.

'Thanks – I might need to talk to you again,' I said.

'Always here. You can't give me a clue what this is about, I suppose?'

'I can't, I'm sorry, but I think it may make the papers if it's what I think it is,' I nodded

'Blimey, I bet I won't come out smelling of roses.'

'If you bought it in good faith, you are just as much a victim as anyone else,' I said.

'Now, why doesn't that put my mind at rest I wonder?'

I left him to ponder that and made my way back to the Hornet.

The address he had given me proved to be a mile or so away on the Burton Road. The house was large but not very well kept, the sort of house that had started life as a desirable abode but time and tight finances had reduced its face value. I parked outside and walked the short path to the front door. A lady very much as described by the pawnbroker answered the door.

'Mrs Tremaine?'

'That's right,' she said, holding her head in a way that asked an unspoken question.

'I'm DC William Dexter, Crammingdon CID,' I said showing my card.

'Crammingdon, what's up have yer lost yer way?' she smiled.

'I'm off patch agreed, but I'm here investigating this suit,' I said holding up the parcel.

'Been a naughty boy has it? Can't yer just lock it up?' she chuckled.

'It's a bit of a delicate matter, could I come in?'

'I suppose so – I've just filled the teapot, can I offer yer one?'

'That would be very nice Mrs Tremaine, thank you.'

'Make yerself comfy in the front room, I won't be a tick.'

The front room, like the house, showed signs of a tight budget. The three piece suite had once been of good quality and still was of course, quality like a Rolls Royce car can always be seen, but fashion and age take their toll. I parked myself on a settee under the window. It's a great place to see the reaction of the person you are talking to; with the window behind you, your face is in shadow whilst theirs is in full light.

'Here we are, help yerself to milk and sugar. Now what's this about a suit?'

'I believe you recently sold a suit through the pawnbroker at the end of Sadler Gate?'

'I did. My late husband's suit, too good to bury him in, so I sold it. Is that what's in your parcel?'

'Yes, at least I think so. Would you mind taking a look and confirming that this is the suit you sold,' I asked, once more unwrapping the thing.

'Yes, this is the suit. It was his idea to sell it; cash is a bit tight at the moment. *"Put me in the grey one, I like the grey one!"* he said when he knew he was near the end. It was his favourite, the grey one that is, so I sold this one like he said. Not that it made a fortune exactly.'

'Can I ask where you bought the suit?'

'Where we bought it?'

'Yes can you remember where you bought it?'

'I can or at least I can picture the shop; now where was it! Oh yes, I remember, middle of Green Lane, on the right going up.'

'Can you remember the name?' I asked, taking a sip of tea.

'I can't but you can't miss it; big shop with a window each side of the door. The window's always full of second-hand suits.'

'You bought it second-hand?'

'Of course, it was only for his mate's retirement do. His grey suit was looking a bit the worst for wear so I made him get another, not that we could really afford it!'

'I think I know the shop, the left hand window has a rack of shoes against the wall. It's Perry's or something like that.'

'Perry's, that's right!'

'Can you tell me roughly when that was, Mrs Tremaine?'

'Hold on a mo`, what's all this about?'

'All I can tell you is that the suit should never have been in Perry's window in the first place.'

'Are you saying it was stolen?' she asked, her eyes narrowing quizzically. 'Cos if you are, don't look at me. We bought it from a shop fair and square.'

'I'm sure you did Mrs Tremaine. I wonder, would you mind making a statement to that effect?'

'If I have to, now do you mean?'

'No, if I need one I'll call back. Have you a phone number I could call on if I need to?' She gave me the number of a neighbour and I thanked her for the tea.

The shop on Green Lane was about to close as I pulled up outside, a tall young man was carrying a rack of ladies shoes back inside.

'Mr Perry?' I asked as I got out of the car.

'No he's inside, but I'm afraid we're closing.'

I quickly explained who I was and the young chap asked me to follow him.

'Mr Perry, there's a policeman to see you.'

'What's it about and make it snappy, I've a doctor's appointment in half an hour!'

I explained and asked him if he recalled the suit. He didn't of course, claiming that dozens of suits and dresses passed through his shop every year.

'I've a chap from your neck of the woods who brings in two or three suits every six weeks or so. It could be one of them. Chap named Butterworth, tip top suits they are, even though they all smell a bit of... er... mothballs. Yes, that's it, mothballs! Have to hang 'em out in the fresh air for a couple of days before we can put em in the shop or they'd smell the place out; bad for business – mothballs!'

'Could you describe the chap?' I asked.

'I certainly can, he was in the end of last week. Brought two suits in; they're out the back in the lean-to, freshening up!'

He described the man in question and it could certainly have fitted Mr Watson the undertaker. Quickly he unlocked the door to the lean-to. The smell he thought was mothballs was faint but unmistakably formaldehyde; embalming fluid.

'Have you ever asked where this chap manages to get so many good suits?'

'Only in a roundabout sort of way, I didn't want to frighten him off. He's brought me a lot of good business over the years.'

'What was his explanation?'

'He said that he and a mate clear houses, so they come from the estate of dead folk.'

'It is something like that,' I admitted.

'Are you thinking he's nickin' them?' he asked, scratching his chin.

'Would you mind holding on to these suits for a day or two? I might need to speak to you again,' I asked.

'He is, isn't he? He's pinchin' the damned things!'

'As yet I don't know, but something doesn't ring true. I'll be in touch Mr Perry.'

'Everything seems to point to Mr Watson or his partner removing the suits and taking them to Perry's in Derby, far enough away to be unlikely to be recognised. Within weeks Perry's sold the Garret's suit to the Tremaine's. They had it until Mr Tremaine died and his wife took it to the shop where Mrs Garret's brother-in-law spotted it,' I said to DI Brierly, next morning.

'I think we certainly need to have another word with Mr Watson, Dexter.'

'Yes. I think so, sir.'

'Right, sir.'

'I wonder if Watson and Marchbank are the only undertakers who make an extra bob or two like that, sir,' suggested DS Whittington.

'It would be hard to prove,' said the DI.

'Especially since it seems that the suits are sold miles away from the undertaker's premises,' Ellen added.

'Like I said sir, Mr Perry had to hang the suits in an outhouse to get rid of the smell. If it is widespread, chances are that other shops have found the same problem. Perhaps we should ring around to see if that's the case. What do you think, sir?' I asked.

'We'll do better than that! You two,' he said looking at Whittington and Harrington, 'go around the second hand shops in town first, ask if they ever get any suits brought in smelling heavily of mothballs. We'll spread it to Derby tomorrow.

'Right lads, *and lady* – Mm, I'd better start saying "Right team" – any news on Jenny or Mr Jellicoe?' he asked.

'Not really sir. Except Ellen had an idea yesterday afternoon; tell him Ellen,' said DS Whittington.

'Go on lass, let's hear it. We can't rule anything out no matter how small,' the DI nodded.

'The school tea-lady, Mrs Ecclestone, said that she had seen Mr Jellicoe doing a magic act!'

'Well he's certainly made himself and Jenny disappear! Carry on.'

'Well sir, I wondered if he might be performing somewhere under another name,' she said, rather shyly.

'On stage, you mean?'

'Just a thought, sir,' she shrugged.

'I can't think of anything better,' he said, looking around the group.

We all shook our heads.

'Okay Ellen, see what you can turn up, though how you'll do it, I've no idea,' he said.

'I thought of ringing the theatrical agents to see if they have anyone on their books that fits Jellicoe's description, sir.'

'Right, I've the Chief Constable's okay to take the case in any direction I see fit and a few extra phone-calls won't break the bank. Do it, Ellen, ring those theatrical places. Come on Dexter, we are going to put a little gentle pressure on Messrs. Watson & Marchbank,' he grinned.

The DI had arranged for a patrol car to be our transport, since he was sure his plastered leg would make it difficult for him to get into the Hornet, not to mention the room for a set of crutches. Our driver dropped us just before ten o'clock at the undertaker's office, and agreed to pick us up again from the little café just down the road when we were finished.

As I opened the door I was instantly aware of a faint smell; mothballs Mr Perry had called it, but I knew better of course. There was a small entrance hall before a second glass door into what seemed to be laid out like a

129

parlour, gold-leaf lettering on the glass telling us that these were the premises of Watson & Marchbank and asking us to "please enter". Two large leather settees arranged in an L shape faced a small counter covered in black satin stood in front of a curtained doorway. A small Egyptian style vase of silk roses in a subdued maroon colour sat on one end of the counter and a highly polished brass bell, like a hotel reception bell, stood at the other. A young lady in her early twenties dressed in a black jacket and skirt, her white blouse decorated by one of those large Victorian broaches of Whitby jet worn centrally close to her neck, answered our summoning ring a few moments later.

'Good morning how can help you?' she asked, giving an obviously well practiced smile; welcoming without being jolly.

'I'm Detective Inspector Brierly and this is Detective Constable Dexter, could we speak to Mr Watson or Mr Marchbank, please,' asked the DI.

'Mr Watson is conducting an interment at the moment, but Mr Marchbank is in our joinery shop. Please sit down, I'll go and find out if he can see you,' she said, clearly trying to puzzle out our business.

'I'll stand thank you, not quite as mobile as normal,' the DI grinned.

'Of course,' she nodded

The DI, wobbling dangerously on his three points of contact, flicked through a brochure of flower arrangements; "Floral Tributes", the cover announced in large flowing copperplate script.

'Any you particularly fancy, sir?' I asked with a bright smile.

'When I go that'll be some other bugger's problem, Dexter,' he said with raised eyebrows.

'If you'd care to come through, Mr Marchbank will see you in his office,' she said holding the curtain aside and then showing us through a corridor out into the yard that Mr Henchcliffe, the sacked assistant undertaker, had described. The faint buzz of modern machinery increased considerably as she opened the door into what was clearly an up-to-date joinery shop, well away from the front parlour. Mr Marchbank, a man I guessed to be in his late fifties, or early sixties, stood at the door to a glass partitioned office within the main workshop.

'Come in gentlemen. That will be all thank you, Miss Benson,' he said, holding the door open and inviting us to sit down, once again we declined. The sound of the circular saw became a gentle background hum as he closed the door.

'Now, what can I do for you gentlemen?' he asked.

'I'll put my cards on the table. Two days ago a lady came into the police station at Whitecross Yard, complaining that a suit belonging to her husband had been found in a second-hand shop in Derby!' said the DI. 'The suit had been recognised by her brother-in-law as one in which her husband should have been buried. A burial carried out by your company.'

'Mr Watson did discuss this with me and we concluded that she must be mistaken or perhaps trying to make some sort of claim upon us!' he shrugged holding his hands out in a gesture of innocence.

'Detective Constable Dexter has made enquiries with the tailor who made the suit and has followed a lengthy trail which leads back to this company,' the DI stated, forcibly.

'Suggesting we are in some way complicit in selling off the suit, for some purpose or other. A suggestion I strenuously deny,' Marchbank said, raising his voice.

'Come now, Mr Marchbank, I have good reason to believe that is actually the case!' the DI said.

'This is a respectable firm Inspector. Why would we do such a thing?'

'Presumably for the same reason you exchange top quality coffins for inferior versions after the deceased's relatives have seen the coffin closed,' the DI stated.

For a moment, Marchbank's face was a picture. His reaction was one I'd seen many times in petty criminals suddenly confronted with something they didn't think we knew. Quickly he regained his composure even though his face had coloured up. The DI looked at him awaiting his reply.

'That is preposterous! I resent and deny the implication of your accusation,' he said, though the shakiness of his voice betrayed the fact that we had hit on the truth.

'We have a witness to the exchanging of coffins and the removal of suits!'

'Ah, from young Herbert Henchcliffe no doubt! Then you may take that information with a pinch of salt. He has reason to besmirch our good name; we sacked him for unprofessional behaviour.'

'Mr Henchcliffe has stated that this practice happened on many occasions!'

'An accusation neither we nor he, can possible prove or disprove since the evidence is either six feet under or away to the heavens in smoke, Detective Inspector. If that is all, I must ask you to leave as I have a busy work load.' he shrugged.

'I have to say that I am unhappy with the outcome of this meeting and request that both you and Mr Watson come into Whitecross to assist with my enquiries.'

'We can't just drop everything, we have strictly timed funerals to conduct!'

'I recognise that you have commitments that need to be carried out. If you could give me an idea when you will be available I shall make suitable arrangements to ensure that there is the minimum of inconvenience to you,' the DI smiled.

Mr Marchbank slid open a drawer in his desk and took out a large diary.

'I see that both Mr Watson and I will be available this afternoon between about two-thirty and four o'clock. I suppose it would look bad on the firm if we refused to help the police with their enquiries, Detective Inspector.'

'Thank you, sir. As early as possible please, I am also a busy man.' the DI said as we opened the door. I'm not sure but I fancy I heard Mr Marchbank say, "Busy-body, more like". I was still grinning at it as we sat ourselves in the café having phoned for our lift.

'Why the cheesy grin, Dexter?' the DI asked sticking his plastered leg into the narrow gap between the tables.

'I think we put the wind up him, sir,' I said as we ordered two teas, thinking it best not to give him the real reason.

'Oh, to be privy to the conversation when those two get back together,' the DI grinned.

'Think they'll be cooking something up, sir?'

'That's for sure! When we get back to the station, you nip off and get our Mr Henchcliffe to pop in about one o'clock to make a statement. We'll confront them with that if need be.'

'I'll go now sir. I'll walk there and catch the bus back.'

'Better than that, we'll drop you off and you can take the bus back!'

'Good enough, sir; drink up, your chariot awaits!' I said, pointing through the window.

They dropped me at Mr Henchcliffe's house and carried on to Whitecross Yard. Mr Henchcliffe agreed to come in and make a statement at one o'clock and I caught the bus to the railway station and walked the five hundred yards back to the DI's replacement office. As I entered the DI was on the phone. From his conversation it was clear that he was making his excuses to his wife for not being home on time. I crept out and left him to it.

I guessed Ellen was up in the CID office and I

ran up the stairs to see if her enquiries had taken us any-where. She was also on the phone and nodded to me as I entered. I pointed to the kettle and she nodded, as it came to the boil she put the phone down.

'Well that was interesting; it seems that our Mr Jellicoe has been pestering a number of theatrical agents in the area to see if they can get bookings for him!' she said.

'Fed up with teaching, eh?' I smiled.

'So it would seem. As yet I can't find any that have taken him on; it seems that magicians are two a penny and unless you are outstanding, forget it!'

'Mrs Ecclestone the tea lady said he was pretty good,' I commented.

'It seems they didn't even get as far as asking him to audition, but one of them told me he was trying to get work using the name "The Great Gondello". I'm go-ing to pop down and tell the DI how far I've got before he goes home.'

'No rush, he's staying on a bit to interview our two undertakers, get your coffee first,' I said.

'Are they looking more like suspects then, Will?'

'Something's going on but they are denying all knowledge, as you'd expect, so the DI has decided to confront them with what we know so far,' I smiled.

'I'd love to see how he handles it!' she said.

'Nip down, give him your report and ask him if you can sit in.'

'Would he let me?' she asked, her eyes opening wide.

'I don't know, but my guess is yes,' I grinned, 'especially if you present him with a cup of tea,' I said and she turned and made a cuppa and took to the stairs.

Mr Henchcliffe came in as agreed and gave a statement, being careful not to incriminate himself but giving us details of the three most recent burials that he was aware had been tampered with. I swiftly typed it up with two carbon copies. Our office lady would normally have done this but due to the delicacy of the subject I thought I'd better do it. He duly signed them and was on his way out as Mr Watson and Mr Marchbank were coming up the steps. For a moment or two it seemed as though there might be some sort of affray, but good sense prevailed, probably because of where they were. Even so, it caused me to suppress a chuckle as I asked them to take a seat in the front office.

'Mr Watson and Mr Marchbank have arrived, sir.'

'We'll speak to them separately. Put Mr Watson in interview room one, we'll see him in there. Ellen has asked to sit in with us on these. I think it will be good for her don't you?' he asked.

'I'd say so; she's pretty keen isn't she, sir?'

'Strictly between us, Dexter, I intend to see if I can get her on our little team permanently. Do you reckon she'd be willing?'

'I think she'd bite your hand off, sir,' I smiled.

'Not a word, Dexter.'

'Understood, sir.'

Mr Watson was taken to interview room one and allowed to stew for a few minutes, whilst the DI gave Ellen and me his plan of action.

'Dexter, I want you to open. Then I'll take over when you've stirred him up a bit. Ellen I want you to take notes. Don't say anything, but if you think of something that might be relevant ask to have a word with me outside.'

'Right, sir!'

Mr Watson was biting his thumbnail as we entered the room. The DI and I sat at the table opposite him; Ellen took a seat in the corner and took out a notebook and pencil.

'Good afternoon Mr Watson. As you know, I'm DC William Dexter, this is Detective Inspector Brierly and acting DC Parsons is here to take notes.'

He nodded and gave his thumbnail a rest.

'I think you know why you are here?' I asked.

'Some silly misunderstanding about a suit!' he snapped.

'My enquiries lead me to believe that a suit belonging to a Mr Garret, which Mrs Garret had given orders he was to be buried in, was removed from his corpse at some point after the official closure of the coffin.'

'As my partner, Mr Marchbank said yesterday and I told you this morning, we are convinced that this is an attempt by Mrs Garret to make some sort of claim on our good name!'

'Leaving that for the moment, do you deny exchanging top quality coffins for ones of a lesser quality after the relatives of the deceased have seen the coffin closed?'

'I suppose that rubbish comes from Herbert Henchcliffe? A young man whom I have already told you I dismissed for unprofessional behaviour.'

'Mr Watson, I will read the statement given to us a few minutes ago by Mr Henchcliffe,' said the DI picking up the typewritten sheet I'd handed him in his office.

"For about three years, prior to being dismissed by Mr Watson I lived in the flat in the yard above the garage of Watson and Marchbank the undertakers. Being a very light sleeper, I was awakened on many occasions by noises coming from the room across the yard from the flat that served as the small chapel of rest. I remember thinking on the first occasion, shortly after taking up residence in the flat that the place was being broken into. Looking out of the window, being careful not to be seen, I saw the two owners of the firm coming out of the chapel carrying a coffin and what looked like a man's suit. Undertakers are used to acting quietly and unobtrusively and most people would I'm sure have slept

through the occurrence."

'The words of a young scoundrel, the inference of which, I strongly deny.'

'He goes on to say, *"I was intrigued to see what they had been up to and having made sure they had gone I went down to the chapel, and using the keys supplied to me went inside. I recognised the coffin to be one of our cheaper types, even though it had originally been of the highest quality when I had assisted in its closure that afternoon. On unscrewing and lifting the lid I found that the deceased's suit had been removed and the corpse wore only shirt and pants."*

'I repeat. The words of a scoundrel!'

'Yesterday I made enquiries at the second hand shop, where Mrs Garret's brother-in-law found the suit,' I said.

I went on to explain how I had obtained the route by which the suit had ended up, or rather, begun its travels at Perry's shop on Green Lane in Derby.

'Mr. Perry told me that a person fitting your description often brought suits in to him. Suits that smelled so strongly of "mothballs" that he had to hang them in his lean-to outside the rear of the shop to disperse the smell, a smell I recognised to be formaldehyde!' I said.

'Rubbish. Nothing to do with me,' Watson snapped.

'Could I have a word, sir?' asked Ellen.

'Excuse me for a moment, Mr Watson,' said the DI and took Ellen out of the room.

'What's that all about?'

'Perhaps DC Parsons has noticed something we are missing,' I suggested.

A few moments later, the DI poked his head into the room.

'DC Dexter, get Mr Watson a cup of tea then join me in interview room two.'

'Very good, sir.'

137

'No tea for me, thank you, but a glass of water would be very welcome. I presume my colleague is to be interviewed now?'

'So I would imagine, sir,' I said and went to collect his glass of water.

Ellen and DI Brierly stood in the corridor outside interview room two. The DI gave me a crooked smile as I joined the pair of them.

'Guess what DC Parsons wanted to tell me?' he asked.

'No idea, sir!'

'She didn't actually want to tell me anything! She thought that if she asked to speak to me outside, it would rattle our friend just that bit more,' he smiled.

'I think she's done that alright. You should have seen his hand shake when I handed him his glass of water,' I laughed.

'You're getting the hang of this, aren't you Ellen?'

'I'd like to think so, sir,' she agreed.

We went into interview room two and the DI made the introductions.

'Mr Marchbank, I'll start by reading you a statement from Mr Herbert Henchcliffe, who I believe you used to employ.'

'That young reprobate!'

'Never the less I will read it…'

The DI read the statement as far as he had read it to Mr Watson.

'What have you to say to that, sir?' he asked.

'Total rubbish, young Henchcliffe has a personal axe to grind!'

'Mr Henchcliffe said a little more than I've read so far; shall I continue Mr Marchbank?'

'If you wish, though I can't see what good it will do,' he shrugged.

'Mr Henchcliffe's statement concludes, *"These things happened so regularly that I can't remember all of the names or dates. I can remember the last three, though!*

> *6th May Mr George Williams, Central Cemetery*
> *18th May Mr Arthur Madison, Central Cemetery*
> *27th May Mr Daniel Portree, St Steven's Churchyard, Washington Road.*

In each case the coffin was changed from that shown to the relatives of the departed, and the corpse left naked, or in only underclothes, after the burial suit had been removed." I think that puts a different complexion on the matter, especially since Mr Perry took delivery of three suits, smelling of what he thought was mothballs, on the 1st of June, from a man answering the description of Mr Watson!' the DI smiled.

For a few moments, Mr Marchbank was silent, then he said, 'I still deny any wrongdoing, and since the evidence is beyond reach I fail to see how this matter can be resolved.'

'I intend to put Mr Watson in an identity parade and ask Mr Perry to identify, if he can, the person who supplied the suits,' the DI pointed out.

'What does that prove?' Marchbank asked, defiantly.

'If Mr Perry identifies Mr Watson as the person he has been dealing with for several years, I will apply for an exhumation order!' the DI said.

Marchbank's face went deadly white. 'You'd never get one,' he stuttered.

'It won't be easy, but I think that this matter is serious enough to apply for one.'

'Could I confer with my colleague? After all as far as I am aware I, we, are not under arrest!'

The DI thought about it for a second of two. 'As you say, neither of you are under arrest so I see no reason why you shouldn't review your position! However unless I make considerable progress in the next few minutes, I will carry out the strategy I have outlined. DC Parsons, take Mr Marchbank to interview one and give them ten minutes in private.'

'Right, sir.'

'That'll stir the buggers up a bit, Dexter,' he laughed, after they had left the room.

'What's it all about, sir? They are a good firm, surely they could just add a bit on to the price if they find things tight.'

'Yes I agree; I'm not aware that undertaking is particularly cut-throat. Anyway, didn't young Henchcliffe tell you that it wasn't every burial?'

'That's right, sir! According to him it was only certain ones and he couldn't see any reason why they did it to one but not another!'

'Maybe we are about to find out! Get a brew on the go Dexter, I'm dying of thirst and I certainly don't want to end up in the hands of those two!' he grinned.

'Right, sir!' I said as Ellen came back into interview two.

'They went straight into a huddle, whispering so I couldn't hear but they know they've been rumbled, sir! My guess is they'll make a full confession any time now!' she said.

'Go back and wait at the door, bring 'em both here as soon as they contact you!'

'How much longer should I give them, sir?'

'Don't worry about that, they'll probably be ready right now!' he said.

As it was, quarter of an hour went by and there were raised voices from the undertakers as they argued about what they intended to say.

'Right, I've had enough of this! Bring 'em in here, Dexter,' the DI snapped.

'Right, sir.'

I got to the corridor as Ellen was bringing them out of interview one.

'Sit down please gentlemen. Now I want to know what this is all about.'

'Some years ago,' said Mr Marchbank, 'several of our competitors started to provide funeral insurance plans.'

Mr Watson sat with his head in his hands.

'Yes, a good idea; I've got one myself!' agreed the DI.

'Indeed they are. They generally tie the person to a particular undertaking establishment.'

'I'm with the Co-op!' the DI nodded.

'We were left with no alternative than to provide one ourselves. They normally operate in conjunction with a major insurance company, but Mr Watson suggested that we cut out the middle man and have all of the premiums ourselves.'

Mr Watson raised his head and looked annoyed with his partner; clearly, he was still in favour of stout denial.

'We sold two hundred or so of them at five shillings a month. A nice little income of fifty pounds a month for nothing, at least that's what we thought.'

'We set a price we thought was realistic, however we weren't aware that the big companies were carrying out strict vetting of individuals for health problems and therefore increased risk. We ended up with most of our policy holders being the ones turned down by the big companies!' Mr Watson interrupted.

'The ones the most at risk?' the DI suggested.

'Exactly! We were losing money hand over fist. One chap snuffed it after two years. Twelve quid he'd paid, and guaranteed a first class funeral,' Marchbanks nodded.

'So you hit on the idea of swapping the coffins?' Ellen asked.

'Not for about a year or so; we stood the loss until it was clear that we couldn't carry on unless we did something. I confess swapping the coffins was my idea. It meant that we more or less broke even, it was Mr Watson's idea to take the suits and rings!'

'Oh, bloody hell! Why did you say that?' asked

Watson.

'They're on about getting an exhumation order! We can't do that to folk!'

'Are you saying that you took the rings from people's fingers?' asked the DI, with a look of disgust.

'Yes! Can't say I'm happy about it but we couldn't carry on without it. Anyway, most wives want to keep their husbands wedding ring as a keep-sake. So we didn't get every one! And only the funerals on the insurance plan, those paid for outright were always dealt with correctly!' said Watson, and Marchbank agreed.

'In view of your confession, I am going to speak to the Assistant Chief Constable to see how he wants me to proceed with this. In the meantime you are not under arrest but do not continue with these goings-on!'

'Does this mean we can continue in business?' asked Watson.

'For the time being, yes. In due course I will quite possibly be charging you with various offences, either together or individually.'

'Are we free to go, Inspector?'

'Yes! You are on your honour gentlemen, not to leave town.'

'With funerals to perform, that is hardly likely, Detective Inspector!' Marchbanks said.

10

On Thursday the fifteenth of June, Ellen's idea finally paid off. Mr Jellicoe, "The Great Gondello", had found an agent. Not only that, the agent lived locally and was something of a local celebrity. DI Brierly sent Ellen and me off just before ten in the morning to make some enquiries of the man.

I headed the Hornet out on the Sheffield Road. Mr Brandon's house was about a mile outside the town; technically not our patch but since the county force were loath to cover the area it often fell to us, being nearer, to police it. A gravelled driveway ended in a large circle in front of the house. I stopped the car outside the most unusual house I had ever seen. The whole building was of white pebble dash with a striking green-tiled roof. The front was not unlike an American ranch house or perhaps that of a Jamaican sugar planter seen on the newsreels or in the glossy magazines, but certainly like nothing I'd ever seen in real life. The front door was on the first floor with a double staircase of marble steps, sweeping around to the left and right, enclosed by pebble dash walls and ending in a lavish landing area with miniature Japanese maples either side of the door.

We'd both heard rumours, the locally circulating story had become almost legend. If it was in fact true, Mr Brandon was a very shrewd man indeed. It seemed that when he was a young lawyer trying to make his way in the world he had gone to work in one of the Caribbean islands, no-one seemed to know which, and joined a well-respected local law firm. After several years, he had made some influential contacts and gained a reputation for outstanding ability, especially in company law. There had been two partners, one had retired and the other had died quite suddenly leaving Mr Brandon as head of the firm. When two large plantation owners decided to merge their interests on a legal footing, they requested the three legal firms on the island to quote a price for the necessary work. Mr Brandon played a masterstroke. Instead of asking a huge fee for the work, he asked a very modest price plus a one percent share in the resulting business for himself and a half of one percent share for his retired partner. His bid was accepted, the plantation thrived and the resulting regular income allowed him to retire to Derbyshire, his original home, at the age of forty-five, and to build the house we were looking at as we got out of the car.

We climbed the staircase and Ellen rang the bell. The door was opened just as Ellen was about to ring again, by an elderly woman in a flowered pinafore dress.

'Mrs Brandon?' I asked, showing my warrant card.

'No! I am Mrs Mavers, Mr Brandon's housekeeper,' she said with raised eyebrows.

'I'm Detective Constable Dexter and this is Detective Constable Parsons, would it be possible to have a word with Mr Brandon, please?'

'Mr Brandon is at his breakfast at the moment, if you'll come through to the sitting room I'll ask him if he's prepared to see you. Could I ask what it is about?'

'Just a few questions to assist with our enquiries,' I said.

'I see; if you'd kindly follow me, please.'

The house was equally as strange on the inside as it was outside. After a short entrance hall, the first floor opened out into a balcony running all the way around an open space looking down on the ground floor. It was easy to see that Mr Brandon had spent some time in the Caribbean. The floor we were looking down on was some sort of display area, almost a natural history museum of the islands. Mrs Mavers took us, anti-clockwise, along the balcony and opened a door on our right into a large but cosy room, furnished with wicker chairs cushioned with folded rugs.

'Please sit down, I'll see if Mr Brandon will see you. Can I offer you tea?' she said. We both declined, and she left us.

'It rather looks like our Mr Brandon is not short of a bob or two!' Ellen whispered.

'Makes you wonder why he's involved with Jellicoe, if indeed he is,' I agreed.

My background as an apprentice electrician with Maddox Engineering had given me a feel for buildings. This house was misleading. The front, surrounded by trees looked quite modest, but the size of the ground floor that we had looked down on, plus other doors beyond the far side of the balcony proved that the front was only the tip of the iceberg. The house clearly ran back a considerable distance.

'Mr Brandon has agreed to see you, come with me please,' said the housekeeper.

She took us along the balcony towards the back of the house and showed us into another large room. We were immediately aware of a noticeable increase in temperature.

'Come in, please sit down. I must apologise for the temperature, I spent some years in the Caribbean and I'm afraid it made me something of a hot-house plant,' said an elderly gentleman, in a blue smoking jacket embroidered with exotic birds. I made the introductions and enquired if he was indeed Mr Brandon.

'Yes that's right, I'm Charles Brandon. Mrs Mavers please take the coats of these officers, they look most uncomfortable.'

'Thank you,' we both said, glad to be a bit cooler.

'Now, please sit down. I never took to the British habit of tea drinking, but about this time of day I enjoy some of Mrs Mavers elderflower water, I find it most refreshing, could I offer you a glass?' he asked pointing to a large glass jug of clear liquid, with ice floating in it, on a silver tray with several glass tumblers.

We both nodded and Mrs Mavers poured out three glasses.

'What can I do for you?' he asked, selecting and filling a pipe with a bowl the size of an eggcup.

'We are looking for a Mr Ronald Jellicoe, otherwise known as "The Great Gondello". We believe you may be acting as a theatrical agent for him,' I said.

'Indeed I am. Has he broken some law or other?' he asked striking a match, applying it to the pipe and blowing out a cloud of pleasant nutty aroma.

'We need to talk to him quite urgently. However he seems to have disappeared,' Ellen replied.

'I regret that was probably my doing,' he chuckled.

'Could you explain, please sir?' I asked.

'Ronald, and I should point out that we have known each other for many years, asked me a couple of years ago if I could help him with his career as a magician. He knew that I'm one of the people known as *angels*!'

'Angels?' I asked.

'The term is clearly one with which you are not familiar. I'm a financial backer. I back theatrical productions, plays and musical comedy. I have a considerable income, more than a man who's never married could ever need, so I back the thing I love most; the theatre!' he smiled.

'That must be a very chancy thing to do,' Ellen suggested.

'It can be a gamble and I have had losses, but I pride myself on being able to pick out a production that will fill a theatre. That's not an easy thing to do, especially now when people can sit in their own homes and listen to first class entertainment on the wireless. No need for scenery or costumes on the wireless, every listener fills in their own canvas, so to speak.'

'Mr Jellicoe is not an actor, he's a magician. Where do *you* come in?' I asked.

'My other passion is the local orphanage! It's not common knowledge that I was an orphan myself. I support the place where, I have to say, I was happy and well looked after. I had an uncle who lived out in the Caribbean who kindly put me though the necessary education to become a lawyer on the understanding that I went to work over there when I graduated, but my younger day to day welfare was down to the orphanage. I believe we have to thank you for introducing Mr Tizoni to the orphanage Detective Constable,' he smiled.

'Mr Tizoni is a friend, but it was another constable who first took him to entertain there at Christmas a few years back. But you were explaining about Mr Jellicoe,' I said bringing him back to the point.

'Ronald, Mr Jellicoe, has performed on a couple of occasions to help raise funds for us. As I said, he knew that I support the theatre and asked me to try to get him work. He confessed years ago that his heart is not in teaching. His mother, a somewhat domineering woman, had forced him into it when he was demobilised after the war. I asked around among my contacts but with nothing really on offer. It seems that magicians and ventriloquists are more than plentiful and a little old hat. Then Tuesday last week a producer from Middlesbrough rang me up to say that one of his music-hall acts had suddenly been taken ill, could I help him out with a first class act, ideally a really good magician. Well, obviously I thought of Ronald. I rang and told him but I explained that if he wanted it he had to decide there and then, drop everything and get himself over there in time for first rehearsal on Thursday afternoon. It seems he must have done just that!'

'Can you give me the address of this theatre?' I asked.

'It's the Westgate Music Hall. I can't give you an address but here's the telephone number of the manager Mr Edward Westgate,' he said scribbling it on a slip of paper.

'Thank you Mr Brandon. That has been most helpful!' I said rising from my chair.

'Only too pleased to help, though I can't see how I have been. But, tell me, is there any news of the little girl that went missing from the school where Ronald worked? He was telling me about it when... Ah! That's it isn't it? You need to talk to Ronald about the child?' he squinted.

'There's little point in denying it, we are hoping he can help us with her whereabouts,' I admitted.

'Then I sincerely hope he can!'

'So do we, Mr Brandon, so do we!'

As we drove back down Mr Brandon's drive, Ellen asked; 'If Mr Jellicoe is in Middlesbrough, will we have to rely on talking to him on the phone?'

'Possibly, but I bet the DI will arrange for us to meet him.' I replied.

I showed DI Brierly the phone number of the theatrical producer just as he was preparing to leave for home just after midday.

'That's a coincidence, guess where I was a bobby when I first started with the force?' he said.

'Middlesbrough?' we both said together.

'No, not that much of a coincidence. I was a bobby in Scarborough. My mate Walter, he was a year or so older than me, took me under his wing, showed me the ropes, you know how it is. Well, he moved to York when he became a sergeant, then to Middlesbrough as a DI. We keep in touch. I'll give him a ring. Ask him to have a word with our Mr Jellicoe or "The Great...?"

"Gondello"!' I said. 'Meantime, what do *we* do, sir?'

'You won't like it!' he smiled.

148

'What?'

'I've been putting this off for as long as I could; I hate having to do it but the time has come to allay our suspicions!'

'You want us to search the Parminter house?' Ellen asked.

'I honestly don't think they are in any way involved, but I can't overlook the possibility that one or other of them has done away with the poor kid. Ellen, go with Will and break it to them gently that we have to do this as a matter of routine. It's a bloody hard thing to ask of you, but I know you'll do it with more tact and sympathy that any of us mere men.'

'Thanks for the back-handed compliment, sir. But I'll do my best.'

'Have your dinner break then get off down there the pair of you.'

'Yes, sir,' we said.

For once the sun had come out and the yard at the back of the station was a little sun-trap at that time of day so we decided to eat our sandwiches sitting on the rail of the bike shelter.

'Why did you decide to become a policewoman?' I asked.

'Because, they wouldn't let me in as a *policeman*!' she chuckled, with a twinkle in her eye.

'Sorry I shouldn't have asked; forget it.'

'There's no secret, Will. I always wanted to join the force. My grandad was a policeman; a parish constable in his early days before there was a police force as we know it. The stories he used to tell me were always funny; I think he loved to make me laugh. As I got older he brought in a bit more of the realities. I think he began to realise that he had whetted my appetite and was trying to put me off a bit. But he only made me more determined to join up,' she smiled. 'So here I am.'

'Still enjoying it?' I asked.

'I love every minute of it, though I can't say I'm

looking forward to searching the Parminter house!'

'I know, but it has to be done. It's only a formality; dotting i's and crossing t's. I don't honestly suspect either of them, do you?'

'No, I see only genuine concern, living on a knife-edge of hope and despair with grief as a half expected finale. Having their home searched says that we think their daughter is no longer alive. That's the bit I dread when they realise that we are also thinking along those lines,' she shrugged.

'You said it yourself, on your first day. Most murders are committed by the nearest and dearest in a fit of rage.'

'I know and I can't see an easier way to do it.'

'There's no way to soften the blow, and I bet one or two of the less friendly neighbours are already thinking it, if not saying it. A search will put a stop to that,' I said.

'True! Strangely that doesn't seem to make the prospect any more agreeable,'

'I know,' I agreed.

She shrugged again and sat quiet for a while before changing the subject.

'Tell me the funniest thing that's ever happened to you in the force, Will; cheer me up a bit,' she smiled.

'There's often a funny side to most things, black humour my mate Bong used to call it.'

'Bong, he's the Australian chap isn't he?'

'He's lived over here for about fifteen years, but he's still that Australian chap to us all,' I laughed.

'You know what I mean,'

'Mm, he was supposed to be giving us a hand, I don't know what's happened to him. Anyway, perhaps it's not the funniest thing but it springs to mind as the first. I was still new to the job; it was my first time working days on my own. As I walked past an entry between some houses on Penny Down Lane, a lady came running down the entry…'

'Shouting, "HELP, HELP!' Ellen said and grinned.

'That's right! How did you know?' I asked.

'Just a guess!'

'Her washing line had broken and she wanted me to tie it back together again for her! No problem of course, all part of the service, except that when I'd tied it together it no longer reached to the hook on the wall. "It's always reached before; what have you done to it?" she asked.'

'And then you spent ages trying to convince her, as she got madder and madder, that tying a washing line together *will* make it shorter,' she smiled.

'That's it. Go on, how did you know?'

'Then you heard giggling coming from over the garden wall and four or five of the lads were there having a laugh at your expense,' she chuckled.

'They've done it to you?' I smiled.

'They couldn't do it to me.'

'Why not?'

'Because that was my Auntie Mable, and my grandad put her up to it to give the lads a giggle. They did it to every new bobby, didn't you know?'

'I didn't, but that makes it all the funnier!' I laughed.

'You were probably the last one it was done to, grandad died about five years ago.'

'I'm sorry to hear that, he sounds like a real card.'

'He was, nothing malicious just a keen sense of fun; I really miss him,' she sighed.

'Mm, come on, into the great unknown,' I said.

'Trouble is, we already know we can only bring more heartache to the Parminters, but putting it off just makes the prospect worse,' she said, brushing the crumbs from her skirt.

I parked the Hornet on Duke Street opposite Mill End. Two uniformed constables stood waiting for us as we got out.

'Good afternoon, we've been detailed to assist in the search,' said one of them.

'We haven't got a court order so we can only search with their permission, this isn't a murder enquiry,' I pointed out.

'Not yet!' said the one who'd introduced them.

'Not yet; let's hope not ever,' Ellen said.

'Hard to believe anything else, after all this time,' said the second bobby.

'I'm afraid you could be right, but for now there's still hope,' Ellen replied.

'Come on, this is getting us nowhere,' I snapped.

Although I was only a DC I was superior to Ellen and so took the lead.

'Mr Parminter, could we please come inside?' I asked as he answered our knock.

'Aye, what is it now? It's just me in, Liz has taken Tommy to do a bit of shopping.'

'It's not easy to say this and there's no alternative at the moment. I'm afraid we need to search your house. I'm sorry but our senior officers have requested us to look in case your daughter is hiding somewhere,' I stumbled over the words.

'In case we've done her in, you mean!'

'Sadly we have no option, just routine, I wish I didn't have to add to your sorrow, I really do,' I said.

'Aye, I'd not be in your shoes for a thousand pounds, any of you,' he shrugged and beckoned us in. 'Just one thing, try to be done by the time Liz gets back, this'll crease 'er!'

'I promise we'll be as quick as we can but we must be thorough. I'd hate to have to do this to you again because we've missed something,' I said.

'Aye, go on then. Be quick mind, she's only taken our Tommy into town, for new shoes so I don't expect she'll be long. He's a right little bugger in the shops,' he said and grinned for a moment. 'Where d' yer want t' start?'

'Right, you know what to look for. Ellen search Jennifer's room please, you two lads start at the top and work down,' I said and off they went. 'Mr Parminter could I ask you a few questions?'

'I've told you all I know but if you think it will help, ask away. Come through to the kitchen, I'll make us all a cup of tea while we talk.'

'Thanks but no! We've just had a lunch break and I want this done with as soon as possible. I think we should sit down, though.'

'Come through to the parlour then, we might as well be comfy,' he nodded.

'This might sound a strange question Mr Parminter,' I said as we sat ourselves on opposite sides of the tiny parlour, 'but has Jennifer ever assisted a magician on stage?'

'Not exactly on stage, but she did go with one of the teachers at her school to do a bit of a show to get money for the local orphanage. She really loved it. She says she wants to be an actress when...!' His eyes filled with tears and he looked away as he recognised that this might never be.

'Can you remember which teacher Mr Parminter?' I said, turning a blind eye, to the man's embarrassment.

'No I can't but it wasn't her teacher; one of the lad's lot. He sent a note to us asking if we minded Jennifer helping him out one Friday evening doing a little turn to help raise funds for the orphanage. It seems he took two or three of the girls after school for a sort of rehearsal and finally chose our Jen to help him. We weren't keen but she was so set on it that we finally gave in, after all he was one of the teachers at her school, and he'd sent us that note asking our permission.'

'Do you still have the note, Mr Parminter?'

'Liz'll have it somewhere, probably in the kitchen drawer. She keeps all of the important stuff there; rent

153

book, gas bills, letters and notes from school, all in their own elastic bands. Do yer want me t' look?'

'It might be helpful,' I replied.

He nodded and made his way through to the kitchen just as the front door opened and Mrs Parminter walked in with Tommy. Her face was already a picture of sadness and stress, becoming more so when she noticed me.

'Why…? What are you…? Arthur, are yer there? Is somebody upstairs?' she asked as light began to dawn on the poor woman.

'We were hoping to be done and gone before you returned,' I said.

'Done, done what?'

'They're searchin' the 'ouse, luv!' Arthur Parminter said, handing me the note.

'Why…? Oh, god. They think we've done 'er in!'

'They 'ave to cover all the possibilities, luv!' he said putting his arm around her.

'I'm sorry Mrs Parminter. I don't for one minute think you've harmed your daughter, either of you, but the order has come down to search, just routine in case she's hiding somewhere unknown to you,' I said feeling more embarrassed than I could ever remember.

The three searchers came down the stairs and Ellen shook her head. The downstairs was easy enough; the kitchen, the parlour we were sitting in and a small scullery-cum-pantry. A door from the kitchen led outside to a small yard with a coalhouse and privy, one of the few in Crammingdon still serviced by the night-soil men. Nowhere to hide anything, certainly not as large as we were looking for.

'The detective asked about our Jen and that teacher, the magician bloke,' he said.

'They're together! That's what yer thinkin' aint it?' she looked at me with eyebrows raised.

'It is a possibility,' I agreed.

'That'll be it! The silly little madam has gone off to be on stage with 'im!'

'He is missing as well, so it is another area that we are looking at,' I admitted.

'Nothing, Will!' Ellen said coming back into the parlour.

'Mr and Mrs Parminter, I'm so sorry to have put you through this, but at least we have a new lead. We think we've located the teacher in question, and are trying to have a word with him. Hopefully we will soon have some more positive news for you,' I said and bid them good-day. I told Ellen about the girl and our magician, "The Great Gondello", in the car.

11

Detective Sergeant Whittington was sitting at the DI's desk up in the CID room when we returned to White-cross Yard just before four o'clock, DC Harrington sat reading over some notes. They both nodded as we walked in.

'She's not at the Parminter house, dead or alive,' I said.

'So we've achieved nothing by the search,' said the DS.

'We now know for sure that she's not there, but I don't really think any of us thought that she would be, Sarge,' Ellen replied.

'Well actually, we are a bit further forward, Sarge. I asked Mr Parminter if the girl had ever appeared on stage with a magician.'

'What did he say?'

'He said she had been on stage with Mr Jellicoe, or the "Great Gondello", at the orphanage, so it looks as though he might have taken her against her will, or per-haps talked her into helping him. It appears the girl is stage-struck, Sarge,' I said.

'Mm! The DI was leaving just as I got back. He'd left a note explaining about a phone call to an old colleague in Middlesbrough. This chap, a DI Boothby, has agreed to get a couple of his chaps to have a word with our Mr Jellicoe and get back to us in the morning. A thing I don't get, if the girl is with him, safe and sound, why take the trouble to walk half a mile down a canal path to dispose of her school bag?' the DS asked.

'To put us off the scent,' suggested Ellen.

'I'd go along with that, so long as the thing was where it could be reasonably easily spotted. That wasn't the case though was it Will?'

'No! The uniform lads had walked past it twice and I'm sure George and I would have walked by it as well if the dog hadn't tugged it out of the bramble bushes.'

'Too well hidden to be a decoy, then?' DS Whittington asked.

'I'd say it was, yet it ties in with the statement from Harry Sumpter the bargeman,' I said and Harrington agreed.

'The odd laces are pretty conclusive.'

'And the small briefcase we now know was the girl's school bag because her story was still in it,' I agreed.

'Why bother to go all that far in the pouring rain?' asked Ellen. 'Why not just chuck it somewhere at the bottom of the steps?'

'Sumpter said the rain had eased a bit by then and Jellicoe, if it was him, was wearing a posh gabardine mac. Only he didn't say that, he called it er…'

'An Aberdeen mac,' Ellen reminded me.

'That's right!'

'That and the odd laces in Mr Jellicoe's shoes; if Sumpter hadn't seen him, how could he possibly know that?' asked the DS.

'So it leaves us with the probability that Jenny is with Jellicoe. That asks the question, was it spur of the moment or had they spoken of it before?' suggested Harrington.

'I interviewed Jenny's friend, the one she often stayed with until the rain eased. She said that Jenny didn't want to wait there that night, even though the rain was heavy. She wanted to race home and show her story to her dad,' I pointed out.

'There's another thing that doesn't quite fit,' said DS Whittington. 'If Jellicoe had taken the girl, or

157

talked her into helping him on the day she went missing, why did he appear at school the next day and admit to giving her a lift, then disappear himself? It makes no sense, well not to me anyway.'

'It seems to hinge on when Jellicoe learned about Middlesbrough and if Jenny was willing to go with him,' Ellen suggested.

'Mr Brandon, the chap who's acting as Jellicoe's agent reckons he learned of the vacancy in Middlesbrough on Tuesday last week and phoned Jellicoe there and then. Jellicoe didn't turn up to work at the school on Wednesday morning so that ties in, but Jenny went missing on the Monday. So where the hell was she between times?' I asked.

'Can I suggest that *I* interview Jenny's school friend, she could possibly have confided in this girl and sworn her to secrecy,' said Ellen, showing once again the benefit of having a female mind on the team.

'You think she'd be more open with you?' asked Whittington.

'Got to be worth a try, Sarge,' she nodded.

'I agree; she should be home from school by now, get over there and have a word. Will, can you nip Ellen over in your car? Don't get involved, stay outside and let it be girls together.'

'Okay, Sarge.'

I parked on the road a little way up from the Richmond house and Ellen went off to talk to Nelly, Jenny's friend. I had no idea how long Ellen would be and my thoughts turned to her; how well she had fitted into the team, her quick enquiring mind, her happy personality. Suddenly I found myself comparing her to my lovely Alice! The shock was electric! I sat there stunned for what must have been several minutes because, the next thing I knew was a little leap of the heart as Ellen stepped out of the Richmond's front door. Ouch!

She walked to the car with one of those "oh-well" looks on her face but gave me a big smile as she opened the door and sat down.

'A waste of time?' I asked.

'I was right there was a secret, something that Jenny didn't want her parents to know,' Ellen smiled.

'You said, *was*. There *was* a secret, so she told you?'

'Only after her mam put her arm around the girl and told her that finding Jenny was much more important than a secret. Nelly looked at me and I nodded my agreement, then she told us and I had to work hard to conceal my disappointment. The secret was so little, so unimportant I felt almost let-down, until I saw the look on Nelly's face; the intense guilt at having betrayed her friend's confidence.'

'So what did you do?' I asked.

'I did what we always do, thanked her for her help and came away.'

'Go on then, what was the secret?'

'Jenny takes sandwiches and an apple for her school dinner, but she never eats the crusts,' Ellen shrugged.

'That's it?'

'Guess what she does with them?'

'Oh, I don't know,' I laughed, '*feeds the ducks*!'

'YES; and the apple core.'

'I thought Arthur Parminter was out of work, how can he afford apples at this time of year?'

'According to Nelly, Jenny took an apple every day, winter and summer. Jenny had told her that her dad grew them on his allotment.'

'Arthur has an allotment?'

'According to Nelly; yes.'

'Now that *is* interesting.'

'But does it get us anywhere?' Ellen asked.

'It gives us somewhere we haven't searched,' I pointed out.

'Oh! How the heck do we handle that one?'

'We see what the DI thinks in the morning,' I

said.

It was now Saturday 20th of June, nearly a fort-night since Jenny disappeared. We were again in the DI's makeshift office and the call came through at 10.15.

'Bugger!' DI Brierly said as he put the newly installed phone down. 'That was my mate at Middles-brough, Our friend Mr Jellicoe has moved on; it's the end of the show last night.'

'Do we know where he's gone?' I asked.

'The show's moved on to Leek and I don't know anybody there.'

'*I* do, sir!' Ellen smiled.

'Have you got a number for them?' the DI asked.

'I *have*, but he's not on the force, sir.'
Why did I get a little jab of disappointment when she said *he*?

'Could he find out if our friend is on the bill in the town?'

'Yes, sir.'

'Right, give him a ring,' he said offering the phone.

'He might not be home but I'll give him a try,' she said picking it up. 'Could I have Leek in Stafford-shire: three-three-seven-two, please?'

'Do we know where Mr Parminter's allotment is, Dexter?' the DI asked turning to me.

'No, sir.'

'Following yesterday, I don't really want to make an official search of the place. If we can find out where it is we could just take a look on the QT.'

'There's some allotments a couple of streets away at the end of Bloom Lane, I'd say that's the most likely place, sir,' I suggested.

'Aye, so there is, go and have a poke around Dexter. If he's there, just say you were thinking of get-ting an allotment and happened to notice him.'

'Right, sir.'

'If he is there, ask him how he manages to keep his apples right through the winter, still eatable in June.'

'I wondered that, sir,' I nodded.

'Sorry, sir, he's not answering,' Ellen said, putting the phone back down.

'Okay, try again in half an hour, when we've had a cuppa…' he smiled.

'Right, sir! I wonder if Mr Brandon knows where Jellicoe's gone?' she said, going to the sink and filling the kettle.

'Jellicoe seems to have made a decision to abandon teaching. It would be hard to go back to school again as though nothing has happened,' I said, rinsing the five mugs.

'If that's the case, any time now he'll be off to one of the seaside resorts for the summer season,' suggested DS Whittington.

'That's if we've not had to put a halt to his new career, after all even if the girl is with him willingly, it's still abduction of a minor,' said Harrington.

'Ah, but I think we've got that sorted. My pal in Middlesbrough said the girl was not appearing on stage with him, he was getting a girl out of the audience to help him.'

'That's what he did at the orphanage. He asked for a volunteer out of the audience, and it was a fix, he chose Jenny!' Ellen pointed out.

'That's right, sir,' I agreed.

'Okay then, she could still be with him.'

The phone rang and DS Whittington answered it.

'Crammingdon CID, DS Whittington speaking… Yes sir, he's here. DI Boothby, from Middlesbrough, sir,' he said handing the phone to the DI.

'Hi Jacko, have you found them?'

There was a longish period where it was clear that DI Boothby was imparting some news that the DI was unhappy about. The smile that he'd had at the start of the

161

conversation quickly faded and a look of deep concern replaced it.

'Thanks Jacko, keep me posted,' he said putting the phone down. 'Oh, bloody hell!'

'Bad news, sir?' Ellen asked, what we were all thinking.

'As you know that was DI Boothby again. In a nutshell, there's a piece of common ground, not far from the theatre where Jellicoe was working. Earlier this morning a chap walking his dog had let it off its lead and it wouldn't return when he whistled. It had gone into some bushes and wouldn't come out. It had found what looked like a shallow grave, a child sized shallow grave. Their lads are about to dig it up!' he said, wearily wiping his hand over his face.

It was one of those moments when our normally chatty little band was stunned into silence. I looked at Ellen; she was biting her top lip and her eyes were filling with tears. I had a desperate urge to put my arm around her shoulder, but that wouldn't do at all of course.

'We need to find this chap Jellicoe. Now! Especially if this turns out to be Jenny's grave. Ellen, try that number again,' said the DI.

'Right, sir,' she said grabbing the phone and asking again for the number. 'Good, could you keep trying please operator, it's very important. Right thank you.'

'It's engaged now so he's at home, the operator is going to connect us as soon as the line is free, sir.'

'Who is this chap? You say he's not in the job, boyfriend is it?' asked the DI with a wink and a cheeky smile.

'Bert, he's a reporter on the local paper in Leek, sir,' she said, adding nothing more.

'Try not to give him too much information, then please Ellen.'

'Understood, sir, but he's a nose for a story, he might guess.'

'Tell him to keep it under his hat until you give him the okay,' the DI replied.

The phone rang and Ellen made a grab for it.

'Crammingdon CID! Oh, right, yes he's here,' she said handing the phone to the DI.

'DI Brierly speaking; who's that? ' he said shaking his head. 'Pete, you'll be the first to know, now get off the line please I'm expecting a couple of important calls... Yes about the missing girl... Okay I'll meet you in the Greyhound tomorrow lunchtime.'

'Pete Warrell, from the Argus, sir?' asked DS Whittington, as the DI put the phone down.

'Yes! It seems that one of his mates in Middlesbrough has got wind of the grave and put two and two together and given Pete the nod,' the DI said, shaking his head.

'What will you tell him, sir?' asked Ellen.

'Gawd knows! Hopefully we might have something positive by then.'

The phone rang and the DI nodded for Ellen to pick it up.

'Crammingdon CID! Oh, hello Bert it's Ellen . . . What do you mean Ellen who, how many Ellen's do you know?'. . . 'Ellen Parsons! . . . Very funny, listen you fool, could you tell me if a magician, "The Great Gondello", is on your local music hall bill?' she asked. 'No, I don't want to go and see him, I just need to know if he's appearing there . . . Sorry Bert I can't say why.' . . . 'Yes it's very important.' . . . . 'Thanks, as soon as you can and I owe you one.' . . . . 'As soon as my DI says that I can.'. . . 'Thanks Bert.' she said and put the phone down.

'He's going to have a nose around and get back, sir.'

'If he is there, how do we play it, sir?' asked DC Harrington.

'I'll have to approach the Assistant Chief Constable to arrange for us to be on Staffordshire's patch. It should be just a formality since Jellicoe *lives* on ours. But it's no good us all sitting on our arses all day, oops sorry Ellen, sitting wasting time. Dexter and Harrington, find that allotment. Whittington, go and have a little poke around at Jellicoe's mother's house. I think she might know more than she's letting on.'

'Thanks, sir; she sounds like a real dragon.'

'She is!' I laughed.

12

The allotments at the end of Bloom Lane were a very run-down affair. It was obvious that the sustained bad weather ever since the beginning of winter, together with soil that seemed not to be draining well, had put off all but the keenest gardeners. An old chap in a flat cap and worn out trousers and jacket, was half-heartedly forking over his plot. He slammed his fork into the ground, and pointed out Mr Parminter's section then tagged along with us.

'Any news of Arthur's young un?' he asked.

'Not as yet,' I said, and the old chap grimaced and shook his head.

'Four apple trees: doesn't he grow anything else?' I asked.

'It's three apples and a Conference pear. He sells a few but mostly he stores 'em in the shed,' he said nodding to a sturdy structure that seemed to be built from old railway sleepers held together with massive bolts.

'How can he store 'em till now? His little lass always take's one to school every day,' I asked.

'She'll not be taking many next year no matter what!' he said.

'Why do you say that? Mr...?'

'Goodward, Bill Goodward, I'm his next door neighbour. And there's no need to look like that, what I meant was look on the ground under the trees. The wind and rain took most of the blossom before the apples set, and the early June-drop has taken most of the rest!'

'June-drop; what's that?' asked Harrington.

'You're not a gardener then. It's a natural thing

165

that happens every year, I reckon it's the tree gettin' rid of diseased and badly formed fruit. It's nearly all on the ground this year, look. I doubt he'll get more than a basket an' 'arf off the whole lot. Not just 'im neither. Nobody local 'as done much better.'

'That's right! I live with my sister and her husband. They have a small orchard and they have suffered from the effects of the weather as well,' I said. 'But if his daughter has had one of his apples every day since last harvest, how does he manage to keep them?'

'Like it's always been done; after he's picked them, he sorts through the crop and selects the ones with bruises and other damage, they won't keep yer see so they get used first. To eat if they're not too bad or crushed into cider. The best ones are carefully wrapped in old newspaper and stored here in his shed.'

'Simple as that?' asked Harrington.

'Mm, but I'm guessin' you're 'ere to look for his young lass. You'll not find 'er 'ere!'

'No?' I asked.

'Not a chance, he'd no more 'arm that gal than fly in the air. Apple-of-his-eye and no mistake,' he said, with a nod. 'Anyway you can ask him yerself, he's just come in the gate.'

Arthur Parminter was heading towards us with a down turned head, and a listless step.

'Now what?' he asked as he recognised us.

'They've been askin' about yer apples,' Mr Goodward said.

'Oh aye; I can see that. No doubt they think my little 'un is all chopped up in my shed, or sommat,' he said and burst into tears. Harry put his arm around his neighbours shoulder and passed him a none-too-clean handkerchief.

'We just wondered why you hadn't mentioned your allotment when we were looking over the house,' I said.

'I never give it a thought, tis just apples and a

166

few carrots and spuds,' he said, drawing a key from his pocket and unlocking the shed. 'Take a look for yerselves.'

The door creaked as we opened it revealing a small bench with odd gardening tools neatly cleaned and ready for use. My old dad would have been proud of Mr Parminter's shed with its sturdy racking stacked with boxes, no doubt for the storage of apples. The sweet smell of produce, and the total absence of flies, said quite clearly that there was no decomposing body in Mr Parminter's shed.

'My dad was a gardener; he'd have given his best boots for a shed like this. He hadn't the room you see!' I said.

'Mm, well if yer satisfied my Jenny is not 'ere, I'll ask yer to bugger off; no offence intended.'

'None taken Mr Parminter,' we said, and buggered off.

'I hate having to do that!' said Harrington.

'There's no easy way to do it and it's one more place eliminated. It was clear even from outside that there was no corpse in there,' I said.

'No smell, no flies; no body!' he nodded.

'It's not a smell you can miss or mistake; once smelt never forgotten, eh?'

'Too bloody true, Will!' he said, though it was clear his mind was on something else.

'What is it?' I asked.

'Something put me in mind of my old dad; not sure what it was, maybe seeing the tools all cleaned and hanging up in Mr Parminter's shed. He wasn't a gardener he was a plumber, but he made models in his shed, beautiful model railway engines. He cleaned and polished his tools and laid them out on his bench, like he loved each one. We got on all right, but we were never close if you know what I mean. He'd missed the war, just a bit too old; I'm not sure if I perhaps thought he hadn't done his bit, yer-know. And, I was at that age when you happily know all there is to know and Dad's ideas weren't mine. I considered him old fashioned, out of tune with modern thinking. I looked on him with pity I suppose. Now I can see the sense in most of what he said, I just wish he was still around to tell him so. Tell him I loved him; he died when I was twenty-one!' he said with a sigh.

'My dad died last year, sadly in the end he didn't know me, kept calling me Joe, I think that was one of his mates at work. I got the chance to tell him I loved him but he didn't know me!'

'Sorry Will, I'd forgotten. Life has a way of givin' yer little stabs in the heart every now and then eh? Anyway, what do you reckon about this grave in Middlesbrough?' he asked, moving to a less personal subject.

'Perhaps the DI has had some news by now,' I said.

'That's not what I asked.'

'I hate jumping to conclusions on only half the story, but a fresh grave, hidden in bushes close to the theatre where we know Jellicoe was appearing, we are pretty certain that Jenny is or was with him. A whole heap of coincidences, I'd say,' I said.

'Mm; not looking good, is it!' he agreed.

'It's hard to feel anything positive after all this time. At least it looks as though we've tracked down Jellicoe,' I said as we walked back to the Hornet.

'If Ellen's mystery man can get in touch with him; she seemed very cagey about him, I wonder who he is. Is there a romance we don't know about do you think?' he chuckled.

'None of our business,' I said, harshly enough to cause Harrington to raise his eyebrows, aware he had touched a nerve.

'Do I detect an interest in our new DC?' he asked tongue in cheek.

'I just think it's her business and we should respect her privacy if that's what she wants,' I replied.

'Mm… okay, you're right of course,' he said, looking away with a big smirk on his face.

Back at the temporary CID room, the DI and Ellen sat reading some of the statements from the teachers at Jenny's school to see if perhaps we had missed something; one of the more boring parts of police work. It was necessary because rereading what people have said, can suddenly bring into focus an answer or statement that has been thought wrong or misleading as new information moves the investigation along. They both nodded as we walked in.

'I take it you found Mr Parminter's allotment?' he asked.

'Yes, he turned up as we spoke to one of his neighbours,' I replied.

'That must have been a bit awkward.'

'He guessed why we were there and unlocked his shed for us,' said Harrington.

'And told us to bugger off once we'd had a look,' I added.

'I can understand that. He's gradually coming to the conclusion that his little lass isn't coming back. I hate to say it but the way things are shaping, so am I!'

'It doesn't look good, does it, sir?' Ellen agreed.

'We seem to be going around in circles at the moment and the weekend is against us. I think I'll scale this case down until Monday,' he said. 'Dexter, go and spend the rest of the day with those lads of yours, back in midday tomorrow.'

'Right, thank you, sir!'

'I'll work out how we'll man things when DS Whittington gets back, meantime Dexter, bugger off before I change my mind.'

'Right, sir; not often I'm told to bugger off twice in one day,' I said putting on the coat I had just taken off.

The puddle just inside the gates at my sister's drive, had dried slightly but was still deep enough to give me a smile as I waited to turn in. Two welly-booted little boys and one welly-booted sister were engrossed in puddle jumping and having a whale of a time. The game came to an abrupt end when the boys recognised the car and came running. Flossie smiled, gave me a cheerful little wave and started to make her way back to the house.

'Come and puddle jump, Daddy,' they yelled together.

'No time now, we need to get ready to go into town to buy you some new trousers; you are both growing so fast the ones we bought at Easter don't fit you anymore,' Flossie shouted over her shoulder.

'Oh! Not now Aunt Flossie, I want Daddy to puddle jump,' said George.

'I can't jump right now, Inspector Brierly will shout at me if I turn up for work in dirty clothes. Go off with Aunt Flossie and get your new trousers and I'll puddle jump when you get back. Promise,' I said.

'When you've changed into your scruffy clothes,' Will suggested.

'Yes, that's right,' I agreed. 'Go on, the quicker you get your new trousers, the quicker we can start puddle jumping.'

'Upstairs, this minute and get changed out of those mucky clothes. Put them in the laundry basket, no mucky clothes lying about please. Daddy can you run a bath for these two ragamuffins?' she said with a warm-hearted smile.

'Yes, come on. No messing about, Aunt Flossie has spoke,' I laughed clapping my hands and shooing them inside.

'Henry's out on a call, can you drop us in town and we'll catch the bus back?' Flossie asked.

'Can I come with you?' I asked. 'I spend so little time with them and I'm back on duty again midday tomorrow.'

'Yes, of course, they'll like that.'

'Should we be thinking about clothes for school?'

'That's nearly three months away, the way they are growing they'll need some more by then,' she chuckled.

She was right, though George was growing slightly faster than William, they had to be side by side to really notice any difference. They hadn't yet cottoned on to the twins trick of pretending to be each other when it suited them. In any case that wouldn't work all that well; although their hair was almost identical in colour, where Will's hair always stayed put and neatly combed and parted George's would always stick up at the crown of his head, no matter how he tried to plaster it down with water. We could always tell them apart!

Sunday, as requested I signed in at Whitecross Yard a few seconds before midday. The DI was again in the rest room cum CID office. He sat behind his desk with a glum expression.

'Problem, sir?' I asked.

'Yes, I'll tell you about it in a second. Yesterday afternoon, after you had gone I had a phone call from my mate in Middlesbrough. The grave they found contained a freshly buried Great Dane pup thank god. But that puts us right back to square one again, of course,' he said.

'Can't say I'm sorry,' I agreed.

'But this thing is something I could do without! Ever heard of Donald Porter?' he asked, wagging the bit of paper he had been reading.

'The only person I know by that name is the chap in the news, Sir Oswald Mosley's mate,' I suggested.

'That's the chap! I've just heard he's organised a meeting in the Miner's Social Club!'

'Here in Crammingdon, sir?'

171

'This Thursday, at seven in the evening, you know what that means, Dexter.'

'It means we'll have all on to keep a lid on the event, feelings are sure to run high, sir,' I said.

'Thankfully that will fall mainly to our uniformed colleagues but we're being asked to mix with the crowd and make a note of any trouble makers on both sides. In short, as usual, do the bloody impossible!' he snapped.

'There's a good many of our lords and masters agree with what they are preaching, sir.'

'Do you agree with the reports coming out of Germany? Innocent people being attacked in the streets, businesses burned just because they happen to be Jewish or any other race that Mr Hitler chooses to point the finger at?' he asked.

'No sir! But it won't happen here in Crammingdon, surely.'

'Don't be so sure, Mosley's Black Shirts stir up hatred wherever they go.'

'Can't we just ban it, sir?'

'Freedom of speech and as you say, a good many of our leaders are supporters of the Nazi party.'

'The new King and Mrs Simpson have been guests of Hitler on more than one occasion if the newspapers are to be believed, sir.'

Aye, as the Prince of Wales he was a very popular figure, but a good many people can't take his friendship with that man; not to mention a King of England wanting to marry a divorced woman, divorced American woman. I can't see it happening!' the DI said. 'There's another factor that could influence how things go here this Thursday. Sir Oswald happens to be staying with some friends about fifteen miles from here. He's sure to want to visit the meeting, and no doubt speak to the assembled masses.'

'Can't say I'm looking forward to hearing that, sir.'

'Nor I, and you can bet our boys in blue will be running around like blue-arsed-flies in the morning trying to get things arranged, so we can forget about requesting any help with finding our little girl.'

'They can't refuse to help us sir, surely?'

'We'll get a couple of coppers if we're lucky; a pair of brain dead flat-foots about as much use as a cardboard cut-out.'

'You've got us, sir! A crack team if ever there was one!' I said, tongue in cheek.

'Mm!' he said and gave me a pitying look.

'We do make a good team, sir. Especially now we've got Ellen's input.'

'Oh, we get there in the end but I just wish we could find Jenny, one way or the other. Her parents are sick with worry and the press don't help. The story went national on Friday and the Chief Constable's laying into me with a vengeance; "Why is there no positive news, Detective Inspector Brierly?" as though I can conjure clues and witnesses out of thin air.'

'Talking of conjuring sir, any news from Ellen's friend in Leek?'

'Yes! Yesterday afternoon the chap rang back; he's located Jellicoe and I've arranged for you and Ellen to interview him tomorrow morning.'

'I assume you've got the okay with the local lot, sir?'

'They are only too pleased for us to do the job, but you've got to introduce yourselves to a Sergeant Danvers.'

'Early start, sir?'

'Sign on at seven, on the road by half-past! I've said you'll be there around nine o'clock so no messing about. Meantime, let's take another look at all the statements and information we have on the case. Ellen looked at it all yesterday but who knows, she could have missed something.'

If she had, then so did we. After a couple of

hours going over and over the same documents, statements and timings nothing had been added to our knowledge or made us think along anything but the same old unfruitful lines.

'Sod this Dexter, let's call it a day and hope that your talk with Jellicoe gives us a new direction tomorrow. Come on, get your coat on, you can run me home.'

'With pleasure sir, but will you manage in my little car?'

'I'll stretch out on the back, it's only a bit over six miles, Dexter.'

'If you're sure sir,' I replied.

'Come on let's get going.'

13

For once, the weather was fine and bright and the run from Crammingdon through to Leek took us across the Derbyshire border just beyond the sleepy market town of Ashbourne, then on into Staffordshire. There's an arduous but spectacular climb out of Ashbourne up to the tiny village of Swinscoe. The Hornet engine was struggling to reach the top even in second gear. As the ground levels out at the crest, there's an inn on the left, The Dog and Partridge and we took the opportunity to let the Hornet cool down.

My knowledge of country inns told me that at this time of the morning the kitchen would be open, preparing breakfasts for the guests. The smell of sausage and bacon frying directed us to the kitchen door and a polite introduction got us in for a welcome cup of tea and use of the lavatories. Ellen and I were back on our way about ten minutes later each armed with a bacon sandwich. The Hornet was still a bit over heated but cooling as we sped along. About three or four miles on there's an equally spectacular hill down into the village of Waterhouses. The area was new to me, but Ellen had known it for a while, and pointed out the view from the top across towards Buxton. In the bright morning air, the landscape lay below us, picked out in crystal-clear detail.

This time I was using second gear to save the brakes on the steep downhill. I was becoming even more aware that, perhaps against my better judgement, I was falling in love with acting WDC Parsons! I was also aware that her gentle perfume added to her attraction, at moments when the Hornet's engine smells were whisked away by the downhill breeze. I realised that she was probably already spoken for, which of course made matters worse.

As requested we carried out the formality of introducing ourselves to Sergeant Danvers in the Leek police station. He nodded his approval and asked us to let him know when we were finished and off his patch.

DI Brierly had arranged with Ellen's friend for us to meet Mr Jellicoe in the small café attached to the theatre, and we arrived only a few minutes late for our nine o'clock appointment. After making the introductions and a suitable apology, we set to business.

'Mr Jellicoe, as you are probably aware Jennifer Parminter is still missing. Can you shed any light on where she might be?' I asked.

'I am aware that is still the case, and I can imagine the distress of her poor parents, however I really have nothing to add to my statement on the day following her disappearance. I really have no idea where the child can be,' he said, looking from one to the other of us.

'You still admit giving Jenny a lift?'

'Of course, it is the truth, I gave her a lift of half a mile or so. I left her at the end of her lane; you can't get a vehicle down to her house or I'd have dropped her at the door!'

'It was raining heavily. That was why you offered her a lift?'

'That and the fact that I was intrigued as to how much input her parents had made to her little story,' he nodded.

'Mrs Leonard had shown Jenny's story to you?' I asked.

'Indeed, as I told you we had discussed it in the staff room that lunch time.'

'Was it still raining when you dropped her at the end of her lane?' Ellen asked.

'It had rained in heavy squalls most of the day with intervals of fine misty rain, it was one of these less miserable periods when she got out of the car.'

'I seem to remember you saying that she ran off down the lane towards her house, is that correct?' I asked.

'She did, and that was the last I saw of her!'

'There is the matter of your own disappearance, Mr Jellicoe. Can you explain that please?'

'I am sure you are both aware by now that I am a stage magician. It is something I am rather good at, a passion you might say, and have always wanted to do it professionally. My heart has never really been in teaching though it has always paid the bills. If I am honest there have been times when seeing a pupil suddenly blossom it has felt worthwhile but on the whole it was a job and nothing more.'

'We have spoken to Charles Brandon. I believe he is acting as your agent?'

'Charles rang me shortly after I got home the evening that I spoke to you. He told me that work existed in Middlesbrough but he said, rather jokingly I thought, that I needed to drop everything and be there in time to rehearse the following afternoon,' he shrugged.

'I spoke to your mother; she had no idea where you had gone,' I pointed out.

'I did not tell her, she would only have tried to talk me out of my one big chance. I packed one bag with my costume and props, and another with my general belongings and some overnight things and sneaked out to the car in the dead of night. My mother takes a sleeping draft each night so I had little fear of awakening her,' he replied, then continued. 'I can tell from your combined expressions that you find my actions somewhat incredible. Perhaps I should explain. In ten years of trying to break into the theatre this is the one, the only time, that someone has actually offered me work. I am fifty-three years of age, how many more chances are going to come my way? Turn this down and even my good friend Mr Brandon would be unlikely to offer more. Oh, I thought it over, should I, shouldn't I, as one does when something life changing needs to be decided. Eventually I asked myself, do I want to be teaching for the rest of my life? The answer was a resounding no!'

'You didn't inform the school or us that you were going away.'

'I am not a strong person, I am easily swayed. Had I spoken to the headmaster he would surely have tried to talk me out of it, perhaps more effectively than my mother! As for the police, I saw no point; I had already told you everything I knew,' he said.

'Do you have a briefcase, Mr Jellicoe?'

'A briefcase? Yes of course, it's in the boot of my car. Why do you ask?'

'Could you describe it please?'

'I can do better than that. I can show it to you,' he said surprised by Ellen's question.

'For the moment, if you'd just describe it, sir, please,' she said.

'Very well, it's brown leather, it has three pockets that open in a concertina fashion, a flap with a chromium catch, and a little lock which doesn't lock. Well I suppose it would but I bought it second hand and there was no key. Oh yes, the lock is etched with the makers name, Mitford and Sons, Doncaster. I remember that because I once did some research into the Mitford sisters,' he nodded.

'Does it have a shoulder strap?' I asked.

'No!'

'Jenny had a school satchel, could you describe that sir, please?'

'Just exactly where is this line of questioning leading Detective Constable?'

'Please bear with me sir,' I said.

'Mm… she had a school satchel slung over her arm, as she got into my car she slipped it off her shoulder and sat with it on her knee. It was old and battered brown leather but well-polished in an attempt, I suppose, to keep out the rain. Now, that did of course have a long strap.'

'Do you possess a gabardine raincoat, Mr Jellicoe?' Ellen asked.

'Yes, it's in my dressing-room back at the theatre. I would have been wearing it this morning had the weather been less clement. I don't see…'

'An eye witness puts you at the London Road Bridge at about four thirty on the afternoon that Jenny went missing; is that correct?' Ellen asked.

'I remember a bargeman but I didn't know him from Adam. I fail to see how he could possibly have known me, though I don't deny I was there.'

'For what purpose, sir?' she continued.

'My mother makes me a packed lunch, always cheese. I admitted once that I liked cheese and from then on every day she packs me cheese. Often I eat them; occasionally I buy something on the way to school. On those days I feed my uneaten sandwiches to the ducks at the bridge on the London Road.' he said.

'The witness suggested that you were carrying what he described as a small brief case with a long strap,' I pointed out.

'Now that, I do deny; a packet of sandwiches in greaseproof paper, yes. A briefcase, no!'

'The man described the person he saw sir, and something in his description could only have been you sir,' I said.

'As I said, I do not deny being there, but I fail to see how this man could know me.'

'When we were informed that you were missing Mr Colchester your headmaster agreed, subject to him being present, to us opening your locker. What we found there confirmed that you were in fact the person seen by the bargeman,' I said.

'So he did not in fact name me, not that it makes

179

any difference. I was there but certainly not with a brief-case. Nor, as he seems to suggest, Jennifer's school satchel!'

'I agree. I don't think he knew you in person but he described your shoes in sufficient detail to make it certain he had seen you!'

'My shoes? Ah, the lace, the black laces!' he smiled.

'We found the shoes with the missing laces in your locker and that fitted exactly with the bargeman's description, sir! I admitted.

'Mr Parminter has told us that Jennifer once as-sisted you on stage with your act, is that correct, Mr Jel-licoe?' Ellen asked.

'She did indeed, a few months ago, I was part of a fund-raising concert for Crammingdon orphanage. I had invited several of the girls to rehearse with me to see which one was the most suitable and I eventually chose Jennifer since she was the most natural! Ah, I see, you thought she was with me – performing on stage?'

'There seemed to be a distinct possibility, sir,' Ellen admitted.

'Apart from a couple, in fact three occasions for rehearsal, that was the only time she has assisted me. The only other contact that I have had with her was on the evening that I gave her a lift,' he shrugged.

'And you have no idea where she might be, Mr Jellicoe?'

'None, I'm afraid; I only wish I did!'

'We could possibly need to speak to you again. Can you provide us with a list of your future venues?' I asked.

'Of course, I am here until Saturday night. Next Monday I open at Nottingham, the week after at Nor-wich. I have a printed list in my car, I'll provide you with a copy!'

'There is just one more thing Mr Jellicoe. The bargeman suggested that when he saw you at the London

Road Bridge, the time would have been about four-thirty; would that be correct, sir?' Ellen asked.

'I cannot say that I noticed the time, but that seems about right,' he agreed.

'Well that does seem to leave us with a slight problem! School finishes at four o'clock, you must have picked Jenny up at say two or three minutes past for a journey you admitted took only a couple of minutes. The bargeman claims it was half-past four when you were descending to the towpath; that seems to create a discrepancy of twenty-five minutes or so on a one-mile journey! Can you account for that, please sir?' I asked.

'This is now nearly a fortnight ago, I can't think of any reason why I was delayed that long, perhaps I jotted something in my diary,' he said feeling in the inside pocket of his jacket. 'Ah here is indeed the answer,' he said as he picked up a slip of paper that had fluttered to the floor.

He handed it to me, and explained;

'After dropping Jennifer off at Mill End I went to London Road Garage to fill up with fuel and get them to check the oil. I have an account with them and normally pay them at the end of the month but after Mr Brandon's telephone call on Tuesday evening, I called in next day to pay what I owed to clear the account since I had no idea when I would be requiring their services again. That slip of paper is my receipt for payment on the morning I left to go to Middlesbrough!'

'With respect, sir, it says you cleared your account that morning but it doesn't prove you filled up on the evening Jennifer disappeared,' Ellen pointed out.

'Indeed it does not! However they keep very accurate records of each account transaction, not only the date and amount but also the time.'

'Do you have a document showing that then, sir?' she asked.

'No, the statement is typewritten at the end of each month and since we were only a few days into the month I simply paid off what I owed at the time. The point I am making is that they will be able to confirm, from their records, time and date!' he said.

'Were you *anticipating* a long journey, Mr Jellicoe?' I asked.

'I see your reasoning Detective Constable; most drivers only think of checking oil when considering a longer than normal journey, however my car is old and has covered many miles so it has become almost a ritual once a fortnight to get them to check the oil to be on the safe side,' he said, with a little nod.

'I think that's all for now Mr Jellicoe, if you wouldn't mind showing us your briefcase just to ensure that your description is accurate?'

'Yes, of course; it's in my car boot at the back of the theatre, if you care to follow me.'

Satisfied that it was as he had described, we bid him good day and headed back to the police station to tell Sergeant Danvers that our enquiries had concluded, and that we were heading back to Crammingdon.

'Thank you, but I've some bad news for you,' he frowned.

'Oh! What bad news?' I asked, fearing that there was a new and unfortunate development regarding Jenny.

'A lorry has crashed on the main road, on the downhill from Swinscoe to Ashbourne. The road is completely blocked at the junction to Mapleton. Looks like brake failure but according to my lads on the scene the driver hasn't survived, so that's just speculation at the moment,' he added.

'I'm sorry to hear that. What alternative route do you suggest, Sergeant?' I asked.

'Either the road to Buxton and down through Bakewell, but it's a long way. Or you could map-read your way across country; it's a pretty route but likely to take just as long!'

'I can get us home through the villages; I know

182

this area reasonably well,' Ellen said.

'That's your best bet then. I'll ring your boss and tell him you'll be delayed.'

'Thanks Sergeant, we'll be on our way,' I nodded.

The road chosen by Ellen twisted and turned up hill and down dale until I became completely lost. Only the near midday sun suggested that we were heading roughly east, certainly heading towards home.

'You seem to know these roads pretty well,' I said.

'I used to cycle them as a girl on my way to see Grandpa in Crammingdon!'

'The policeman?'

'That's right,'

'It's a heck of a long way to cycle!' I said.

'For a girl you mean?'

'For anybody; it must be hard work on a bike?'

'I have a secret; in the next village there's a pub that does, or used to do, home-made ginger beer. We could take a break there, I need the loo anyway,' she smiled.

'Sounds like a good idea. We've already been excused our time limit, if Sergeant Danvers has rung the DI,' I nodded.

'I think you'll love it, just wait till you see Jedidiah Small the landlord!' she chuckled.

The pub was just opening for business. A woman I guessed to be in her mid-fifties, was tending a flower bed at the side of a small car park.

'That's Mrs Small,' Ellen said.

Just then, a huge man, looking rather like a mix between the jolly fisherman on the Skegness adverts and Oliver Hardy, carried a board out and placed it on the pub sign post.

'That's Mr Small!' she smiled.

'He looks a happy sort of chap,' I said.

'Salt of the earth, I wonder if he'll remember

183

me,' she said getting out of the car.

We followed him in through the low doorway and into the bar.

'Good morning to you, what can I get you?' he asked in a deep rumbling voice.

'Do you still make you own ginger beer Mr Small?' Ellen asked.

'That I do, miss. And I seem to know your face,' he said, squinting at her.

'I used to call in on my bike, but that's six or seven years ago now!'

'I remember a blue cycle with a massive saddle bag!' he said, snapping his fingers. 'I never forget a face.'

'That was me. So, two glasses of your ginger beer please Mr Small.'

'Sit yourselves out in the sun if you've a mind and I'll bring it out. A shame to miss a nice bit of sun; we've not had a deal this year and that's a fact.'

We thanked him and went to sit ourselves at a table looking out onto the bit of garden Mrs Small was tending. The little area was quite a suntrap and Mr Small carried out our drinks as we struck up conversation.

'We don't seem to be any further forward, especially if the records at the garage confirm why there's a time discrepancy,' I said, noticing that each time our eyes met as I looked at her she turned away a little, as though reading my mind and unsure how to react. Was there perhaps a degree of mutual attraction? I knew that our superiors wouldn't look very kindly on a romantic involvement between their officers. Not to mention Diana Penworthy; life looked like getting very complicated.

'Feeding the ducks! It seems to be a bit weak; if he wasn't going to eat his sandwiches, why not just put them in the bin at the school or take them home?'

'You've clearly not met his mother,' I chuckled. 'It'd be a brave chap who took his sandwiches back to

184

her.'

'Is she really that bad?'

'I don't suppose she actually does bite heads off but I for one wouldn't want to give her the opportunity,' I said and she giggled.

'So you think he was going to feed the ducks?' she asked.

'Why not, thousands of people do every day.'

'I suppose so and he does seem genuine, if a bit straight-laced,' she agreed.

'Meaning we are back to square one. Except why would the bargeman, Mr Sumpter, even suggest a bag with a strap unless he had known one existed?' I asked.

'You think he'd seen the bag, and was trying to lay the blame elsewhere in case the thing was found?'

'Meaning; he knew where it had been thrown. Perhaps even, he had thrown it,' I said, and that of course started a whole new train of thought.

'We told him there had been a search when we spoke to him at Swarkstone Lock, he was covering himself if Jenny's satchel was found,' she nodded.

'Looks like it, I think we need another word with our Mr Sumpter.'

'Trouble is where will be by now?' she asked.

'He has to be on the canal network somewhere, presumably he will have completed his run to Liverpool and be on a return journey. We'd better ring the DI and get him to start a search for the man,' I said.

I used the pub phone to contact the DI to explain what we thought, and he agreed to get the thing moving. I explained that we would probably be with him in about an hour and a half. We finished our ginger beer and set off. Now we were well clear of the lorry crash site we dropped back onto main roads and the little Hornet was seldom below sixty where traffic permitted.

The front of the Hornet is a snug fit at the best of times and whether Ellen would have preferred to have a little extra space between us or not, the confines dictated that we sat shoulder to shoulder. There was no sign of tenseness in the way she sat so I took that to mean she didn't feel threatened. We were travelling along in one of those comfortable, amicable silences.

'Do you know where your name comes from, Will?' she asked, the question coming out of the blue.

'William or Dexter?' I asked.

'Dexter, do you know where Dexter comes from?'

'I don't, but does it matter?' I couldn't see where this was taking us.

'My Grandpa got me interested in where names come from, and how they seem to be an indicator of people's background, even the job they are doing!' she grinned.

'Mr Baker, the baker: Mr Farmer, the farmer, that sort of thing?'

'Sort of; take my name, Parsons; it has a religious context obviously. Though it is related not to the parson himself but to anyone who worked in his household or sometimes to his son,' she said.

'Mm... interesting, but what's brought this on?' I asked.

'It's just something that fascinates me. My Grandpa had a book listing all the surnames and where they come from. "Vickers" means more or less the same, but is mainly applied to the son of the vicar. I think it originated in Durham with the Prince Bishops.'

'Okay; I can see you're dying to tell me mine!' I grinned.

'That's just it, I can't remember what the book says; can't even be sure that it's in the book.'

'You'll have to look it up.'

'I wish I could, Grandpa left the book to me but I've mislaid it!'

'Oh, I get it, you want to look it up and can't 'cos you can't find the book,' I laughed.

186

'That's right,' she admitted.

'So, *what* can you remember? What about DI Brierly, where does his name originate?'

'Oh, that's easy, that is where the person comes from. Briar comes from the rose briar and lea from meadow. The meadow of briars,' she said.

'So, somewhere in the distant past, the DI's family came from a place known for a lea of briars!'

'Yes, but it could go back to way before the Romans.'

'What about Whittington and Harrington; where do they come from?'

'I've no idea,' she admitted.

'You're going to have to find that book!' I laughed.

We arrived back at Whitecross Yard at a little after one-fifteen and made our way to the temporary CID room.

'We've been busy while you two were swanning around the country. Mr Sumpter made his delivery at Walker Brothers in Runcorn, as we already knew, and picked up another load nearby, assumed to be heading back in this direction. Walker Brothers weren't sure which one of his normal customers he would be picking up from but they gave us a list of three that it might be. We are in the process of checking them out now. Ellen, since you've been chauffeured all over the country whilst the rest of us have been working, would you take over from Harrington; give his ear a rest please?' the DI smiled.

'Yes, of course, sir,' she agreed.

'Dexter, put the kettle on and let's make notes on how this changes our perception of the case!'

'Right, sir.'

DS Whittington came into the office just as we seated ourselves around, drinks in hand, for an informal case discussion. He had been liaising with the uniform

187

boys as to how the forthcoming black-shirts meeting would be organised.

'Is it all in hand, Whittington?' the DI asked.

'Uniform seem to be overreacting if you ask me! I can't see the people of Crammingdon going in for the sort of brawling and rioting that has happened at other meetings,' he replied.

'What sort of brawling and rioting do you see them going in for then, Detective Sergeant?' the DI chuckled.

'You know what I mean, sir; Crammingdon is a sleepy old place, folk don't get stirred up all that easily.'

'The fascist movement is gaining ground among the people who see Britain as being overrun with foreigners and communists. Rightly or wrongly, they see our values being worn away as we accommodate these groups. Don't underestimate Mr Porter, if he's half as good at public speaking as his leader there could be fireworks,' the DI pointed out.

'Especially if Sir Oswald does turn up and stands up to speak!' Ellen said.

'The plan is, all available uniform in and around the hall, and they'd like us to provide at least three to infiltrate the crowd looking out for troublemakers, sir!'

'Right then; any volunteers for an interesting evening out with our colleagues in uniform?' he chuckled.

'I'd like to be included, please sir. I think there's just as likely to be women getting fired up as the men. A friend was at one of Donald Porter's meetings just outside Buxton and he said that the women there were, if anything, more aggitated than the men, sir!' Ellen said.

'Was that your reporter friend?' the DS asked, putting the question we were all thinking.

'Yes, he was there to cover it for his paper.'

'It passed off quietly though, surely?' DC Harrington asked.

'The mood was getting ugly when someone

asked him what he thought of what is happening in Germany; the murder and plunder of ordinary folk by mobs in fascist uniforms. He was unable to give a satisfactory answer, saying that Heir Hitler could not be held responsible for the actions of the mob!' Ellen replied.

'He stirs them up to fever-pitch but is not responsible for the outcome; that's ridiculous!' the DI said.

'That was the next point raised from the floor, and then the meeting broke up in disarray, according to my friend.'

'I bet our Mr Porter didn't like that. Are you sure you want to be involved in this, Ellen?' the DI asked.

'I think I might even shout out the same question, sir!'

'I'm not sure I like the idea of that, Ellen. If you could arrange for someone you know to do the shouting, then the force can't be accused of being involved in the politics of the thing,' the DI pointed out.

'I think I know just the person, sir,' she said.

'Good, I'll leave it to you then. So, two more volunteers; Whittington, and you Dexter,' he smiled.

'Right, sir,' we both said, though I for one didn't much like the idea.

'So how did your meeting with Jellicoe go?'
We quickly filled in the details of our meeting and the reasons why we thought we needed to talk to Harry Sumpter again.

'It certainly seems to put Harry Sumpter back into the frame; find him Ellen.'

'Right, sir.'

'Dexter, get your interview with Jellicoe written up and on my desk in the morning, I've agreed to be home before four o'clock or get my ears chewed off, so I'm heading into the sunset,' he grinned.

'Right, sir.'

Using the notes from Ellen's pocketbook as my prompt, I summarised what Mr Jellicoe had told us, and our feelings on the matter. Ellen had put the phone down and was looking up the number for her next call, I asked her to read what I had put and add anything she thought relevant.

'That covers the facts and I agree with you that Mr Jellicoe seems to have addressed our questions in a straightforward way. The only thing we haven't checked is if he actually did call into the garage that evening as he said,' she pointed out.

'I could do with a break. I'll nip round and see them,' I replied.

London Road Garage is a new feature in Crammingdon, having opened about two years ago. Constructed in the futuristic art deco glass and concrete style, it sported three modern electric petrol pumps, displaying the sign of a huge American oil company on a slightly raised concrete island in the middle of the forecourt. I was surprised that such a staid figure as Roland Jellicoe would have used it but it was on his way home so I suppose convenience was a major factor. Choosing a place on the forecourt to park that was clear of anyone wanting to use the pumps, I walked into the reception office. A smart young lady in a mid-blue blazer with the company crest on the breast pocket sat behind a desk in the corner.

'Good afternoon, I'm Detective Constable Dexter, I wonder if I might have a word with the owner please?'

'We are owned by the Magnum Oil Company, but I will enquire if the manager Mr Andrews can see you,' she smiled. 'Can I ask what it's about?'

'I would like his help in an ongoing enquiry,' I replied.

'Give me a moment, please,' she said, getting up and walking over to a door in the centre of the back wall and having politely tapped on it, went in. She appeared a few moments later and asked me to go in. Mr Andrew's office was light and airy, again in the modern style, with a large window looked out onto the driveway running down the right hand side of the premises as you looked at it from the road. Another equally large window and a glazed door looked out onto the workshops.

'Detective Constable, what can I do for you?' the man asked, holding out his hand. His shirtsleeves were rolled up to his elbows, displaying a gold wrist-watch the size of a half-crown. I got the impression he was a hard man to like or work for.

'I wonder if you could confirm that Mr Roland Jellicoe is one of your account customers please sir?'

'Mr Jellicoe, the school teacher – yes he gives us his trade, though I can't see how that helps you, Detective Constable.'

'Could you also confirm that he purchased petrol and possibly oil on Monday the eighth of June?' I continued.

'I don't have that information in this office, it will be out in the cabin,' he said pressing a bell push on his desk. A moment or two later the receptionist opened the door.

'Yes, Mr Andrews.'

'Would you pop to the cabin and get Mr Roland Jellicoe's account details please?'

'No need sir, they are all paid up and on my desk for typing at the end of the month!'

'Get them please Gwen.'

'Yes, sir.'

A few moments later, she returned with a sheet of paper and handed it to him.

'Thank you Gwen that will be all.'

She gave a little nod and closed the door behind her.

'Mm, just three dates; first of June four-fifteen pm, two gallons of Magnum Super, eighth of June four-twenty-five pm, two gallons of Magnum Super and half a pint of Magnum Lubro oil. You should try it; it reduces friction in moving parts and improves MPG,' he smiled.

'The time is important, how can you be sure it is

correct?' I asked, ignoring the sales pitch.

'There's a big clock in the petrol cabin; the attendant has to record the time at the completion of the transaction and ask the customer to sign, see,' he said passing the sheet to me.

'Yes, I see. This last item on the eleventh at six-forty-five am: it shows account closed. Do you know why that was?' I asked.

'No, but perhaps Gwen knows. He will probably have come across from the cabin to pay by cheque,' he said, pressing the bell again.

'Ah, Gwen; when Mr Jellicoe paid his account, did he give a reason?'

'Yes Mr Andrews, He settled his account in the cabin, it was before seven o'clock, I wasn't here that early but he told the night attendant he was moving away and wasn't sure if he'd be coming back, sir!'

'Thank you, Gwen,' he said, quite dismissively. 'Mr Jellicoe won't exactly be sadly missed, he was hardly a massive spender. I can't see Magnum Oil collapsing at his loss,' he laughed.

'Thank you Mr Andrews, that was most helpful.'

'What has he done anyway?'

'I simply needed to check his whereabouts at a particular time; you have confirmed that and eliminated him from our enquiries, thank you sir.'
I could tell he wasn't happy but he was getting nothing more from me.

Ellen had made real progress in tracking Harry Sumpter's movements.

'He unloaded in Runcorn, as DC Harrington found, picked another load a few hundred yards away at a company called Watson Cotton, and is bound for Wolverhampton.'

'Brilliant! Do you know his route?' I asked.

'Yes, he went back along the Trent & Mersey as far as the Middlewich branch and has just entered the Shropshire Union Canal; my guess looking at the map is that he'll make an overnight stop at Nantwich Junction.'

'You seem very sure of that.'

'There's a mooring with a pub, fresh water and supplies; it seems to make sense.'

'I see, what's your next move?' I asked.

'I rang the DI at home, is wife wasn't very happy but when I told her it was about Jenny she put him on the line. He rang Cheshire Constabulary and they have agreed to pick Mr Sumpter up in the morning or if they miss him at Nantwich, the flight of locks at Audlem will slow him up and they'll pick him up there!'

'Are they bringing him here, or are we going there?'

'I think they'll decide that once they've got him. So until morning, there's not a lot we can do. The DI suggested that we call it a day if the DS is in agreement.'

'Where is the DS anyway?' I asked.

'Still consulting with uniform over the Black Shirts meeting and getting pretty fed up with it all. He doesn't see what all the fuss is about. On top of that, Pete Warrell from the Argus is on his back about our incompetence with the Jenny case.'

'The joys of command,' I laughed.

Just then, the man in question entered along with DC Harrington and quickly dismissed us for the night.

14

The boys were in the garden playing on the swing when I drove through the gates, and Flossie was kneeling tending a flowerbed. The boys jumped off the swing and came running and grabbed my hands as I got out of the car.

'Come and listen to us read!' said George, and I guessed Flossie had been busy teaching them again.

The boys had finished reading to me, had their supper and been tucked up in their beds. I walked quietly down the stairs looking forward to a couple of hours to relax. Henry sat doing the crossword in the local paper.

'What do you make of this Will?' he asked, handing me the front page.

What I read made my jaw drop!

SCANDAL AT LOCAL UNDERTAKER!

Have you ever wondered what happens to your deceased loved ones once the coffin is closed? Read on for an unbelievable story, straight from an eyewitness. Our source, an undertaker's assistant, at what has always been considered a reputable company, has revealed these disturbing facts exclusively to the Argus!

Read his words:

"I lived in a flat on the premises of a local undertaker. One night I was awoken by a noise coming

from across the rear yard in the Chapel of Rest. Thinking we were being burgled I got dressed as quickly as possible in the hope of apprehending the villains. Before going down I took a last look out of the window, trying to decide the best means of attack. Only to find, that the noise had been made by the owners themselves. As I watched, they came out of the chapel carrying an empty casket and what was clearly a suit of men's clothes. Once they had gone I went down to the chapel, removed the lid of the casket and found that they had exchanged the fine oak one for an inferior plywood affair. Even more shocking they had removed the suit from the deceased who lay in his cheap, shoddy coffin in just a shirt!"

Is this an isolated case I wonder? How often does this sort of thing happen? I approached the company in question and was told that they were unable to make any comment at this stage.
I will not let this rest; follow the unfolding story in tomorrow night's Argus.

Pete Warrell (Crime reporter)

'Did you know about that, Will?' Henry asked.

'Strictly between us, I was part of the investigation. As far as I'm aware the case is being looked at by the Chief Constable to decide what action to take.'

'It's true then? A local undertaker has been defrauding his customers!'

'So it seems,' I agreed.

'But this just sounds like the word of a disgruntled ex-employee. Why has it gone as high as the Chief Constable? How could you have taken this man's word? He seems clearly to have an axe to grind, the truth of which cannot be verified.'

'The revelation didn't initially come from the person in the paper. A lady came into Whitecross Yard, claiming...' I gave him a quick outline of the way the thing had run.

'So how will this article change things do you think?'

'At the moment there's a degree of anonymity, but once Pete Warrell gets onto anything he'll soon have, or create, as much sensation as he can handle. Tom Brierly will have something to say about this in the morning, that's for sure,' I laughed.

'I assume you have all seen the front page of last night's Argus?' the DI said, once we had all assembled in the office next morning.

We all nodded and mumbled, 'Yes.'

'The Chief Constable rang me last night and gave me the roasting of a lifetime. Anyone would have thought that *I* had passed the story to our local newshound. The point *is* how do we handle it now the story is out of the bag?'

'It *was* in the CC's hands, did he give you any idea how he intends to pursue the matter now, sir?' asked DS Whittington.

'I get the impression he was hoping to, er, sweep it under the carpet with a quiet reprimand; I think that Mr Watson is a golfing and drinking pal. That stays in this office by the way.'

'That seems unlikely now though, sir, and immoral,' Ellen suggested.

'Certainly now that Pete Warrell has got his claws into it; problem is it opens up a floodgate of folk all wondering if the same happened to their deceased loved ones. I'm beggared if I can see where it's all going to end.'

Just then the phone rang and Ellen picked it up.

'Crammingdon CID ... Yes he's here, I'll hand

you over… Cheshire Constabulary, sir!'

'DI Brierly… So where is he now? If you could hold him there… it'll take us about three hours from here. Thanks,' the DI said and put the phone down. 'They've stopped him at Audlem, holding him there until we arrive. I'll see if one of our motor patrols can take us. Who was it drove you to York, Dexter?'

'Sergeant Byland, sir.'

'Find out if he's on duty Dexter, if so raise him and get him to run us to Audlem.'

'Have you sorted out the arrangements for this fascist meeting, Whittington?'

'There's another meeting, this morning sir, at ten o'clock. Uniform are shitting themselves in case it all gets out of hand, sir.'

'I apologise for the uncouth language of my staff, Ellen, but I think we all get the picture!'
We all nodded sheepishly.

'Go and get that sorted, Dexter.'

'Right, sir.'

Having checked with Sergeant Youngman on the desk that Sergeant Byland was on duty, I got him to alert the motor patrols with the police box lights and ten minutes later was talking to the sergeant-driver. He agreed to pick us up from Whitecross Yard as soon as he had filled up with fuel.

Our choice of driver again proved to be a good one; he handled the big MG saloon with flair and panache, getting along the often twisting roads with commendable progress but complete safety. Only on two occasions, when passing through narrow town streets did he resort to using the warning bell. However, when he did, the wake-up effect on the local inhabitants was clear, and often amusing to see. One poor chap arranging a stall outside his shop dropped a tray of what must have been two or three dozen eggs. Turning to look out of the rear window, I could see him, shouting and shaking his fist at us before he disappeared from view as we rounded

197

a bend in the road.

Audlem locks are an impressive sight. Trent Wanderer, Sumpter's boat was moored at a small quayside with a police constable standing alongside. Sergeant Byland pulled up by the boat and we got out, glad to stand up and stretch after the long journey. We introduced ourselves to the PC on duty and he directed us to the small office used by the lock keeper. Built in brick with a grey slate roof, the centre of the building was an open fronted shelter like a market stall, covering a water tap and dustbins, between a small WC on the right and the office on the left. Sumpter sat on a form in this area clearly upset at having his journey held up.

'Good morning, I assume you are the canal manager,' the DI said, introducing ourselves as a tall man in a blue uniform came out of the little office.

'Walter Springer, lock keeper actually' he said holding out his hand. 'Look, I've things to do so please feel free to use my ivory tower,' he grinned pointing to the office.

'Thank you Mr Springer, we shouldn't be too long,' the DI said indicating for Sumpter to enter.

'Good morning Mr Sumpter, I'm Detective Inspector Brierly of Crammingdon CID,' the DI said, struggling to sit down.

'Pleased to meet you I'm sure, now get on with it, I've a load to deliver.'

'I believe you told DC's Dexter and Parsons that you had seen someone descending to the towpath at the London Road Bridge in Crammingdon?' the DI continued.

'That I did and described him quite well, I reckon.'

'Could you describe him to me, please Mr Sumpter?'

'It's to do with that missin' gal aint it?'

'It is, yes sir.'

'Er… Black trilby hat, light grey gabardine

198

coat…' he continued to give us more or less word for word the description he had given to Ellen and me earlier.

'I rang the next day, I think it was. I'd remembered what first made me notice him, he 'ad brown brogue shoes with black laces! That's it, I can't tell you anything else!'

'Could you describe his briefcase again, please Mr Sumpter?' the DI asked.

'Like I just said, brown leather two straps at the front with little buckles and a long strap, like it was for carrying over your shoulder. It looked sort-of old but well-polished yer know.'

'Do you mean a bag like this? Ellen, would you show Mr Sumpter the sort of bag we think he is describing?'

'Yes, sir.' Ellen replied lifting the little school satchel from the bag she had brought with her.

'That's it! That's the one; or one as could be its twin.'

'We've traced the man you described; does the name Ronald Jellicoe mean anything to you?'

'No, and it's not a name as you'd forget is it?' he smirked.

'You see we have a problem. Mr Jellicoe admits to being at the bridge at the time and date you suggested, but he claims only to have been feeding the ducks.' the DI said.

'Maybe he was, I can't say. All I know is I saw him where and when I said! Show me that bag again, love.'

Ellen passed it across to him.

'Ere this aint a briefcase is it? It's one o' them school satchels! Bloody hell.' he said and looked wide-eyed from one to another of us in turn.

'We believe this to actually belong to the missing girl!'

'Bloody hell; 'e was going to chuck it in the water! That's it aint it?'

'Why do you say that, Mr Sumpter?' asked the DI.

'Why else would he be comin' down the steps?'

'Do you mind if we take another look at your boat?' I asked, ignoring his question.

''Elp yerself, yer will anyway,' he shrugged. 'I aint kidnapped no young gal and I aint even seen 'er like I told these two last time,' he shouted and thumped his fist on the office desk.

The DI nodded and Ellen and I walked over to the Trent Wanderer.

'Do you think he's involved, Will?' Ellen asked as we stepped aboard.

'He's a good actor if he is, but then so is Jellicoe. They each throw doubt on the other just like it's some sort of conspiracy,' I replied.

'He was genuinely shocked when he realised it wasn't a briefcase.'

'Or he recognised it as the one he had thrown into the undergrowth by the canal, but if that's the case he's quick thinking, I'll give him that,' I said.

'When I looked last time I only looked in the living part of the boat; I'll look again if you'll look in the cargo hold,' Ellen suggested.

'Okay,' I agreed.

The cargo hold; was covered with a heavy canvas tent arrangement, to shed rain away from the hold. Unable to move it on my own, I commandeered the PC to help me remove it. The hold was full to the top with heavy bolts of cotton fabric about four feet wide. If the girl had ever been in there, there was no way to prove it without removing every bolt of cloth and that was an impossible task without a gang of labourers and possibly an on-shore derrick.

'I think we can cover this up again constable,' I said and he nodded.

'What were you looking for?' he asked.

'Any sign of a missing girl, we just needed to eliminate this chap from our enquiries.'

'Did you think she was on board?'

'Not really, just routine,' I said and he nodded looking up into the sky.

'We only just covered it over in time,' he said as the first few drops of rain fell.

Back in the cabin, Ellen was just concluding her search.

'There's a couple of kiddies reading books and some clothes for a girl a good deal younger than Jenny but otherwise nothing. My guess is that they are a few keepsakes from his wife and daughter. He lost them to the flu a couple of years ago if you remember?'

'Yes. I can't see any reason why he would have taken Jenny anyway,' I said.

'Canal families work the boat together, losing his wife and daughter must have made it very hard work all on his own. Perhaps he might have taken her to force her to give him a hand.'

'Do you remember what Nelly Richmond, Jenny's friend, said in her statement? She said Jenny had saved her crusts each day to feed the ducks.' I reminded her.

'That's right; what's your point, Will?'

'When the dog pulled her school bag from the brambles it couldn't get it open and it gave up after a minute or so and left it on the towpath.'

'Yes I know; you and Harrington picked it up and opened it,' she nodded.

'That's the point; her story was there and a couple of school books, a couple of pencils, a rubber, but no crusts!'

'She'd *already* fed the ducks! She *must* have been down to the towpath!' Ellen exclaimed.

'Looks like it. I'm not sure our Mr Sumpter is in the clear yet,' I said, and Ellen gave a low whistle.

'I don't think Jenny has been on this boat, but it seems there's something he's not telling us,' Ellen agreed.

We ran back to the lock keeper's office as the rain began to worsen.

'Could we have a word with you, please sir?' I asked as we opened the door.

The DI struggled to his feet and looked at us both, quizzically.

'Go on, what have you found?' he asked as he closed the office door and we stood in the tiny sheltered area.

'Nothing, but Will has remembered something,' Ellen explained.

I quickly put him in the picture.

'So you are saying that Jenny had already fed the ducks?'

'Why else would there have been no crusts in her bag?' I asked.

'Because she'd already eaten them at lunch time, she'd taken something other than sandwiches, she'd swapped her sandwiches for a slice of cake with one of her pals; any number of reasons,' he suggested, shaking his head.

'Sorry, sir, I don't think so,' I shrugged.

'So it could be. All I'm saying is the crusts could be missing from the bag for lots of reasons; we need to check it out. Meantime let's see what he has to say about it,' the DI said, heading back into the office.

'Mr Sumpter, we now have reason to believe that Jenny had been down to the towpath at about the same time as you were passing under the bridge by her house. What do you have to say about that?' asked DI Brierly.

'Why would she go down to the towpath, with 'er 'ouse just over the bridge?'

'To feed the ducks,' the DI pointed out.

'Lots of folk feedin' the bloody ducks all of a suddin',' he snapped.

'Never the less new information suggests that

she was on the towpath for that purpose at about the time you, by your own admission, happened to be passing by,' the DI said.

'Like I said if she was on the towpath, feeding the ducks, it was before or after I got there. I didn't see no girl!' Sumpter yelled.

'Thank you for your time Mr Sumpter, I'm sure you'll understand this is a very serious matter and we might need to talk to you again. Could you give me a rough idea where you are likely to be, in the next two or three days, please?' the DI asked.

'I'll be along this stretch until I unload at Cotton Printers in Wolverhampton.'

'When will that be?'

'If I get a move on and run till last light I'll just about make my right time; middle of the day after to-morrow.'

'Thank you Mr Sumpter, you're free to go,' the DI said.

'Thank gawd for that,' he moaned.

The DI thanked the lock keeper for the use of his office and we set off back to Crammingdon, without the urgency of the outward journey.

With the evidence into the whereabouts of Jenny drying up and the trail, fragmented as it was, getting colder by the minute, three days of useless effort followed. The Black Shirts meeting was in the middle of that period and proved to be more of a problem than any of us expected.

The meeting at the Miner's Welfare Club had been advertised in the local newspaper and on posters all over the town and surrounding villages. There had been a massive gathering, mostly of menfolk, far too many to fit into the relatively small building, meaning that many people were left outside in the drizzle. The organizers had foreseen the possibility of a large turnout and installed outside loudspeakers.

As the meeting was about to begin, a chap I didn't recognise walked out onto the platform.

'Ladies and gentlemen, it is my pleasure to introduce Sir Oswald Mosely, here to support Mr Donald Porter of the Nationalist Party.'

They both walked on stage, Sir Oswald gave a little bow and then seated himself at the back and to one side of the stage.

'Please show your appreciation for Mr Donald Porter who is here to speak to you tonight,' the Master of Ceremonies said.

The applause, such as it was, was muted, a good half of the audience remaining silent or muttering in a discontented way. If Mr Porter expected to have the meeting all his own way, he was sadly mistaken. The good people of Crammingdon had turned out to support him or to shout him down in equal numbers. His speech met with silence to start with, giving him the chance to put his thoughts before the assembly. Mostly, his point was, *Britain for the British* and we were being over-run with undesirable aliens, especially pointing a finger at Jewish and eastern Europeans. His mistake came when he praised Hitler for the way he was rescuing the German nation from the tyranny of those peoples.

"Whether we like it or not, Mr Hitler has restored Germany's standing in the world. He is the choice of the German people, democratically elected by them!" he shouted amid almost equal cheers and boos.

"And once elected, he promptly banned future elections; Hitler is a dictator!" shouted a voice from the crowd when the noise had subsided.

"Mr Hitler has taken steps to ensure that his policies are carried out. The people of Germany have entrusted him with that," Porter replied, his amplified voice drowning out other adverse comments.

"The people you complain are flooding here are doing so to flee from Hitler's tyranny!" shouted another voice.

"Nonsense; Heir Hitler is a strong and fair leader seeking only to return self-respect to the German people!" Porter retorted.

"Some self-respect when anyone who disagrees with the tin-pot dictator is hounded and has their businesses and belongings plundered by Hitler's young thugs?" shouted the first voice again.

No doubt Porter replied to that, though something distracted me from it. From where I was in the hall, I noticed three young men in Black Shirts approach the person who had been the main heckler and start to forcibly remove him from the crowd. His mates were having none of it and grabbed them and pulled them off the chap. The meeting erupted into a number of localised pitched battles in which the Black Shirts produced cudgels; and quickly become sorry that they had. Miners can fight dirty when they need to and although we were forced to make several arrests, as the fighting continued, many of them were for carrying offensive weapons, particularly among the Black Shirts. In general, the only offensive weapons the miners carried were fists like shovels and muscles honed at the coal face. Mosely never had a chance to speak. The meeting broke up in disarray about eight-fifteen, the more sensible folk left the scene as quickly as possible without becoming involved, and some scuffles carried on out into the street.

The open fighting among some sections of the crowd was the main feature in the Argus the next day, effectively pushing the stories of the undertaker's scandal and Jenny Parminter's disappearance into the background. Friday therefore was taken up with bringing to justice those who had been arrested, seeing them through the courts and dealing with the vast amounts of paperwork that it generated.

Apart from a few hours each day in the office doing my share of cover, Saturday and Sunday was spent with the boys. Diana came along with us on Sunday afternoon as we retraced the walk that had become the boy's favourite, watching the trains hurtle across the Monsal viaduct on their way to or from Manchester.

It became clear that since Diana had declined my marriage offer things between us were on a different footing. She loved the boys of that there was no doubt, but she thought of me as a valued friend, nothing more. With my feelings for Ellen growing stronger every time I saw her, was I really sorry Diana had had the good sense to say no? I wasn't sure; especially since I was unsure if Ellen was already spoken for.

Monday morning, Ellen came into the office just as I was putting the kettle on ready for our daily exchange of ideas. The others arrived more or less at the same time.

'Right, my merry men, er, and woman, what has the weekend turned up for us?' asked the DI.

'One of our uniform lads has been rushed to hospital; got a crack on the head Thursday night, thought nothing of it, collapsed on duty last night. In a coma at the moment and I'm told it doesn't look good,' said DS Whittington.

'Bloody politicians, they make me sick! Ordinary people around the world get on okay for the most part. Agreed there's the odd dispute about garden boundary lines and somebody's bonfire blackening someone else's washing, or a tiff at the pub; but folk get on with their lives, choosing to boycott each other or forgive and forget. Not bloody politicians, it always has to be dramatic. Stirring folk up into hatred not for any other reason than I don't like your religion or the colour of your skin. And who has to sort it all out? Not them, they are safe in their ivory towers while Joe Soap fights their wars for them or cleans up their bleedin' mess! Sorry Ellen it really gets my goat,' said the DI.

'One of the Black Shirts hit him?' asked Harrington.

'According to the report the PC gave that night,

he had actually been hit by one of the miners, a chap he had run in several times for drunk and disorderly. Two other uniform lads arrested him on the spot but PC Drummond said it was probably in the heat of the moment and asked that the chap be released,' the DS said.

'If Drummond doesn't pull through, this chap will be facing a manslaughter charge,' the DI replied. 'I assume we know who he is?'

'Aye, he's well known to our lads, I was involved with his arrest one night. No harm in the chap; just can't hold his drink!' Ellen said.

'We'll just have to pray that Drummond recovers, but I think we should look at pulling this chap in on a GBH charge; serious assault on a police officer in the line of his duty. I won't have folk thinking they can nobble our lads and get away with it. Let's get some more information on the incident, look into that Harrington.'

'Right, sir.'

'Anything else cropped up over the weekend?'

'Possibly, sir,' Ellen said.

'Let's have it then.'

'Yesterday I happened to be biking through Backridge, and called in to see Mr and Mrs Durose, the lock keepers. A social call really, just a chat about old times. But it came up in conversation that Mr Sumpter had taken on a chap to help on the boat, about a year back.'

'Had he now?' the DI put in.

'That's not all. It seems, according to Mr Durose, that this new chap had eventually bought the boat from Mr Sumpter, and Sumpter now works for this new bloke,' Ellen said, raising her eyebrows.

'So, where was this new bloke when we interviewed Sumpter at Audlem? More to the point why didn't Sumpter mention him?'

'The plot thickens, sir. Mr Durose said that the new chap was on the boat with Harry Sumpter when they went up to turn in the basin at the mill, but not on the way back!'

'Perhaps he was in the cabin,' the DI suggested.

'But where was this new bloke when we interviewed Harry Sumpter at Swarkstone lock?' I asked.

'Good work, Ellen. This is the first new lead we've had in days.'

'Thank you, sir.'

'I think we need yet another word with our Mr Sumpter and this new bloke. He's been withholding information; I wonder why? Find out where he is now, Ellen.'

'Right, sir.'

I suddenly remembered that the Hornet had a punctured tyre clamped to the rear of the boot.

'I had to change the wheel the other night, sir and now I haven't got a spare. Is it okay if I nip round to Cox's Garage and get it repaired?' I asked.

'Provided it doesn't take all day.'

'I'll just leave it there and collect it at lunchtime.'

'Off you go then... rush there and hurry back,' he said with a nod.

You'll no doubt remember that I had in mind a full overhaul of the little Hornet. Mr Cox was standing on the forecourt as I drove in. He was chatting to a fellow leaning on a large blue Vauxhall but waved as I got out. As I was removing the spare wheel from the back the Vauxhall drove away and Mr Cox walked over to me.

'Morning Mr Dexter, bumped into any trees lately?' he chuckled, referring to an unpleasant incident a few years earlier that had put us both in hospital.

'Once in a lifetime is more than enough thank you Mr Cox,' I replied.

'Amen to that! Got a flatty?'

'Mm, happened a couple of nights ago; only just remembered it,' I said, lifting the wheel off its cradle.

'She still looks nice, still happy with her? I

could give you a good price.'

'Yes, but I was wondering what it would cost to give her a full overhaul, engine, brakes, steering the lot?'

'Won't be cheap… take a while too… thinking of keeping her, are yer?'

'Rather sentimentally attached to the old girl!' I replied.

'Some would say that being attached like that to a motorcar is like backing the gee-gees. Only one winner and it's not you!' he laughed.

'I'd still like a price, though.'

'Look, I'll do you a deal… Trade price on the bits plus labour at five bob an hour so long as you let us fit it in between other work; what do you say?'

'Sounds good, but would I be better to bring it in say once a month and have one item done at a time, as a proper booked-in job?'

'Up to you. I can see your thinking; if you leave it with us then suddenly at the end get saddled with a hundred pound bill; that's it isn't it?' he smiled.

'I know you'll be fair with me. But a DC's pay sets pretty close budgets.'

'Okay then, how's this; leave her here now and we'll get her on the ramps, assess the work and give you a rough idea, what do you say?'

'I'll need a car while you look,' I said.

'Take the Rover saloon over there, it doesn't look much but it's sound. Bring it back this evening and I'll have an idea of price for you!'

'That sounds very fair, don't forget about the tyre!'

'Roll it into the workshop while I get the Rover keys!'

So less than twenty minutes after leaving I was back at Whitecross Yard at the wheel of an aging Rover. Ellen was speaking as I walked in.

'…dropped his load at Wolverhampton two days ago, picked another up at the same place, made up stuff to come up to Nottingham via Trent Lock; I reckon he should be there about midday today, sir.'

'Right we'll have another word with him there. I'll get the local lads to hang on to him. Dexter arrange for our driver again!'

'No need sir, I've borrowed a big Rover saloon, plenty of room for you *and* your leg, sir!'

'How come you're borrowing a car? I thought you had only gone in to get a puncture repaired,' the DI asked.

'I had, but I've left the Hornet for them to get me a price on some work that needs doing. I've got this until this evening, sir.'

'Fair enough and it'll save asking the traffic boys again.'

The door opened and in walked Arthur Milford, the Assistant Chief Constable. We all stood up and saluted.

'I need a word in private with DI Brierly; make yourselves scarce for a minute or two please!' he said nodding to us all, and we did as we were told.

Ellen and I went out to the yard and stood enjoying the sunshine and each other's company. DS Whittington and DC Harrington were due in court to give evidence against the worst of Thursday evening's rioters and so they nodded and asked us to remind the DI that was where they would be.

'Okay, now tell me why you really went to Backridge Lock yesterday,' I said.

'It's true, I went out for a bike ride and found myself about half a mile away and just thought it would be nice to drop in and have a chat with the pair of them. I think they must get a bit lonely now that there's so little canal traffic.'

'Mm…'

'Don't look at me like that, it's true!' she smiled.

'Mm…'

'Not much gets past you, does it Will?'

'So go on, why did you *just happen* to drop in and see them?'

'I had started to wonder, as I rode along, if anything had occurred to them that they hadn't told us when we interviewed them.'

'The copper's nose, that's what Sergeant Bell used to call it. You get the feeling that there's something that's not been said.'

'That's it! I'd no idea what it might be. But, finding that Harry Sumpter had a shipmate, then it seems this new bloke bought the boat; well, what's all that about?' she said.

'Not only that, why was this chap there on the way up past the lock but not there, as far as we know, coming back down?'

'I think our Mr Sumpter *or his mate* could well be back in the frame for whatever has become of Jenny,' Ellen said and pursed her lips.

'Look's that way,' I agreed.

'Why do you think the ACC didn't call DI Brierly over to his office, instead of slumming it in our restroom?' Ellen asked.

'Heaven!' I said and smiled.

'Heaven?'

'That's what we call the senior offices across the yard,' I chuckled.

'That's very naughty. But go on why is he using our office?'

'Not a clue, but I bet there's dirty work at the mill.'

Twenty minutes went by and the conversation turned to other things.

'So, what's up with your lovely little car, Will?'

'Nothing really, I want to hang on to it as you know, I had a word with Mr Cox when I took the spare wheel in, and he agreed to give it the once over and report anything he thinks needs doing,' I said.

'I don't want to pry, and tell me to bugger off if

you think I'm being too personal, but you said the car was your wife's. I guess that's why you want to keep it?' she asked, and just for a moment her hand touched mine, then she quickly withdrew it with a little half-smile of embarrassment. It was only the merest of touches but the effect was like a lightning bolt.

Where things might have gone is anyone's guess but the tension was broken by the sound of the DI clumping along the passage to the back steps.

'Okay you lot, he's gone. Where's the other pair?' he asked as he came to a halt at the top of them.

'In court about the arrests at Thursday's meeting, sir,' Ellen said.

'Oh yes, so they are. Come into the office, I've some interesting news,' he smiled.

'Close the door and put the kettle on Dexter,' he said as he settled himself behind his desk and stood his crutches within easy reach. 'I'll be glad when I'm rid of these blasted things,' he added.

With kettle filled and the pair of us sitting in what was rapidly becoming our normal places, he started to smile.

'Ellen, as from now, you are no longer an Acting DC!'

'I'm sorry sir, have I done something wrong?'

'No, from now on you are a DC, you are on the team, such as it is, full time if you want to be?'

'Thank you, sir!' she said eagerly.

'Is that what the ACC came to see you about, sir?' I asked.

'No!' he smiled. 'He came on quite a different matter. Once again what I'm telling you stays in this room. It seems Pete Warrell, our local newshound, had put one of his mates in the crowd at Thursday's meeting to stir things up a touch. It seems that *Mr Someone* and *Mr Someone's* wife are big mates with our Mr Warrell and *his* wife. That *Mr Someone* was arrested by our boys in blue on Thursday night and charged with inciting a public disturbance and Mrs Warrell is giving our news sleuth a massively bad time since she blames him for the fact that *Mr Someone's* wife is now giving her the cold shoulder,' he chuckled.

'So; Pete's in trouble with his missus?' I suggested.

'Oh yes, so much so that he came in early this morning to do a deal with the Chief Constable!' the DI smiled.

'Are we allowed to know what the deal is, sir?' asked Ellen.

'Stays in this room remember. Like I said, Pete came in asking for his mate to be treated leniently or let off all together. I think Pete sent this *Mr Someone* into the meeting to get things stirred up and he was too effective. In exchange Pete has agreed to let the story about the undertakers *die the death*. No pun intended! They are, or at least one of them is, a golfing, drinking mate of the Chief Constable and he has agreed to the deal. The ACC came to put me in the picture,' the DI grinned.

'That's a bit naughty, sir. They are nearly as bad as the olden-day body snatchers, definitely not what you expect from an undertaker,' I said.

'I agree but something I learned in this job long ago is *'don't rock the boat,'* the shit'll all sort itself out in due course. These things always come to the surface sooner or later. Meantime, make use of their embarrassment,' he said.

'Not with you, sir,' we both said together.

'I just happened to mention what a massive help it has been having Ellen on the team, and what a shame it would be if she had to return to uniform duties,' he laughed. 'The ACC agreed that we are understaffed and suggested that if Ellen was to make the appropriate application together with a recommendation from me, it would be approved as a matter of course. We'll sort that out this morning!' he smiled.

'So I really am on the team full time?'

213

'Bank on it, Ellen. Welcome to Crammingdon CID full time.'

'Thank you, sir.'

'My pleasure. Now *DC* Ellen Parsons, find me Sumpter.'

'Yes, sir.'

Within minutes she had located the Trent Wanderer at the basin at Trent Lock.

'There's a problem, sir!'

'Let me guess, our Mr Sumpter has gone missing.'

'Afraid so, sir,' she nodded.

'I can't believe he's left his boat just like that,' the DI remarked.

'It's not his boat now though is it, sir?' Ellen replied.

'Mm, the boat no longer belongs to him and the new owner is also missing, where the hell do we go from here?'

'I don't know, sir' she said and I shook my head.

'This chap has lost his wife and his daughter, now it seems, his boat no longer belongs to him, he's being hounded by the police, or at least that's how he sees it. Where would he go?' the DI said, ticking the points off one by one on his fingers.

'There's a good chance he's drowning his sorrows in a pub somewhere,' I suggested.

'With bloody good reason, I'd say,' the DI agreed. 'How many pubs in the immediate area, do you reckon?'

'How far do you think he'll have gone from the boat, sir?' ask Ellen.

'I'd guess no more than a mile or so.'

'Trouble is it's right on the county boundary, sir.'

'So long as he stays on the Derbyshire side, I've got agreement to follow it up as I see fit. Let's get over there now, all three of us, and find our friend Mr Sumpter and get some answers.'

The big Rover saloon proved more than capable of swallowing up a DI with a plastered leg and a set of crutches, and we set off for a very dry pub-crawl, starting in Sawley with the three most likely inns. We arrived at the Waterman's Tavern, the third on our list, just as a very drunk Harry Sumpter was very forcibly, told to leave.

'Standing on the doorstep when I opened, he was. Already had a few by then, but pleasant enough so I let him in. Regular customer, he is, when he's here on his travels. Gets two pints down him then he's shouting the place down about injustice,' said the publican.

'What exactly was he saying?' asked the DI.

'About somebody swindling him out of his boat; said he'd kill the child snatching bastard! Excuse my language, miss, but those were his words.'

'Say that again please,' the DI said.

'Said he'd kill this bloke, who'd swindled him out of his boat!'

'Not that, the other bit,'

'Not with you?'

'What name did he call this person?'

'Oh – child snatching bastard!'

'Are you sure those were his exact words?' the DI asked.

'Hardly likely to forget, he yelled 'em at the top of his voice!'

Meantime Sumpter had thrown up about three pints of ale in the gutter and backed up against the pub wall, gently sliding down to sit on the pavement groaning and slowly shaking his head.

'Now I've got to wash that bloody lot away. I should never have let him in! Bloody hell,' the landlord snapped.

'I think we need a cosy little chat with our Mr Sumpter,' the DI said.

'I don't fancy having him in my car in that state,

sir,' I pointed out, 'especially since it's not my car anyway!'

'My days of riding around with drunks are long past, Dexter we'll phone for the boys in blue and the Mariah. Could I use your phone please landlord?'

The man led the way inside and the DI followed a little unsteadily. Sumpter was now merrily snoring away coming close to rattling the pub windows.

'What do you make of that?' Ellen asked.

'I'd say it's our best bit of evidence for days, but he's not going to tell us much until he's slept it off!'

'Could just have been the drink talking,' Ellen suggested.

'Maybe, but why call his mate that?'

'Hardly his mate, but I know what you mean,' she smiled.

'If this new chap did snatch Jenny from under the bridge at the mill, it answers why her school bag was thrown into the brambles,' I pointed out.

'Snatching her right outside her home? A bit risky don't you think, but probably he wouldn't know where she lived?'

'She'd be well out of sight down on the towpath. A quick grab, hand over her mouth and down into the cabin.'

'That's just speculation, Will!'

'Agreed, but I bet it's not far from the truth,' I shrugged

'Why would Sumpter lie about this new chap?' she asked. 'And why would this new chap take the kid?'

'He'll claim he didn't actually lie, just didn't volunteer the information. At the time we spoke to him we had no idea there was anyone else,' I suggested.

'True! I suppose he was just looking after his job. Perhaps he was hoping to get his boat back at some point. Or maybe, Barber is blackmailing him somehow!'

'Now you're speculating,' I chuckled.

'Mm!'

'Right, the vans on its way; cuff him Ellen. I can't see him running away in that state but yer never know!' the DI said as he eased himself down the pub step, still moving very carefully on his crutches.

'Right, sir.'

A purpose built Ford one ton van, had replaced our old 1917 Bedford custody van a few months back and it turned up about twenty minutes later. Sumpter was unable to walk and the driver and his mate had to carry him into the back, with looks of distaste on their faces.

'Make sure he doesn't get injured, he has important information,' the DI said.

'Can't really hurt himself in here, sir; plush seats, even a bed for them as can't sit up.'

'Even so, one of you sit in with him, I don't want him choking on his vomit.'

'Right, sir. In yer go, Jack,' the driver indicated to his mate.

'Why is it always me, 'Arry?'

'Cos' I'm the driver!' Harry pointed out.

Grudgingly Jack climbed aboard; muttering that he'd had to do it last time, a statement that made no difference, and the driver locked the door. Moments later the van drove off. After taking a statement from the landlord, we followed them back to Whitecross Yard, arriving just as Sumpter's cell door was clanging shut.

'Can't see you getting anything out of him for a couple of hours at least!' the desk sergeant chuckled.

'Any way to sober him up a bit smartish?' the DI asked.

'In the old days we used to take 'em in the yard and chuck a bucket of cold water over 'em, sir,' he chuckled. 'Can't do it these days, sir!'

'You have my permission to do it now sergeant.'

'I will if you insist sir, but it never did any good, except make the arresting officer feel better, sir,' he replied, with a big cheesy grin.

'Forget it then, just keep a close eye on him. I

want to know the moment he's even half-coherent,' the DI nodded.

'Right you are, sir,' the desk sergeant said tossing the keys from hand to hand.

Back in the temporary CID office, we sat ourselves down to discuss how the questioning should progress when Harry eventually resurfaced. Ellen was doing the kettle honours as heavy and rapid footfall in passage from the front office suggested someone in a hurry. There was a knock on the door and a PC opened it when the DI shouted, "Enter".

'PC Drummond died a few minutes ago, sir!' the PC gasped.

'Hell! The lad who was hit on the head by the miner?'

'Yes, sir!'

'Does the Chief Constable know?'

'Sergeant Youngman has gone to inform him now, sir, I'm to hold the desk till he gets back.'

'Thank you constable, get back to the desk then please.'

'Yes, sir,' he said and a much slower footfall went back along the passage.

Moments later the phone on the DI's desk rang.

'Yes sir, I've just been informed... Very good, sir,' the DI said putting the phone down. 'I've been called to Heaven to decide the next move. It would be a good idea if I knew the offender's name; Ellen you've arrested the bloke in the past!'

'Thomas Norton, sir. Ireland Place, number 61 I think!'

'Good girl!' he said and disappeared as quickly as a plastered leg would allow.

The shock of the situation had us both deep in thought. PC Drummond had a wife and two small children, a boy and a girl a bit older than my own. I couldn't help thinking what the effect on my boys would be if they were to lose me as well as their mother.

'His poor wife; what's her name I can't remember?' I asked. I'd worked with him on a couple of day shifts during my time in uniform, but that was several years ago now.

'Sylvia! She'll be devastated. I suppose she was at his bedside?'

'I should think so,' I agreed.

'I'm going to ask the DI if I can go and see if I can help; we were at school together!'

'Mm,' was all I could say.

The DI was gone about twenty minutes and when he returned, Ellen asked his permission to go to PC Drummond's wife.

'I agree you should be with her but his nibs is going himself right after he's done his bit for the assembled press,' the DI said, clicking his tongue.

'I'll go around tonight, though what I'm going to say to her, I have no idea!'

'Ellen, there aren't any words; a friendly shoulder to cry on is the best any of us can do. Go to her as soon as the Chief gets back.'

'Thank you, sir.'

'The uniform boys are tracking down Thomas Norton so we'd better go back to thinking about Jenny and how this new accomplice of Harry Sumpter fits in with everything.'

'We can't do a lot until he's back from the land of nod and in the land of the living,' I said, instantly thinking that land was now short of one of the good guys!

Thomas Norton had already gone down the mine by the time the uniform boys had found out which pit he worked at. The mine owners refused to stop the flow of coal up the shaft to extract him, pointing out that he was going nowhere! His shift ended at seven the next morning and by the time he had walked the mile and a half from the coal-face to the bottom of the shaft for his ride to the top it was likely to be quarter to eight before he was on the surface. We had arranged that two uniformed officers would meet him as he stepped from the cage.

At six o'clock Harry Sumpter was still snoring away merrily like a saw-mill in full production, and the DI dismissed us all having got the duty sergeant's agreement to contact him as soon as the slumberer, woke so I took the big saloon back to the garage. Mr Cox had gone by then but my little Hornet was parked on the forecourt with an envelope on the passenger seat containing a full written report on the car. I put the envelope in my inside pocket, collected the Hornet and headed home.

As I put the boys to bed George said,

'Uncle Henry told us about two other George and Williams, the ones in…er…'

'Your cousins in Canada, you mean?' I suggested. It hadn't occurred to me that my boys had never met them.

'Yes; he said that you and Auntie Flossie had a sister and she went to live in Canada! Why?'

'It's a long story, so I'll tell you the first part, come on now snuggle down,' I said wondering where to start.

'Your Granny and Grandpa had three children – me, Auntie Flossie and Auntie Edith.'

'Is Auntie Edith the one in Canada?' asked Will.

'That's right, Auntie Edith and Uncle Joe have two children and called them George and William. Your Mammy and me had two children, you are my children,' I said and kissed them each on the forehead.

'Auntie Fossie is our Auntie!' said George looking a bit worried. 'Will we have to live in Canada with them?'

'No; of course not! You live here with me and Auntie Flossie and Uncle Henry. Auntie Flossie and Uncle Henry don't have any children, except two rascals who should be asleep by now.'

'We are Auntie Flossie's children!' George exclaimed.

'You are my children but Auntie Flossie's nephews,' I said and gave them a big hug. 'Auntie Edith sends us letters and photographs of her George and William so that we can see how fast they are growing, that's all. I'll ask Auntie Flossie to show you the photographs in the morning. Come on now snuggle down, time for sleep.

'Can we see them now?' asked Will.

'I suppose so, just one and the rest another day. I'll get the one that's Auntie Flossie's favourite.' I ran down to the front room and collected the framed photo of them all, pointing out Edith and Joe and their boys standing smiling beside a huge snowman.

'I wish we could build a snowman as big as that,' Will sighed.

'I like them. Do they like us?' George asked.

'Oh yes! Everyone likes you two scallywags. Come on, night night.'

Henry and my sister were sitting in the front parlour, listening to a play on the wireless. As I joined them I became aware of a large vase of flowers in pride of place on the window sill. A little card sat at the side of them and another larger one stood on the mantelpiece. My dear sister Florence's birthday and I had forgotten! The sister who had taken me and my boys in, given us her home as though it was our own. The sister my boys looked as their replacement mother. How could I forget?' I walked over to her and put my arms around her.

'Oh Flossie, I'm so sorry, I quite forgot it was your birthday!' I said.

'I guess you've had a lot to think about,' she smiled and squeezed my arm. 'Is there any news of the missing girl?'

'No, though we do have a couple of new ideas

that need chasing up.'

'Find her Will; that would be the very best present you could give me.'

'I'd give you that right now if I could, though I fear finding her might not be as happy an ending as we would all like,' I said.

'You think she's…?'

'It seems more likely with every minute that passes,' I said. 'Though we never put it into words, I think we are all preparing ourselves for the worst.'

'With that on your plate, is it any wonder that you forget your sister's birthday,' she said, giving me a hug in return. 'You have given me a birthday present every day. Your boys are a joy and being allowed to at least pretend to be their mother has been a constant pleasure. I'm only sorry that they came to me because you lost your lovely Alice,' she said and burst into tears. I hugged her, crushed her to me as my own tears began to fall. Henry got up from his easy chair and put his arms around us both. 'I think I'd better put the kettle on!' he said, shaking his head.

I finally got around to reading the report about my car as I sat in bed that night. Basically, it was still in good condition, a fact I think I already knew. There was a slight problem on one of the steering joints, not dangerous but in need of replacement in the near future. All of the tyres were showing signs of age cracking; and the report suggested that they were the original ones and since *I* had never replaced them I guessed that was probably the case. A couple of loose spokes in the front wheels also needed attention, but that would be done as a matter of course, when the tyres were replaced. I was given the option of having each thing done in turn at my convenience, or I could leave the car with them to fit in the jobs to suit their other work and have the Rover on loan for as long as it took. The prices quoted looked very fair either way so I thought I'd have a word with Henry the next morning to see what he thought.

'I know you love the Hornet and this report says it's basically sound. It just needs a bit of service. Your decision of course but you can't afford a *new* car and buying a second hand one could just be buying someone else's trouble, Will!' Henry said as we sat over breakfast.

15

Harry Sumpter woke about the same time as a very coal blackened Thomas Norton was brought into the station. Since DS Whittington and DC Harrington had been in charge of the Black Shirt event, the DI asked them to carry out the initial arrest procedures on the hapless miner.

A very sullen Harry Sumpter awaited us in number two interview room as the DI, DC Parsons and I entered the room.

'Good morning Mr Sumpter,' the DI said.

'Is it?' Sumpter snapped, clearly wishing he hadn't since he grasped his forehead with a groan.

'I think you know the three of us but I'll re-introduce ourselves if you prefer!'

'I know who you are! What do you want now?'

'I think you've not been strictly honest with us Mr Sumpter I think you've been withholding vital information,' the DI glared.

'Like what?' Sumpter asked in a somewhat quieter manner.

'Like you didn't tell us that you no longer owned your barge.'

'Oh, that?'

'Yes, that! You also failed to tell us that the new owner was assisting you with the day-to-day workings of the boat,' the DI said, raising his eyebrows.

'Assisting with the bloody working, that would have been good. Along for a free ride more like the swindling bastard!'

'What's his name and how did he come to own

your boat?'

'Maurice Barber; beat me in a game of cards that I swear was rigged. Got me drunk one night and like a fool I kept raising the stakes, till all I had with any chance of clearing what I owed 'im was the "Wanderer"; swindling bastard!' Sumpter moaned.

'What can you tell me about him?'

'That 'e's a swindling bastard!'

The DI nodded to me to take over.

'You already said that. Where can we find him?' I asked.

''E's a bit of a drifter, been about for years on and off. On the boats, workin' supposedly, for one then another; never lasts all that long, idle sod soon gets the push. Met 'im this last time in Nottingham, more's the pity.'

'That's when he won your boat?'

'I'm not daft enough to play cards with 'im in the normal way but I was already in the school when he replaced a chap who dropped out!'

'A card school?'

'Yes, one by one the others dropped out till it was just me an' 'im. I was deep in it to 'im by then, an' that's a fact. Then 'e suggests the boat to clear me debts. Like a bloody idiot I agreed.'

'How did you feel when you lost?'

'How did I feel? How the bloody hell do you think I felt? The Wanderer's my life; all my memories are on her, my missus, my little gel,' he said, shaking his head.

'What can you tell us about the missing girl, Jenny Parminter?' Ellen asked when the DI nodded at her.

'He snatched her, from under the bridge. She was feedin' the ducks, like you said. It's sheltered under there yer see, though it wasn't raining all that bad at the time. Took her down into the cabin, kickin' she was but 'e 'ad 'is 'and over 'er mouth!'

'What did you do about it?'

'Keep yer mouth shut 'e says or I'll sell your silly bloody boat to someone who won't give a damn about you and through you on the canal bank!'

'So that is why you kept quiet?'

'Mm!'

'***Even though a young girl had been abducted?***' Ellen yelled.

'I'm not proud of it; don't think I'm proud of it! 'E 'ad me with me boat, didn't 'e?'

'Then what?' the DI asked.

'I think 'e must 'ave knocked 'er out or given 'er somethin' cos five or six minutes later 'e come up on deck and looks around to see if there's anyone knockin' about on the towpath, then 'e chucks 'er school bag in the bushes!'

'That's why you came up with the story about the chap you saw coming down the steps at the London Road Bridge?'

'Like you said, he was already on the path feedin' the ducks. I made the bit up about 'im comin' down the steps.'

'If he was already on the towpath you must have seen his shoelaces then, why didn't you mention them when we first questioned you?'

'I'd forgotten them until just as we were movin' again at Swarkstone. I thought I'd ring up and add a bit more to this bloke's description; muddy the water a bit, see!'

'You weren't worried about this little girl, Mr Sumpter?'

'Of course I was, but 'e tells me to keep me mouth shut or 'e'll sell the boat to somebody who'll want me off! That boat's me life, all me memories; know what I mean?'

'So what happened after he'd thrown the satchel in the bushes?' I asked.

'Barber gets me to pull the boat into the side of

the canal opposite the tow path and gets off with the girl over his shoulder, like firemen carry somebody. He disappeared into the bushes, that's the last I seen of him, an' good riddance!'

'And the girl: *how* was she?' Ellen asked.

'Sort of limp, like; out for the count I'd say?'

'And that didn't bother you?'

'It all happened so quick; he's a nasty piece of work is Maurice Barber. I did as I was told!'

'Even though, this young girl might be in great danger?'

'Do yer think I'm 'appy about that? I just didn't know what to do.'

'When we spoke to you at Swarkstone, and at Audlem, you denied all knowledge of the girl. Are you saying that was because Barber threatened to sell your boat and throw you on the canal bank?' ask the DI.

'Yes... bloody hell what have I done!' Sumpter said holding his head in his hands.

'Now, tell me everything you know about Maurice Barber, and I mean everything before I charge you with aiding and abetting child abduction and wasting police time,' the DI shouted more angry than I'd ever seen him before.

'Oh, bloody hell. I'll tell you all I can but it's not much; I've always steered as far away from him as I could. He was only with me on the boat for two days, I won't say helping 'cos my little gel, God rest her little soul, was ten times the use that he was. He's a bit taller than me, runnin' to fat. As regards his strength and willingness to work, my dear lass could have worked him under the table; aye and my young 'n God rest their souls!'

'How tall are you Mr Sumpter?' the DI asked.

'About five foot nine I think!'

'Let's check you against the wall; stand over there would you please,' the DI said pointing to the measure painted on the wall.

Harry had had his boots removed and been given a cheap pair of canvas pumps by the custody officer. Harry got up and stood against the wall, and Ellen recorded his height.

'Five-nine and a half sir, say five-nine without his pumps!'

'Thank you, if Maurice Barber is a bit taller than you, we'll say he's just under six feet tall, would that be about right, sir?' asked the DI.

'About that I'd say!'

'Carry on with your description, Mr Sumpter,' the DI said, indicating him to sit again.

'Thick hair, mousey, going grey at the sides.'

'What do you mean by mousey?' asked Ellen.

'A sort of grey-brown and like they say, salt and pepper, greying over his ears. His sort of colour...' he said pointing at me. '...but, more grey!'

Ellen placed a hand over her mouth to stifle a giggle as she looked at me.

'His eyes are a sort of light blue, with black flecks in them. I don't normally look at *men's* eyes that close but that day as I dropped him off he pushed his face close to mine and said malicious like, and said, "You seen nothin' remember." I seen 'em then!'

'Facially, what does he look like?' asked the DI.

'Ugly bugger, wi' a double chin. Reckons he used to be quite an athlete in his day, but I'd take that wi' a pinch o' salt. Fat face wi' a snub nose a bit like a pig. Wears them thick glasses, like the bottoms of a pair o' bottles; that's what made 'is eyes stand out that day!'

'Anything else, Mr Sumpter?' Ellen asked.

'Mm, 'e talks like Brummy; like that copper that brought m' tea!'

'You've no idea where he is or where he has taken the girl?'

'No!'

'Where exactly did you let him off your boat?' the DI asked.

228

'There's a tumble-down old cottage on t'other side from the towpath, about a mile past the London Road Bridge, I dropped him near there, suppose he might have taken her there!'

'The uniform lads will have searched there I guess, sir. It should have been searched the day that Harrington and I found Jenny's school bag. The day you fell off the fire escape, sir,' I said.

'Thanks for reminding me, Dexter, I fear I'd almost forgotten. This cottage Mr Sumpter; what can you tell me about it?'

'It's the other side of the canal, not the towpath side if yer get me.'

'So how do you get to it?'

'I don't know. I suppose it must be on a path of its own! But like I said, it's all falling down.'

'Fetch the maps Ellen, let's see if we can sort this out.'

'Right, sir,' she said and headed for the front desk.

'What else can you tell us about Maurice Barber or the cottage?' the DI asked.

'Can't think of anythin' else!'

'Take Mr Sumpter back to the cells, please Dexter.'

'Right, sir. Come on Mr Sumpter let's get you back in your plush little suite,' I sneered. I took him along the passage and handed him to one of the lads behind the counter, then followed a few steps behind Ellen back to the office; an unsettling experience in the nicest sort of way!

'How is the ankle, sir?' I asked a moment or two later, to bring my mind back to business.

'Itching like bloody hell and I can't get down the plaster to scratch it, but they tell me that's a good sign that things are on the mend,' he shrugged.

'Glad to hear it, sir!' I said and Ellen nodded.

229

'The cottage *is* the other side of the canal, sir. It seems to have a track down to it,' Ellen said pointing to the map. 'It runs from the bridge to the cottage, sir.'

'The London Road Bridge?'

'Yes, sir.'

'So it's got no canal access?'

'Can't really tell, sir, but the towpath is only shown on the other side. It might have access to the water but not along the canal, as far as the map shows.'

'Right! Both of you, go and take a look, see if Jenny is there, or has been there and find out where the track goes after the cottage,' the DI said, pointing to the fact that the track disappeared off the map. 'I'd better go and see how the others are getting on with our miner.'

'Right, sir.'

As we settled ourselves in the Hornet, Ellen said, 'Well, did you like what you saw?' and smiled.

'Mm… sorry I'm not with you,' I said.

'Come off it, Will. I could feel your eyes on my backside like red hot pokers,' she grinned.
She was wearing a well-tailored skirt and it was flattering to say the least.

'Wow, how do I answer that? I find you very attractive and I admit I did rather like… er… the cut of your jib,' I said with an embarrassed little chuckle.

'Well that's a new way of putting it… I find you attractive too, Will!' she said and gently touched my hand for a moment as I released the handbrake.

So there it was. We had a mutual admiration; where should it go from there? Diana Penworthy had declined my offer of marriage, though she wanted to remain a friend. I thought Ellen had made a pass at me and it felt rather nice. Life suddenly seemed both simple and extremely complicated at exactly the same time!

The cottage wasn't exactly as Sumpter had described.

'Seen from this side the place looks reasonably

habitable,' Ellen pointed out as we stopped on the narrow overgrown track outside. It was true, from the canal the place was a wreck but from here the roof was intact and the windows and doors looked serviceable. At the side of the cottage was a small piece of ground where a car had been kept, and from the tyre tracks, had recently been driven away. The front door was unlocked and I called out as we opened it,

'Hello! Police, is anyone there?'

I called a second time without a reply so we entered. The place seemed dry but smelt a bit fusty. Remains of several, rather basic, meals were in the sink and across a table. There had clearly been a couple of days of occupation if not more. But now, the place was empty, and whatever it might tell us was down to us to find out. We both jumped as a plate crashed to the floor and a little furry something, leapt from the makeshift draining board and scurried off into a corner disappearing among a pile of old newspapers.

The place had an upstairs or attic room, though we discounted it from having been used in the recent past since the open wooden stairs, really only a sturdy ladder, had several rungs missing. Downstairs there were two habitable rooms; the one we had entered into, a sort of living room cum kitchen, and a small area off to the left with a single metal bedstead, with a chamber pot under the bed, which had been recently used, emptied, but not cleaned. A small ottoman style chest sat at the foot of the bed. Ellen opened it with a little gasp.

Fearing the worst I went over to peer at the inside. Thankfully, it did not contain the missing child's body! It did however contain clothes; child size clothes. Gently Ellen lifted them out and spread them on the bed. I had read the description of the clothes Jenny had been wearing on the day she disappeared enough times to realise that these were what we had found!

'We know she has been here. I think we need to call in the finger-print boys from county,' I suggested, knowing that there would be the usual wait for them to fit us in.

'I'll stay here, Will, make sure no-one touches anything till you get back,' Ellen said.

The closest phone was back along the track at the Bridge Inn, where we had parked on the day we stopped to look at the steps to the towpath. Not wanting to destroy any evidence that might exist where the other car had been parked I drove further up the lane and turned, with some difficulty, in a field gateway. I rang the station from the pub, and was told that the DI was still in the interview with the miner. I asked to talk to him and a few seconds later, he came on the line and agreed to arrange the fingerprint mob from county.

'Stay at the cottage, I'll get a uniformed officer to take over as soon as I can,' the DI said.
I thanked him and went back to the cottage.

As things turned out, although we were replaced at the cottage by a PC Millar within the hour, the fingerprint boys wouldn't be available that day. We made our way back to the station, leaving PC Millar to his lonely vigil, no doubt to be replaced at some point.

'A penny for them, Will,' Ellen said, as we got under way.

'Sorry?'

'A penny for your thoughts; you are clearly troubled by something!'

'Mm, I don't know where to start.'

'About me, you mean?'

'Us… Yes!' I agreed.

'Has our relationship changed *so* much? We're still work colleagues but now, I think, we are friends as well. *What's* the problem, Will?' she asked.

'I'd like it to be more than that, but I've a lady already. A lady my boys like a lot!' I admitted.

'I see, sorry I didn't know. Look, forget I said anything,' she said turning away, clearly embarrassed.

'It's not that simple. I asked her to marry me a

few days ago and she turned me down!'

'I see!' she said, though it was clear that she didn't. 'Can I ask why?'

'She's a music teacher and wants to carry on with that. Her heart's in that rather than me, at least I guess that's the reason,' I said.

'I see,' she said again. 'So, where do we go from here? *I'd* like us to be more than just friends as well!'

'I'm damned if *I* know,' I admitted.

'You like her a lot don't you?'

'Yes, but I suppose it's the way my boys react to her.'

'You were really after a mother for them!' she turned to me and raised her eyebrows questioningly.

'I suppose so.'

'Do you still want to work with me?'

'God, yes! Why wouldn't I?' I asked.

'I just thought I'm an unnecessary complication in your life. I'll refuse the CID job if that makes life easier for you!' she said biting her lower lip.

'Please don't do that. You're a natural; you'll go a long way!'

'Let's just step back from this for little while; see how we feel in a few weeks!' she suggested and leaned over and kissed my cheek, then wiped a little lipstick smudge away with her hankie.

I was sure where I'd still be!

On arriving back in the office, DS Whittington put us in the picture with regard to the arrest of the miner.

Thomas Norton, accused of assaulting PC Drummond at the rally was provided with a duty solicitor to advise him. It seems that he had made a statement at about the time we were leaving the cottage. In it he admitted hitting PC Drummond with a cudgel captured from a Black Shirt. Norton, had been arrested by another officer, at the time of the incident. It had happened in the heat of the moment and Norton had apologised to Drummond as soon as he had regained consciousness. PC Drummond had accepted his apology and had arranged to have him released. He stated that he had not gone to the rally with any intention of causing trouble and like all of his mates had gone unarmed. "They searched us at the door before we were allowed in," he had pointed out. He stated that if his actions had caused the death of PC Drummond he was deeply sorry.

The DI had him taken to a cell and had gone to ask the Assistant Chief Constable how he wished to proceed with this unfortunate case.

'I have left it in the hands of the ACC! He's taking it to the Crown Prosecution Service to get advice on how to take it forward. I'm personally a bit loathe to push for murder, I don't think for one minute that there was any intention to assault PC Drummond. I think like the chap said, it was in the heat of the moment, but it's out of my hands now!' the DI said. Then continued, 'So… are you both sure that Jenny has been kept at the cottage?'

'Yes, sir,' we both agreed.

'The clothes we found were Jenny's without a doubt and there is evidence of a couple of days habitation at least, and probably considerably more,' Ellen stated.

'The more I hear of this case the less I like it. We need to trace this chap Maurice Barber as soon as possible. He's undoubtedly the key to all of this but where the hell is he and where's Jenny?'

'I wonder if the cottage belongs to him; should I try to find out, sir?' Ellen asked.

'Yes! Do that please, Ellen. I assume you went to see PC Drummond's wife last night?'

'Yes, sir. She's much as you'd expect; still deeply in shock. Her mother and sister were there helping with the children and they made me feel a bit like a representative of the enemy. I said my bit and didn't stay all that long, sir. It's never easy in that sort of situation, but I really was uncomfortable!'

'I've been in that situation myself, Ellen; it's not, as you say, an easy one. Perhaps the Chief Constable's visit didn't... help all that much. I guess he would have been very...'

'Official, sir?' I suggested.

'Mm!' he sighed.

'I told her if she needed anything to be in touch. "My bloody husband back you silly cow." she said and she burst into tears, sir!' Ellen said, her own eyes needing the application of her hankie.

'Don't take that personally, Ellen; it was just the grief talking,' the DI said. 'It's totally understandable, she needed someone to hit out at and you just happened to be there.'

'I know, sir, I just felt so bloody useless.'

'Mm...

'Find out about the owner of that cottage as soon as you feel able,' the DI said gently touching her wrist.

'I'm all right, sir; I'll do it now,' she said.

Tuesday the first of July started as a beautiful day. I was awakened by the sun streaming through a slight gap in my bedroom curtains. A blue sky with the merest wisps of clouds turned vivid orange by the rising sun seemed to herald an amazing day. It was clear that the dawn chorus had been in full swing for some time, a blackbird close by was making an especially good job of wakening the world. I could hear the boys quietly talking and giggling together, and slipping my dressing gown on I tiptoed to their room not wanting to wake Flossie and Henry.

'Good morning you pair!' I whispered.

'Morning Daddy!' they said together.

'What were you giggling at?' I asked.

'Last night Uncle Henry said a naughty word!' George said, and giggled again.

'Perhaps he didn't know you could hear.'

'He said it when he had put the phone down,' Will said.

'He said "Oh, BUGGER" and went outside to his car and drived away,' George said, and they both giggled again.

'Sometimes when grown-ups are very angry or upset, they say things they don't mean. I think we should keep that as our secret. Uncle Henry is a very nice and kind man; something must have really upset him to make him say that. I don't want to hear you two say it again,' I said holding up a warning finger.

'Sorry Daddy,' they both said, 'but that's what he said.'

'It's only just gone five o'clock so snuggle down and go to sleep for a bit longer!'
They settled down and as I sat on my bed wondering whether to try to do the same I could hear them quietly giggling and shushing one another. I had to smile and shake my head. Oh Alice, you're missing so much.

The fingerprint crew had started at the cottage a little after eight o'clock and found some useable prints; those of an adult and also of a child. A glass on the little bedside table showed traces of the last drink the girl had. It had been taken away to be analysed by a chemist in Matlock who regularly carried out tests like this for the police.

Ellen had worked her usual magic and had somehow come up with the fact that the cottage had belonged to one Clarence Barber, Maurice Barber's father.

'I remember a Clarence Barber when I was just a bobby just after the war. I can see his face as plain as plain, but not the reason why I remember him. I don't think he was ever arrested or in real trouble but something rings a bell… I bet there are dozens of Clarence Barbers out there so it's quite possibly someone else,' the DI said.

'It's a shame we haven't got a picture of Barber, something the uniformed lads could carry with them,' I said.

'Thank you for telling us the bloody obvious Dexter,' the DI snapped.

'Could we get a local artist to *draw* him from Sumpter's description, sir?' Ellen suggested; an equally obvious suggestion, yet none of us had thought of it.

'Got anyone in mind?'

'Not really sir, it just occurred to me.'

'Why don't we see if Pete Warrell, on the Argus knows of anyone?' DS Whittington asked.

'That's not a bad idea, sir! We could let the Argus have an exclusive to print the picture and say we need to talk to him in connection with the missing girl,' DS Harrington added.

'Mm! Ellen, check if the Assistant Chief is in, I'll see if I can hop over and get his approval on this. Good thinking you lot… I might make coppers of you yet!' he grinned.

The DI returned a few minutes later with the Chief Constable's approval to go ahead.

'The Chief has had a word with Pete Warrell and made arrangements for one of their artists to come over and sit with Sumpter and draw a likeness from his description. Pete agreed to have the chap here within the hour!' the DI said as he slumped back in his seat with a little grimace of pain and tried to scratch under his plaster.

It was in fact much sooner than that. The artist was lead through to us in less than half an hour, then taken to number one interview room and introduced to Harry Sumpter. The DI asked me to sit in with them to assist with anything they might need.

'Can you describe the man in as much detail as possible please Mr Sumpter?' Tommy Darton, the artist, asked.

Harry repeated the description he had given to

us and the artist listened, then drew a quick sketch on a pad and showed it to Sumpter.

'Not bad, but the ears don't stick out enough. And the lips are not puffy enough.'

The artist carefully erased those bits and amended the drawing, and again showed it to Sumpter.

'That's better! The mouth is still wrong though, it needs to be a bit smaller, not so wide if yer get me. Not a lot but sort of mean and sullen like,' Sumpter added,

Again, the artist did some adjustments and showed it to Harry.

'His nose is about right but it needs to be a bit wider, an' there's somat wrong with his eyes. They're a bit closer together than you've got 'em. 'Is eyebrows aren't as bushy as you've done 'em!' Sumpter commented. 'He wears heavy glasses.

Again amendments were carried out and Harry shown the result.

'Bloody 'ell; that's 'im! That's Maurice Barber to a tee,' he chuckled.

'Let me re-draw it to get rid of the messy lines and see if you're still happy with it,' Tommy said, tearing the first sheet off his pad and placing it on the table as a guide.

The artist turned out to be very much a cartoonist, exaggerating Barber's features, yet capturing in a very few lines a picture that not only created a face but gave an impression of his personality and character, probably better than a photograph could have done.

'His eyes are a bit baggier than you've drawn 'em but other than that it's right.'

'Like that?' Tommy suggested after a few more strokes of his pencil.

'Aye that's it... E's an ugly bugger, aint 'e?'

'No film star, that's for sure. Thank you Mr Sumpter,' the artist said.

'Thank you Mr Sumpter, I'll have to put you

back in the cells for a while longer I`m afraid,' I pointed out.

'Aye, I know. Yer couldn't rustle-up a cup o' tea could yer lad? I'm dyin' o' thirst, it's as 'ot an' dry as a bloody desert in there!'

'I'll see if I can arrange that,' I said.

'I hope that helps to find yon lass in good 'ealth! I keep wantin' to tear me 'air out for bein' so bloody stupid,' he said as I turned the key to the door.

'The drawing should be a great help,' I said.

'Pray God, she's all right!' he said as I looked through the little spyhole in the cell door.

'The drawing's done, and it's pretty good. The artist has gone back to the paper, promising fifty copies for us early this afternoon, sir,' I said to the DI as I sat down.

'Don't sit down Dexter, put the kettle on.'

'Right sir. Is it okay if I take one down for Sumpter, sir?'

'CID *do not* provide room service to the cells Dexter, however since the chap has been helpful, you can arrange for the uniform lads to do it.'

'I'll do that, sir; I've got to take the maps back!' Ellen said.

'Mm, okay. Check to see if we've a map that covers where the track goes after the cottage,' the DI nodded.

'If we haven't, I've got some maps of most of Derbyshire in the car,' I offered.

'Nip and get 'em anyway, Dexter. They're likely to be more up to date than any the force has got!'

'Right.'

We arrived back at the office from our errands at much the same time, and this time Ellen indicated that I should go down the passage first. Half way along she said "Mm" and pinched my bottom with a little giggle. Phew! That was a surprise I shan't forget.

My maps were of a smaller scale than the ones behind the counter, but combining the information from the extra sheet Ellen had found and that on my maps we were able to trace the track beyond Barber's cottage and follow it as far as Blackmills Moor, though the last three or four miles were shown only as a footpath. Apart from two isolated cottages a mile or so from Barber's place there were no signs of habitation further on towards the moor.

'Better check those two places out, Dexter,' the DI said.

'Yes, sir.'

'Ellen, see if you can find out anything else about Clarence Barber, Maurice's dad. There's something rolling around my brain about him and it just won't surface. My copper's nose tells me it's important but just how I've no idea.'

'Right, sir.'

The track beyond Barber's cottage became more and more overgrown and I eventually decided to stop the car at a place I could turn around fairly easily, then walked the rest of the way. From over two hundred yards away, it was obvious that the cottages were beyond use, in each case the only bit that remained standing was one gable end wall and that was only because of the extra support given by a chimney. The rest was little more than an outline of the walls. At a guess, the rest of the stonework had been robbed for other, newer work somewhere. I'd promised the DI that I'd investigate them and so I walked into each one in turn just in case they provided any further information. In the second ruin, there was what must have been an oven of some sort at the side of what was left of a fireplace. The metal door to the oven was rusty, but swung open surprisingly easily, showing signs that the hinges had been lightly oiled. Inside were two little Egyptian style models, cheap, cast replicas of the Sphinx and the mask of the young Tutan-

240

khamun. Howard Carter, the Egyptologist, had discovered his tomb about twelve years before, long after the cottages had gone out of use, so what were they doing there, I wondered. I couldn't see how they could possibly have anything to do with our case, but I decided to take them back to the station just in case. Carrying them carefully in my handkerchief, so as not to damage any fingerprints there might be, I placed them on the back seat of the Hornet and headed back.

As I entered the office, Ellen was just finishing saying something to the DI:

'...from Woolworth's shop in the High Street, sir.'

'That's it! I remember now; we were sure he'd nicked the stuff but we never did find it. He was a queer old sod, used to reckon he was the reincarnation of... er?'

'Tutankhamun, sir?' I suggested.

'Ye... how the bloody hell did you know that?'

'Are these what you were looking for?' I asked holding up my prize finds. His open mouth was all the answer I needed.

'Where the hell did you find them? We looked high and low for them at the time.'

I explained how I had come to discover them.

'If the oven door was that easily opened, do you think that Maurice was aware where they were and... I don't know, is making use of them in some way?' the DI asked.

'Perhaps carrying on the Egyptian thing, sir?' I suggested.

'In those days it was quite common for a Pharaoh to marry girls of ten or eleven, or at least that's what historians think now that they are beginning to read and understand the hieroglyphs, sir,' Ellen said.

'Are we starting to think that Maurice Barber is carrying on the practices that his father started?'

'Perhaps, taking them on to new heights! You

don't think he was going to marry Jenny do you, sir?' Ellen suggested with a shudder.

'Whatever the answer it looks increasingly like the poor kid's not going to come out of this unscathed,' the DI nodded.

'How far did his Father go then, sir?' I asked.

'Clarence was the head of a little group they worshiped him as the leader; like I said he claimed to be the reincarnation of the Tooting-common bloke! Nutty as a bloody fruit cake; but as far as we know he never harmed anybody!' the DI said, shaking his head.

As good as his word, a small stack of the drawings of Barber jnr. was handed in at the front desk, a little after four-thirty, by a young messenger boy. They were about half the size of a postcard and had been done on a stiff photo-paper; just the right size to slip into a PC's notebook. Someone must have done their homework since there was a copy for every police officer, plus a couple of large copies for notice boards at the front desk and in our office. For once the Argus had done us proud; Pete Warrell was rewarded with an interview with the Assistant Chief Constable had given as much as we wanted the public to know in an exclusive briefing on the state of the investigation into the disappearance of little Jenny Parminter. That night's paper carried a front page story together with a photo of Jenny, supplied by her parents, and the drawing of Maurice Barber.

Readers are no doubt aware that eleven year old Jennifer Parminter went missing on the 8th of June; over four weeks ago. Police urgently need to talk to this man believed to be Maurice Barber who was seen in the vicinity at the time of Jennifer's disappearance. Anyone with information as to his whereabouts or that of the girl

are requested to contact Crammingdon CID at Whitecross Yard on Crammingdon 3399 or the Advertiser office on Crammingdon 3838. I'm sure our readers will join with me when I hope this new police lead will bring Jenny back safe and sound to her parents...

Pete Warrell Crime correspondent   (Turn to page 2)

From the moment the article appeared on the street, there was an almost non-stop flood of phone calls all claiming to have information regarding Maurice Barber. Much of it related to months ago and was of no or very little use. One caller did seem to have recent information and the DI asked me to follow it up on my way home.

'Goin' back to me great-grandad's day we was traveller's; Gypsies yer know! Grandad sold the caravan an' bought a boat when canals were makin' money. He used the 'orse to pull it along. In them days it was easy work, see! The Barbers had a barge but the old man sold it when it became clear that Maurice was about as much use as a cardboard fryin' pan. The old man bought an old cottage by the canal and Maurice worked, and I use the word worked in its loosest sense, on the canal boats when folk would 'ave 'im. Worked for me for a while the lazy, useless bugger! That was when I still 'ad a boat,' said Norris Wheeler, the man I had come to see.

'My DI seems to think that Clarence Barber had an unusual hobby!' I suggested, resisting leading the man with great difficulty.

'Oh, that! When what's-'is-name found that tomb in Egypt, Clarence, Maurice's dad, took to this idea that 'e was the mummies spirit released back to life. Silly old sod! Of course, Maurice was all of a suddin the son of an Egyptian king! 'E played that card pretty well as an excuse not to pull his weight. Reckoned 'avin' 'im

243

on board brought the boat good luck!'

'So Maurice carried on his father's beliefs?' I asked.

'Oh, yer. 'E was always talkin' about 'ow it used to be, the rituals and stuff. 'E 'ad books on it all; spent about ten time more time readin' that rubbish, then ever 'e did 'elpin' with the boat, an that's a fact!'

'Do you think he honestly believed that he was a pharaohs' son?'

'Made 'isself believe it more like! At night 'e'd come up on the deck in a long white nightshirt and chant stuff at the moon; bloody scary that was!'

'What did the other boat owners think of it?' I asked.

'They all used to go down below and leave 'im to it!' he shuddered.

'The DI suggested that Clarence had a bit of a following!' I said.

'Now they *were* a queer lot! The sort of folk who'd follow a muck-cart if you told 'em it was a weddin'! Held court at an old cottage by the canal just up from the bridge on London Road.'

'What did they get out of it?'

'I think 'e offered 'em eternal life; an everlasting life, as a favoured priest of the re-what's-a-named king of Egypt. It all fell apart literally, when one o' the chosen ones fell in the canal an' drowned. Clarence claimed it was because the chap wasn't a true believer but the spell was broke! They all went off to be the next daft thing that drove their fancy. Balmy bloody lot!'

'So Maurice had no other followers?'

'Not while 'e worked for me!'

'Thank you Mr Wheeler, that is most helpful,' I said.

'I'm not done yet; I saw Maurice Barber 'angin' around that old cottage of 'is dad's a couple of days ago. He ducked inside when he spotted me, like he 'oped I 'adn't seen him. It was 'im all right, and in that silly bloody nightshirt, but 'e wasn't on 'is own. There was an old Austin I think it was, its back was to the canal so it was 'ard to tell but this other bloke dropped down in front of it; thought I 'adn't seen 'im!'

'You still run a barge, then Mr Wheeler?'

'No, gone long ago, I was helpin' a mate that day!'

'When was it you saw them exactly?' I asked.

'Let me think; Tuesday was the last day of June, it'd be Monday, I remember seein' 'em on the way from Blacks Boatyard. He'd got a bit o' trouble with is rudder and we went to get it fixed, saw 'em on the way back. Yes Monday 29th.'

'Could you describe this other man?'

'I only seen 'im for 'alf a mo. I reckon 'e 'ad a black suit an' a bowler 'at on, but like I said, he dropped out of sight pretty bloody smartish when 'e seen me.'

'Would you be able to recognise him, if you saw him again?'

'No, I don't think so. Like I say, I on'y seen 'im for a split second.'

'Thank you Mr Wheeler, that's been a great help. I might need to talk to you again.' I said.

'Not for a couple of days you won't, I'm on me way to Durham in the mornin' to see me son!'

'Can you let me know when you get back, please Mr Wheeler?' I asked handing him a card.

'Okay, but I reckon I've told yer all I know.'

I drove home with something buzzing around the back of my brain: something that kept nudging me, telling me that it was important, but what?

The following morning I put the DI in the picture with what I had learned from Mr Wheeler and now we had a likeness of the man we were looking for the whole of the force started again with as much vigour as had been the case on the first day. Around midday, Ellen again proved her value to the team by coming up with the registration number of an elderly Austin saloon, registered to Clarence Barber, believed to now belong to Maurice Barber; presumably the one seen by Mr Wheeler outside the cottage. However, there was a problem; there was no record of a current Road Fund Licence registered in any of the local authorities. The last time the duty was paid was two years before at Derby Vehicle Licencing Office.

'Great work again Ellen,' the DI said.

'Thank you, sir,' she said, and smiled at me.

'I think it's a pretty safe bet that Barber is using his dad's car and we can add that to the information for the men on the ground. Dexter, organise a police box alert and get this new bit of information out to the lads,' the DI continued.

'Right, sir.'

'Ellen, get out all of the statements and reports we've got so far and the pair of us will go through it all over again; see if we've missed something, now that we know a bit more.'

'Right, sir.'

After making sure that all of the foot soldiers and the motor patrols were aware of the car registration, I went back to the office and assisted with reading through the mountain of paperwork that now existed on the case. Unfortunately, nothing new turned up and the DI threw down the sheaf of papers he had been reading through with a shake of his head.

'I don't like the way this case is progressing,' he said, 'we are getting nowhere. Every move we try to make we hit a blank and have to interview witnesses two and three times.'

'Each new bit of information, changes what we think we know and we need to recheck the details again. It's coming together, sir; slowly,' DS Whittington pointed out.

'I know, but I wish it would bloody-well hurry up! This is gettin' us bloody nowhere. It's nearly six o'clock, let's go across to the Barley Mow and sink a couple,' the DI snapped. 'It wouldn't be the first time that a pint of ale has awakened the flagging grey cells.'

The Barley Mow is probably the oldest of the many inns in Crammingdon, built as a stop and over-night resting place for travellers on the road from London to Sheffield, York and Edinburgh. It became a coaching inn in the early 1800's, adding the route to the rapidly growing Manchester, somewhere in the 1850's. It was now just a humble spit and sawdust pub. It wasn't the normal watering place for the force but the landlord brewed his own ales and the DI was rather partial to the chap's draught bitter.

As we walked in a familiar voice shouted to us, it was my old sergeant, the long retired John Bell, and sitting next to him my old pal Bong; 'Aussie Bobby' as Blind Marco used to call him.

'Over here, come and join the discussion,' yelled Bell.

We collected our drinks and went over.

'What are we discussing?' asked the DI as we all settled ourselves at a table in the near deserted pub.

'We've been doing a little bit of investigation off our own bat,' said Bong.

'Now why doesn't that surprise me,' the DI chuckled. 'What happened to you anyway? I thought you'd offered your services days ago,' he added looking at Bong.

'Like you said I offered me services to the Assistant Chief Constable over three weeks ago and was told that he had sufficient manpower and I was dismissed like a naughty school boy. A couple of days later I went back to Manchester with the missus, I was a bit bloody miffed I can tell yer. Then her mother takes bad. I put in for extended leave and back we came. The following morning, by chance I met John in the Market place and we got chatting,' Bong replied.

'I was out doing a bit of shopping with the wife, and walked into this old reprobate so we decided to sink a couple for old times' sake!' John said taking up the story. 'He told me about how he had been sent packing by the ACC and I suggested that he gave me a hand with something I had been looking into.'

During all of this Ellen sat quietly sipping a glass of lemonade.

'You're Ellen Parsons, aren't you?' asked Bell. 'Joseph Parsons granddaughter.'

'Yes, Sergeant!' she smiled.

'Ex-sergeant,' John said, 'so it's just John now.'

'Sorry Ellen, I should have introduced you. Bong, this is our newest recruit to CID, Ellen Parsons, as John said, as of a couple of days ago DC Ellen Parsons.'

'I remember you. You were in the north division,' Bong said and Ellen nodded.

'How come I didn't know about that?' laughed the ex-sergeant. 'My grapevine is not keeping me up to date.'

'It's part of a deal with the Chief Constable, involving one of his golfing mates. I can't really say any more, just that Ellen's appointment only needs the rubber stamp.'

'You can't say any more but we can! Does this deal include a pair of unscrupulous undertakers?' John asked.

'Is that what you've been working on?' I asked.

'Yes.' they both nodded and winked.

'How come you know about that?' the DI asked.

'Mrs Garret, the lady whose brother-in-law found her husband's suit in a shop window, came to me initially and I suggested that she came to see you, Tom,' John said nodding at the DI.

'The deal is a bit complicated but it seems, in the end, that the undertakers will get a smacked wrist and no further action!' the DI said shaking his head.

'Seems like we've wasted our time then Bong. Perhaps what we've found out about Maurice Barber will be of more use?'

248

By now we were talking in whispers as the pub began to fill up.

'Now you're talking, what can you tell us that Ellen hasn't already got for us?'

'Bugger, so you know Maurice Barber has been working for Watson and Marchbank,' Bong said.

'What?' the DI said, and the three of us leaned forward to hear better.

'It seems you *didn't*! Well by chance, because we had been looking into the funeral suits I suppose, we came across the fact that they had sacked one of their staff...'

'Herbert Henchcliffe!' the DI said.

'That's the chap. Well we went to see him. He wouldn't tell us much except what he'd told you about the thefts but that he'd seen the drawing of Maurice Barber in the paper. He said Maurice was one of Watson's big mates and that they were into some queer stuff; worshiping mummies and Egyptian stuff.'

'So Henchcliffe thinks that Watson is into this Egyptian thing?' the DI asked, looking from one to the other.

'Swore on it, Tom!'

'The Chief Constable and his assistant will have gone home long ago so I think we'd better continue this little discussion in the CID office where we are less likely to be overheard, if that's okay with you two?' the DI suggested.

'You reckon Henchcliffe said Barber was involved with the undertaking business, or do you think they were just mates?' I asked as we made our way back to Whitecross Yard at the DI's faltering pace.

'According to Henchcliffe, Barber occasionally used to help with the embalming and as a pallbearer, but he didn't think that there was anything other than the casual employment of a mate with the similar interests,' Bong said, and John agreed.

'I don't like the sound of all this, sir,' Ellen said,

as we settled ourselves in the substitute office.

'I agree, give us your thoughts on this, Ellen,' the DI said.

'Just that the Egyptians were into human sacrifice, sir!' she said with a shudder.

We all nodded.

'I assume at some point you would have brought this information to me?'

'That's why we were in the Barley Mow, trying to decide how best to tell you without the top brass finding out we had been having a little nosey around, then in you three walked!' John chuckled.

'Well thank you lads, I think that in the light of this new development we should have another word with our undertaker friends. Especially since they haven't come forward with information on Barber; they must have seen the front page of the Argus!' the DI said.

The following morning, Wednesday second of July, DS Whittington and I went unannounced to the shop cum reception office of Watson & Marchbank, Undertakers. The young lady who had dealt with the DI and me a few days earlier invited us to take a seat and went off to ask if we could be seen. Suddenly the thing that had been rolling around my brain since I found the Egyptian trinkets in the tumbledown cottage, clicked into place. The reception desk was exactly as I remembered it; the same black satin cover, the little silver reception bell that DS Whittington has just rung to announce our presence, the same maroon silk roses and the same vase. Having looked up a bit of the history of the Howard Carter Egyptian finds in Henry's little library I now recognised the vase as a beautiful china replica of the head of one of the Egyptian Queens, complete with a faithfully reproduced chipped nose.

I nudged the DS but it was unnecessary, his eyes were firmly fixed on the same vase.

'Isn't that King Tooten-something or other?' he

whispered.

'No, I think it was one of his wives, but it's a bit complicated, I think they are still trying to decide who's who and just how it all fits in. It's definitely meant to be Egyptian, though,' I agreed.

'Looks like our pair of off-duty detectives have come up with a new line of enquiry!' the DS whispered as the young lady returned and told us that both Mr Watson and Mr Marchbank would see us now if we cared to come through.

They sat behind what I remembered as being Mr Watson's desk, looking very prim and proper, expecting to send us off with a flea in our ears.

'I consider this nothing less than police harassment!' said Mr Watson, and Marchbank nodded. Then he continued, 'It has already been decided at way above *your* level, that there is no case to answer with regard to the preposterous allegation that we removed and disposed of goods belonging to one of our clients,' and Marchbank smirked.

Strange, as I seemed to remember that they had both admitted as much in written statements, but I held my tongue.

'So I understand, sir. We are here about another, unrelated matter, gentlemen!' the DS smiled.

'Oh!' they both said together and looked at one another.

'Mr Watson, I believe you are acquainted with a Maurice Barber, is that the case, sir?'

'I think I've heard the name, yes,' Watson replied.

'I have it on good authority that he has in fact helped out with certain duties for your company, is that correct, sir?' the DS continued.

'Possibly, I can't remember all the people who have been pallbearers for us!'

'I don't think I mentioned any specific duty, sir, however that is just one that has been suggested, also on

251

occasions, he was involved in the embalming of bodies, sir. Is my belief correct?'

'Ah! Yes, now I think about it, I do seem to remember him. What is the problem Detective Sergeant?'

'I would have thought that the embalming of bodies was a fairly important and specialised job, yet you seem only to know this person vaguely. Is it the normal practice within your company to let casual acquaintances do this sort of work for you?' the DS asked, keeping a straight face.

'I don't think there is any need to be facetious, Detective Sergeant. I have admitted that I know the man. He has on occasions been involved with the company, possibly in the capacity you suggest,' Watson flustered.

'Can you remember when you saw or had dealings with him last, please sir?'

'Months ago, perhaps years!'

'Not on Monday last, sir?' asked the DS and Marchbank gasped.

'Certainly not!' said Watson.

'What about you Mr Marchbank?' the DS asked and Watson glared at Marchbank.

'No… Er… no!' he stuttered.

'I find that hard to believe since we have an eye witness who puts you at a cottage by the canal. A cottage owned by Maurice Barber!' the DS said, rather overstating the facts of the case.

'Say nothing more Frederick, we need to see the Chief Constable about this intrusion,' Watson blustered.

'I think that's a good idea, I'll ring for a motor patrol to take you both to the station and we'll continue this interview there, with the Chief Constable in attendance if you wish! If I might use you telephone please, sir?' the DS suggested picking it up anyway.

'We are just about to set out on an interment; the hearse is ready and the bereaved are no doubt waiting at the deceased's address for the cortege to arrive, Detective Sergeant!'

252

'Very well, Mr Watson, I will expect you both to present yourselves at Whitecross Yard to answer some very important questions,' the DS agreed putting the phone down again. 'What time might that be, sir?'

'We will be there with our solicitor at two thirty,' snapped Watson.

'I look forward to it, good morning sir,' DS Whittington said and nodded to me that we were leaving.

'Do you think we can trust them?' I asked as we got back in the Hornet.

'Oh they'll turn up all right but how much sense we'll get out of 'em with a solicitor there and the Chief at their side, who knows,' he shrugged.

'Is the Chief Constable likely to come to their aid if what we are thinking is true?'

'Go on then, Will, what are we thinking their involvement *is* exactly?' asked the DS.

'Well er... I'm not sure exactly... only that they have failed to come forward and admit knowing a man the police want to talk to.'

'Mm... a bit bloody thin, don't yer think?'

'Perhaps the DI can come up with an angle we can work from,' I suggested.

'Time's ticking away, we need to get back and see if between us we can get a few searching questions put together.'

'Well, the pair won't get a lot of support from the CC; he's at a crime prevention and detection conference in Harrogate today,' the DI grinned.

'They'll have their solicitor with them though, sir,' the DS pointed out.

'What exactly are we suggesting they've done?' Ellen asked.

'From the way Marchbank jumped when I mentioned him having been seen at Barber's cottage, he or possibly both of them are involved in this Egyptian thing; whatever it is!' Whittington said.

'Do you think that Barber has a following after all?' I asked.

'Like his father? Perhaps even some of his father's ex-cronies?' Harrington suggested.

'Speculation of course, but it doesn't seem far from impossible. I wonder if we could find out if there's some sort of secret society, like witchcraft, that type of thing. Ellen you've got a nose for rooting things out, sniff around, see what you can come up with,' the DI nodded.

'Right sir, I think I know where to start. It'll mean a lot of phone calls, sir!'

'Get ringing, Harrington give her a hand. Meantime the three of us will hammer out what attack we intend to make on our undertaker friends,' the DI said.

At two-thirty, the two undertakers turned up with their solicitor; a Mr Goodison, an over-weight, blustering man with a red face. The DI, DS Whittington and I joined them in interview room one, where the desk sergeant had installed them.

'For the benefit of Mr Goodison I will introduce the three of us; I'm Detective Inspector Brierly, this is Detective Sergeant Whittington. He and I will conduct the interview, whilst DC Dexter will take notes!'

'My clients have prepared a statement which I have here; they do not propose to answer any questions and once I have read this statement which I have advised them both to sign in front of you, they request to be allowed to leave in order to attend to important matters at their business,' the solicitor said, with wobbling jowls.

'I'm not sure I can accept that. I will require some very important questions to be answered; if this statement fails to address them I must request your clients to remain and give me adequate replies,' DI Brierly replied.

'As far as I am aware, my clients are not under arrest and have agreed freely to this imposition upon their time. However their statement does seem to be pretty far-reaching and I feel sure it will answer many if not all of your questions, Detective Inspector!'

'Very well, please read it out but I reserve the right to ask about anything that is unclear!'

Goodison looked at the two undertakers with raised eyebrows. Reluctantly they nodded their agreement, so he turned to us and said, 'I wish it to be recorded that my clients have agreed to those terms, though they will of course be guided by me with regard to their answers. With your permission I will now read their joint statement?'

'Go ahead please Mr Goodison!'

'Before I do, I think I should make you aware of certain details. I was called to my clients' premises at eleven-fifteen this morning having been requested, at short notice, to take a statement from them, following the visit of DS Whittington and DC Dexter. Their statement reads –

"Following the visit this morning of DS Whittington and DC Dexter, we discussed the points raised by them and feel we need to address certain issues. This is a joint statement.

1,   *We the undersigned, realised after discussing the matter following the visit this morning of the two police officers, that we do in fact know one Maurice Barber and have indeed employed him on occasions to carry out various tasks with our business, though only on a casual basis*

2,   *The reason that we at first were unable to place him was that he is known to us simply as "Mo".*

3,   *Mr Marchbank did indeed visit Mr Barber at his cottage on Canalside Lane on the morning of Monday twenty-ninth of May, for the purpose of requesting him to assist us with some work later next week.*

4,   *That is the total of our knowledge with regard to Mr Maurice Barber."*

'I shall now ask my clients to sign and date this in front of you, Detective Inspector and beg leave for my clients to return to their lawful business!' Goodison said.

'Just a minute, Maurice Barber's face, together with that of Jenny Parminter was on the front page of the Crammingdon Argus. Are they suggesting that they were unaware that we were looking for him?' the DI asked.

'My clients suggested that you might ask that, having become aware of the news item *after* the visit this morning of DS Whittington and DC Dexter. They both state quite categorically that they never read the Argus newspaper!'

'Mr Marchbank, if your visit to Barber's cottage was as innocent as you suggest, why did you dodge out of sight when you thought you had been seen?' the DI asked.

'I wasn't aware that I did "dodge out of sight", Detective Inspector.'

'I advise no further comment,' Goodison said.

'Mm… Did either of you follow Clarence Barber, Maurice's father, in his Egyptian Worship group?' I asked, with a little wink at the DI.

Goodison answered without even looking at his clients, 'No comment!'

'Are you, either of you, followers of Maurice Barber in his current Egyptian worship group?'

'No comment!'

'You were aware that this group exists, though gentlemen?' the DI added.

'No comment!'

'Gentlemen, as the newspaper article suggested, we are certain that Maurice Barber abducted a young girl, for reasons unknown, but possibly to do with some form of ancient ceremony. Having admitted that you both know this man, yet refuse to give other information regarding your involvement with what seems to be some sort of cult, you leave me with no alternative other than to believe that you were, probably still are, involved with this cult in some way!'

'No comment, Detective Inspector! Now, I believe my clients are free to leave?'

'Yes!' the DI nodded. 'Please sign your statement, such as it is, gentlemen. It could prove useful at some point in the future after all!'

'What exactly do you mean by that, Inspector?' Goodison asked.

'No comment,' the DI smiled.

Back in the CID office, Ellen was on the phone. She nodded as we all sat down and I received a now familiar command.

'Put the bloody kettle on Dexter. That's left a nasty taste in my mouth!' the DI said.

'Right, sir.'

'Well that could have gone better, we don't seem to be any further forward,' DS Whittington complained.

'Will, cast your mind back to Mr Brandon's house; the place like a ranch house,' Ellen said as she put the phone down.

"The Great Gondello's" agent?' I asked.

'Yes. Can you remember, walking around a sort of upstairs balcony looking down on a kind of central display area, a bit like looking down on a museum?'

'Yes, absolutely crammed full of mostly Caribbean tribal art!'

'Mostly, yes, but something else, what was in pride of place right in the middle?' she asked.

I screwed up my eyes and tried to visualise the place and all I could really remember was a display of strange carved masks in a dark wood, possibly ebony, hanging on the wall facing us, among a collection of spears. I was vaguely aware that there was a large white stone carving on the floor in the middle of the display but I couldn't make it take shape in my mind.

'I give up. I noticed something but I can't think what it was,' I admitted.

'A large copy of the Sphinx!' she said.

'Is that true, Dexter?' ask the DI.

'I didn't really look at it, sir! There was so much to look at and other things took my attention in the few seconds before we were ushered into a little side room to wait for Mr Brandon to see us,' I had to admit.

'I did, sir; I'm one hundred percent certain that was what it was,' Ellen stated.

'Just what does it mean?' the DI asked.

'Possibly nothing, sir, but it is another coincidence,' Ellen shrugged.

'Mm. What have you found out about Maurice Barber?'

'It seems he is some sort of Grand Leader of a cult with some of those followers who used to be followers of his father,' she replied.

'How did you find that out?'

'My reporter friend in Leek, he's been looking into a similar cult in his area and Barber appears to be at the centre of it, sir,' she smiled.

'I think we need to sit down tomorrow and make a list of all the goings-on and timings as best we can, to see if anything emerges. Don't sigh like that Harrington. Going over and over the same information until something clicks is all part of the job. We've got to make sense of this one way or the other.'

'Sorry, sir!' Harrington shrugged.

Unbeknown to us at the time, events were unfolding thirty miles away.

The phone rang just as we were about to call it a day and the DI picked it up.

'Nothing to report as yet, I'm afraid, sir……. Yes sir, first thing……. In that case perhaps I should pop across and have a wor……. Very good, sir.'

'The Chief Constable, sir?' Whittington asked, with a big cheesy grin.

'It was, he's been given a dressing-down by Alderman Tippett, and he's now turning the screw on me! I wanted to go over and discuss a thought I've had but it seems he's too busy. "You are the detective in charge DI Brierly, find the paintings and the culprit, and I don't care how you do it!" were his exact words,' the DI said. 'Ellen, arrange a patrol car and a driver for eight o'clock in the morning.'

By midday, the next day the DI was sitting at his desk, his bad leg resting on a chair and his crutches in their now familiar place leaning against the wall.

'I think we can call that a successful end to the case of the missing paintings!' he grinned.

'Have you found them, sir?' asked Whittington.

'No, Ellen did! We roused the household at five past eight, to carry out a search, oh you tell him Ellen. I'd better go and let the Chief know what happened,' he said, his grin a mile wide as I helped him across the yard to the garage.

'You'd better make yourself scarce Dexter, I'm not sure if his nibs is going to like this.'

'Right sir,' I nodded.

By the time I got back to our office, Ellen had told her story and DS Wittington and DC Harrington were chuckling away merrily. Therefore, I suppose I'd better relate it.

The car picked us up, the DI, Ellen and me, as arranged at eight o'clock sharp. On the way to the Mayor's house, the DI told us his thinking and I have to say it seemed like the only logical answer to the problem. At five past eight, the DI had me ringing the bell, which I admit I did a little apprehensively. It was opened by the old manservant who let us in and led us to a room, clearly the library and offered us a seat. Alderman Tippett came blustering in a few minutes later, dressed it an expensive looking blue dressing gown tied together with a gold tasselled cord.

'What is the meaning of this Detective Inspector?' he growled.

'I have been given permission to search the house in the belief that your paintings never left the premises, sir!'

'What! Just what are you suggesting?'

'It seems to me that the thief or thieves removed the paintings from the wall and hid them in the house to collect them at a later date. That seems to me the only answer as to why the household was not awakened, sir!' the DI pointed out.

'And you now propose to search my house, is that it?'

'If only to eliminate my suspicions, yes sir.'

'This is preposterous, Detective Inspector. I shall have words with the Chief Constable this minute,' the man said foaming at the mouth.

'Your privilege of course sir, however the Chief Constable has given me the right to conduct this investigation in whatever way I see fit, sir!'

'Right I'll see about that!' the Alderman said lifting the phone.

'Of course sir, in the meantime I'll organise a search.'

'You will not!'

'I'm sorry sir; I need to eliminate this theory from the enquiry. I'm sure you'll agree, we would all look very silly if the paintings turn up here after we have instigated a full, nationwide investigation, sir,' the DI said.

The DI detailed the driver to search the garage and outbuildings, Ellen the upstairs and sent me to search the ground floor and wine cellar. The cellar, divided into two by a central support wall with a wide doorway between the two parts, showed nothing but a few dusty racks which containing a few small groups of bottles. I quickly dismissed it but as I was climbing the wooden staircase, I noticed a large wooden case, big enough, I thought for the three paintings, but the thing was old and covered in the dust of ages and I discounted it almost as soon as I saw it.

'The man's not in his office, and not expected in until nine-thirty. Neither is he answering his home telephone. Rest assured I will complain in the strongest way possible about this outrage!' the Mayor said and stormed off, no doubt to get dressed.

'Oops, won't expect a Christmas card from him this year,' the DI chuckled.

'Nothing in the cellar, sir,' I said.

'Nothing under the beds and the airing cupboard is too small to take anything of the size we're looking for sir.'

'Is there a trapdoor up into the attic?'

'Yes. But much too small to get a large painting through, sir!'

'Oh bloody hell. If this doesn't turn something up, I'll be back pounding the beat again.'

'On crutches, sir,' Ellen grinned.

'Watch it my girl, you're only here with my say so!'

'Sorry, sir.'

'Okay, search this floor and find me those bloody paintings.'

We split up and I consider I did a thorough search, though it didn't take all that long. The things were too big to hide in a drawer or under a cushion, so it wasn't long before I was joining Ellen back in the library with the DI.

'Nothing, sir,' I said.

'Nor me, sir.' Ellen agreed.

'You've looked everywhere?'

'There's a door that's locked sir, opposite this room across the hall,' Ellen said.

'I seem to remember that it's the music room, sir,' I suggested, as Alderman Tippett entered the room.

'Well, how fruitful has your search been?' he asked, placing his thumbs in his waistcoat pocket and standing as though making a point in the mayoral chamber.

'Nothing as yet, though we can't get into the music room, sir.'

'Well they're not in there are they? The blasted things were taken from there,' Alderman Tippett pointed out.

'Never the less sir; we need to take another look, in case there is something we've missed,' the DI said, clutching at straws.

'There's only the grand piano and five or six chairs, I can't see what you hope to gain from looking again.' the Alderman said, though he seemed very reluctant to open the room.

'If you wouldn't mind, please sir,' the DI pressed.

'Oh, very well,' he said fumbling in his pocket for his keys.

The room was exactly as I remembered it; the grand piano was in the same place more or less in the middle of the window wall, covered with its pale green dustsheet, reaching to about a foot from the floor. The three legs of the piano were visible augmented by the four smaller legs of the piano stool, which was underneath the middle of the instrument. The sofa and armchairs completed the furnishings. The spaces on the wall where the paintings had been grabbed the attention like a sore thumb.

'Satisfied?' the Alderman snapped.

'Yes, thank you, sir,' the DI nodded.

Ellen, like me, had carried her notebook and pencil around in her hand ready to make notes as she carried out her search. As she made to slip it back in her shoulder bag, she dropped the pencil and making a ham-fisted attempt to catch it knocked it under the grand piano. I was the nearest to the instrument and dived to retrieve it, throwing the edge of the dustsheet up onto the top. Alderman Tippett dropped onto one of the chairs, looking decidedly groggy. There nestling on top of the piano stool, were the three paintings, less their frames.

'Oh, dear, you look a little unwell, sir!' the DI said.

'No, no. Just a bit surprised that they must have been there all the time, Inspector,' he said sweating visibly.

'I'd better get the fingerprint boys back again, to see if we can find who's handled them, sir,' the DI suggested.

'Er... no, no. Don't bother, I'm only too pleased that they have been found. Forget all about it, Detective Inspector.'

'If you're sure, sir. Would you mind signing a statement to that effect, sir?' The DI asked with an almost imperceptible wink at us both.

'I'll enjoy informing his insurance company that we've found them!' the DI sniggered as we settled ourselves back in the squad car. 'I think our highly esteemed Alderman was trying to pull a fast one; can't prove it of course. It was lucky you happened to drop your pencil, DC Parsons.'

'*Was it sir!*'

'What, you mean...? Oh, bloody brilliant,' he laughed.

'The Chief Constable has asked me to give him a full report on the Alderman's paintings,' the DI said as we sat with a well-earned cuppa an hour or so later. 'That's no problem, but he's also asked for the same on those suits and how the undertakers are involved. I suspect that's so that it can be quietly filed away and forgotten about. I know you've already told me once but explain it again.'

'It is a bit complicated sir,' I said referring to my notebook. 'Would it be easier to tell how it actually happened rather than the order in which we found things?'

'Yes, do that. Ellen, jot it down,' the DI said as Ellen found paper and pencil.

'About five years ago Arthur Garret bought a suit for his daughter's wedding,' I said. 'The suit, together with two similar ones for his brother and brother-in-law, were made to measure by Thompsons on Crammingdon marketplace.

Arthur Garret died three years ago. On the afternoon before the funeral his wife watched as the coffin was closed and claims her husband was in the suit then.

I took the suit to Thompsons and Mr Thompson confirmed that they had made the suit and from its actual measurements related it to Mr Garret rather than either of the others.'

'He actually stated the suit had been made for Arthur Garret?' the DI asked.

'Yes, sir. His body was supposed to be at the Garret house overnight before the funeral, but the undertakers Watson & Marchbank claimed to be short of transport and Mr Garret's body remained on their premises.'

'Supposedly, that's when the suit was removed!'

'The suit next turns up in Perry's window in Green Lane, Derby. A Mr Tremaine bought the suit for the retirement party of a work colleague. Mr Perry couldn't identify the actual suit due to the vast number they sell every year. However he did state that a chap from "our neck of the woods", meaning Crammingdon, supplied him with three or four suits most months, but that he had to hang them outside in a lean-to at the back of the shop to get rid of the smell of mothballs.'

'Or embalming fluid?'

'Yes, sir. He was able to give me a description of the person, and it closely fits Mr Marchbank.

'When Mr Tremaine died about nine months ago, he had asked to be buried in another suit and told his wife to sell the suit in question. She sold it through E M Chandler of Sadler Gate, Derby and that's where Mr Garret's brother saw it and bought it.'

'Okay, give me all the dates and names and addresses and I'll get it across the Assistant Chief asap. Ah, better still, this looks like a nice little job for you, Ellen!' he chuckled.

'Thank you, sir!'

16

'I see, thank you, I'll arrange that,' DI Brierly said as he put the phone down. The changing expression on his face as the conversation had progressed told us that it was far from good news.

'Bad news, sir?' Ellen asked, and the DI nodded.

'That was Detective Inspector Morton from Buxton CID. The body of a young girl has been found,' the DI said rubbing the worry lines on his forehead.

'Earlier this afternoon a couple of walkers up on Blackmills Moor were making the most of a spell of good weather looking for an ancient stone circle; "the Fallen Stones", does anyone know it?' the DI asked.

'I know it!' DS Whittington said. 'As the name suggests it's a ring of stones that are laid flat and because of the way they are lying, fanning out like a giant clock face, it is thought they were never standing up in the first place. In any case they're not easily seen from a distance. The ground for miles around is a soft peat bog, not a good place to get lost. Unless they knew the area they must have had an Ordnance Survey map and a compass, sir.'

'It seems the girl's body is lying on a flat stone in the middle of the circle!'

'They reached the circle about three-fifteen this afternoon. What they found there had them racing back to the Needle & Yarn Inn where they're staying. They arrived at the inn breathless and worn out just after five o'clock. They used the pub phone to ring the County Police Headquarters in Matlock, who informed Buxton police station,' the DI said, with another rub of his brow.

We sat in stunned silence waiting for him to continue. Ellen turned away, dabbed her eyes and blew her nose.

'Although it should still be reasonably light until about ten o'clock, DI Morton has taken the decision to leave the search until morning because of low-lying cloud, heavy rain and the nature of the land. I think it goes without saying that DI Morton suspects that they had found the body of our missing girl. He thinks it only fitting since the case is ours that we are involved in their search mission tomorrow. They want to start as soon after first light as possible. They'd like us to be at the Needle & Yarn about five in the morning; any volunteers?' the DI asked.

All four hands shot up simultaneously.

'Okay, DS Whittington, DC's Dexter and Parsons, I want the three of you to go, let's show the presence on this one; it's our case after all.

'Why not me, sir?' asked DC Harrington, clearly a bit put out.

'It should be *me* leading our party, but with this bloody leg in plaster there's a limit to what I can do even if I'm here and who knows what else may crop up. I've got to send my most senior officer. I'm going to ask Dexter to use his car, and I think Ellen needs the experience; plus I need someone I can trust here as my right hand man, to cover my limitations. That's you Harrington. As I see it, the best, most effective way to use my team,' said the DI.

'Understood sir,' Harrington said with a little grin.

'Right Dexter, I'll leave it to you to arrange to pick up the other two, meeting at The Needle and Yarn as soon after five as possible in the morning.'

'Okay, sir. Have you both got wet weather walking gear?' I asked Ellen and DS Whittington. They both nodded.

'I reckon it will take us about three-quarters of an hour to get to the pub, so I'll pick you both up here at

267

around four o'clock,' I said and again they both nodded.

'Make sure you're ready for Dexter, please. I don't want us to look bad in front of the county mob!' the DI warned.

'Right, sir,' we all agreed.

It was with a heavy heart that I drove home. Although I think we had all more or less come to the conclusion that Jenny was dead, there had always been that tiny flicker of hope that by some miracle she would be found, somewhere, safe and sound. This news dashed that hope. Jenny was the only girl reported missing in the area, certainly in the last few months; who else could it be?

'Why are you looking sad, Daddy?' asked Will as I walked into the kitchen.

It never ceases to amaze me how perceptive my two boys are.

'Am I?' I asked, forcing myself to cheer up for them.

'We have helped Auntie Flossie bake some cakes for the school picnic,' said George. 'Can you come, Daddy?'

'When is it?' I asked vaguely aware that I had seen a letter from school inviting them as part of the new term intake to their little picnic.

'Tomorrow afternoon, at two o'clock!' George replied, always matter of fact.

'I can't I'm afraid, I've got to keep looking for that little girl!' I sighed.

'Is that why you is sad?' asked Will.

'I think so yes,' I nodded.

George came across to me, squeezed my hand and said, 'I hope you find her tomorrow, Daddy, then you won't be sad anymore.'

I remember thinking that we were almost certain of finding Jenny the next day but not in the way meant by my innocent young boy.

'Thank you George. Come on let's read a story, then time for bed,' I suggested, changing the subject.

'I wish I could take them to the picnic, but we think we've found her,' I told Henry and Flossie once the boys had settled down for the night.

'That doesn't sound good,' Henry said, and Flossie put her hand to her mouth with a little gasp and ran out to the kitchen.

'Two walkers found what they think is the body of a young girl at the ancient stone circle on Blackmills Moor. I'm taking a team up to meet the county lads first thing in the morning.'

'Stone circle; "The Fallen Stones"?' Henry asked.'

'Yes.'

'It may not *really* be all that ancient; rumour has it that it was *found* in the early eighteen-hundreds, and many believe it was actually built about then!' Henry shrugged. 'Personally I think they're probably right; our ancient ancestors would have stood the stones up no matter what the cost in time and labour.'

'DS Whittington has seen them and thinks the same. He reckons all of them point outwards from the centre, not fallen in a random pattern as would almost certainly have happened.

'I agree; I think it was definitely built then!' Henry nodded.

'But for what purpose?' I asked.

'There seems to have been a semi-religious group around that time, sun worshipers or some such thing. Possibly they built it, no-one knows, but again, the popular suggestion, since there were several unexplained disappearances around then, is human sacrifice,' Henry said rubbing his chin.

'From the couple's description the body is on the centre stone, what would have been the altar stone I suppose, meaning that has to be a possibility!' I shuddered.

Flossie returned from the kitchen. 'I'll take the boys to the picnic, I'll see if Diana can come as well shall I?' she asked.

'Er… Yes, okay,' I said. What else could I say?

'What time do you need breakfast in the morning?

'I'll sleep down on the settee tonight. I've got to pick the others up at four o'clock at the station so I'll see to myself!' I replied.

'No you won't, you'll need a good breakfast inside you out on that bleak place. Get off to bed now and at least rest as I doubt you'll get a deal of sleep with this on your mind!'

'She's right!' Henry agreed.

'Rest and the odd snooze is about as good as you can expect. The sooner you start the better rest you'll get. I'll wake you at quarter past three with a bowl of sweet porridge,' Flossie said, and made it an order.
Their suggestion made good sense and I made my way quietly up the stairs so as not to wake the boys. I'm not a great lover of porridge but how could I complain when it was made with love?

I was awakened next morning at just after quarter past three. Flossie was tapping gently on my door so as not to wake the boys in the next room.

'Come on Will, your porridge is ready!'

'Thanks, two minutes, Flossie.'

Washed and shaved at the kitchen sink and with the warm glow of the hot sweet porridge inside me, not to mention a cup of tea and a couple of slices of toast, I set off to Whitecross Yard about twenty to four. My two fellow officers were waiting at the steps in the rear yard, and with simple greetings they piled into the little Hornet and we were on our way.

'I've made us a big pack of bacon sandwiches; I thought we might need something inside us out on a bleak moor,' Ellen said, opening a paper bag and filling the warm little Hornet with the delicious smell of freshly cooked bacon.

'Brilliant! I think we'd better eat them on the way, the county boys will no doubt want to get started as soon as we arrive,' DS Whittington suggested.

'I've just had a massive bowl of porridge and two rounds of toast, but you two get cracking on them,' I said.

'I'll save some for you Will, but they're still warm if you want them now!'

'I'll eat his if he's not hungry,' Whittington nodded..

'No you won't, I'll save them for later,' Ellen laughed.

We kept the conversation, such as it was, as light as possible; silly little topics with no bearing on the mission we were involved in. The first dim wisps of daylight broke as we were about to start on the long and twisting climb to the pub. I dropped the car into second gear at the start of the hill, to give the tiny engine the chance of a clear run to the top without the need of a gear change half way up.

The Needle & Yarn Inn is on the main road to Manchester. A few yards further on the road reaches its highest point and then runs more or less level across the flat boggy summit for a mile or so before dropping down into the next valley via yet another series of double bends. The little Hornet climbed willingly in second gear, even with the three of us and loads of walking boots and wet weather gear. As the road twisted its way up to the lonely public house, we caught occasional glimpses of the police vehicles of the county force, half a mile or so ahead of us. We arrived to find that DI Morton had already knocked on the inn door. It swung open a few seconds later and we all trooped in.

'DI Morton introduced himself and his team of four, DS Waterman, DC Ferguson and two uniform bobbies, Briggs & Jones. DS Whittington did the honours in return and we all shook hands.

'Now gentlemen, I'm sure we are all aware of what our task is this morning?' DI Morton asked.
We all nodded.

'I am aware that if what we find turns out to be the remains of the missing girl, Jenny Parminter, then the initial enquiry was carried out by Crammingdon force. However as senior officer on this part of the enquiry I trust I can have your permission to be in charge of the site and the procedures we might need to adopt?' asked DI Morton.

'As I see it, *we* are here as your guests, and I'm sure DI Brierly would have no objections to your suggestion, sir!' the DS agreed.

'Before we actually go out, I arranged over the phone last night to have a word with Mr & Mrs Hardacre; the young couple who reported the find. They agreed to make themselves available this morning,' DI Morton said.

Two large pub tables had been pushed together to form one long one, surrounded by ten chairs in a cosy room with a roaring coal fire. The young couple sat at one end hand in hand. DI Morton did the introductions once again, and the pair nodded, though whether they actually took the names on board or not seemed doubtful.

'Did you *find* her last night?' John Hardacre asked, looking at DI Morton.

'No, as I said last night, our search is about to start as soon as we've asked you a few questions!' he replied.

'Then it wasn't *your* lights up on the moor last night?' Kathy Hardacre asked.

'You saw lights up on the moor last night?' DI Morton asked.

'Yes!' said John, and Kathy nodded.
'When was this?'

'Neither of us could sleep thinking of it; we stood at the window and said a little prayer for the poor little… Anyway, we can't see the "Fallen Stones" from our window. Although the bog is pretty flat it's a long way to the stones but we could see two or three hurricane lamps swinging about in roughly the right direction. Then they disappeared off in the opposite direction after about half an hour!' John said. 'It was about half-past one this morning!'

'And you assumed it was us?' Morton asked.

'Naturally; I think we assumed you had come up from the other side of the moor,' John Hardacre replied.

'I can assure you it wasn't us! I think we'd better set out right now. Thank you Mr Hardacre, Mrs Hardacre. I'll have to ask you to remain here please until I get back to take a full statement from you,' Morton said.

'We had plans to go into Glossop today, but we can leave it until tomorrow,' Kathy suggested.

'If you'd be kind enough to do that please. Right lads, sorry miss, right team, wet weather gear on please, even though we don't look like getting rained on. Does anyone know the way to the stones?' Morton asked.

'I know it vaguely,' admitted DS Whittington.

'I know it well, sir!' said one of the coppers, PC Briggs I think. There was a plane came down onto the moor about five years ago and I was one of the rescue team, sir.'

'I remember it, constable. Can you take us straight to the "Fallen Stones"?'

'I reckon so, sir.'

'Can I say something?' asked the pub landlord.

'Go ahead,' said DI Morton.

'We often get what people think of as heavy mist up here, though it's more likely to be low lying cloud rolling in over Wales from across the Atlantic. I've just had a look outside and there seems to be a bank rolling in right now. It's a long way off over the Wirral

273

at a guess. It seems to be stationary or very slow moving at the moment, but keep an eye on it. If the wind freshens from the west, it'll be on you in minutes and you won't see a thing. Abandon what you are doing and get back here as soon as the wind changes. If you are caught out by it, stay together as a group! Divide and die... Honest I mean it!'

'Thank you, we'll keep that in mind. Briggs, an eye on the clouds and warn us the moment the wind changes,' Morton said.

'Right, sir,' the copper nodded.

'You can borrow our ex-army compass. From the stones, keep heading south east,' said John Hardacre. 'And don't be tempted to leave the well-trodden path.'

'That's right, keep to where the peats well-trodden and you *should* get back here. Better still, head back before you get misted-in,' the landlord repeated.

'Right, is everyone ready? Let get started,' DI Morton said, taking the hefty little compass from Mrs Hardacre. 'Get the equipment Jones.'

'It's here, sir,' he replied picking up a collapsible stretcher and a small canvas body bag, instantly reminding us all, as though that was necessary, of our sad task.

The path, such as it was, was spongy, wet and extremely difficult to walk on, sapping our strength with every step. Heavy walking boots and wet-weather coats didn't help of course and although the rain kept off, the air was loaded with moisture; within minutes we were soaked and miserable. The cloudbank that the landlord had mentioned still seemed to be in the same place and we began to discount it. The sun was up above the horizon, and had begun to draw the moisture from the water-laden peat up into the air.

It was clear that there had been recent activity at the stone circle. The area around the centre stone was like the goalmouth on a football pitch after a rainy match; so many overlapping footprints as to be evidentially useless. The stone appeared to have been scrubbed clean, so although there was no sign of Jenny, something had happened and the Hardacres seemed certain about what they had found. Since the Hardacres were almost certain that the lights they had seen in the night had gone off across the moor in the opposite direction, DI Morton decided that we should try to follow in that direction rather than return to the Needle & Yarn. The three of us from Crammingdon were far from happy about the idea but went along with it since the PC who had been part of the aircraft rescue was adamant that he knew where to go.

I suppose we had been walking in the new direction for about three or four minutes when DI Morton's Trilby flapped a little at the brim before flying off in a sudden and unannounced gust of wind. Instinctively we all looked at the cloudbank, to find it had advanced towards us and was now only half its original distance and approaching slowly but noticeably. The wind was now quite gentle but persistent from the west.

'I thought you were supposed to be keeping a bloody eye on that lot, constable,' snapped Morton as he stepped off the path to retrieve his hat and went shin deep in soft muddy peat.

'Sorry, sir. It must have moved a lot since I last looked,' said PC Briggs a bit sheepishly.

'That's a bit bloody obvious!' said Morton, trying in vain to wring out the bottom of his right trouser leg, his hat dripping brackish water from the brim as he shook it and returned it to his head.

'Sorry, sir!' the copper repeated.

'Do you think we should head back to the inn, sir? That cloud bank could catch us out anytime,' asked DS Whittington, and Ellen and I stared at the DI.

'How far will our lantern gang have come to get to the stones, Jones?'

'A couple of miles, sir!'

'*A couple of miles,* of this?'

'Yes, sir, perhaps we should turn back, sir.'

'I think we'd better, that bank is really rolling in now, sir,' said Briggs.

'Okay, back to the pub. Double-quick, we don't want to get caught out in that lot,' Morton said, apprehensively.

We set off back and by the time we had reached the stone circle again the cloud was noticeably nearer and threatening to be on us long before we gained the inn.

'Step it out everyone, don't straggle, keep up,' Morton said extracting the compass from his raincoat pocket, flipping open the lid and striding off at a rapid pace.

About halfway back the wind dropped but the air was suddenly laden with moisture, we were breathing mist and it was thickening by the minute. With the dropping of the wind the temperature plummeted and we were soon deep in almost freezing cold mist, then dense fog. Morton was striding out making it difficult for us, fit though we were, to keep up.

'Please slow down, sir; I'm tired and I'm struggling, sir,' Ellen shouted.

'Okay, you have the compass and set the pace,' Morton snapped, tossing the robust little instrument to her.

Not expecting this to happen, she fumbled the catch, and our means of escape disappeared into the mist and the peat, with a soul destroying plop!

'Oh, well done DC Parsons,' he snapped.

'I wasn't expecting you to throw it, sir!' Ellen replied.

There was no point in looking for it, its heavy steel case was instantly lost in the mist and the plop suggested it was already submerged in one of the many deep puddles along the edge of the pathway.

'If we just keep to the path, sir, we should find our way easily enough,' said Briggs.

'Right Parsons, lead the way as fast as you can manage, keeping to the path,' demanded Morton, a little unfairly I thought.

'Yes, sir,' she agreed and set off quite obviously as fast as she could.

If you've ever walked on wet peat in heavy mist you'll know that it's a very hard and tiring slog. The mist plays tricks with sounds, killing them almost stone dead, then amplifying them so that they seem close by. Its swirling nature creates mirages; twice I was sure I had seen the outline of the inn in the distance only to have it melt away in moments. Then we came across a point at which the path had been cut away into a step, down to where peat had been cut in the distant past. We hadn't seen it on the way out and certainly hadn't stepped up it. Somehow we had strayed onto a different path. I suspected that in the confusion of the episode with the compass we had set off again in a wrong direction. We had no alternative but to stop and take stock, decide our next move. Clearly, we were lost in what was now thick fog.

'I suggest we go back to the stones and start again,' Morton said.

'Any idea which way that is, sir?' asked Whittington.

'Back the way we came sergeant, unless you have a better idea?' snapped Morton.

'Perhaps we should stay put and see if it clears, sir?' Ellen suggested.

'Stay put? Is that the best that the cream of Crammingdon can come up with?'

'There doesn't seem to be any way that we can determine where we are, sir. Perhaps staying put makes the most sense,' suggested Whittington.

'When we were rescuing the crew from the wreck site, this happened to us, sir. The chap in charge had been a keen hill walker. He said once you realise you are lost, try not to panic and stay where you are, sir.'

'And what happened?' asked Morton.

'Within half an hour the sun burned through the mist and we could carry on, sir.'

'What are the chances of that happening today?'

'You never know, sir,' said PC Briggs. 'It's only nine o'clock and the sun's still rising!'

'Quiet!' Ellen snapped. 'Listen!'

There was the faint and distant sound of a bell ringing, seeming to come from our right. On the counter of the Needle & Yarn the landlord had a hand-bell, to ring time I suppose, though this far from civilisation I doubted if his customers stayed till closing time and had ever given him much cause to use it.

'I think that must be the landlord's bell, sir,' Ellen said.

Unable to go any further in our present direction because of the step in the peat, we back-tracked along the path we had followed eventually coming to a point where we were sure we had taken a wrong turning. Heading along what we thought was the correct route we now seemed to be heading towards the bell, but after a few seconds it stopped.

'He's listening for our shouts!' Whittington said.

'Ok, all shout "Keep ringing,' said Ellen. 'One… two… three!'

'Keep Ringing!' we all shouted in unison. Almost instantly, the bell began ringing again but now every so often the bell would stop and we gave a responding shout. The sound was still a little way off to our right and the path seemed to be taking us slowly away from it, though still in the general direction.

'This *is* the right way!' said Morton, 'I remember that rusted lunch tin lying by the path!' I had noticed it myself on the way out and added my agreement.

We continued to follow the sound of the bell, which reassuringly got closer or at least seemed to. After what seemed like an age, an age that felt like trying to walk in treacle wearing walking boots, the mist suddenly cleared and the day became bright and sunny. And, there straight in front of us, was the inn, two or three hundred yards away. Kathy Hardacre was ringing the bell. Her husband and the pub landlord were standing by her. It seemed that they had been taking it in turns to shake the heavy little bell, and she stopped ringing and waved as we suddenly became visible.

'There's been a phone call for you, Glossop Police need you to ring them,' the landlord said to DI Morton as we all arrived at the pub. 'Come on in, I've got the kettle on the boil; unless you'd prefer something a little stronger?'

'A nice cup of tea with a dash of whisky for us all, please landlord.'

'Coffee for you again, Miss?' the landlord asked and Ellen nodded.

'That's an experience I don't want to repeat again! Right where's that phone?' Morton asked.

We made ourselves comfortable by the fire and chatted to the Hardacres asking where they had come from and how they were enjoying their holiday, where they had been to, what they had done since they arrived, trying to help them forget what they had seen at the stones. The tea and coffee arrived along with a bottle of Johnnie Walkers and we all settled down to enjoy its warmth. A few seconds later DI Morton came in and sat at the table, one of the PC's poured him a cup of tea and the DI splashed a goodly dollop of Johnnie Walkers into it.

'Glossop police have found a car answering the description you gave us. It was in the railway station yard, unlocked, and the body of a young girl was in the boot. I suggest we all get over there as soon as possible,' said DI Morton. 'I think you'd better ring your boss!' he continued looking at DS Whittington.

'Right… right, I'll do it now,' said the DS.

I looked at Ellen, her face was ashen and her

eyes watery with tears. I think we all knew that at last we had found, our little girl. No doubt she was wondering, as I was, what horrors little Jenny Parminter had endured since her disappearance nearly four weeks ago.

-

Two sturdy police officers stood guard over the old Austin saloon, now presumably run by Maurice Barber. It was a very poor looking specimen, a front wing was tied on with heavy string and it was a close run thing whether there was more rust than paint. Not that that was of any real importance compared with what the boot contained. The body of Jenny Parminter was in remarkably good condition, suggesting she had not been dead for very long, but the unmistakable and overwhelming smell of formaldehyde told a different story. Little Jenny Parminter had been embalmed; a technique that we already knew Maurice Barber was familiar with.

'I'm going to suggest that now we have found the child you've been looking for, that I contact DI Brierly to see how best we can combine our investigations. Does that meet with your approval DS Whittington?' asked DI Morton.

'Yes! Thank you, sir,' the DS replied.

'In the meantime I'll arrange for the removal of the body to the local morgue, after the police photographer has done his stuff. We can make further arrangements once we've decided a plan of action.'

'That certainly seems best, sir.'

'Come with me then; once I finish talking to your DI I'll hand the phone to you, no doubt he will want to sort things out,' DI Morton said and strode off in the direction of the local police station with DS Whittington in close pursuit. The photographer arrived on a motorbike and sidecar with the usual assortment of flash bulbs, tripod and a couple of cameras.

'This won't take long,' was his only comment on the distressing little scene that had stunned us all, even though we knew what to expect.

'Do you notice the smell?' I asked.

'Yes, is it embalming fluid?' Ellen asked.

'Yes, our little girl has been preserved!'

'Do you think Barber did the embalming?' Ellen asked.

'Probably; he probably got the fluid from our pair of undertakers,' I suggested.

'That's speculation, Will!'

'It's the most logical place to get it. Especially since we are pretty sure they are, or at least one of them is, a follower of his little Egyptian cult,' I shrugged.

'I admit they are a strange pair! Struggling to keep the business running; selling funeral suits to make a few bob extra, yet getting involved with Barber and all this lot,' Ellen said shaking her head.

'Right; that's me done, no doubt they'll want me to do some more shots at the morgue!' the photographer said, packing his kit into his sidecar.

'I suspect that the examination will actually be done at Crammingdon Hospital,' I said.

'No skin off my nose mate; so long as I get paid,' he said and kicking the bike into life roared off.

'Callous little sod!' Ellen snapped.

'His way of dealing with it, I guess he sees some sad and disturbing sights like us, he can't afford to become too involved,' I said with a shrug.

I glanced in through the car window, white powder was on the things likely to have been touched by the driver, suggesting that Glossop fingerprint boys had already given it a thorough going over.

'Is it okay for us to have a look inside?' I asked one of the on guard coppers.

'Our boys said they'd done, so I don't see why not,' he said with a nod.

I opened the driver's door and Ellen opened the front passenger door. The car smelt old and fusty with its worn and torn leather seats and the scratched and cracked dashboard. Formaldehyde overpowered what

281

other smells there might have been. On the passenger's side of the dashboard there was a glovebox that had once had a hinged cover. Ellen felt inside and, satisfied that it was empty, shook her head. Finding nothing of interest in the front, we opened the rear doors. The wooden lid to the glovebox had been fingerprinted, then placed in the middle of the back seat, together with two pieces of thin card still stuck to the back of the hinges where they had been used as packers; they were clearly the remains of a business card. Carefully I pealed them from the hinge and placed the two bits one below the other. They had been roughly torn to size and although the characters had been torn the remains clearly read: **tson &** **Marchb** on the upper piece and **undertakers** on the lower. I passed the two bits across to Ellen who looked at them in amazement for a moment or two.

'Watson & Marchbank – undertakers!' she whispered.

It didn't tell us anything we didn't already know, and anyone could have ended up with an undertaker's business card. However it was another piece of evidence, if that was necessary, that they were known to each other. I placed the two fragments of card in my wallet just as the stationmaster stepped out into the yard. We returned his greeting.

'I'm DC William Dexter, and this is DC Ellen Parsons of Crammingdon CID. I wonder if you would mind answering a few questions please, sir?'

'Of course, anything I can do to help in this dreadful business, please ask.'

'Thank you, sir. What can you tell us about this vehicle?' I asked.

'It was here, with its owner, when my ticket clerk opened up this morning at five o'clock. The last train arrived exactly on time at eleven-fifty-eight last night. This is a terminus station and the train stands here overnight; the station was closed until five this morning, opening for the five-fifteen to Manchester and Liverpool. The man bought a ticket to Newton le Willows, and boarded the train. I'm afraid that's all I know,' he said.

'The same train that has stood overnight in your station, sir?'

'That's correct.'

'How can you be sure he bought a ticket to Newton le Willows?' I asked.

'The man was standing by his car when my ticket clerk unlocked the station. He remembers the man; he was the only person in weeks to buy a ticket to Newton, that early in the morning.'

'There was nothing to arouse any suspicions?'

'I live in the Station house across the road. And my staff are aware that they can alert me at any time, if they feel unsure or unhappy about anything. Since this did not happen I assume they considered this person to be just another traveller along with the twenty-one other travellers on that train this morning.'

'I don't know the Manchester area too well; Newton le Willows is beyond Manchester, is that right?' I asked.

'Oh yes; half way to Liverpool!'

'When did you become aware that the vehicle was of interest to us?'

'At eleven-seventeen this morning, Sergeant Jones tapped on my door. He had been alerted by one of his officers that a vehicle answering the description of one they had been asked to look out for, was parked in my station yard!'

'Then what, sir?'

'He asked my permission to break into the car, a formality since it was on my station property. I agreed and asked him if he required me to be an official witness to the event. He thanked me for the offer and together we went out to the car. These two officers were standing guard on it,' he said nodding to the two coppers. 'We found the vehicle to be unlocked and as you know, the boot…!' the Station Master shuddered.

'Thank you, sir! Our senior officer Detective Sergeant Whittington has gone across to the police station to inform our Detective Inspector of events; he might want to ask you some further questions, if that's okay, sir?'

'Of course, in any case, as I said, I live across the road if I'm not here that's where you'll find me!' he said pointing to the house.

I thanked him again and he returned to his duties.

'Jenny's mam and dad… in their hearts they must already know… now they really have got to identify her!' Ellen said, looking away.

'How on earth will they ever come to terms with this?' I asked.

Ellen still had her back to me and after a short pause she said:

'I had a sister, six years older than me. When I was about three, she contracted Meningitis. The doctor told my parents, that Annette needed to rest, no exertion of any kind. It was the school summer holiday, all the local kids were out playing and as soon as Mam's back was turned Annette was out playing with them. At nine, I suppose, she had no idea how seriously ill she was. I can't exactly remember how often she sneaked out, maybe only once or twice, often enough for Mam to be at her wit's end. She collapsed one hot afternoon, out in the street skipping with her friends. By the time Dad got home from work, she was dead. I was only three, like I said but I can see it now. Mam standing blank-faced in bewilderment, Dad cradling my sister in his arms, sobbing, sobbing. I just thought she was asleep; couldn't see what all the fuss was about. I remember the doctor came a little while later, I peeped through a crack in the door and saw her being put in a little polished box and carried away by a man in a black suit and bowler hat. They *never* got over it! Mam had a little school photo, just a little black and white photo, enlarged to almost life size, had it coloured, just tinted, you know; kept it in pride of place on the sideboard and kissed it every night before she went to bed, we all did. I can't honestly say I can remember my sister, only a photo of a happy smiling face with little sticky-up pigtails and freckles,' Ellen said, still turned away.

'Sorry Ellen, I had no idea! That must have been... I don't know!' I stumbled my words; wanting to put an arm around her. As I said it I realised that our true friendship had been cemented at that moment by this very personal insight.

'Water under the bridge, Will!' she said with a sniff. 'I've been thinking more and more about it as the case has gone on, as you can imagine, she said with a sigh. 'Now I suppose I'll have to break the bad news to the Parminters!'

'I'll do it if you prefer,' I offered.

'It's up to the DI to decide, but thanks Will,' she turned and gave me a little smile.

DI Morton returned and told us that he had left DS Whittington on the phone to Whitecross Yard.

'Your DI has agreed to us removing the body from the car, but has asked if we can get it down to Crammingdon. I've agreed to that and it's all arranged. This car is to be moved into the police station yard until such time as we can decide what to do with it,' he said.

'Thank you, sir,' I said just as DS Whittington appeared around the corner.

'DI Brierly has asked me to thank you for your co-operation sir, and has ordered us to return to Crammingdon as soon as possible, if that's okay with you, sir?' Whittingham said.

'I can't see that there's much more any of us can do here, I've already set up a search for Maurice Barber in Manchester and Liverpool, so, until that produces a result we are all stumped. I'll wish you good day and get back to my local duties,' he said.

285

'According to the Station Master, Barber bought a ticket to Newton le Willows, sir,' I pointed out.

'Did he indeed, then I'd better get things reorganised. I'll keep you informed,' he said, and left us.

As we were ready to leave, a large black Rolls Royce hearse pulled up, I remember thinking that at least we were too far away from Crammingdon for it to be from Watson & Marchbank. In the back, visible through the darkened plate glass windows, was a small shiny coffin. Ellen was in the back of the Hornet and I looked at her in the driver's mirror. She was looking at the coffin, wide eyed; I put my foot down and made our escape.

'Something cropped up when I was gathering information about Barber!' Ellen said, a few minutes into our journey.

'Something important?' asked the DS.

'It could suggest where he's headed,' she replied.

'Go on then!'

'The Barber family originally come from what is now Eire, Southern Ireland; two brothers came over to help dig the canals four or five generations back. At some point the Barber family became boat owners, presumably when the canal system was complete, I suppose. The rest we more or less know,' she said.

'Are you suggesting that he could be headed for Ireland?' asked DS Whittington.

'Chances are he will have family still living there.'

'His ticket was to Newton le Willows,' I said. 'But what if he got off, bought another to Liverpool to throw us off the scent, then a ferry to Dublin.'

'He could almost be there by now,' DS Whittington nodded.

'Five fifteen from Glossop to Liverpool, what, say two and a half hours maximum?'

'His ticket was to Newton, but if he got off at Manchester, would there be enough time to buy a ticket for Liverpool and get back on?' Ellen suggested. 'Or, he could just stay on and hope his ticket wasn't checked!'

'Possibly, but what if his ticket was checked after the train had passed Newton, think how much attention he would bring on himself. That would be taking a real chance, would he want to do that?' I replied.

'Okay, let's say he has to catch the next train, an hour later for the sake of argument. Glossop to Manchester, an hour, lose an hour between trains, makes it seven fifteen, or thereabouts. That would mean he'd be heading for Liverpool by nine o'clock. He could be waiting for a ferry. I wonder how often the ferries cross to Dublin,' Whittington said

'There's probably two, perhaps three a day,' I suggested.

'Seven, maybe an eight hour crossing, he *could* be halfway there!' the DS agreed.

'What if we are jumping the gun, and he really is going to Newton le Willows?' asked Ellen.

'We need to get Harrington working on this, pull up, that shop will be on the phone,' Whittington said, pointing to a little greengrocer's shop.

The shopkeeper wasn't all that happy to let us use the phone, but a half-crown placed on his counter persuaded him fairly effectively.

After a long delay because of repair work on the Mam Tor road, known locally as Shivering Mountain due to it being little more than a huge mound of loose shale, we arrived back at Whitecross Yard just after four-thirty. On the go for twelve hours we were all shattered. We quickly exchanged progress reports only proving how little of a positive nature we had actually achieved. However, the DI added, 'I've started an investigation into the possibility of there being other murders with an Egyptian cult background.'

DI Brierly reached for his crutches, staggered to a standing position and made a pronouncement:

'We've alerted the Liverpool ferries and also those at Holyhead to look out for Barber, given them his description, I can't see the point of sitting around on our arses, oops... sorry Ellen! Let's finish for the day. I'm already in for a roasting when I get home!' he grinned, referring to the lunchtime deadline imposed by his wife.

I arrived back home to be jumped on by the boys wanting to play pirates on the latest thing that Henry had made for them, a frame about six feet high, with scramble nets like the rigging of a sailing ship, together with an arrangement of planks to walk and a sand pit.

'Your Daddy's tired, he's been at work all day and needs to rest,' Auntie Flossie said.

'Come on Daddy, just for a little while,' said George.

'When I shout tea's ready that's it, in straight away,' Flossie demanded, with a sly wink to me.

'Yes, come on Daddy!' Will said grabbing my hand.

I took command of the good ship Dexter, giving them orders to climb the rigging, walk the plank and hoist the flag; there wasn't a flag but at that age a detective constables blue hankie tied to a broomstick will do just as well. Seeing them playing together, okay, with the odd little argument now and then but mostly quite harmoniously, I found myself thinking about Alice, and how cruel life can be sometimes. Then my mind skipped to the Parminters and I wondered which was worst, a child losing a parent or parents losing a child in such terrible circumstances.

'Come on Daddy, now what?' yelled George from the top of the rigging nets.

'Tea time, that's what,' Flossie shouted from the kitchen door.

When the boys had gone to bed, Henry, Flossie and I settled in the front room.

'I took the boys to the school picnic this afternoon,' Flossie said as we relaxed.

'Oh yes, I'd forgotten, did they enjoy themselves?' I asked. 'They didn't mention it.'

'I'm surprised, they were full of it when we got home. Yes, they were given a great welcome and sat and talked with Miss Kent; she'll be their teacher; she was impressed how well they can both read.'

'You've really made them love books, as you did me,' I smiled.

'I'm not all that sure if the picnic was a good idea,' Flossie said.

'Oh, why is that?' I asked. 'You said they enjoyed it.'

'I worry that the boys will think that school will be a daily picnic.'

'Could be a rude awakening; is that what you're thinking my love?' Henry asked.

'Something like that, yes.'

'I asked Diana to come with us; she seemed very off hand and said she had a couple of lessons so, sorry she couldn't make it. What's wrong Will, have you fallen out?' Flossie asked

'No, just a cooling of the relationship, we're still friends but it seems that's it,' I replied.

'I got the idea that she's found someone else, do you think that could be it?'

'Or *Will's* found someone else!' Henry chuckled, and I know I blushed.

'You know she turned me down, I suppose once that has happened things can never be the same. I think we both accepted that it wouldn't have worked out. I realise now that I liked her but I don't think there was that spark of love that was there with Alice!' I admitted.

'I think she's drawing away gently, for the boy's sake as much as yours,' Flossie said.

'There's a twinkle in the lad's eye. He's found someone else mark my words. Go on deny it!' Henry laughed, pointing a mildly accusing finger.

'There is someone I feel, well, special about. Someone I'd like the boys, and you, to like,' I said.

'Told yer so. He's your brother, but I can read him like a book.'

'Who is she? Have you told her how you feel? Does she feel the same?' Flossie asked gabbling her thoughts.

'He'll tell us in his own good time. Leave the lad alone,' Henry scaled.

'She's the new DC, Ellen Parsons. We, I think we feel the same about each other. She knows about Diana and the fact she has turned me down. We've agreed to soft pedal for a while to see how things progress. The difficulty is that our lords and masters don't look kindly on marrying within the force,' I said. 'Two people working opposing shifts doesn't bode well for a marriage or for harmony in the force, or at least that's the way they see it.

'CID seems to be very much a daytime thing, so surely that argument goes out of the window,' Flossie said.

'I think I'm going to put my cards on the table with Diana; tell her I've found someone else and ask her blessing.'

'I half think *she's* found someone, I got that notion; how do you feel about that, Will?'

'I feel very glad for her and wish her all the happiness in the world,' I admitted.

'See her tomorrow if you can, sort it out and if she is fixed up elsewhere, do like you just said, wish her well,' Henry said and Flossie nodded her agreement.

'So what has happened today? Was your early start worth the effort?' Henry asked.

I told them as much as I could without compromising the case, and as to be expected, they were both upset by our find in Glossop.

'We need something to cheer us up,' said Henry

clicking the wireless on a few minutes into a radio play that turned out to be quite light-hearted and amusing.

It was Saturday the fourth of July. Ellen and the DS were sent to break the bad news to the Parminters The DI had arranged for them to identify the body around lunch time. I had no doubt in my mind that this was their daughter; I remembered that Mrs Parminter had remarked on the fact that two of her daughter's toes were webbed together and such was the case with the body in the boot.

At around lunchtime, about when the Parminters were making their identification, there was a phone call from Glossop. DI Morton reported that there had been no sightings of anyone meeting the description of Maurice Barber at Newton le Willows, Liverpool or indeed Manchester, other than him buying the ticket to Newton at Glossop station; Maurice Barber seemed to have disappeared off the face of the earth.

Ellen and DS Whittington arrived back at Whitecross Yard just after one having returned the Parminter's to their home following their positive identification. Ellen had arranged for Violet Goodward, their next door neighbour to make them a pot of tea and sit in with them for a while.

'Let's call it a day, it's nearly two o'clock; I've given DI Morton my home phone number if anything crops up. So let's make fresh start eight o'clock Monday morning,' the DI said, and wobbled on his crutches to arrange a lift home at the front desk.

I went to see Diana on Sunday afternoon and explained about Ellen. She dropped a bombshell of her own. It seemed that months before we first went out together, she had applied for the post of music teacher at a posh school near Bristol. That's why she had turned me down, not feeling totally sure about our relationship. She'd got the job and would be starting a few days before the new term in late August. After sitting for several minutes in silent reflection, we wished each other well and agreed to meet for a cup of tea in the teashop on the market place. But, I don't suppose we will.

Even Crammingdon market was changing, lacking Marco's music on a Tuesday and Friday. He had given up his little room above the shop at the corner of the market, to live with his new wife in her neat little house a couple of miles from the town centre. On Saturday's he took his usual place and played for all his worth. He has placed a little sign in the front of his open shelter; "Please give generously – all donations to Crammingdon orphanage".

Dear old Marco; generous as ever.

17

On Monday morning, DI Brierly presented the details of the case to the Chief Constable and requested that, with the autopsy report together with the comprehensive collection of photographs of the body and the fact that the Parminters had made a positive identification, the body be released for burial. The Chief, making an exception to the rule that underlings present themselves over at "heaven" had condescended to visit the DI in our makeshift office. He had been in touch with the town coroner, and had agreed to the request. The inquest was set for Tuesday at 2pm.

'Look Tom, once this case is sorted, I want you to take a few days off, until then I've set up a rota of patrol cars to be at your service, starting now,' he said pointing out of the window as PV2 pulled into the rear yard.

'Thank you, sir,' the DI said. 'I could have done with that a month ago, still better late than never,' he muttered as the Chief closed the door.

'I'll go and let the Parminters know that they can start making arrangements,' the DI said.

'Do you want me to come with you?' Ellen asked.

'No! Thanks for the offer but I need you to set a real search in progress for Maurice Barber; you've a nose for that sort of thing and quite frankly Harrington and I got nowhere!' he replied.

'Right sir, I have got an idea that might be worth looking into.'

'Okay I'll leave you all to it,' the DI said and

stumped his way to the front steps, as I waved the driver to the front of the building.

'I think Harrington and I should take another look at Barber's cottage by the canal. Will, can you go to Watson and Marchbank; see if they supplied the embalming stuff. Have a nose around, see if there's anything to tie them with what happened up on the moor,' said DS Whittington.

'Right, Sarge,' I said.

Both Watson and Marchbank were carrying out a burial and the young receptionist wouldn't agree to me making a search of the place in their absence. As I returned to the station, a newspaper placard caught my eye. I seldom buy a newspaper these days, Henry has two nationals and the local one delivered every day, and I read these if there's time after playing with the boys and getting them to bed. For some reason that I couldn't put my finger on, the seven word headline stuck in my mind and I determined to read the story in his paper when I got home.

Back in the office Ellen was scribbling on a piece of paper and looking perplexed.

'No luck?' I asked.

'Not really, I need the Ordnance Survey maps from Glossop to Liverpool, to try to work out where Barber has gone to. He can't just disappear off the face of the earth!'

'I'll pop down to the library and see if I can borrow some,' I said.

'I'll put the kettle on. Oh, pick up some biscuits on you way back please, the tin's empty!'

'Okay,' I agreed, little realising that the simple act of buying biscuits could suddenly move us a long way forward.

The library supplied me with the necessary maps on production of my warrant card and I walked the few yards to a small newsagent who I knew would have an assortment of biscuits and chocolate. Pete Warrell was at the counter buying a couple of national newspapers.

'Buying the opposition, Pete? Looking for something more interesting than the church bazar and the Mayor's ball?' I said, tapping him on the shoulder with a cheeky grin.

'Interested in this story, flavour of the day with Fleet Street but they'll drop it as soon as something else comes along,' he said pointing to the story that had caught my eye earlier.

'Going to feature it, Pete?'

'If only. I think there's more to it than meets the eye, but my editor says it's out of our region so I have to leave it to the big boy's. I'm going to dig around, see what I can find though and I think I know just the bloke to ask, do me 'omework, see!' he nodded and shuffled out of the shop.

Back in the restroom-cum-office Ellen and I moved the DI's desk against the wall and laid the maps end to end on the floor. Ellen traced the railway line across the map from its start at Glossop, shouting out the names of the stations and I wrote them down.

'Let's have those drinks, sort them out please Will, I could do with powdering my nose!' she said, and disappeared in the direction of the station WCs.

With the tea made and coffee and a couple of biscuits each, we perched on the edge of the DI's desk looking down on the maps.

'Do you think Barber actually got off at Newton le Willows and he just wasn't seen?' I asked.

'Probably, or perhaps that's a smoke screen and he did get off somewhere, anywhere, bought a Liverpool ticket and caught a later train, like was suggested,' she said, shaking her head.

'Or got off somewhere and just disappeared.'

'What I can't understand is, why did he leave Jenny's body in the car? We would almost certainly

295

trace it to him if we hadn't already.'

'My guess is he was pretty confident of escaping to somewhere we'd find difficult to follow,' I said.

'Ireland?'

'Eire, but yes,' I agreed.

'That wouldn't be cheap. I wonder how much money he had on him or could call on.'

'From the state of his cottage and that car I'd say not a lot,' I said with a shake of my head.

'It doesn't always follow, Will. My Uncle Jeff had a little drapery shop, quite a modest little one-man business in the High Street in Blackburn I think it was; he was a real old skinflint. My dad had worked with him for a short while, said Uncle Jeff used to carefully unwrap all of the incoming parcels and save the brown paper and string and then use it again on outgoing parcels. He died four years ago and I happen to know he was almost a millionaire!' she nodded.

'From saving string and brown paper?' I asked in amazement.

'No! *His* uncle had died years before and left him a dollop of shares in a Texas oil well!' she grinned.

'I see,' I nodded realising I had had my leg pulled pretty effectively.

'The point remains, he might not be as badly off as he seems. It could all be a big act, like "The Great Gondello",' she said.

'True,' I agreed.

'Let's suppose, just for argument that he has several thousand pounds squirrelled away somewhere, enough to be more than comfortable; what would a man like Barber do with it?'

'I'd have flying lessons and buy a plane!' I laughed.

'Would you really?' she asked suddenly serious.

'With enough money, yes I think so.'

'That's interesting. Ever heard of Barton Moss?'

'The name seems familiar, who is he?' I asked.

'It's not a person, it's a place!'

'Okay, so where is it?'

'Well Barton Moss is a station on the line to Liverpool just outside Manchester. Here look,' she said getting down on her knees and pointing to the little red dot on the line. As I knelt beside her I was once again aware of that delicate perfume she was wearing.

'Is this some new parlour-game of which I am unaware?' the DI asked as he entered the office. 'No, don't get up, I'm intrigued, I assume that there is a logical explanation?'

Luckily I had heard the tap and creak of his crutches, or he might well have walked in on our first kiss.

'We are working on the assumption that since Maurice Barber has probably still got connections with Southern Ireland that is where he is ultimately making for,' Ellen said.

'We suspect he may have got off the train at some point and bought a new ticket extending his journey to Liverpool,' I added.

'Or lying low for a while, until the heat is off!' the DI suggested.

'There's another thing that caught my eye, sir. I was about to show it to Will when you came in,' Ellen said.

'Go on.'

'Here, look sir,' she said pointing to the map.

'Bring it up on my desk I can't get down there with this bloody thing!' the DI said slapping his plaster with his crutch.

'Here, just above Barton Moss station, sir!' she said dropping her finger on the spot.

'Now that is interesting, well done Ellen.'

'There's something else, sir,' I said. 'Is it okay if I arrange to buy Pete Warrell a pint in the Market Inn?'

'I think I might just join you both, give him a ring, Dexter... er... this is in the course of duty I trust?'

'Earlier this morning, Pete drew my attention to

a story he's looking into. It's a long shot but it might just link into what we are on with.'

'Ring him,' the DI nodded.

Pete beat us to the Market Inn due to the slow progress the DI made on his crutches, and was sitting in a corner by the window when we arrived.

'Mob handed, eh!' he smiled.

'Just fancied a pint that's all, and anyway I promised you an exclusive,' the DI smiled.

'That you did, Tom! What have you got for me?' Pete asked, his face lighting up.

'A bit of information from you first Pete, then you'll have the lot, here and now.'

'Nothin' bloody changes, does it! You want mine first, right?'

'*I* do,' I said. 'When we met in the newsagents you were going to look into a story that was interesting you; how far have you got?'

'Not far at all really. I reckon there's a story in it, but why does it interest you?'

'I can't say at the moment, maybe not at all but it could tie up some loose ends,' I shrugged.

Pete opened his briefcase, and pulled out one of the newspapers with the relevant story on the front page and pointed to the pertinent paragraph.

'They reckon it's a Taylor Cub light aircraft, range with a full tank of fuel about a hundred and sixty miles, a hundred and eighty possibly with a following wind, allowing a bit in reserve. I've checked and nothin' is missin' from Ireland so it must have come from the UK. That's as far as I've got!' Pete said.

'You're sure about the range?' I asked.

'I am, I rang a mate who knows these things, and I can vouch that nothin` is reported missin on the Irish mainland, north or south!'

'Thanks, Pete!' I said and nodded to the DI.

'Okay, get yer notebook out Pete!' the DI said.

'The body of a young girl, since identified as Jennifer Parminter, was found…'

'I nodded to them both and with my new found information headed back to Whitecross Yard. I called in at the library on the way and borrowed a school atlas.

'Where's the wooden ruler Ellen?' I asked, laying the book on the desk on top of the map.

'It's in my drawer,' she answered, opening it and sliding the ruler across to me.

I opened the atlas at a double page spread, showing about half of Ireland, centred more or less on Dublin on the left hand page, and England and Wales on the right hand page. The scale at the bottom, showed a handy twenty-five miles to the inch. The phone rang and Ellen answered it.

'That was the stationmaster at Barton Moss, returning my call. He was busy dealing with a VIP on the morning in question, but he has asked the porter who was on duty and he remembers a man answering Maurice's description getting off the train that morning. It had been slightly delayed but arrived at Barton at twenty minutes to seven. The man was in a tearing hurry, I suppose that's why he remembered him… What are you doing Will?' she asked, as the DI entered.

'A hundred and sixty miles at twenty-five miles to the inch is just under, six and a half inches, agreed?'

'Agreed!' she said and the DI nodded.

'I'm measuring an arc, six and a half inches from Dublin on this old atlas, starting where it touches the English coast at its most northerly point. That's Ayr. If I swing it down, keeping this end on Dublin, the next place is Douglas on the Isle of Man.'

'Hang on I'll write them down,' Ellen said, 'Okay got them!'

'Next one is Blackpool, then Manchester, Holyhead, Shrewsbury and Swansea; everywhere else is out of range,' I said.

'What's your point, Will?' Ellen asked.

'Just bear with me a moment: how many of these places have airports, airfields or aerodromes?' I asked.

'I still don't see your point. However, I know there's one at Aye, Prestwick it's called, it was on the wireless in the news the other day,' she said.

'There's one at Blackpool, the ACC flies from there to the Isle of Man. As far as I know there's nothing further south within the range that Pete gave us!' the DI said.

We looked again at the Ordnance Survey map in the DI's desk. Ellen put her finger again on the area just above Barton Moss station, it was clearly marked Manchester City Airport!

'That's in range,' she said.

'Ellen, ring them to see if anything out of the ordinary happened on the day in question!' the DI said. 'Dexter go and get a copy of the newspaper article, I wanted Pete to give me his but the awkward bugger refused.'

'Right, sir!' we both agreed.

The newsagent where I'd met Pete Warrell had sold out, but grudgingly suggested that "that old bugger", meaning Cawson's in Blacksmith Lane, "might still have one." I managed to get the last copy. It was a bit dog-eared and scruffy but the front page, which had clearly been quickly reshuffled, to take the late news item, told the story well enough. Ellen was talking to the DI as I entered the office.

'…flight book, two aircraft failed to log flight plans on that morning, naughty but not uncommon apparently. One was a De Havilland Rapide on a regular flight to Edinburgh, returned the same day so no problem; the other was a Taylor Cub, they've no idea where it went but it was last seen heading west, sir.'

'There's our answer, or as near an answer as we are likely to get,' the DI said laying the newspaper on

300

top of the map and Ellen read it aloud,

WRECKAGE OF LIGHT AIRCRAFT FOUND IN IRISH SEA.

Reports have just been received that the wreckage of a light aeroplane, believed to be that of a Taylor Cub, has been recovered about three miles off the coast of Southern Ireland. At approximately three o'clock this morning, just as we were about to go to press, an Irish fishing boat reported recovering several pieces of wreckage. There is no news, as yet, of any survivors and the chance that there will be any seems slight. No doubt we will have more details in tomorrow's edition.

'Certainly looks like that, sir!' Ellen nodded.

The rattle of earth on Jenny's coffin lid as the vicar said the familiar word of the burial service brought me back to the present; knowing that the mystery of what happened to little Jenny Parminter would probably never be fully known. I found myself saying a little prayer of my own, that whatever had happened she knew nothing of it; felt no pain.

Epilogue

The crashed plane was identified as the Taylor Cub from Manchester Airport, two days after Jennifer's funeral. So far, no bodies have been recovered, and the most likely hypothesis is that Maurice Barber perished in the crash along with the pilot. Sometimes a negative outcome to a case is as much as can be expected.

The Trent Wanderer is laid-up in a Northampton boat yard, and of Harry Sumpter there is no sign, although I expect him at some point to reclaim his boat and continue his livelihood, with all its sorrowful memories.

Alderman Tippett, is standing down from his council duties due to ill health!

Watson & Marchbank, the undertakers have gone into voluntary liquidation after having settled out of court with Mrs Garrett. The Crown Prosecution Service is considering what action, if any, to take in the case. Since Mrs Garrett is no longer pressing charges, my guess is that it will all be dropped and quietly forgotten!

DC William Dexter   Thursday 16[th]July 1936

Perhaps you missed the first in the Whitecross Yard Murders.

"The Killing of Cristobel Tranter"

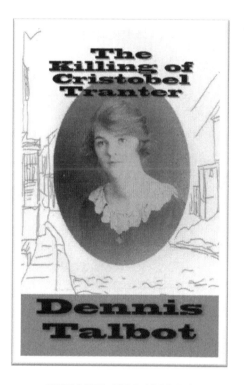

(ISBN 978-1985-1808-95)

Young police officer Will Dexter finds the body of a 20year old girl in the entry to a yard of slum houses. The local CID investigate the case. A chance car crash weeks later, starts a chain of events that sees him involved in the crux of the investigation and deep in the blood-soaked ending.

Also available

"Death in the Back Row"
A Whitecross Yard Murder

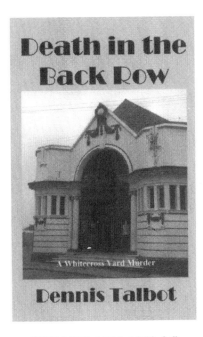

(ISBN 978-1725-1393-36)

The second in the Whitecross Yard Murder series, *"Death in the Back Row"* sees PC Will Dexter again seconded to Crammingdon's small CID department, assisting the investigation into the death of a very portly picture-goer. Enquiries suggest that several suspects might have wanted him dead!

Natural death – suicide – murder, but which?

If it was murder, it was with a clever and unusual weapon!

And

"Too Many Wrong Notes"

A Whitecross Yard Murder

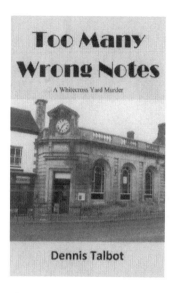

(ISBN 978-1729-2789-56)

Just as PC Will Dexter is coming to terms with a devastating personal tragedy and his move from pounding the beat as a local bobby to joining DI Brierly's CID team as a Detective Constable, he is involved with a series of crimes.

A shoebox full of pound notes donated to the local church turn out to be forgeries. This together with the theft of sugar from a Government warehouse, and missing works of art are just the lead up to several murders, as tracks are covered and clues fudged.

Could there possibly be a connection between these varied crimes?

Printed in Poland
by Amazon Fulfillment
Poland Sp. z o.o., Wrocław

54796866R00186